About the Authors

Michelle Smart is a *Publishers Weekly* bestselling author with a slight-to-severe coffee addiction. A book worm since birth, Michelle can usually be found hiding behind a paperback, or if it's an author she really loves, a hardback. Michelle lives in rural Northamptonshire in England with her husband and two young Smarties. When not reading or pretending to do the housework she loves nothing more than creating worlds of her own. Preferably with lots of coffee on tap.
www.michelle-smart.com

Lucy Ellis has four loves in life: books, expensive lingerie, vintage films and big, gorgeous men who have to duck going through doorways. Weaving aspects of them into her fiction is the best part of being a romance writer. Lucy lives in a small cottage in the foothills outside Melbourne.

Lynne Graham lives in Northern Ireland and has been a keen romance reader since her teens. Happily married, Lynne has five children. Her eldest is her only natural child. Her other children, who are every bit as dear to her heart, are adopted. The family has a variety of pets, and Lynne loves gardening, cooking, collecting allsorts and is crazy about every aspect of Christmas.

D0717150

Italian Summers

Italian Summers
Scandalous Demands

MICHELLE SMART

LUCY ELLIS

LYNNE GRAHAM

MILLS & BOON

First Published in Great Britain 2022
By Mills & Boon, an imprint of HarperCollins*Publishers*
1 London Bridge Street, London, SE1 9GF

www.harpercollins.co.uk

HarperCollins*Publishers*
1st Floor, Watermarque Building,
Ringsend Road, Dublin 4, Ireland

ITALIAN SUMMERS: SCANDALOUS DEMANDS
© 2022 Harlequin Enterprises ULC.

Once a Moretti Wife © 2017 Michelle Smart
A Dangerous Solace © 2013 Lucy Ellis
Roccanti's Marriage Revenge © 2012 Lynne Graham

ISBN: 978-0-263-30492-3

MIX
Paper from
responsible sources
FSC C007454

This book is produced from independently certified FSC™ paper to ensure responsible forest management.

For more information visit: www.harpercollins.co.uk/green

Printed and Bound in Spain using 100% Renewable electricity at CPI Black Print, Barcelona

ONCE A MORETTI WIFE

MICHELLE SMART

This book is for Jennifer Hayward,
writer extraordinaire and a wonderful friend. Xxx

CHAPTER ONE

How much had she *drunk*?

Anna Robson clutched her head, which pounded as if the force of a hundred hammers were battering it.

There was a lump there. She prodded it cautiously and winced. Had she hit her head?

She racked her aching, confused brain, trying hard to remember. She'd gone out for a drink with Melissa, hadn't she? *Hadn't* she?

Yes. She had. She'd gone for a drink with her sister after their Spinning class, as they did every Thursday evening.

She peered at her bedside clock and gave a start—her phone's alarm should have gone off an hour ago. Where had she put it?

Still holding her head, she looked around but saw no sight of it, then forgot all about it as her stomach rebelled. She only just made it to the bathroom in time to vomit.

Done, she sat loose-limbed like a puppet on the floor, desperately trying to remember what she'd drunk. She wasn't a heavy drinker at the best of times and on a work night she would stick to a small glass of white wine. But right then, she felt as if she'd drunk a dozen bottles.

There was no way she could go into the office… But

then she remembered she and Stefano had a meeting with a young tech company he was interested in buying. Stefano had tasked Anna, as he always did, with going through the company's accounts, reports and claims and producing her own summary. He trusted her judgement. If it concurred with his then he would invest in the company. If her judgement differed he would rethink his strategy. Stefano wanted her report first thing so he could digest it before the meeting.

She'd have to email it and beg illness.

But, after staggering cautiously around the flat she shared with Melissa, holding onto the walls for support, she realised she must have left her laptop at the office. She'd have to phone Stefano. He could open it himself. She'd give him the password, although she was ninety-nine per cent certain he'd hacked it at least once already.

All she had to do was find her phone. Walking carefully to the kitchen, she found a pretty handbag on the counter. Next to it was an envelope addressed with her name.

She blinked hard to keep her eyes focused and pulled the letter out. She attempted to read it a couple of times but none of it made any sense. It was from Melissa asking for Anna's forgiveness for her trip to Australia and promising to call when she got there.

Australia? Melissa must be having a joke at her expense, although her sister saying she was going to visit the mother who'd abandoned them a decade ago wasn't the slightest bit funny to Anna's mind. The letter's postscript did explain one thing though—Melissa said she'd gritted the outside step of the front door so Anna wouldn't slip on it again, and asked her to see a doctor if her head hurt where she'd banged it.

Anna put her hand to the lump on the side of her head. She had no recollection whatsoever of slipping. And no recollection of any ice. The early November weather had been mild but now, as she looked through the kitchen window, she saw a thick layer of frost.

Her head hurting too much for her to make sense of anything, she put the letter to one side and had a look in the handbag. The purse she'd used for a decade, threadbare but clinging to life, was in it. It had been the last gift from her father before he'd died. Had she swapped handbags with Melissa? That wouldn't be unusual; Anna and Melissa were always lending each other things. What *was* unusual was that Anna didn't remember. But they must have swapped because in the bottom of the pretty bag also sat Anna's phone. That was another mystery solved.

She pulled it out and saw she had five missed calls. Struggling to focus, she tapped in the pin code to unlock it.

Wrong pin. She tried again. *Wrong pin.*

Sighing, she shoved it back in the bag. It took enough effort to stay on her feet, never mind remembering a code with a head that felt like fog. It was times like this that she cursed their decision to disconnect the landline.

Fine. She'd flag a cab and go to the office, explain that she was dying and then come home again.

Before getting dressed, she took some headache tablets and prayed her tender belly could keep them down.

She always put the next day's clothes on her bedroom chair and now she hugged them to her chest and gingerly sat back on her bed. Where had *this* dress come from? Melissa must have muddled their clothes up again. Not having the energy to hunt for something else, Anna decided to wear it. It was a black long-sleeved, knee-length jersey dress with a nice amount of swish at the hem but it took her an age to get it on, her limbs feeling as if they'd had lead injected into them.

Damn, her *head*.

She didn't have the energy to put on any make-up either, so she made do with running a brush gently through her hair and then she staggered to the front door.

On the rack in the entrance porch was a pair of funky black boots with thick soles she hadn't seen before. Surely Melissa wouldn't mind her borrowing them. That was the best thing about living with her sister; they were the same dress and shoe size.

She locked the front door and treaded carefully down the steps. Finally luck was on her side—a vacant black cab drove up her street within a minute.

She got the driver to drop her off across the road from the futuristic skyscraper near Tower Bridge from where Stefano ran his European operations. As Anna waited at the pedestrian crossing next to the road heaving with traffic, a shiny stretched black Mercedes pulled up outside the front of the building. A doorman opened the back door, and out came Stefano.

The green light flashed and, working on autopilot, she crossed the road, her eyes focused on Stefano rather than where she was walking.

A tall blonde woman got out of the car behind him. Anna didn't recognise her but there was something familiar about her face that made it feel as if nails clawed into Anna's already tender stomach.

A briefcase whacked her in the back and, startled, Anna realised she'd come to a stop in the middle of the road, dozens of other pedestrians jostling around her, some swearing.

Clutching a hand to her stomach to stem the surging rise of nausea, she forced her leaden legs to work and managed to make it to the pavement without being knocked over.

She went through the revolving doors of the building itself, put her bag on the scanner, waited for it to be cleared, then went straight to the bathroom, into the first empty cubicle, and vomited.

Cold perspiration breaking out all over, she knew she was an idiot to have come in. Her hangover—was it a hangover? She'd never felt anything like this—was, if that was possible, getting worse.

Out of the cubicle, after she'd washed her hands and swirled cold water in her mouth, she caught sight of her reflection in the mirror.

She looked awful. Her face was white as a sheet, her dark hair lank around her shoulders...

She did a double take. Had her *hair* grown?

After popping a mint in her mouth, she inched her way around the walls to the elevator. Two men and a woman she vaguely recognised were getting into it, chatting amiably. She slid in with them before the doors closed.

She punched the button for the thirtieth floor and held onto the railing as it began the smooth ride up.

All talk had stopped. She could feel their eyes on her. Did she really look so bad that she'd become a conversation stopper? It was a relief when they got out on the floor below her.

A gaggle of secretaries and administrators worked in the open space in front of the office Anna shared with Stefano. They all turned their heads to stare at her. A couple were open-mouthed.

Did they have to make it so obvious that she looked

this awful? All the same, she managed to get her mouth working enough to smile a greeting. Not one of them responded.

She looked around for Chloe, her newly appointed fresh-faced PA who cowered in terror every time Stefano made an appearance. Poor Chloe would not be happy to know she'd have to take on Anna's duties for the day.

Anna hadn't wanted a PA of her own. *She* was a PA! But Stefano had thrown so many responsibilities her way in the year and a half since he'd poached her from Levon Brothers that when he'd caught her working at nine in the evening, he'd put his foot down and insisted on hiring someone for her.

'Do I get a new job title?' she'd cheekily asked, and been rewarded with a promotion to Executive PA and a hefty pay rise.

Maybe Chloe was cowering in the stationery cupboard, waiting for her arrival so she could hide behind her. The girl would get used to Stefano soon enough. Anna had seen it with most other employees. It was that mixture of awe and fear he inspired that curdled the stomach, but eventually the curdling settled and one could hold a coherent conversation with him.

Anna had skipped all these stages herself but had seen the effect Stefano had on others too many times not to sympathise with it. He inspired terror and hero-worship in equal measure.

She let the office door shut behind her and came to an abrupt halt. For a moment she forgot all about her pounding head and nauseous stomach.

When Stefano had offered her the job and she'd learned it entailed sharing an office with him, she'd said on a whim that she would only do it if he decorated her side in shades of plum. Her memories of her first day working for him were ones of laughter, when she'd walked into the sprawling office and found one half painted a functional cream, the other varying shades of plum.

Today the whole office was cream.

She'd just reached her desk when the door flew open, and Stefano stood there, as dark and menacing as she'd ever seen him.

Before she could ask if he'd had an army of decorators in overnight, he slammed the door shut and folded his arms across his broad chest.

'What are you doing here?'

'Not you too,' she groaned, half in exasperation and half in pain. 'I think I had a fall. I know I look awful but can't you pretend I look like my usual supermodel self?'

It had become one of those long-running jokes between them. Every time Stefano tried to cajole her into coming on a date with him, Anna would make some cutting remark, usually followed by a reminder that his preferred dates were the gorgeous supermodel type, whereas she barely topped five foot.

'You'll get neck-ache if you try to kiss me,' she'd once flippantly told him.

To which he'd immediately replied, *'Shall we find out now?'*

She'd never dared mention kissing to him again. Imagining it was more than enough, and wasn't something she allowed herself to do, not since the one time she'd succumbed to the daydream and then had spent a good week pretending not to have palpitations whenever she got close to him.

There was no denying it, her boss was utterly gorgeous, even when her eyes were struggling to focus as they were now. There was not a single physical aspect of him that didn't make her want to swoon. Well over a foot taller than her, he had hair so dark it looked black, a strong roman nose, generous lips and a chiselled jaw covered in just the right amount of black stubble. He also had eyes capable of arresting a person with one glance; a green colour that could turn from light to dark in a heartbeat. She'd learned to read his eyes well—they corresponded exactly with his mood. Today, they were as dark as they could be.

She wasn't in the right frame of mind to dissect what that meant. The paracetamol she'd taken hadn't made a dent in her headache, which was continuing to get worse by the second. She grabbed the edge of her desk and sat down. Straight away she saw something else that was wrong, even with her double vision. She strained to peer more closely at the clutter on her desk. She never left clutter. It drove her crazy. Everything needed to be in its correct place. And...

'Why are there photos of *cats* on my desk?' She was a dog person, not a cat person. Dogs were loyal. Dogs didn't leave you.

'*Chloe's* desk,' he said in a voice as hard as steel.

Anna tilted her head to look at him and blinked a number of times to focus. Her vision had blurred terribly. 'Don't tease me,' she begged. 'I'm only twenty minutes late. My head feels...'

'I can't believe you would be so brazen to turn up here like this,' he cut in.

Used to Stefano's own brand of English, she assumed his 'brazen' meant 'stupid' or something along those lines. She had to admit, he had a point. Leaving the flat feeling as rotten as she did really did rank as stupid.

'I know I'm not well.' It was an effort to get the words out. 'I feel like death warmed up, but I left my laptop behind and needed to get that report to you. You'll have to get Chloe to sit in on the meeting.'

His jaw clenched and his lips twisted into something that could be either a snarl or a smirk. 'Is this a new tactic?'

Was her hearing now playing up along with the rest of her? One of the things she liked about working for Stefano was that he was a straight talker, regularly taking his more earnest employees to task for their corporate speak. 'I taught myself English,' he would say to them with disdain, 'but if I'd tried learning it from you I would be speaking self-indulgent codswallop.'

She always hid a grin when he said that. 'Self-indulgent codswallop' was a term she'd taught him in her first week working for him. His thick Italian accent made it sound even funnier. She'd taught him a whole heap of insults since; most of which she'd initially directed at him.

Which made his riddle all the more confusing.

'What are you talking about?'

He stepped away from the closed door, nearer to her. 'Have you been taking acting lessons, Mrs Moretti?'

'Mrs...?' She closed her eyes and gave her head a gentle shake, but even that made the hammers trapped in it pound harder. 'Have I woken in the twilight zone?' It didn't sound completely mad when she said it. Quite credible in fact. She'd felt disjointed from the moment she'd woken, Melissa's letter stating that she was flying to Australia only adding to the incoherence.

When she opened her eyes again, she found Stefano by her desk, his large frame swimming before her eyes.

'You're playing an excellent game. Tell me the rules so I know what my next move should be.' His tone was gentle but the menace behind it was unmistakable, his smooth voice decreasing in volume but increasing in danger.

Anna's pretty hazel eyes widened. She had clearly been practising her innocent face in the month since he'd last seen her, Stefano thought scathingly.

It had been a whole month since she'd humiliated him in his own boardroom and walked out of his life.

He placed his hands palm down on her desk and gazed at her, taking in the beautiful face that had captivated him from the start.

'I honestly don't know what you're talking about.' Anna got slowly to her feet. 'I'm going home. One of us is confused about something and I don't know which of us I hope it is.'

He laughed. Oh, she was something else.

'You should go home too,' she said, eying him in much the same manner as a person cornered by a dangerous dog. 'If I didn't know better I'd think you were drunk.'

For a moment he wondered if *she'd* been drinking. Her words had a slurred edge and she seemed unsteady.

But those luscious lips were taunting him. *She* was taunting him, playing a game he hadn't been given the rules to, trying to catch him on the back foot. Well, he wouldn't fall for her games any more. He wrote the rules, not this witch who had spellbound him with lust.

She'd planned it all from the start. She'd deliberately held off his advances for eighteen months so he'd become so desperate to possess her he would agree to marry her just so he could sleep with her.

He'd admit it had been a bit more involved than

that but that had been the crux of it. He'd thought he'd known her. He'd thought he could trust her—*him*, Stefano Moretti, the man who had learned at a young age not to trust anyone.

She'd set him up to marry her so she could divorce him for adultery, humiliating him in front of his staff for good measure, and gain herself a hefty slice of his fortune.

He couldn't believe he'd been stupid enough to fall for it.

When he'd received the call from his lawyer telling him his estranged wife was going to sue him for a fortune, he'd quelled his instinct to race to her home and confront her. He'd forced himself to sit tight.

Sitting tight did not come easily to him. He was not a man to wait for a problem to be solved; he was a man to take a problem by the scruff of the neck and sort it. He reacted. He always had. It was what had got him into so much trouble when he'd been a kid, never knowing when to keep his mouth shut or his fists to himself.

He'd spent nearly two weeks biding his time, refusing to acknowledge her lawyer's letter. In ten days they would have been married for a year and legally able to divorce. Then, and only then, would Anna learn what he was prepared to give her, which was nothing. And he was prepared to make her jump through hoops to reach that knowledge.

He would make her pay for all her lies and deceit. He would only stop when she experienced the equivalent humiliation that he'd been through at her hands.

One hundred million pounds and various assets for barely a year of marriage? Her nerve was beyond incredible.

But despite everything she'd done, seeing her now, his

desire for her remained undiminished. Anna was still the sexiest woman in the world. Classically beautiful, she had shoulder-length silky dark chestnut hair that framed high cheekbones, bee-stung lips that could sting of their own accord and skin as creamy to the touch as to the eye. She should be as narcissistic as an old-fashioned film star but she was disdainful of her looks. That wasn't to say she didn't make an effort with her appearance—she loved clothes, for example—but rarely did anything to enhance what she'd already been blessed with.

Anna Moretti née Robson, the woman with the face and body of a goddess and the tongue of a viper. Clever and conniving, sweet and lovable; an enigma wrapped in a layer of mystery.

He despised her.

He missed having her in his bed.

Since his release from prison all those long years ago he'd become an expert at masking the worst of his temper and channelling it into other areas, but Anna could tap into him like no one else and make him want to punch walls while also making him ache with need to touch her.

She wasn't a meek woman. He'd understood that at their very first meeting. All the same, he'd never have believed she would have the audacity to walk back into this building after the stunt she'd pulled.

'I'm not drunk.' He leaned closer and inhaled. There it was, that scent that had lingered on his bed sheets even after copious washes, enough so that he'd thrown out all his linen and bought new sets. 'But if you're having memory problems, I know something that will help refresh it.'

Alarm flashed in her widened eyes. He didn't give her the chance to reply, sliding an arm around her waist and pulling her to him so he could crush her mouth with his own.

He felt her go rigid with shock and smiled as he moulded his lips to hers. If Anna wanted to play games she had to understand that *he* was the rule maker, not her. He could make them and break them, just as he intended to eventually break her.

The feel of her lips against his, her breasts pressed against his chest, her scent... Heat coiled in his veins, punishment turning into desire as quickly as the flick of a switch...

All at once, she jerked her face to the side, breaking the kiss, and at the same moment her open hand smacked him across the cheek.

'What do you think you're doing?' She wiped her mouth with the back of her hand, her tone half shocked, half furious. 'You're...' Her voice tailed off.

'I'm what?' he drawled, fighting to control his own tone. The potency of the chemistry between them had become diluted in his memories. He'd forgotten how a single kiss could drive him as wild as an inexperienced teenager.

She blinked and when she looked at him again the fury had gone. Fear now resonated from her gaze. The little colour she'd had in her cheeks had gone too. 'Stef...'

She swayed, her fingers extending as if reaching for him.

'Anna?'

Then, right before his eyes, she crumpled. He only just caught her before she fell onto the floor.

CHAPTER TWO

WHEN ANNA AWOKE in the sterile hospital room, her head felt clearer than it had all day. The heavy pounding had abated but now came something far worse. Fear.

She didn't need to open her eyes to know she was alone.

Had Stefano finally left?

The memory of their kiss flashed into her mind. In a day that had passed as surreally as if she'd been underwater, his kiss was the only memory with any real substance.

He'd *kissed* her. It had been almost brutal. A taunt. A mockery. The blood thumping through her at the feel of it had been the final straw for her poor, depleted body. She'd collapsed. And he'd caught her.

He seemed to think they were married. The hospital staff were under the same impression.

Swallowing back the panic clawing at her throat, Anna forced herself to think.

Her memory of the day might be blurry but she remembered snapshots of it. Stefano had carried her to his office sofa while shouting for someone to call for an ambulance. He'd travelled to the hospital with her. He'd been with her through all the prodding, probing and questioning she'd endured when she'd been awake and coherent enough to answer. He'd even come to the scan with her. If it weren't for the dark tension radiating from him she would have been grateful for his presence, especially since Melissa hadn't shown up.

Where on earth was she? It wasn't possible that she could be on a flight to Australia. She wouldn't have done that without telling her. No way. Besides, they lived together. Anna would have known!

Just what the hell was going on?

Never mind all the so-called marriage nonsense, which had to be some kind of elaborate hoax, but since when had Stefano hated her? They'd always sniped at each other and communicated through sarcasm but it had always been playful, with no sting intended. Today, despite his seemingly genuine concern for her health, it had been like having a Rottweiler guarding her with its teeth bared in her direction.

The door opened and the consultant from earlier stepped into the room, clipboard in hand. She was followed closely by Stefano.

Anna's heart rate accelerated and she eyed them warily. They had the look of a pair of conspirators. Had they been talking about her privately?

'What's wrong with me?' she asked.

The consultant perched herself on the edge of Anna's bed and smiled reassuringly. 'You have a concussion from your fall last night.'

'I don't remember the fall,' Anna said. 'My sister wrote it in a letter…have you got in touch with her yet?'

'Her flight hasn't landed.'

'She can't be on a flight.'

'She is,' Stefano chipped in. He was seated on the

visitor's chair just a foot from her bed, his stance that of a man who had every right to be there. Even if she were to ask for his removal, no one would dare touch him.

His break away from her bedside seemed to have done him good though as he'd lost the Rottweiler look he'd been carrying all day. He looked more…not relaxed, not happy exactly, but…pleased with himself.

'Melissa's taken a month's leave to go to Australia and celebrate your mother's fiftieth birthday,' he finished.

'That's not possible.' The stab of betrayal pierced her hard. 'She couldn't have done that. I'd know.'

'The chances are you *did* know,' the consultant said. 'Your scan has come back clear…'

'What does that mean?'

'That there's no bleeding on the brain or anything we need worry about in that regard, but all the evidence is pointing to you having retrograde amnesia.'

'Amnesia?' Anna clarified. 'So I'm not going mad?'

The consultant's smile was more like a grimace. 'No. But it appears you have lost approximately a year of your memories.'

Anna exhaled in relief. Amnesia she could cope with. There had been moments during the day when she'd thought for certain she was losing her mind. And then she remembered Stefano's insistence that they were married…

'Don't tell me I'm actually married to him?'

Now the consultant looked uncomfortable. 'You're on our records as Anna Louise Moretti.'

There was silence as the meaning of this sank into Anna's fragile head.

She didn't know what was worse. Being told Melissa

had gone to Australia to see their mother or being told she was married to Stefano. Discovering that there was life on Jupiter would be easier to comprehend.

She turned her head to look at the man who claimed to be her husband. His long legs were stretched out before him, his tie removed and top button undone. He was studying her with an intensity that sent little warning tingles through her veins. It was the look he always gave when he was thinking hard, usually when he was debating to himself whether he wanted to risk his money and reputation on a particular venture.

When Stefano chose to back a business he didn't hold back. He gave it everything. He thrived on the gamble but liked the odds to be in his favour. He liked to be certain that he wasn't going to be throwing away his time, resources and money. It didn't matter how many reports she produced, he would play it all out in his mind, working through it on his own mental spreadsheet.

And now that gaze was directed at her, as if she were a business venture that needed to be analysed. He was mentally dissecting *something* and that something had to do with her.

'We're really married?' she asked him.

A slow smile spread across his face as if she'd said something amusing but the focus in his eyes sharpened. '*Sì.*'

None of this made sense. 'Why would I have married you?'

He shifted his chair forward and leaned over to speak directly into her ear. His warm breath stirred the strands of her hair, making her pulses stir with them. 'Because you wanted my body.'

His nearness meant she had to concentrate hard

to form a response. 'This is no time for your jokes. I wouldn't marry you. I have self-respect.'

He sat back and spread out his hands. 'No joke. We're married.'

'I don't believe you.' The very idea was preposterous.

'I can give you proof.'

'We can't be.'

There was no way she would have married Stefano. He was gorgeous, funny when he wasn't being brooding and impatient, and rich, but he also had a revolving door of girlfriends. She had always maintained that she wouldn't touch him with a ten-foot bargepole and had told him so on numerous occasions.

Always he'd responded with a dazzling grin and, 'You can't resist me for ever, *bambolina*.'

To which she'd always replied with her own grin turned up to full wattage, 'Watch me.'

This time there was no comeback. He pulled out his phone and started tapping away. After a few moments he leaned over to show her the screen. Her pulse made another strange leap at his closeness and the familiar scent of his tangy cologne that had always filled their workspace. She blinked and focused her attention on what he was showing her.

It was a photograph of them standing together on a beach. Stefano was dressed in charcoal trousers and a short-sleeved open-necked white shirt. She wore a long white chiffon dress that had a distinct bridal look to it, and was clutching a posy of flowers. Oh, and they were kissing.

Anna stared at the screen for so long her eyes went dry. Her heart was pounding so hard its beats vibrated through her. When she dared look at him she found him watching her closely.

'Did you drug me?' She could hardly believe the evidence before her. It wasn't possible. It had to be fake.

'We married on the twentieth of November. Our first anniversary is in ten days.'

'That's impossible.' She did some mental maths. She remembered as far back as her Spinning class, which had been the day after bonfire night, November the fifth.

He expected her to believe she'd married him two weeks later? Did he take her for a complete idiot?

But then she looked again at the photo on his screen.

'We married in Santa Cruz,' he supplied. 'It was a very…I can't think of the word, but it was quick.'

'Spontaneous?'

'That's the word, *sì*.'

Despite the mounting evidence she still couldn't bring herself to believe him.

'If we're married, why did I wake up in my own bed in mine and Melissa's flat?'

There was only the barest flicker of his pupils. 'We'd had a row.'

'About what?'

'Nothing important. You often stay the night there.'

'Why were you so angry to see me in the office this morning? And why has Chloe taken my desk?'

'I told you, we'd had an argument.'

'Cheating on me already?' she asked, only half jesting.

There was a tiny clenching of his jaw before his handsome features relaxed into the smile that had always melted her stomach. 'I've never cheated on a woman in my life.'

'You've never stayed with a woman long enough *to* cheat.' Stefano had the attention span of a goldfish. He thrived on the chase, growing bored quickly and moving straight onto the next woman to catch his eye.

'We've been married for almost a year and I've never been unfaithful,' he stated steadily.

'Then what were we arguing about?'

'It was nothing. Teething problems like all newly-weds deal with. You weren't supposed to be in this week so Chloe's been working at your desk.'

The image of the blonde woman following him out of his car popped back into her mind. She had no memories of that woman but the way she'd reacted to her, the way her already tender stomach had twisted and coiled, made her think she *had* met her. 'Who was that woman in your car this morning?'

Before he could answer, the consultant coughed unsubtly. Anna had almost forgotten she was there.

'Anna, I appreciate this is hard for you. There are a lot of gaps in your memory to fill.'

She sucked in her lips and nodded. A whole year of memories needed to be filled. A *whole year* that she'd lost; a big black void during which she had married her boss and Lord knew what else had occurred. 'Will I get my memories back?'

'Brain injuries are complex. There are methods that will help retrieve the memories, things we call "joggers", which are aids to help with recall, but there are no guarantees. The country's top specialist in retrograde amnesia will be here in the morning to see you—he'll be able to give you more information.'

Anna closed her eyes. 'How long do I have to stay here for?'

'We want to keep you under observation for the night. Providing there's no further issues, there's no reason you can't be discharged tomorrow after you've seen the specialist.'

'And then I can go home?'

But where *was* her home? Was it the flat she'd shared with her big sister since she was fourteen? Or with Stefano?

The nausea that had eased with the help of medication rolled back into life.

She couldn't have married him. Not Stefano of all people.

'You'll need to take it easy for a few weeks to recover from the concussion but your husband's already assured me he'll be on hand to take care of you.'

'So Stefano knows all this? You've already discussed it with him?'

'I'm your next of kin,' he said, his thick accent pronouncing 'kin' as 'keen', something that under ordinary circumstances would make her laugh. Right then, Anna felt she would never find anything funny again.

'No, you're not. Melissa is.' Melissa had been her next of kin since her sister had agreed to take sole guardianship of her when she'd been only eighteen and Anna fourteen.

The uncomfortable look came back to the consultant's face. 'Anna, I understand this is difficult for you but I can't discharge you unless you have somewhere to go where you will be looked after, for the next few days at least. Your husband is your next of kin but you don't have to go with him. Is there anyone else we can call for you?'

Anna thought hard but it was hopeless and only made her head start hurting again. The only person she was close to was Melissa. They both had friends—lots of them—but it was only each other that they trusted. Their friends were kept on the fringes of their lives and there wasn't a single one she could impose herself on for however long it took to be deemed safe to care for herself.

But Melissa was on an aeroplane flying to the other side of the world to visit the woman who'd abandoned them for a new life in Australia with a man she barely knew.

The betrayal sliced through her again, tears burning in her eyes.

'Anna, your home is with me.'

She closed her eyes in an attempt to drown out Stefano's hypnotic voice. She wished she could fall into the deepest sleep in the world and wake to find the normal order of things restored.

The sad truth was there was no one else who could take her in or, if there was, she couldn't remember them.

Whatever was wrong with her head though, wishing for something different wouldn't change a thing. Her world might be all topsy-turvy but this was her reality now and she needed to deal with it. Bawling her eyes out and burying her head in the sand wouldn't change anything.

She looked directly at him. 'I don't remember it being our home. I don't remember a thing about us other than that you're my boss and the bane of my life, not my husband.'

Was it her imagination or was that satisfaction she saw glimmer in his eyes?

'I will help you retrieve the memories. I don't deny our marriage can be...what's the word? Like many storms?'

'Tempestuous?' she supplied, fighting the urge to smile.

'That's it. We are very tempestuous but we're happy together.' He straightened his long frame and rolled his shoulders before flashing his irresistible smile. 'I need to get back to work and get things arranged so I can care for you like a good husband should. I'll be back in the morning for when the specialist gets here.'

He handed a business card to the consultant. 'If you have any concerns, call me.' Then he leaned over and placed the briefest of kisses on Anna's lips. 'Try not to worry, *bellissima*. You're the most stubborn woman I know—your memories won't dare do anything but come back to you. Everything will feel better once you're home.'

The endearment, *bellissima*, sounded strange to her ears. The most endearing term Stefano had ever used towards her before had been *bambolina*, Italian for little doll, which he'd thought hilarious. He'd often said he would mistake her for a princess doll were it not for her blunt tongue.

Anna watched him stroll from the hospital room, the good, faithful husband leaving to sort out his affairs so he could dedicate his next few weeks to caring for his poor, incapacitated wife, and all she could think was that she didn't trust him at all.

Until her memories came back or until she spoke to Melissa, whichever came first, she would have to be on her guard. She didn't trust Stefano any further than she could see him.

Stefano strode through the hospital entrance with a spring in his step. It was at times like this, when he had something to celebrate, that he wished he still smoked. But smoking was a habit he'd kicked a decade ago.

He was going to bring his wife home. The woman who'd used, humiliated, left him and tried to blackmail him was going to be back under his roof. He had big plans for her.

Those plans would have to wait a few days while she recovered from the worst of her concussion but in the meantime he fully intended to enjoy her confinement. Anna hated being fussed over. She was incapable of switching off, always needing to be doing something. Having to rest for a minimum of a fortnight would be her worst nightmare.

It cheered him further to know he would be there to witness her live through this horror.

Stefano intended to keep his word and ensure she was well-looked-after while back under his roof. He might despise her all the way to her rotten core but he would never let her suffer physically. He could still taste the fear he'd experienced when she'd dropped in a faint at his feet and knew he never wanted to go through anything like that again. It amazed him that she'd been able to get into his offices without collapsing, something the consultant had been surprised by too. If he hadn't been so angry at her unexpected appearance and unprepared for seeing her for the first time in a month, he would have paid more attention to the fact she'd looked like death warmed up.

Fate had decided to work for him.

Anna didn't remember anything that had happened between them. The whole of the past year had gone, wiped clean away. He could tell her anything and with her confined to his sole care and her sister on the other side of the world, there was no one to disprove it. Judging from the way she'd blanched when she'd learned Melissa had gone to Australia, she would be too angry to make contact with her any time soon.

All he had to remember was to keep his bitterness that she'd fooled him into marrying her inside. Anna could read him too well.

He'd called Melissa as soon as they'd arrived at the hospital, knowing Anna would want her sister there. He'd been put through to her boss and told that Melissa was on leave and had been planning her trip for months. Considering Anna had never mentioned it—and she surely would have done—he guessed Melissa had put off telling her for as long as she could. Certainly, when the two sisters had gone away for their trip to Paris, which *he* had paid for as a treat for his wife and which Anna had returned from early, determined to catch him up to no good, she hadn't known anything about it.

He found Anna alone in her private room flicking through a magazine, dressed in the same black jersey dress from the day before. She greeted him with a wary smile.

'How are you feeling?' he asked.

'Better.'

He sat down in the visitor's chair. 'You look better.' Then he grinned and ran a finger down her soft cheeks, causing her eyes to widen. 'But still too pale.'

She jerked her face away and shrugged. 'I slept but it was patchy.'

'You can rest when we get home.' The consultant had told him in private that the best medicine for concussion was sleep.

'I just can't believe I've lost a whole year of my life.' She held the magazine up. 'Look at the date on this. To me, it's the wrong year. I don't remember turning twenty-four. There are stories in here about celebrities I've never even heard of.'

'Once we get you home I'm sure your memories will start to come back.' But not too soon, he hoped. He had plans for his wife. 'Do you not remember *anything* about our marriage?' He wanted to make double sure.

'Not a thing. The last I remember you were dating that Jasmin woman.'

Jasmin had been the date who'd got food poisoning an hour before his scheduled flight to California for the industry tech awards. It had been her illness that had given him the chance to coerce Anna into attending with him in her place. It was only because it was far too short notice for him to get another date that she'd agreed. That, and the designer dress he'd had couriered over from the designer personally had helped make her decision. The awards evening had ended with Anna insisting the only way she would have sex with him was if he married her.

He didn't doubt her memories of their time together would eventually return. If anyone could bring them back, it would be his wife, the most stubborn, determined woman he'd ever met in his life. But in the meantime...

'Our marriage is a shock for you.'

'That's one way to describe it,' she murmured. 'I'd promised myself I would rather date a baboon than go on a date with you, never mind marry you. Have you really never cheated on me?'

He forced his tone to remain light through the blood roaring in his veins. 'Not once. We've had a few issues but nothing serious. We've been working through them.'

A few months ago he'd been pictured dining with one of his new Swedish directors, a blonde statuesque beauty he hadn't felt even a flicker of attraction towards. Anna had shrugged the ensuing press melee off but he'd known it bothered her. A second photo a fortnight later, this time of him dining with one of his female employees in San Francisco, had only added fuel to the fire. He'd explained his innocence, proving the picture had cropped out the other half-dozen employees also dining with them, and she had outwardly accepted it. But her distrust had grown and she'd no longer bothered to hide it. Her attitude had infuriated him so much he hadn't cared to explain that he liked socialising when he travelled abroad without her because it made the time pass so much quicker.

He should have known from that point that she'd wanted to catch him out just as much as the media had. She had wanted proof of his supposed infidelity.

Her hazel eyes were filled with the suspicion he'd become too familiar with. 'What kind of issues?'

'You've found it hard to be my wife. You don't like the media.' That much at least was true. Anna loathed being under the media spotlight. 'There have been many stories about our marriage being in trouble. If we were to believe the press we've split up a hundred times since we married. It is all poppycock. We married quickly. It is natural for us to have the teething problems.'

Her nose wrinkled. 'When you found me in your office it was as if you'd found the Antichrist trespassing. What was the argument about that made me sleep at Melissa's? Was it that woman I saw you with?'

Dio, even with amnesia her mind ran to suspicion. He'd already told her there was no one else. There hadn't been anyone else since they'd flown to California and their relationship had irrevocably changed.

'That woman you saw me with is my sister.'

'Oh. Sorry.' She looked shamefaced. 'I saw her getting out of the car after you and...'

'And you assumed I was having an affair.' She'd made that exact same assumption when she'd found Christina in their apartment. Finally she'd found the proof she'd been waiting for from the very moment they'd made their vows. If she'd bothered to ask for the truth he would have given it, but she hadn't cared for the truth. All she'd wanted was evidence of infidelity so she could bleed him for as much of his hard-earned money as she could get her grasping hands on.

He'd planned to reveal his sister in court, in front of a judge, so the law could see Anna's accusation for the entrapment it was. He'd looked forward to her humiliation. Now he had a different kind of humiliation in mind, one that would be far more pleasurable. If she retrieved her memories before he could pull it off then so be it. He would enjoy it while it lasted.

'Sorry,' she repeated. 'I thought you were an only child.'

'So did I until recently. I'll tell you about it when you're not so exhausted.'

On cue, she covered her mouth and yawned widely, then blinked a number of times as if trying to keep her eyes open.

'Lie down and rest,' he said. 'The specialist will be here soon and then we'll be able to go home and you'll be able to sleep as much as you need.'

As much as he despised the very air she breathed, seeing her vulnerable and weak sat badly inside him, made him feel strangely protective. It made him want to hold her close and stroke her hair until she fell asleep. He much preferred it when her wits were sharp. It put them on equal footing. Her amnesia was a weapon in his own arsenal that he would use to his advantage but he wouldn't unleash its full force until he was satisfied she was over the worst of her concussion.

She nodded and lay down, curling up in the foetal position she always favoured when she slept. After a few minutes of silence when he thought she'd fallen asleep, she said, without opening her eyes, 'What did we argue about that was so bad I spent the night at my flat?'

'It wasn't anything serious. It's still your flat too and you often stay there. We've both been playing games. We're both stubborn, neither of us likes to admit to being wrong, but we always make it up.'

'If it wasn't serious, why were you so angry with me yesterday? You were grumpy for most of the time in the hospital too.'

Typical Anna. When she wanted an answer to something she was like a dog with a bone until she got it.

'I was hurt that you rejected me. I didn't understand you had amnesia. I was out of my mind with worry about you. Worry makes me grumpy. I'm sorry for behaving like that.'

Her eyes opened, an amusement he hadn't seen for a long time sparkling in them. 'An apology and an admission to hurt feelings? Have you damaged your brain too?'

He laughed and leaned over to press a kiss to her cheek. She scowled at the gesture, which made him laugh more.

It was as if this Anna beside him had been reset to factory settings before marriage had even been mentioned between them.

'I know you have no memories of us. I have to be hopeful they will return.' But not too soon. Too soon and he wouldn't be able to fulfil the plan that had formed almost the instant the consultant had informed him that his estranged wife had amnesia.

Their wedding anniversary was now only nine days away. To celebrate it, he had a surprise planned for her that no amount of amnesia would ever allow her to forget.

CHAPTER THREE

ANNA GAWKED AS the driver came to a stop along the Embankment. She'd always been curious about Stefano's home, situated in a high-rise residential complex overlooking the Thames, which, at the time of building, had been the most expensive development in the world. So naturally, Stefano owned the most expensive apartment within it: the entire top floor.

The driver opened Stefano's door. Before he could get out she touched his arm, only lightly but with an instinctive familiarity she'd never used before. 'You could be telling me anything about our relationship. I can't disprove any of it. How do I know I can trust you?'

'In all the time you worked for me did you ever know me to lie?' he answered steadily.

'I never caught you out in a lie,' she conceded. In the eighteen months she'd worked for him their relationship had been nothing less than honest, brutally so on occasion.

'So trust me.' He held her gaze with that same intense look that sent tendrils of something curling up her spine.

'It doesn't seem I have much choice.'

If she could remember her phone's pin code she could reach Melissa and ask her but even if she could, she knew she wouldn't make that call. Not yet. The thought of speaking to her sister made her feel sick. She wouldn't call her until she could trust she wouldn't scream down the line at her and say things she knew she would regret.

She must have known about Melissa's trip. Melissa's letter had said as much. She'd asked for her forgiveness.

How could she forgive that? After everything their mother had done and put them through? Their father had been six feet under for less than six months when their mother had started seeing an Australian man she met through a dating agency. Anna, who'd been desperately grieving the loss of the father she'd adored, had tried to understand her mother's loneliness. She really had. She'd resisted the urge to spit in the usurper's tea, had been as welcoming as she could be, believing Melissa's private assertion that it was nothing but a rebound fling by a lonely, heartbroken woman and that it would fizzle out before it really started. If only.

Three months after meeting him, nine months after she'd buried her husband, Anna's mother had announced she was emigrating to Australia with her new man.

Stefano pressed his thumb to her chin and gently stroked it. 'When your memories come back you will know the truth. I will help you find them.'

Her heart thudding, her skin alive with the sensation of his touch, Anna swallowed the moisture that had filled her mouth.

When had she given in to the chemistry that had always been there between them, always pulling her to him? She'd fought against it right from the beginning, having no intention of joining the throng of women Stefano enjoyed such a legendary sex life with. To be fair, she didn't have any evidence of what he actually got up to under the bed sheets; indeed it was something she'd been resolute in *not* thinking about, but the steady flow of glamorous, sexy women in and out of his life had been pretty damning.

One of her conditions for accepting the job as his PA was that he must never ask her to be a go-between between him and his lovers. No way would she be expected to leave her desk to buy a pretty trinket as a kiss-off to a dumped lover. When she'd told him this he had roared with laughter.

When had she gone from liking and hugely admiring him but with an absolute determination to never get into bed with him, to marrying him overnight? She'd heard of whirlwind marriages before but from employee to wife in twenty-four hours? Her head hurt just trying to wrap itself around it.

Had Stefano looked at her with the same glimmer in his green eyes then as he was now? Had he pressed his lips to hers or had she been the one...?

'How will you help me remember us?' she asked in a whisper.

His thumb moved to caress her cheek and his voice dropped to a murmur. 'I will help you find again the pleasure you had in my bed. I will teach you to become a woman again.'

Mortification suffused her, every part of her anatomy turning red.

I will teach you to be a woman again?

His meaning was clear. He knew she was a virgin.

Anna's virginity was not something she'd ever discussed with anyone. Why would she? Twenty-three-year-old virgins were rarer than the lesser-spotted unicorn. For Stefano to know that...

Dear God, it was *true*.

All the denial she'd been storing up fell away.

She really had married him.

And if she'd married him, she must have slept with him. Which meant all her self-control, not just around him but in her life itself, had been blown away.

She'd taken such pride in her self-control after her mum had left. Events might fall out of her power but her own behaviour was something she controlled with iron will. All those teenage parties she'd been to when alcohol, cigarettes and more illicit substances were passed around and couples found empty spaces in which to make out... She'd been the one sitting there sipping on nothing stronger than a cola and taking great pride in the fact that she was in control of all her faculties. Her self-control was the only thing she'd *had* control of in a life where she'd been powerless to stop her father dying or her mother moving to the other side of the world and leaving her behind.

A different heat from the mortification ravaging her now bloomed as her mind suddenly pictured Stefano lying on top of her...

His eyes still holding hers as if he would devour her in one gulp, Stefano trailed his fingers down her neck and squeezed her shoulder. 'Let's get you inside. You must rest. You're exhausted.'

Anna blew out a long breath and nodded. For once she was completely incapable of speech.

She'd shared a bed with him.

She'd shared more than a bed with him.

Trying desperately to affect nonchalance, she had no choice but to allow him to assist her through the grand atrium of his apartment building to his private elevator. It was either that or have her unsteady legs collapse beneath her again.

She'd always been physically aware of him before but with his arm slung protectively around her shoulders that awareness flew off the scale.

The dividing line she'd erected between them and worked so hard to maintain... Noting Stefano's easy familiarity with her; the way he was so comfortable touching her now along with the flirting she'd long been used to... Yes, that dividing line had been demolished.

She just wished her body didn't sing its delight at his new proprietorial manner with her.

It was such a relief to be led to a sofa to collapse onto that it took her a moment, catching her breath, to take stock of Stefano's home.

Her home.

It was like stepping into another world.

She was sitting in a living room so vast and wide she felt like a toddler who'd stumbled into a ballroom, the room complete with a gold-leafed crystal chandelier gleaming magnificently above her.

Floor-to-ceiling windows covered the entire perimeter and from one aspect gave the most amazing view of the Thames—was that Westminster Bridge she could see in the near distance?

Not a single memory was jogged by any of it. She'd lived here for almost a year but she was seeing it for the first time.

She looked around wondering where everyone was. 'No staff?'

'I don't have staff. The concierge service runs my housekeeping for me and I pay them a fortune for it.'

When Stefano had first made his fortune in his home town of Lazio, he'd employed live-in staff but had soon learned to dislike having other people in his space.

Housekeeper, cleaners, butler, chef, gardener...the list had been endless. Being waited on hand and foot sounded fantastic in theory but in practice it was a drag and he'd put the staff on day-only duties within weeks.

He was a fully grown man who'd been caring for himself since he was fifteen. He didn't need someone to dress him or run his baths. He saw his peers with their homes full of enough staff to fill a cinema and thought them fools for allowing themselves to revert to infancy.

It was all the fawning he couldn't abide. That was one of the reasons he'd been so keen to employ Anna as his PA. She'd been completely unaffected by meeting him, a reaction he hadn't received in years. In a business setting he was used to fear being the primary reaction; in his personal life he received desire from women and enthusiasm from men, both sexes looking at him with dollar signs flashing in their eyes. Anna had looked at him with disdain.

He'd strolled into the Levon Brothers offices when they'd been in early discussion about him buying the business from them and she'd been behind the desk in the office guarding theirs. He'd handed her his coat as he walked past for her to hang for him and heard a sarcastic 'You're welcome,' in his wake. He'd paused at the door he'd been about to open and looked at her, standing with his coat in her arms, challenge set in her eyes, jutting chin and pursed lips.

'What did you say?' he'd asked.

'I said that you're welcome. I meant to say it in my head just as I'm sure your thanks for me taking your coat off your hands was said in *your* head, but it slipped out.'

It had been a sharp salutary reminder of the importance of manners, something no one had dared to pull him up on for many years and it had taken a scrap of a woman to do just that.

He'd put a hand to his chest, made a mocking bow and said, 'Thank you.'

She'd nodded primly and crossed the room to hang his coat on the stand. Shorter than the women who usually caught his eye, she had the most exquisite figure, perfectly proportioned. He remembered exactly what she'd been wearing that day, a billowing checked skirt that had fallen below her knees, long tan boots with spiked heels, a tight black vest and a fitted khaki-coloured jacket, all pulled together with a thick belt with studs that looked sharp enough to have someone's eye out.

'Do I dare ask if you make coffee?' he'd asked, fascinated by her.

'You can ask but beware—refusal often offends.'

Roaring with laughter, he'd gone into his meeting. Within an hour, when the beautiful, sarcastic secretary had been brought in six times to explain the report she'd compiled for him but which the idiots running the company didn't understand, he'd known he was going to buy the company and poach her to be his PA. It turned out Anna was the real brains behind Levon Brothers. Without her by their side and covering their messes, it would never have taken off. With her by Stefano's side, Moretti's could only strengthen further.

It had been the best business decision he'd ever made. He'd learned to trust her judgement completely.

He'd believed her to be as straight as a line. He'd thought that with Anna what you saw was what you got, when all along she'd been nothing but a grasping gold-digger.

Now the bravado that always shone in her eyes was muted by alarm. 'It's just you and me here?'

'We like our privacy,' he said. 'We can walk around naked without having to worry that we'll frighten anyone.'

Her cheeks turned the most becoming crimson but she raised a tired brow and wanly retorted, 'I can assure you I won't be walking anywhere naked within a mile of you.'

Amused by her stubbornness even when she was so clearly ready to fall into a dead sleep, he whispered into her ear, 'And I can assure you that when you're feeling better you will never want to put your clothes on. Believe me, *bellissima*, we spend a lot of time together naked.'

'If I don't remember it then it didn't happen.'

Studying the firm set of her lips, he remembered what it had been like between them when they'd first married. He'd had no idea she was a virgin until she'd blurted it out when they'd walked into the bridal suite hours after exchanging their vows. She'd stood as defiant as she did now but there had been something in her eyes he'd never seen in her before: fear. That had been a bigger shock than her declaration of virginity.

He'd made love to her so slowly and tenderly that night that when he'd felt her first climax he'd been as triumphant and elated as if he'd been the first man to conquer Mount Everest. That night had been special. Precious. And it had only been the start.

Once Anna had discovered the joy of sex she'd been a woman reborn and unleashed.

She had no memories of any of it. When he next saw her naked, for Anna it would be the first time, and he remembered how painfully shy she'd been then.

He took one of her hands and razed a kiss across the knuckles. 'Can you walk to the bedroom or shall I carry you?'

Her eyes flashed and she managed to inflect dignity into her reply. 'I can walk.'

She allowed him to help her to her feet and held onto his arm as he led her to the bedroom he'd slept alone in for the past month.

The last twenty-four hours had brought such a change to his fortunes that Stefano was tempted to wonder whether it was *he* who had suffered a bump to his head.

His wife was back under his roof and shortly to be back in his bed.

He caught her unconcealed surprise when he opened the door to reveal a room cast in soft muted colours and dominated by an enormous emperor bed.

'We chose the decor together,' he told her. '*You* chose the bed.' It had been the first thing they'd bought as a married couple. He'd known she would hate sleeping in a bed he'd shared with other women.

And now they would share it again. Anna needed to know that this was *theirs*, a bedroom they'd created together, a room they'd made love in hundreds of times. He needed to consolidate in her mind that they were a properly married couple and that it was natural for them to sleep together.

He couldn't begin to dissect his own feelings about sleeping by the side of the woman who had played him for a fool so spectacularly.

'Seriously?' she asked in a voice that had gone husky.

'*Sì*. And when you're better I can promise you'll enjoy it as we always used to. But all that can wait. Consultant's orders are for you to do nothing but rest for the next few

days. I promised I would take care of you and you know
I am a man of my word.'

He always kept his word. To his way of thinking it
was what separated humans from animals. He'd married Anna giving his word that he would be faithful. He'd
given his word that if he ever felt the impulse to cheat
he would tell her before acting on it and they would go
their separate ways.

She'd given him her word too. She'd promised she
would trust him. Her word had been a lie. Her intentions
had been a lie. It had *all* been a lie. Their entire marriage
had been built on lies and deception. No sooner had she
left him than she'd hit him with her demands for a massive slice of the fortune he'd built from nothing.

Anna was a greedy liar who had made a fool of him,
and for that she would pay the price.

But however greedy and conniving his wife was, right
then she was too wiped out for any games.

She slumped onto the bed and sat there blinking to
try and keep her eyes open. He sank to his knees and
unlaced her boots before carefully removing them, then
got her settled and comfortable under the bed sheets.
She was asleep before the automatic curtains had finished shutting.

His guts twisted as he took in the sallowness of her
complexion and the dark hollows under her eyes. He
fought his primal reaction to lean over and smooth the
hair from her face and place a kiss on her cheek.

He closed the door on the darkened room. There was
no place in their relationship for sympathy. Anna's amnesia and her current vulnerability did not change what
she'd done to him. Nothing could change that.

Soon her concussion would pass and she would be physically fit again.

Then the games could commence in earnest.

When Anna next opened her eyes, her first conscious thought was that someone lay beside her.

Not *someone*. Stefano.

When had he come to bed?

She hardly remembered getting into bed herself her exhaustion had been so sudden and so complete.

Stefano had brought her to the apartment early afternoon. Judging by the absolute darkness shrouding her it now had to be the early hours of morning. She must have slept for a good twelve hours straight and she felt better for it. The nausea had gone and her head felt thick and fuzzy rather than pounding. Her throat was parched but even if she knew where the kitchen was she didn't dare move from the bed. She hardly dared to breathe.

That was Stefano lying beside her, sharing this bed. If she moved her foot it would brush against his leg.

Did he have clothes on? Or was he lying there naked…?

The only sounds were his rhythmic breathing and the thundering of her heart.

It was the strangest feeling in the world to be in such an intimate environment with him, especially after eighteen months of doggedly keeping their relationship on a professional footing. She'd spent more time with him than anyone else when their working lives had bound them together. They'd travelled all over the world together, eaten together, had the occasional drink together, sniped at each other, laughed at each other, laughed with each other, sworn at each other, thrown things at each other…yet she had never allowed him to cross the threshold into her private life and had steadfastly refused to cross the threshold into his. They'd never been alone as they were now.

And here she was. Married to him and wholly aware that during their marriage they had done far more than merely sleep in this bed.

Stefano awoke with an almost painfully obvious erection. In their marriage's previous life he would have pulled Anna into his arms and made love to her before either of them had opened their eyes. Today he jumped out of bed and took a shower before he could act on that urge.

While he'd told himself that it was no big deal sharing a bed with his wife again, he'd had to psych himself up to join her in it. That had been unexpected. He'd gazed at her sleeping form in the dim light and experienced the strangest combination of loathing and compassion sweep over him.

He'd never known Anna to be ill before. He'd never seen her vulnerable. He'd lain beside her unable to get out of his mind that she was there, in his bed, the place he had once believed she belonged. It had taken him an age to fall asleep.

As he lathered himself with his expensive shower gel, it occurred to him that this was the first time in a month he'd woken up feeling this kind of desire.

Celibacy was not a healthy state to live by and he could only assume it was his loathing for Anna consuming all his waking moments that had stopped him seeking another woman in the month since she'd gone. He hadn't even thought of another woman to warm his bed; no wonder he reacted so viscerally just to have her back beside him.

But he wouldn't act on it yet. Seduction of his wife would have to wait for now.

Anna was awake and sitting up when he returned to the bedroom with only a towel around his waist. He noted the way her eyes widened at his bare torso and smirked.

'Feeling better?' he asked. She looked better. Her face had regained its colour, although that could be due to embarrassment at his semi-naked form. This was the first time in her memories that she had seen him anything but fully clothed. He worked hard to keep himself in shape and she had made no secret of her appreciation of his body.

She jerked a nod and pulled the covers tighter. That she was still wearing the jersey dress she'd collapsed in two days ago only made her embarrassment more amusing.

He strode over the thick carpet to his dressing room. 'Can I get you anything? A cup of tea?'

Anna was addicted to tea. He'd once counted her drink nine cups in one day.

'Tea would be good, thanks,' she muttered.

'Painkillers? Food?'

'Just painkillers, please.'

Deciding not to torment her further by dressing in front of her, he threw on a pair of jeans and a black T-shirt in his dressing room, then went to the kitchen where her teapot and teabags still lived.

He automatically reached for her favourite morning mug, a vessel so large it could reasonably be classed as a bucket, and a fresh burst of fury lashed through him.

He should have got rid of all her possessions instead

of keeping them here as a constant reminder. He'd given in to his anger only the once since she'd left him, in their San Francisco apartment, and had despised himself for his momentary weakness. Since then, his fury had been internal, simmering under his skin, crawling through him, festering.

Anna's amnesia had given him the perfect means to channel his rage into something far more satisfying than making a bonfire from her belongings.

His rage was back under his full control when he took her tea to her and placed it on her bedside table.

'I've ordered a light breakfast for you,' he said, handing her the painkillers.

'I'm not hungry.'

'You need to eat something.'

Anna took the pills from him and pulled a face, but her retort about not wanting to eat died on her lips when she noticed his bare wedding finger. She looked at her own bare hand and asked, 'Why don't we wear wedding rings?'

'You didn't want to. You said it would make you feel like a possession.'

'You didn't mind?'

'It was a compromise. You agreed to take my name on condition of no rings.'

'I would have thought it would be the other way round and that I'd refuse to take your name,' she mused.

His smile was fleeting. 'You wanted to be a Moretti so when we have children we can all have the same name.'

'We want children?' That shocked her almost as much as learning she was married to him had.

He shrugged then flashed his gorgeous smile. 'At some

point. When we're ready. Until then we've been enjoying practising making them.'

Something poked in her memories, squeezing her heart and making her stomach clench so hard his unsubtle innuendo barely registered. Desperately she tried to capture the feeling but whatever *it* was fluttered out of reach before she could put her finger on it.

'What is it?' he asked, staring at her with drawn brows.

'I don't know.' She shrugged and shook her head. 'Not a memory. A feeling.'

'Good or bad?'

'Painful.' That was the only word she could think of to describe it. She'd always wanted children but it had been something shoved to the back of her mind, a 'one day' want. She'd imagined she would one day reach the stage where her biological clock started ticking furiously and then be forced to make her decision. And that would have been hard as she'd always avoided relationships. If her own mother hadn't loved her enough to stay, how could she trust any man to?

When had she looked at Stefano and decided she could trust *him*?

She'd been attracted to him from the first moment she'd met him but which woman wouldn't be? The outrageously handsome, infamous boss of Moretti's had strolled into her office as if he already owned the building and had arrogantly placed his coat in her arms without a single word of greeting, never mind thanks. When she'd sarcastically responded with, 'You're welcome,' to his retreating back, she hadn't cared about offending him. Being a woman in a heavily male-dominated environment had caused her to grow skin as thick as leather and she'd adopted an unwillingness to tolerate sexism in any form. She'd known her worth to Levon Brothers as well as they had. She'd merely been given the title of secretary because her two bosses there had been too unimaginative to think of a more appropriate title. They'd only been a few years older than her, a couple of eggheads with more brains than an elephant and less common sense than a dormouse.

Stefano had paused and turned to face her and in that moment she had experienced a flicker of nerves at crossing some invisible line with a man with such a ferocious reputation; a billionaire who'd come from nothing and served time in jail, but then their eyes had clashed and something else had flickered inside her. Attraction.

So attractive had she found him that she'd thought long and hard before accepting his job offer. He'd assumed she was playing hardball for more money and increased his offer, but money had been the least of her concerns. Stefano had a magnetism about him, a power that clung to his tailored suits and the dashing looks of a matinee idol. All this and the element of danger that oozed from him had proven a potent mixture and one she'd been wary of committing her working life to.

In the end, the pluses of taking the job had outweighed the minuses. She had never regretted her decision. She enjoyed working with him. Even on those days when they'd be working towards some deadline that would see them in the office late in the evening, bad-tempered and shouting at each other, she had never regretted it. That she'd spent most days fighting her own responses to touch him or act in any way inappropriately was something she had learned to live with. That Stefano seemed to know exactly how badly she desired him was something she had sworn to never give him the satisfaction of confirming.

So how had he worn her defences down enough to persuade her to marry him and consider having children together?

A ring vibrated through the apartment, startling her.

'That will be our breakfast,' he said.

'That was quick.'

'That's why I pay such a high price for the service.' He reached the bedroom door. 'You need to build your strength up, *bellissima*. I need you fit to fly in a few days.'

'Why? Where are we going?'

'California.' The smile he gave was unlike any she'd seen on his lips before. 'It's the industry awards next week. And our first wedding anniversary. Where better to celebrate it than where it all started?'

Stefano waited until he heard the shower running, then dialled the contact on his phone.

Anna had spent her second day in the apartment sleeping on and off. After her small evening meal she'd declared she needed a shower. Her health was improving by the minute.

His call was answered within two rings.

'Miranda, it's Stefano,' he said. 'How would you like the celebrity scoop of the year?'

CHAPTER FOUR

FOR THE SECOND night in a row Anna woke to darkness and the regular deep breaths coming from her right. The covers she'd burrowed under had been pulled down and the chill of the winter night covered her skin.

Holding her breath, she turned her head to look at him. Stefano slept with his back to her, the covers twisted around his waist. As with the night before, he slept deeply. She couldn't keep her eyes off him. Her heart seemed to make a clenching motion and the urge to rest her hand against his warm skin grew almost overwhelming.

Cautiously, she tugged at the sheets, trying to dislodge them without waking him. She managed to free a couple of inches, and tried again.

She didn't want to wake him. There was something about the darkness of night that heightened the intimacy being alone in his apartment evoked in her senses.

She would never have believed he could be so attentive. Nothing was too much trouble for him, not the endless cups of tea, the regular small meals…he'd even had a pair of pyjamas couriered to her from Selfridges. She was certain that if she were to wake him up and ask him for something he would do it without complaint. It made her realise that she must mean something to him as a wife, that he had true feelings for her. If only she could remember what her own feelings towards *him* were.

Eventually she came to the conclusion that she would have to wake him. It was either that or freeze.

'Stefano,' she whispered. When there was no response, she repeated his name, louder. Still no response.

She would have to touch him…

She took a deep breath, then quickly poked him in the back. 'Wake up. You've stolen all the covers.'

It was like arguing with a corpse.

After trying to wake him a few more times with minimal contact, she sat up. Now holding her breath, she put a hand to his shoulder and gave it a quick shake before snatching her hand away.

That did the trick.

He rolled over. 'What's the matter? Are you feeling ill?'

'You're hogging the bed sheets.' She lay back down and fixed her gaze to the ceiling, making sure to keep a good distance between them.

'Sorry.' He yawned widely then untangled himself and breached the small distance she'd created to pull the covers up to her shoulders. Then he settled himself back down next to her, on his side, facing her. A centimetre closer and he would be pressed against her. 'We decided long ago that you're a refrigerator at night and I'm a radiator.'

Going by the heat coming off him now she could believe it.

She swallowed and croaked out a reply that was nowhere near as witty or nonchalant as she wanted. 'I normally sleep with bed socks on.'

Bed socks were as unsexy as they came and right then

she was prepared to grab at anything that didn't make her think of sex.

He chuckled lightly, as if he knew what she was thinking. He was so close his warm breath whispered against her skin. 'You don't need them any more. We both sleep naked. I keep you warm.'

She tried to breathe but suddenly it seemed as if all the air had been sucked from the room. As hard as she tried to resist, her head turned of its own accord to face him.

A flame flickered to life inside her, turning her core to liquid. If she rolled over she would be flush against him.

Help her, she wanted to be flush against him. Her lips tingled to feel his mouth on hers again but this time for her to be coherent enough to savour the moment.

As if he could sense her silent yearning, Stefano breached that last, tiny distance and brushed his lips to hers in the softest of caresses.

And then he pulled away and rolled over so his back was to her again. 'Go back to sleep, *bellissima*.'

Anna only just stopped herself from crying out. She clamped her lips together and lay there rigidly, waiting for her heartbeat to return to its normal rhythm and the flames still flickering inside her to subside.

If they weren't married she would be plotting her escape from this dangerous situation where the biggest peril was herself. Yet somewhere in her past, in the blank space that was her memories, Stefano had worn her defences down. She'd acted on the desire she felt for him.

And now, God help her, she wanted to act on it again.

Anna managed to fall back into a light sleep, a restless state where her body didn't know if it was awake or dreaming. Stefano seemingly had no such problems, sleeping deeply while she lay fidgeting, her mind a whirl, questioning everything: her marriage, her sister's betrayal… When six o'clock finally struck she decided to get up.

Physically, she felt a lot better. Almost normal. Her legs had lost the jelly-like feeling she'd been experiencing every time she stood and the ache in her head was now a dull thud rather than rivalling a pneumatic drill.

Tiptoeing over the thick carpet so as not to wake Stefano, she opened her dressing-room door and closed it quickly behind her so the light wouldn't disturb him. It was the first time she'd entered this room.

She experienced another in a long list of surreal moments. Floor-to-ceiling fitted white wardrobes lined the walls, while at the far end of the room sat a vanity desk, a full-length mirror and a squishy armchair. And it was all hers.

She opened the nearest door and found a row of trousers and jeans. The next door opened to display a row of tops. As she fingered the expensive material of a silk green and black checked shirt that caught her eye, a memory flickered, a sudden image of herself in this very room looking at herself in the mirror wearing this very top.

It was the first concrete memory of her missing year since she'd woken three days ago.

Stefano woke to a bed he knew was empty before he opened his eyes. Through the duration of their marriage he'd become accustomed to waking next to Anna, usually with their arms and legs entwined. He'd learned as a teenager to sleep anywhere he could rest his head but nowhere did he sleep as deeply or as sweetly as when Anna lay beside him. He hated that fact about himself.

He shrugged on his robe and went in search of her. He found her in the kitchen looking through a drawer, dressed in her favourite green and black checked shirt and a pair of slim-fitting dark grey canvas trousers. Her hair was brushed and pulled back in a loose ponytail and on her feet were the fluffy duck slippers he'd bought as one of her birthday presents. He'd chosen them as a joke but of all the things he'd bestowed her with on that day, which included a surprise holiday to the Seychelles, the slippers had been her favourite.

He'd spotted a pair of fluffy lamb ones only a week ago and his first thought had been to buy them for her as an early Christmas present. A split second later he'd remembered that Anna no longer lived with him and the only Christmas present she would receive from him would be his contempt.

'It's good to see you up.' He hooked an arm around her waist, dropped a kiss on the nape of her neck and inhaled her delicious soft floral scent.

Turning his back on her in the early hours of the night had been hard but necessary. He'd sensed her desire simmering beneath her rigid surface and known that with only a little persuasion on his part she would be his for the taking. But it was too soon for her. When he seduced her anew, he wanted his wife to be a tinderbox of desire for him. He wanted her to beg for his possession. He wanted her helpless to do anything but melt in his arms. He wanted her fully fit and knowing exactly what she was doing.

The more heightened her emotions and desire for him, the greater the low that would follow when he exacted his revenge.

She stiffened but didn't pull away or shrug him off.

He pressed one more kiss to her neck and stepped back.

'What are you looking for?'

She cleared her throat but kept her back to him. 'My phone charger. I can't find it anywhere and yours doesn't fit into my phone.'

'You probably left it at the flat.' There was no probably about it.

'Can we go and get it?'

'Sure. What do you need it for?'

She turned her head and cast him with a glance that contained a trace of amusement. 'To charge my phone, obviously.'

Oh, yes, she was definitely on the mend.

Then her amusement turned to a scowl and she flung the phone to one side. 'I guess it doesn't matter if I get the charger when I can't remember the pin code to get into it. Do you know what it is?'

'No.'

'Can I use your phone?'

'What for?' he asked cautiously.

'I want to call Melissa.' There was the slightest tremor in her voice. 'You must have her number.'

'I do,' he admitted. It was pointless to lie. If Anna was determined to speak to her sister she would find a way. His job at this point was to deter her. 'Are you sure it's wise to speak to her yet?'

'I want to know why she's gone to visit our mother... unless you can tell me?'

'Her decision to go was very sudden,' he said, thinking quickly. 'I shouldn't speculate what her reasons were.'

'I only want to know why she's gone. You say you're

my husband—this is the sort of thing a husband would know.'

'I *am* your husband, Anna, but Melissa's reasons are hers alone. I don't think you should contact her until your memories return. If they come back to you before she gets home from Australia then you will know the truth for yourself. If they haven't come back by then, the two of you can sit down and you can hear her reasons from her own mouth.'

Her eyes flashed with anger. 'Our mother abandoned us to live with another man when our dad wasn't even cold in his grave. I don't want to wait for a month to know why Melissa's suddenly decided to forgive her.'

Stefano strove to keep his features neutral. Anna must assume he already knew all this but he'd only known the basics about her mother's emigration to Australia. The way she'd always spoken about it was that staying in England to live with her sister was something they'd all been happy about and that the two sisters' estrangement from their mother had grown organically over time, a simple result of living on opposite sides of the world.

He didn't want to know any more. She'd had a year to confide her secrets to him but had chosen to keep them to herself.

Stefano held no truck with traumatic childhoods. His own was there for the world to see. He wasn't in the least ashamed of his past but could think of nothing worse than sitting down to dissect its effect on him. The only effect had been to act as fuel for his success.

He didn't want to know anything more about his wife than he already did. He didn't want to delve into her psyche and would not allow her to delve into his.

That chance had long gone.

He took her hands in his and brought them to his lips. 'I know you find Melissa's actions painful but all that matters is getting your memories back. Everything will fall into place when they return.'

She held his gaze, the ire slowly evaporating from them until she sighed. 'It's not just Melissa. Or you. I feel so out of the loop with everything. I was watching the news earlier and there's so much happening in the world I know nothing about.'

It was only eight o'clock. 'How long have you been awake?'

'A couple of hours. I've had so much sleep that I'm all rested out.'

'You should have woken me.'

'I knew you'd say that. And I did think about it but, other than my head aching a little, I feel normal. It would have been mean to wake you. Besides, you sleep like the dead.'

'Fed up of being fussed over?' he teased.

The wry smile broadened and she sniggered. 'Fed up and bored rigid. There's not even any housework for me to do. Everywhere is spotless.'

'I knew it wouldn't take long for you to get bored,' he said smugly. 'But I have a cure for your boredom. Let's fly to California tonight. The sun and change of scenery will do you good and being there might act as one of those joggers the specialist spoke about.'

California was where she'd reeled him in like a fish on a hook. It was only fitting he did the same in return.

Her face suddenly brightened. 'I did have a memory come to me when I was in my dressing room. Nothing significant, just a memory of wearing this shirt.'

A sharp stabbing struck at his brain. 'It's your favourite,' he confirmed, forcing his features to relax. 'And that memory must be a good sign.'

'I hope so,' she said reverently. 'It's a start in any case.'

'It is. So do I tell my crew they're taking us to California today?'

She thought for a moment then nodded. 'Do it. It can only help me.'

'I shall make the call now.'

'Aren't we going to San Francisco?' Anna asked when Stefano's driver took them down a different highway from the route she remembered. She'd travelled with him on business to San Francisco a number of times, stopping at a hotel while he would stay in his penthouse apartment.

He grinned. 'Your amnesia means I get to surprise you twice.'

'What do you mean?'

'You'll see.'

They'd landed on a sunny late afternoon. The Californian warmth felt wonderful on her skin, the majestic redwood trees lining the route as they wound through the mountains...

'Are we going to Santa Cruz?' she asked as they drove past a sign with the name of an approaching town she recognised. She'd gone for a hike in the summer through the Forest of Nisene Marks State Park on her day off during a week spent in the Moretti's San Francisco building.

'You'll see,' he repeated. He took hold of her hand and brought it to his lips to breathe a kiss across the knuckles.

She snatched it away. 'Can you stop playing games for two minutes and give me a straight answer?'

Although she'd slept for most of the flight, her body thought it was the early hours of the morning, not the early Californian evening they'd landed in. It was driving her crazy that he wouldn't give her a straight answer to anything, not even their destination.

He cast her with hurt eyes that didn't fool her for a second. 'I like to give you surprises.'

'Don't give me that. You're on one of your power trips. You're loving having me at your mercy.'

'I don't have the power trips.'

'But you don't deny that you love me being at your mercy.'

His voice dropped to a murmur as he leaned close to speak in her ear. 'I love nothing more than having you at my mercy, *bellissima*. And you love it too.'

'And you can stop with the innuendoes,' she snapped. 'You're supposed to be helping me get my memories back. All you're doing is alluding to sex. Is that all our marriage amounts to?'

'It's the best part of it.'

'Well, from now on you can take it as read that I know we have a fantastic sex life.' She could feel her cheeks burn as she spoke but refused to allow herself to be distracted. 'So I would appreciate it if you would remember that I know nothing of our life together and am relying on you to fill the holes—and if you make an innuendo out of that I shall get a flight straight back to London.'

His lips twitched and he settled back and folded his arms across his chest. 'What do you want to know?'

'Where we are going for a start!'

Right on cue, his driver took them over the border into the hip, arty city of Santa Cruz.

'We're going to our beach house,' he confirmed. 'We bought it a few months ago. This is the city we got married in.'

Slightly mollified, she said, 'Why did we marry here?'

'California allows quick marriages. I told you to name your city. You chose Santa Cruz.'

'*I* chose? You didn't frogmarch me to a register office?'

'Marriage was your idea.'

'I don't believe you.'

He shrugged. 'It's the truth. You flew to San Francisco with me as my guest for the awards ceremony. At the end of the evening I got my driver to drop you at your hotel first.' He spread his arms. 'We had our first kiss in this car. Things got a little…hot but you wouldn't let me come to your room. I asked what it would take to get you into my bed and you said marriage.'

'I must have been joking.' She *must* have been. Anna had never even thought of marriage, had assumed she would grow into a grey-haired spinster surrounded by dogs—not cats—and had been comfortable with that. Singledom was safe. It wasn't men specifically that she didn't trust, it was people. People were selfish. People put their own needs and wants first. They broke hearts and left others to pick up the shattered pieces.

'You said you were.' He shrugged again and in the movement she thought she glimpsed a darkening of his features that passed so quickly she guessed she'd imagined it. 'But the idea took hold with both of us. I came back to your hotel in the morning knowing I was going to marry you that day. It was what we both wanted.'

'But *why*?'

'We wanted each other and we'd both reached our limit of you keeping me at arm's length. Think about it, *bellissima*—what couple was better suited to marry? We'd worked closely together for eighteen months. We'd seen the worst of each other. We'd fought. We spent more time together than with anyone else but we never quit. If a man and a woman could truly be friends then that's what we were.'

'You're my boss. I'm paid to be nice to you.' But even as she made the jest she was wondering where love had come into it. That was why people married, wasn't it? Because they trusted someone enough to give them their heart as well as their body? It was why she'd never thought *she* would marry.

He snorted with laughter. 'When did that ever stop you saying what you think of me? We married knowing exactly what we were getting into. It made perfect sense.'

And as Stefano finally explained how he'd worn her defences down, a warm feeling spread through her.

For all their sniping at each other in the workplace, they'd forged a strong camaraderie. A bond. She would attend meetings with him, sit in on interviews for both staff and acquisitions, travel the world with him… She'd got to know him so well she would know his opinion on a person or situation before he'd opened his mouth to vocalise it.

She'd learned that though he was an exacting taskmaster, his word was his bond. She might even have learned to trust him.

Suddenly she could see exactly why she'd married him.

Not only was he the sexiest man to walk the planet, but by marrying her Stefano had proven he wanted her as more than just another notch on his endless bedpost.

Love must have been a gradual progression between them. It appeared Stefano was wisely avoiding talk of it knowing it was pointless to talk of love with someone who had no memory of it. His pride must be so hurt with it all, she thought, feeling a twinge of compassion for him, having to be the one to hold her steady until her memories of the life they'd forged together returned; having to trust that they *would* return and that she would remember all they'd meant to each other.

'I can see how it happened,' she said quietly, nodding slowly as she processed it all. 'But I must have asked for some kind of reassurance that you would be faithful. Your track record with women hardly inspires confidence.'

If he hadn't been such an unashamed womaniser she might have given in to her desire for him sooner. There had been nights when she would lay awake aching for him, filled with pent-up frustration that working so closely with him brought. Day after day of breathing in his scent, watching his throat move while he ate and drank, catching a glimpse of exposed torso when he'd rip his constricting tie off or a glimpse of his forearms when he'd roll up his sleeves... She had become obsessed with those arms. She would dream about them. She would dream about him.

'Your only request was that I tell you if I met another woman I wanted to bed so you could walk away with your dignity intact. It was a promise I was happy to make.'

'It's good to know I didn't completely lose my marbles.'

'You did,' he assured her solemnly but with a glint in his eye. 'I told you I would wear you down eventually and I was right.'

'You're always right.'

'*Sì.*'

'In your own head.'

Catching his eye again, Anna suddenly, inexplicably, found herself unable to stop laughing.

'What's so funny?' he demanded to know.

'Everything.' She covered her mouth with her hand, trying hopelessly to regain some composure. 'You must be an amazing kisser if one kiss in the back of a car was enough to make me marry you.'

The wolfish gleam in his eyes and the way he leaned closer made her suddenly certain that he was going to show her exactly what it had been like, right here and now.

She waited in breathless anticipation for his mouth to press on hers.

But then he grinned and the moment was lost. 'We're here.'

CHAPTER FIVE

ANNA SNAPPED HERSELF back to the present. They'd entered a private enclave lined with clean wide roads fringed with palm trees.

As they got out of the car, the salty air of the Pacific and its accompanying breeze filled her senses, along with a tremendous sense of déjà vu. She *knew* this place.

The house they'd stopped outside was stunning, a modern Spanish-style beach home that, from the outside and despite its grandness, looked surprisingly cosy.

Cosy was a word she'd never used in association with Stefano before.

She followed Stefano through the front entrance and into a home that made his London apartment seem like a shoebox.

'Take a look around. I'll get us a drink.' He disappeared through an arch and into the kitchen.

Intrigued by her surroundings, she trod her way through the ground floor, over marble floors, under high ceilings, soft furnishings and elegant decor. The only room accessed by a door was a cinema with a dozen plush leather seats.

Carrying on with her tour, she found an indoor swimming pool, a gym, a majestic dining room... She finally came to a stop at the rear of the house. The glass walls overlooked a palm-tree-lined patio area and another swimming pool, which in turn overlooked a glorious sandy beach and the deep blue Pacific. On the left of the room was the most enormous rounded sofa she'd ever seen, almost bed-like in its proportions.

'You said this is ours?' she asked in amazement when he joined her a short while later holding two tall glasses of fruit juice.

'*Sì.*' He handed a glass to her. 'I would have poured us champagne but it's not a good idea for you to drink alcohol until you're fully recovered from your concussion.'

She raised a brow. 'How do you know I'm not?'

'Because I know you, *bellissima*. I don't want to rush you. When you're fully better we can celebrate.'

'Celebrate what?'

'You being here.'

She couldn't know what a truth that was. Stefano wasn't about to tell her that they hadn't spent a night together under this roof, that the purchase had been finalised three days before she'd left him. Especially as part of the settlement she'd instructed her lawyer to hit him with had been a demand for this house. Now he would taint the memories of it for her as much as she had tainted them for him. Here, in this house that was supposed to have been their first real home, the one they'd chosen together, he would seduce her so thoroughly that all the pleasure they shared would haunt her for ever. Her humiliation would be twofold: public *and* private. Just as his had been.

Her cheeks coloured. She cleared her throat and took

a sip of her juice, then looked around again and said conversationally, 'You like your glass walls, don't you?'

'What do you mean?'

'Your apartment in London has external glass walls. Is there a theme?'

'I don't like to be…what's the word when things are too near to you?'

'Hemmed in? Cramped?'

He shrugged. 'Both could be it. I like space and light. I had enough of being cramped when I was a child.'

'You weren't put in a cupboard under the stairs, were you?' she asked teasingly.

'I spent a year living in a cellar.'

Anna eyed him warily, unsure if he was joking. Everyone knew of Stefano's torrid childhood—he wore it as a badge of honour: the teenage drug-addicted mother who died when he was a toddler, the teenage drug-addicted father who'd disappeared before he'd been born, the grandfather who'd raised him until his own death when Stefano had been only seven at which point he'd been sent to live with a succession of aunts and uncles. He'd always been fighting and causing trouble and being kicked out to live with the next family member until there had been no family members left willing to take him in. From that point on he'd been alone. At the age of fifteen.

He'd spent years begging and fighting to make a living, finding work wherever he could in the seedy underbelly of Lazio's streets. At the age of nineteen, to no one's surprise including his own, he'd been sent to prison but, within a year of his release, the adolescent who had been expected to spend his life as a career criminal had formed the technology company known to the world as Moretti's and the rest was history.

This was all public information. Stefano was happy to talk about his formative years with the media, proud of being the bad boy who'd made a success of himself.

As a PR strategy it had worked fantastically well, capturing the public's imagination and adding an edgy aura to the Moretti brand. It had the added advantage of actually being true, or so Anna had always assumed. Stefano's past crossed the divide from professional to personal so she'd never asked him anything about it other than in the most generic terms. Well, not in her memories in any case.

'Really? A cellar?'

'That was when I lived with my Uncle Vicente. My cousins there wouldn't let me share their rooms.'

'They made you sleep in a cellar because they didn't want to share?'

'They were scared of me—and for good reason. You do not keep kicking a dog and not expect it to bite. I was an angry teenager who liked to fight.'

Fighting was the only answer Stefano had had. A patchy education had left him severely behind at school, which, coupled with always wearing threadbare clothes either too big or too small, had made him a target for bullies. Once he'd realised he could silence the taunts from cousins and school friends alike by using his fists he'd never looked back. A volatile temper and a rapidly growing body had quickly turned him into the boy everyone crossed the road to avoid.

'Were all your family afraid of you?'

'They were when I hit puberty and became bigger

than all of them. I wasn't the skinny kid they could bully any more.'

'Why did they bully you?'

'My mother was the bad girl of the Moretti family and brought shame on them. I was guilty of being her son. They only took me in because it was my *nonno*—my grandfather—his dying wish. They hated me and made sure I knew it.'

'That's horrible,' she said with obvious outrage. 'How can anyone treat a child like that? It's inhuman.'

'It makes you angry?' he asked with interest.

'Of course it makes me angry! If Melissa had a child and anything should happen...' Her voice faltered and she blanched at the weight of her own dark thoughts. 'I would love that child as if it were my own.'

Yes, she probably would. If his wife was capable of loving anyone it was her sister.

She shook her dark hair and took a drink of her juice. 'Do you ever see them now?'

'You know I don't...' But then he remembered she knew nothing of the last year and how all their time not working had been spent in bed. When they'd been only boss and employee she had determinedly made a point of asking him little about his free time. 'The last time I spoke to any of them was when my Uncle Luigi turned up when I was still living in Italy asking for money. My answer would make a nun blush.'

Her face broke into a grin and she laughed. 'I can well imagine.'

'Do you know, I walked out of my Uncle Vicente's house—was kicked out for breaking my cousin David's arm in a fight—thinking of only one thing. Revenge. I would make such a success of myself that my family would have to see pictures of my face everywhere they went and read details of my wealth and know they would never get any of it. Whatever they did with their lives, I would do better. I would earn more money, eat better food, live in a better home, drive a better car. My success would be my revenge and it was. Everything I gained only drove me to get more.'

His revenge had fuelled him. The cousins who had begrudged him the clothes they'd outgrown, the aunts who'd begrudged feeding him, the uncles who'd treated their pets with more respect than they had their orphaned nephew... None of them would see any of his hard-earned gains.

'If the success you've had is any measure, your thirst for revenge must have been huge.'

Almost as great as his thirst for revenge on his wife.

He kept his voice steady as he replied, 'I am not a man to forgive. I forget nothing.'

Anna sat on the sofa, tucking her feet under her bottom and wishing she could put a finger on the danger she felt herself in. She kept her gaze on Stefano and was met with a sparkling gaze and the curve of his lips, yet there were undercurrents to this conversation that she was missing. She could feel it. A darkness, like a shadow that only showed itself intermittently.

'How did you do it?'

'I told people I was eighteen and found jobs on building sites and in clubs... Work was easy to find and working in the clubs meant it was easy to find a woman and a bed for the night.'

'When you were *fifteen*?'

'I didn't look fifteen. Women like a bad boy. I saved as

much as I could earn. I'd saved ten thousand euros when I was sent to prison and lost it all in legal fees.'

'What did you go to prison for? Fighting, wasn't it?'

'I saw a man in one of the clubs I worked at hitting a woman.' He raised his shoulders. 'I stopped him.'

'You beat him up?'

'He deserved it. He was two times her size. She couldn't defend herself. It was one of many fights I had in those years.' His smile was wry. 'The man I beat up that time was a policeman's son who made sure I went down for it.'

'Was prison really awful?' she asked tentatively.

He pulled a face. 'The worst thing was probably the food. Then the boredom. I had quite an easy time compared to many people but when I left I knew I would never go back. It gave me the focus to change. No more fighting.'

'What about the bedding of beautiful women?' she tried to say in a joking voice.

He pulled another face that quite clearly said she was pushing her luck.

If the thought of him bedding others didn't make her chest contract she would laugh.

'I had a little money left. I took it to a casino.'

'You gambled your savings?'

'A hundred euros. That's all I had left. If I lost it, I would have earned it back the next day and started again but I had a feeling… Like… Like…' His face scrunched as he tried to think of the word, and Anna was reminded that his English was entirely self-taught.

'Do you mean you had a gut instinct?'

'*Sì*. That's it. I played it on the roulette table and I won. I won big. I went outside for a cigarette…'

'Since when do you smoke?'

'I haven't for years but I did then. There was another guy out there. He told me about this app he'd designed to track mobile telephone devices. Apps were babies then. Smartphones were babies compared to now. I didn't understand it but I understood that he did. It was a risk but I'd won that money and decided on one last gamble. I put one hundred euros in my pocket and handed the rest to him. We wrote an agreement on a napkin. Two months later he found me and gave me back my investment plus the interest we'd agreed on. For me, it was the start of everything. Smart technology was my future. I didn't know how to develop it for myself but I'd proved I could spot a winner. I backed the brains and reaped the rewards.'

'You've always seemed so confident and knowledgeable about the technologies you invest in,' she said with bemusement.

'That first deal made me one of the first people to see their full potential. I would say I got lucky but luck had nothing to do with it. Instinct and hard work were what got me where I am.' He grinned. 'The best deal I ever made was investing forty per cent in developing that social media site. I made seven billion dollars when it floated on the stock exchange.'

'I remember that.' It had happened before he'd bought Levon Brothers and she'd begun working for him. 'Have you gambled again since that night? In a casino?'

'Gambling is for morons.'

She laughed and drained her glass. 'Your revenge must taste very sweet.'

'It does. Like strawberries and cream at Wimbledon.'

Another burst of laughter escaped her but there was

anger underlying it. 'I'm glad. Your family don't deserve anything after the way they treated you.'

'If they had treated me better, do you think they would have deserved something then?' he asked.

'That's not what I meant,' she protested. 'Your money is yours. You earned it, you're the only one with a right to it. If you choose to share it with anyone then it's that—a choice, not an obligation.'

'You don't think you're entitled to a share of it as my wife?'

'Of course not.'

His eyes burned intensely. 'But say we were to go our separate ways, would you not be tempted to sue for a large share of it?'

'No. And if I know you at all I would gamble my own money that you made me sign a prenup.'

For a brief moment his lips pulled together and his jaw tightened but then his features relaxed. 'We married too quickly for that.'

'So I'm not the only one who lost their marbles, then?'

That made her stomach settle a bit, knowing whatever madness had caught them in its grip to compel them to marry had been mutual. She'd always known Stefano had worked like a lion to build his fortune and enjoyed the fruits of his spoils like a sultan. Until that moment she'd thought she'd understood it but she'd underestimated him. The fight and grit it must have taken for him to build what he had was mind-blowing and her respect for him only grew.

Stefano finished his drink and smiled tightly. 'I think we both went a little mad that day.'

It was an insanity he would never allow himself to fall into again.

Anna put her empty glass on the coffee table. 'Has getting your revenge helped?'

'*Naturalmente.*'

'But has it helped you emotionally? You had such a lot to deal with...'

'It's over,' he interrupted with a shrug. 'I dealt with it at the time and moved on.'

'That's a lot to deal with and you were so young.' Her pretty eyebrows rose disbelievingly. 'I thought I'd been dealt a crummy hand but at least I've always had Melissa.'

Stefano flexed his fingers. He didn't want her sympathy or attempts to delve into his mind.

Anna's actions had hit him in a place his family had never reached.

'We make our own luck and fortune, *bellissima*. The past stays where it is.'

'I'm not so stupid that I don't know my dad's death and my mum's desertion affected me,' she said stubbornly.

'Are you calling me stupid?'

'Of course not. I'm just saying that I don't see how your revenge could have been enough...'

'It was more than enough.' He could feel his ire rising. Anna was the only person who dared speak back to him. They could argue and shout at each other like a pair of wildcats.

Those arguments had always made him feel so alive even before the days when they'd settle cross words in bed.

'We've had a long flight and you're exhausted. Rest for a few hours and then I'll order some food.'

She got to her feet and folded her arms across her

chest. 'Do you always brush me off like this now I'm your wife?'

'I'm not brushing you off; it's just not a subject worth wasting my breath on.'

Seeing her face turn mutinous, he forced a more conciliatory tone of voice. 'Let's not have an argument when we've only just arrived. Come, I'll show you the rest of the house.'

Anna stepped into a bathroom on the second floor with an external wall made entirely of glass.

'I've been in here before,' she said, the words popping out of her mouth as that feeling of déjà vu hit her again, all residue of their almost-argument forgotten.

This memory was more than a feeling though. This one had substance.

She hurried to the glass wall and looked out.

Just as she'd known, the bathroom jutted out over the sunroom on the ground floor giving an immaculate view of the ocean and their strip of private beach.

Excited at this burst of memories, she faced him. 'I remember this! This glass…you can't see in from the outside, can you?' She pointed to the free-standing bath. 'I remember saying how brilliant it would be to have a bath in here and watch the ocean. I *remember*.'

'I didn't think a bath would act as a jogger,' he said drily but with a stiff undertone that made her look at him.

He'd come to stand beside her. His face was inscrutable as he gazed out. 'Are you remembering anything else?'

Her excitement diminished as more longed-for memories stayed stubbornly stuck in the void. 'No.'

'More will come. I don't think it will be long.'

'I hope so,' she said fervently. 'It's so frustrating. You're going to have to fill me in on everything about work if they don't come back soon.'

'Forget work.' He gathered a lock of hair that had fallen onto a shoulder and smoothed it off her neck. 'I don't want you thinking about it until we return to London.'

'I can decide for myself what I think, thank you.'

'Your beautiful mind is one of the many things I adore about you.' He placed his other hand on her neck and gazed down at her. 'But all I want is for you to get better. I'm thinking of you, *bellissima.*'

'I *am* better.'

'Almost.' He stepped closer and inhaled. 'You're almost there.'

CHAPTER SIX

'Do you miss Italy?' Anna asked some hours later. She'd had a three-hour nap in their four-poster bed, which even had muslin curtains, then a shower, and gone downstairs to find Stefano had ordered Italian takeaway for them.

Now they were sitting outside on the terrace, the roar of the Pacific their music.

'I miss the food.' He removed the lid of one large box to reveal a sharing platter of antipasti.

'What about everything else?'

He thought about it. 'I miss speaking my language.'

'Your English and Swedish are excellent and your Japanese is pretty good too.'

'Is not the same. When I speak my language I don't think about the words before I say them. Is natural for me.'

'Okay, so that's the food and the language. Anything else?'

'Our summers are better than in London.'

She gave him the stern look with one raised eyebrow that she'd often fixed him with when she'd worked for him.

'I am Italian. I will always be Italian. It is in my blood and when I retire I will move back there.'

'You? Retire?'

He laughed. 'When I get to fifty I will stop working and enjoy what I have built for myself.'

She smiled. The soft hue of the patio lights lent her face an extra glow that only enhanced her natural beauty. If Stefano didn't know of the poison that lay behind the beautiful façade, he would be entranced.

'I can live with retiring in Italy.'

He made his lips curve. 'You've said that before but I think you will find it hard not to have your sister on the doorstep.'

Her smile faded into a grimace, pain flashing in her eyes. 'I think so too. I want to stay angry with her but it's too hard. She's my sister and whatever's happened between us I still love her.' She blew a puff of air out and shook her head. 'I need to speak to her.'

'You'll be able to soon. She's only away for a month. You two will sort it out, you always do.' As close as the two sisters were, they often argued. Some days Anna would hear her phone ring, see Melissa's name on it and say, 'I'm not in the mood to talk to *her*,' with a scowl. Other times they were quite capable of spending two hours on the phone, their conversations only coming to a close when one of their phone batteries ran out.

It came to him that when he went ahead with his plan to humiliate her at the awards ceremony she wouldn't have her sister to turn to.

Before his conscience could start nagging at him about this, he opened the bottle of wine he'd placed on the table and poured himself a healthy glass.

Anna stared from him to her own glass and the jug of iced water he'd put beside it, her nose wrinkling.

With equal parts amusement and irritation, he watched her pour herself some wine.

'You shouldn't be drinking.'

She rolled her eyes. 'One glass isn't going to kill me.'

'You have to be the worst-behaved patient.'

'You've lived with me for a year. That shouldn't be news to you.' She took a chunk of focaccia and dipped it in the *pinzimonio* before popping it into her mouth whole and devouring it with relish.

It was the first time she'd eaten anything with enthusiasm since her injury.

Suddenly he remembered all the meals they'd shared together and her love of good food. Anna had an appetite that belied her petite figure. This wasn't the first sharing platter they'd had between them, and when she picked up a tooth pick to swipe the largest bite of Parmigiano Reggiano before he could take it, the boulder that had been lodged in his throat settled in his chest.

'I've never known you to be ill before,' he said.

'Melissa says it's like caring for an adolescent toddler.'

He laughed at the mental image this provoked.

'I haven't taken a painkiller all day,' she pointed out. 'And speaking of sisters, you never did tell me how yours found you. Her name's Christina?'

'*Sì.* Christina. She reached out to me when our father died.'

'So your father was alive all this time?'

He nodded with a grimace. 'All those years I thought he was dead he was living in Naples, not even a two-hour drive away. I even had his name wrong—I always believed he was called Marco but it was Mario.'

'How awful.' Her hazel eyes were dark with the same

empathy he'd seen in them earlier. 'He was so near to you all that time? Didn't he want to see you?'

'He wasn't allowed.' There was little point in evading the subject. Anna had that look about her that meant she would chip away until she had all the answers she desired. It was what made her so good at her job: that refusal to leave any stone unturned. 'My *nonno* paid him to leave Lazio before I was born. He blamed him for my mother's addiction. My father took the money and ran, then he grew up and got himself straight, got a job and a place to live. He tried to get in touch with my mother and learned she had died. Nonno didn't trust him and told him to stay away from me. Rightly or wrongly, he agreed. He didn't trust himself any more than Nonno did but he did stay clean, met another woman and had a child with her—Christina. His wife encouraged him to get in touch with me directly but by then Nonno had died and I'd been kicked out by the rest of my family and living on the streets. He couldn't find me.'

'But he looked?'

'He looked, *sì*, but at that time I often used different names and I never gave my real age. He was searching for someone that didn't exist.'

'What about when you started to make a success of yourself?' she asked with wide eyes. 'Did he not realise it was you, his son?'

'He knew,' Stefano confirmed grimly. 'But he thought I wouldn't want to see him; that I would think he only wanted to claim me as his son to get some of my fortune.'

All those years he'd blithely assumed his father was a no-good junkie who didn't want him. But he *had* wanted him. His father had wanted to put things right. And now it was too late and he would never know him and never be able to tell him that he forgave him. His parents had been little more than children when they'd conceived him, and immature, addicted children at that.

While they'd been talking, they'd cleared the antipasti so all that remained were the pickled vegetables neither of them particularly liked.

'My father left me this watch.' He rolled his sleeve up to show it to her.

She looked at it with a pained expression, taking in the shabbiness of the leather strap and the scratches on the glass, then looked back at him. Her smile was tender. 'At least he died knowing you'd made a success of yourself. That must have given him comfort.'

He nodded and took the lids off their main courses, biting back the sudden anger that rushed through him that she could act so supportive now, when her platitudes were worthless.

Christina had given him a letter written by their father. He'd said Stefano had made him proud.

He'd never made anyone proud before.

He served the *linguine con le vongole* onto Anna's plate. She beamed. 'That's my favourite.'

'I know.' He served his lemon sole onto his own plate and took a bite.

Anna, who was a real pasta lover, twisted some linguini onto her fork, stabbed a clam, and asked, 'When did you learn all this?' before popping it into her mouth.

'A month ago.'

He'd learned the truth about his father while Anna was away with Melissa in Paris, the night before she'd flown back early and stormed into his boardroom to accuse him of having an affair. And he'd thought treating

Anna and her sister to a few days away together would be a good thing!

She'd called and left a message but he'd spent most of the night with Christina, talking and steadily making their way through numerous bottles of wine. He hadn't seen Anna's message until he'd gone to bed at four in the morning; too late to call her back. Then, with hardly any sleep, he'd had to get his heavy head to the office, leaving his new-found sister in the apartment.

While he'd been reeling over the discovery of a grown-up sister and a father who *had* wanted him, Anna had flown home early with the sole intention of catching him with another. Why else would she have come back, armed with accusations, without leaving a message of warning?

He'd been fool enough to think she cared when all she'd ever wanted from him was his money.

They ate in silence for a while before she asked, 'What's Christina like?'

'Very young, not long turned twenty but young for her age and very sheltered.' He pushed his dark thoughts about his beautiful wife to one side and smiled wryly. 'Reading between the lines, our father was afraid to let her out of his sight in case he lost her as he lost me. But we're building a relationship.'

'Has she been staying with us?'

'No.' Anna, damn her, was the only person he'd ever been able to stomach living with. 'I've rented a flat for her in London and she's doing some work experience at the office.'

'She doesn't have a job?'

'She'd just started her second year at university when our father was diagnosed with cancer. They thought they had more time so she arranged with the university to take the year off and return next September. Until then, she's going to stay in London and work for me and improve her English.'

'What about her mother?'

'She's in Naples but will be coming to London at Christmas.' Seeing Anna open her mouth to ask another question, he said, 'How's your meal?'

As with the rest of his life he had no qualms about discussing it but Anna had this way of listening that made him want to talk about more than the facts, to lay bare everything living under his skin.

It was an unburdening he'd fought to escape from in their marriage and he was damned if he would do it now when their relationship was days away from being over for good. The only unburdening he wanted from her was her clothes.

Anna was ripe for seduction, just as he wanted.

If he took her into his arms there would be only the slightest resistance. He could see it in the eyes that undressed him with every hungry look.

But something still held him back from acting on it. Whether it was the hint of vulnerability that still lingered in her eyes or the wine she'd been drinking when she really shouldn't so soon after her concussion he couldn't say, but, either way, not even his deplorable conscience would allow him to act on his desire yet. When he made love to her again he wanted to be certain that it was the Anna he'd married he was making love to. The vulnerability was almost gone. Almost. And when he was certain she was as well as she could be then, and only then, would he seduce her into an ecstasy she would remember for the rest of her life.

'It's beautiful, thank you.'

He raised his glass. *'Salute.'*

'What are we drinking to?'

'To us. You and me, and a marriage you will remember for ever.'

Anna's belly was comfortably full. It was the only comfortable part of her anatomy.

They'd long finished their meal and the bottle of wine and now sat, Stefano's eyes burning into her while she waited almost breathlessly for him to suggest they go to bed.

Heat flowed through her veins as her imagination ran amok wondering what it would be like, what it would *feel* like, to be made love to by him. To have that hard, naked chest she pictured every time she closed her eyes pressed against hers...

'Earth to Anna,' he said, elbow on the table, cheek resting on his hand, a gleam in his eyes that made her wonder if during their marriage he'd developed the power to read her thoughts. 'What are you thinking that makes your eyes glaze over like that?'

He flirted with her, he was tactile, he left her in no doubt he couldn't wait to bed her again...but so far he'd made no real move on her.

Was he waiting for her assent?

When she'd woken up three mornings ago feeling as if she might die, she'd had no idea that she was married. No idea that she'd shared a bed and her body with someone, let alone him.

Stefano was the only man she'd ever fantasised about. The only man she'd ever wanted. Her brain might not remember what he did to her but her body did. It ached for him with an intensity that made her bones liquefy.

And she was married to him! At some point in her past she'd found the courage to confirm her desire for him, both in words and deed.

She took a breath and looked him right in the eye. 'I was thinking that it's time for bed.'

He returned her gaze then slowly nodded. 'Go ahead. I'll join you later.'

She wasn't quick enough to hide her dismay. 'Aren't you coming with me?'

His eyes flashed before he closed them and inhaled slowly. 'I'm not tired enough to sleep yet.'

But she didn't want to sleep and she was damned sure he knew that.

Stung at his rejection, Anna got quickly to her feet. 'I'll see you in the morning, then. Night.'

'Anna.'

She ignored him to dart away from the table, not wanting him to see the mortification she knew would be written all over her face.

After all his innuendoes and hungry looks, he was rejecting her?

She couldn't escape from the terrace quickly enough.

'Anna,' he repeated in a voice that demanded to be obeyed.

Almost at the door, she reluctantly turned to face him. 'What?'

Under the soft glowing light she saw a knowing tenderness on his handsome face that took a little of the sting away.

'You're beautiful.'

His words were so unexpected that she found herself gazing from the simple blue shift dress she'd chosen from her enormous dressing room, slipping it on with thoughts of Stefano in her·mind, to him, the man she ached to make love to.

Then he smiled wryly, poured himself another glass of wine and raised it to her. 'Sleep well, *bellissima*.'

The house was eerily silent when Stefano headed down the stairs the next morning wearing only his robe.

He found Anna at his desk in his office, his laptop open in front of her.

'What are you doing?' he asked with an easiness that belied the impulse to slam the lid shut.

'Trying to hack into your laptop.' She didn't look at him, and nor did she look or sound the slightest bit penitent at what she was doing.

'You can't get into your own phone. What makes you think you can hack into this?'

'Because you're extremely predictable with what you use as your password.'

Stefano had always given her free access to his laptop when she worked for him and he'd trusted her with his often-changing passwords for it. Of course, he only used it for work purposes and it was for this reason he didn't want her getting into it now. It would take her all of a minute to discover that he'd sacked her and then all his plans would come tumbling down. Everything would come out and the revenge he was working so carefully towards would be ruined.

He ignored the nagging feeling in his guts that it might just be a good thing for his plans to be ruined. 'What do you want it for?'

'To get onto the Internet.'

'Why? To email Melissa?'

'I agree with you that I shouldn't speak to her yet but she must be worrying that she can't get in touch with me.'

'If she's worried she'll contact the office. They'll tell her where we are.' And then Melissa really would have something to worry about. She knew all about their vicious split.

All he had to do was stop Anna contacting her for four more days.

Her eyes lifted to meet his. She scowled but not before he read the hurt on her face.

He hid his satisfaction.

She was still smarting at his rejection of her the night before. Declining her open invitation had taken a huge amount of willpower and he'd had to keep himself rooted to the chair to resist following her inside and up to the bedroom. *Dio*, he had wanted her so badly it was a physical pain. Now, in the cold light of day, he could hardly believe he'd been so selfless. Being selfless was not on his list of attributes.

There was no hint of any vulnerability in those flashing hazel eyes now. And she was stone-cold sober.

'Is something troubling you, *bellissima*?'

'No.'

He sat on the edge of the desk beside her, taking in the tight shorts and the coral T-shirt that caressed her small, beautiful breasts.

Her jaw clenched and she stabbed at the keyboard and hit return.

Suddenly her face brightened and she cast him with a wicked grin. 'I'm in!'

The grin fell when she saw what was on the screen.

It was a letter of termination he'd got Chloe to write for one of the men who worked in his development lab.

He'd been reading through it before he'd remembered a meeting he was supposed to be at. Forgetting a meeting would never have happened when Anna was running the place alongside him. He'd left the laptop open and had just arrived at the meeting when a breathless member of staff had run up to inform him that his estranged wife had barged her way into his office.

He'd closed the laptop without shutting it down on his return from the hospital and hadn't opened it since.

'You're sacking Peter?' she said, reading it quickly.

'He's been selling patent application details to one of our rivals.'

'You have proof of this?'

'Enough for me not to give him the benefit of the doubt.'

'Have you confronted him?' she asked suspiciously.

'We had a little chat.'

'Did I sit in on it?'

'It was just me and him. I wanted to give him the chance to confess. His behaviour in that meeting was very…what's the word? When someone can't sit still or talk properly?'

'Nervous? Jittery?'

'Both of those. His body language made his guilt obvious.'

'For heaven's sake, Stefano,' she exploded, sliding the chair back to slam against the wall. '*Anyone* hauled in for a private chat with you is going to act nervous and jittery. You can be terrifying and Peter is a nervous soul as it is.'

'Someone is selling secrets from that department. Too many things are being leaked and he's the only person it can be.'

'Maybe the system's been hacked!'

'Maybe we have a traitor in our team.'

'Who in their right mind would turn traitor on you?'
Now she was on her feet with her hands on her hips.
'You're a terrifying ogre but on the whole you're a good
person to work for. You pay extremely well and you're
generous with perks—you've one of the highest staff retention rates in the industry! I *know* Peter. You hired him
as a graduate only a couple of months after you hired me.
He's as timid as a mouse but one of the brightest brains
you've got, and he's *loyal*. Are you really going to sack
him without concrete proof?'

'I can't risk keeping him on!' He conveniently forgot
to mention that neither Peter nor any of his other staff or
even his business had crossed his mind since she'd collapsed at his feet.

'Have you even looked into the possibility that one of
your rivals has infiltrated the system?'

'Our system is foolproof as you very well know!' he
shouted back.

'Rubbish! If even the Pentagon can be broken into
then your system can be too. Do you want to ruin a life
with no proof? Do you want to be sued for unfair dismissal?'

'No one has grounds to sue me.'

'Of course they do, you moron, if you treat them like
this.'

'Now you're calling me a *moron*?'

'If the boot fits then wear it!'

This was what he'd missed in his month without her;
someone to call him out and make him see things from
a different angle. Everyone else was too damn scared
to speak up.

Everything had gone wrong since she'd left him. He

couldn't think straight, too consumed with his anger and humiliation at her hands to think clearly.

Anna would never have let him meet an employee without a witness to report the unbiased facts and protect both parties.

That he had the highest staff retention rates in the industry was down to her. Sure, all the wages and perks were his to be proud of but with Anna gone there was no one there to fight the staff's corner, no counterbalance, no one to make him listen to reason.

This was just as it had always been between them, Anna thought through the blood pounding in her brain.

Stefano was facing her with the same angry stance she knew she must have, both of them glaring and snarling at each other until one of them backed down and apologised.

Except this time she was wearing only a pair of skimpy shorts and a tiny T-shirt, and he...

He was wearing a loosely tied dark grey robe with nothing underneath.

And then, without her knowing how she got there, she was in his arms, his mouth devouring hers, he was kissing her, she was kissing him, in the way she'd yearned to for so, so long.

Sensation such as she'd never known existed skipped over her skin and down into her pores. His tongue swept into her mouth, their lips dancing to a tune she hadn't known she'd already learnt, and she swayed into him, closing her mind to everything but the feelings firing through her.

This was everything she'd been dreaming of and more. His taste, his scent, the feel of his lips, the roughness of his stubbly jaw, the strength of his arms and the hardness of his chest crushed against her... It was heat in its purest, most carnal form.

He rubbed his cheek into her neck and clasped her to him. His other hand gathered her hair together into a sheath and roughly, yet gently, he pulled her head back.

'Now do you understand why we married?' he asked coarsely. 'That night we both drank more champagne than was good for us and I took advantage of it to kiss you, just as I did now, and you kissed me back.'

His hand holding her ground her to him.

She gasped to feel him huge and hard against her abdomen.

No wonder they'd married so quickly. If she'd felt even a fraction of the desire in that car as was swirling through her now...it was the headiest feeling imaginable. No wonder she'd demanded marriage. It was the only thing that would have a hope in hell of putting him off the idea and leaving her safe.

Yes! It wasn't a memory that came to her then but a feeling, a certainty that this was how it had played out.

She'd had no idea the attraction she'd held so long for him would turn her into fondue at his touch. She would have had to scramble to hold on to her sanity. But Stefano's own sanity had been scrambled too and he'd agreed to her flippant remark.

She didn't need to hold on to her sanity now.

They had made love many times in their marriage, and now she would get to experience it for the very first time all over again...

Fresh sanity suddenly struck her.

She didn't know what to do.

Stefano felt her hesitation.

Cupping her cheeks in his hands, he gazed deep into

her eyes and saw nerves merging with the desire, just as he'd seen the first time they'd made love on their wedding night, and with it he remembered that she had no memories of their lovemaking. None at all.

Sex was the only aspect of their marriage he had no doubts about. Clever little liar that she was, no one could fake those reactions. It had never been a case of going through the motions for a quick release but a real, deep connection that had scorched them both. He knew he would never find that with anyone else and he hated her for it; hated her for destroying his faith in what they'd shared.

For a few more days he could enjoy it all again but this, their first time together in over a month, was the first time for Anna. He had to remember that. When she'd confessed her virginity, although shocked, he could not deny his primal reaction had been elation that he would be her one and only.

'I'm not making love to you in here,' he said hoarsely before sweeping her into his arms.

She hooked her arms around his neck but the trepidation was still there. 'Why did you reject me last night?'

'Because I was waiting for my Anna to come back. When you shouted at me so passionately...' he kissed the tip of her nose '...I knew it was you.'

CHAPTER SEVEN

STEFANO SHIFTED HIS HOLD so she was secure in his arms and carried her up the stairs.

His Anna, he thought with a possessiveness that caught him off guard.

Only his.

But only for a few more days.

He couldn't think of that right now. Right now it didn't matter that the whole reason they were here was so he could seduce her so thoroughly that when he publicly ended things between them she had the added humiliation of knowing she had willingly lost herself to his touch and screamed out the name of the man who was playing with her all along. All he wanted at that moment was to sink himself into Anna's tight heat and lose himself in her.

The bedroom door was open, the bed sheets still unmade from the frustrated, tortured sleep he knew they'd both shared.

Something *more* had made him wait until he'd been certain she would be asleep before joining her, and it wasn't just that he'd wanted to be sure she was truly recovered and sober. It was that nagging in his guts speaking to him, putting doubts in his mind.

Now, having shared those searing kisses and felt her taut and hungry against him…

He laid her on the bed and in a moment had shed his robe and climbed on top of her.

Anna waited for him to kiss her again. He'd placed his hands either side of her head, his legs long and lean between her thighs, and he was staring at her…

He was staring at her as if he could eat her whole.

She thought of all the women that had been before her, those faceless women she had been desperate to keep away from, desperate not to know, terrified that if any of them were to meet her they would recognise the secret feminine signs of a woman in love. She had feared their pity. She had feared she would hate them for it. Now she was the one to pity them.

It wasn't possible that Stefano had looked at another with the hunger with which he was looking at her.

Stefano was hers. All hers. She would never share him with anyone.

How beautiful he was, as if sculpted in marble by a master and then injected with life. To feel him against her inner thigh, hot and ready, his own desire wholly evident even to a novice such as her…

Flames licked her everywhere.

She reached out to touch him again, pressing her hand to his chest, feeling the heavy thuds of his heart. She sighed and closed her eyes.

Never had she imagined his skin would be so warm and smooth to her touch, or that the fine dark hair that covered his chest would feel so silky. Slowly she trailed her fingers down to the hard muscle beneath the damp skin of his abdomen and heard his sharp intake of breath.

Still gazing at her, he took hold of her top and, with
only the smallest movement from her, pulled it off.

His devouring gaze took in every inch of her but she
was far too gone to feel any embarrassment. Her only moment of shyness came when he tugged her shorts down
and exposed her most private area. Even that shyness
flew away at his deep groan.

'*Dio*, you have the sexiest body,' he said in a pained
voice. Then he brought his mouth back down on hers and
she wound her arms around him and responded with all
the passion alive in her heart.

Fresh heat enflamed her body, desire uncurling inside her, the yearning for Stefano's possession growing.

And as she rejoiced in all these wonderful sensations,
she was jolted from the moment with a thought that had
her turn from his hot mouth to gasp, 'What do we use
for contraception?'

'You've had those injections since we got back from
our honeymoon,' he muttered raggedly, hardly pausing
for breath before his lips found her neck and her heart accelerated at the thrill racing over her skin and the burning in her veins, all worries of contraception happily
dispatched.

Everything was heightened, all her senses were con-
verging together. She started as she felt his mouth on her
breast, then shut out the last of her nerves and succumbed
fully to the pleasure being evoked in her every last cell.

His mouth and hands were everywhere, kissing,
nibbling, stroking every inch, bringing her desire to a
boil that was on the cusp of spilling over. Every touch
scorched, every kiss burned and soon she wanted so
much more than this heavenly torture. When his lips

found hers again, she parted her thighs at the same moment he put a hand to them.

He muttered something, shifted, then took hold of himself and suddenly she felt him there, right at the place she most wanted him to be, and just as suddenly her fears returned and she froze.

Stefano must have sensed something wrong for he stopped what he was about to do and, the tip of his erection still poised in the apex of her thighs, stared intently into her eyes.

'There is nothing to fear, *bellissima*,' he whispered. 'Nothing at all. I would never hurt you.'

His lips came back down on hers and she returned the heady pressure of his kiss. As his tongue swept into her mouth she wrapped her arms around him then cried into his mouth as she felt him push inside her, so slowly and with such care that she could have actually shed tears.

But then all thoughts of crying were swept away because *he was inside her.*

All her fears were unfounded. There was no pain. She'd known in her head that there couldn't be, that her virginity was only in her head, but that sensible voice hadn't been enough to quell her anxiety that somehow her body would have forgotten along with her mind.

There was only pleasure. Deep, radiating pleasure.

In their time together Stefano must have learned exactly what she liked because the thrusts he was making inside her felt heaven-sent.

His movements increased, the groans coming from his mouth in her ear making the pulsations inside her thicken. She put her lips to his neck and inhaled his tangy, musky scent, driving him deeper and deeper into her.

The world became a distant blur, shrinking down to

just them and this magical moment. The secret torch she'd carried for him for so, so long had been lit into a furnace and all she could do was let the heat from it burn until it reached its peak and she was crying out his name, over and over, pleasure rippling through her in long waves.

Stefano gave a hoarse groan and drove so deeply inside her at his own climax that she wrapped her legs even tighter around him, wanting to savour every last bit of this incredible moment.

When he collapsed on her with his face in the crook of her neck, she held him tightly. She dragged her hands up the length of his muscular back and up to his head, threading her fingers through the thick dark hair. She could feel his heartbeat hammering in time to hers and thrilled to know that he too had felt the joy she had experienced.

'Is it always like that?' she asked when she had finally caught her breath. Dull pulses still throbbed inside her.

He gave a sound like a laugh and lifted his head. A smile played on his lips. 'Always.'

The next morning Anna woke up in her second strange bed of the week—the third if one counted the hospital bed—and stretched before turning her head to the sleeping figure beside her.

The early morning light illuminated him perfectly and for the first time she allowed herself the pleasure of gazing at Stefano without interruption from the doubts in her own head.

Making love to him had been beyond anything her imagination could have conjured up.

She covered her mouth to stifle the laugh that wanted to explode from her. If she'd ever imagined it to be even half as good as it had been she would have resigned on the spot. There was no way she could have dealt with working by his side day by day with those rampant thoughts.

The second time had been even better. And by their third time the last of her inhibitions had been vanquished.

Having got so little sleep she should be shattered but she wasn't. She had never felt anything like this, as if there were a beehive in her chest, all the worker bees buzzing to make honey inside her.

Climbing out of the bed carefully so as not to wake him—although, as she'd already learned, an earthquake would have trouble disrupting Stefano's sleep—she tiptoed naked out of the bedroom and walked to the bathroom at the other end of the landing.

She shut the door behind her and headed straight to the window to look out at the cerulean sky.

It was going to be a glorious day, she could feel it in her bones.

She ran the bath and added liberal amounts of bubble bath to it, then climbed in.

Doing nothing more than lying there in the steamy suds, she gazed out at the beach. In the distance she could see someone walking a small dog, the first signs of life in Santa Cruz. She wondered if she and Stefano had ever spoken of getting a dog. She'd had one as a child, a soppy cocker spaniel that had been as daft as a brush and as useful a guard dog as a packet of pasta.

An image came into her mind, so vivid that she bolted upright.

Making love to Stefano in their London apartment.

She hugged her knees, the image forming, becoming more than just a picture in her head. This was a memory, pure bona fide remembrance of them being together.

Anna had no idea how long she sat in that bath, her attention wrenched away from the view, thinking as hard as she had ever done, so hard her brain hurt. It wasn't until there was a tap on the bathroom door that she realised the bathwater had turned cold and the bubbles gone.

'Come in,' she called, startled out of her reverie.

Stefano strode in wearing nothing but a pair of white cotton boxers slung low on his hips and a sexy lopsided grin. His sleep-tousled hair swayed as he walked to her and crouched down to rest his arms on the side of the bath.

'You should be in bed.'

She raised a brow at him, her senses jumping in so many directions just to see him so that it took a moment to find her tongue. 'I'm remembering things.'

Stefano's stomach lurched.

He'd woken to an empty bed and with only one thought in his mind, namely finding his wife and dragging her back to it. In the middle world of sleep and waking, and distracted by the ache in his groin, this time *he'd* been the one to forget everything.

He searched her face carefully. There didn't seem to be anything dark or suspicious lurking in her clear gaze, only animation.

He allowed himself a small breath of relief. 'What are you remembering?'

'Us. Patches of us. Our wedding.' Her cheeks flushed with colour and she lowered her voice. 'Making love for the first time.'

'What are your memories of that?'

She palmed his face with her hand, a look of bliss spreading across her beautiful face. 'It was wonderful. *You* were wonderful.'

His chest filled with emotion. 'What else?'

'Business meetings. Did you promote me?'

He nodded. 'Nick retired. I gave the job to you.'

Her eyes widened. 'You put me on the board of directors?'

'Who else would I trust to keep the place running when I had to travel? You're an exceptional businesswoman—the whole board was behind your appointment. And not just because they're scared of me,' he added, before she could quip that they would back anything he said out of fear.

In hindsight he recognised that promoting Anna had been when their troubles had begun. As his PA she had travelled everywhere with him. As Vice President of Moretti's UK, second only to the US in his burgeoning technology empire, she had needed to be on hand in the UK when he travelled to America. They'd gone from seeing each other all day every day and sleeping together every night to spending up to a week apart at a time. That was when those insecurities had set in.

But she'd been—acted—insecure from the beginning, he reminded himself. Her accelerated promotion had only given her the tools to up her campaign.

Yet the wonderment ringing out from her eyes at this moment put more doubts in his head.

Anna was clever and stubborn. She could by turn be sweet then sour. She was good cop to his bad cop but people were always aware that her being good cop did not make her a pushover. If she thought someone was being an idiot she had no qualms about telling them so, just as she had no qualms about telling him. Until she'd hit him with that ludicrous demand for a hundred million pounds of his fortune she would have been the last person he'd suspect of being á gold-digger. The last person he would have suspected of having an agenda. He'd trusted her as he hadn't trusted anyone since his *nonno* had died and to discover it had all been a lie had shattered him in ways he couldn't explain even to himself.

Her fingers gently massaged his cheek. It was such a simple sign of affection but one that made his heart expand.

'I don't remember everything,' she whispered, bringing her face to his so the sweetness of her breath sighed against his skin. 'All that I remember of us as a married couple is spending long days in the office and long nights making love. I don't remember falling in love with you but I know that I did. I *know* I did. I can feel it as clearly as I can feel the bristles on your jaw where you need to shave.'

And then her eyes closed and her lips pressed against his, not moving, just breathing him in.

Stefano gripped the back of her head and held her tightly to him to deepen the kiss, his mind and heart racing.

She spoke of love? *Love?* That was a word neither of them had ever said before.

That was *not* what their marriage was about.

Then what was it about?

It had been about desire. The primal need for a mate. A partner. Someone to have *bambinos* with.

He had long wanted children. To have a child would be to ice the delicious cake that was his life. His hated cousins had an abundance of them, and he'd beaten them in everything except in the *bambino* stakes. But to have children he needed to find a woman to have them with and he hadn't trusted any of the women in his life with a vase, never mind a child. Still, he'd looked forward to seeing miniature versions of himself running around and causing havoc one day; a bloodline to pass his wealth on to.

He'd be damned if he'd leave anything to the other members of his family.

When he'd started making waves in the world of technology, and journalists had learned of his rags-to-riches background, the shady acquaintances of his early years, the prison sentence…suddenly they had wanted to interview him and hear his story from his own lips. He'd been happy to oblige, especially if it involved having his photo taken in front of his yacht or his private plane. Stefano had become a poster boy for the kids of Lazio, an icon to look up to, the local bad boy who'd turned out good. He didn't doubt for a minute that his family, who all still lived in the same homes in the same close-knit area he'd been dragged up in, knew everything about him. And he didn't doubt that his success made them sick.

See? he would say to them through the lens of the camera. *This is what you threw away. If you'd treated me like the orphan boy of your blood that I was and not like some kind of wild animal, these riches would have been yours.* He was Italian after all! Life and its riches were for sharing with family. But he'd decided when he was fifteen that he had no family. Everything he earned, every penny of it, was his and his alone.

When Anna had so flippantly—but trembling after that first passionate kiss they'd shared—declared that if he wanted to bed her he'd have to marry her, he'd known by the next morning that she would be the mother of his children. There was no one better suited. They worked fantastically well together, shared a chemistry that was off the charts and they already knew each other's faults. Marriage and babies together? Well, why not? If not her then who? At least life with Anna would be fun, he'd thought. And she was straight down the line. As sexy as a nymph. He'd trusted her. But love? Love was for romantic fools who needed to put a name to their desire rather than just accepting it for what it was: chemistry.

The only person who had ever shown him love or affection was his *nonno*. When he'd died, Stefano had quickly learned he was not a person to inspire affection. As he'd grown older and started catching the eye of beautiful women, he'd discovered lust but had known their desire for him was based solely on his physical attributes. If they could see him without the outer shell, they would be repelled.

Anna was the only person since his *nonno* to see beneath that shell and still want him. He had never repelled her. He'd infuriated her—yes, he could admit to that—but seeing the real man hadn't made her run. She was level-headed enough not to want to try to change him.

In her own way, she was a misfit like him. They'd understood each other as no one else could.

But then she'd so spectacularly accused, humiliated and dumped him and he'd realised that it had all been an act. What Anna had seen beneath his shell *had* repelled her but she had bided her time until she'd been in a position to go for the kill and take him for everything she could get.

Had she planned her scheme right from the beginning as he'd thought since that torrid black moment in his boardroom? Or had it formed over time…?

Things were getting confused in his head. He had to focus. He mustn't let what was happening between them now and her words of love cloud his judgement any further.

The feelings she was now mistaking for love were its opposite: hate. Only the utmost loathing of him could have made Anna do what she had done. If she'd felt even a flicker of love for him she would never have gone through with her grand plan.

And now he loathed her. *His* grand plan was coming together better than he could have hoped.

Stefano pushed the disquiet in his guts aside with force and concentrated on the desire blazing in his loins. He lifted her out of the bath and carried her wrapped in an enormous towel to their bed.

They spent the day making love but, during the spent times when they dozed, he couldn't shake the voice in his head telling him that his plan was in danger of un-ravelling.

Anna's dressing room in their Santa Cruz beach house was even larger than the one she had in Stefano's London penthouse. It took for ever to rifle through the racks of clothes, all of which still had their tags on. She guessed they hadn't spent much time here since they'd bought the house.

After much internal debate she selected a pear-green silk sleeveless wraparound dress that was cinched at the waist and fell like soft leaves to the knees, held together by a thin belt studded with dainty diamonds. She also earmarked a gorgeous red dress to wear to tomorrow night's awards ceremony.

Delving further into the shelves uncovered a shoe-lov-er's paradise and, after much consideration that involved trying on half a dozen pairs, she settled on sky-high beige diamond-encrusted mesh heels that she suspected she would never have been able to afford even if she'd set aside a whole month of her generous salary.

Stefano had never stinted on displaying his wealth. It seemed that same generosity extended to his wife, a thought that sent a pang through her chest. Four whole days in Santa Cruz, just the two of them, had revealed a side to her husband she had only suspected before. Not only was Stefano an amazingly considerate lover but he was considerate of *her*. It was the little things, like holding her hand to keep her steady when she got out of the swimming pool; taking her beach towel a long distance from her to shake the sand from it…all the little things that made her heart swell and made her rethink her original assumption that she'd lost her marbles by marrying him.

Marrying Stefano had clearly been the sanest thing she'd ever done. Their first anniversary was only days away, proof that they must have been happy together and that Stefano had kept his promise of fidelity. She just wished she remembered more than snapshots of it.

She must find an anniversary present for him. They were going to San Francisco tomorrow morning ahead of the awards ceremony. She'd see if she could sneak out and get him something there.

She checked her reflection one last time and left her dressing room.

She found Stefano hunched over the end of the bed reading something on his phone. He looked up as she entered.

His eyes gleamed and a slow smile spread over his handsome face. '*Bellissima*, you look beautiful.' Then his eyes drifted down to her feet. 'Should you be wearing shoes that high in your condition?'

'What condition?'

'You've had severe concussion,' he reminded her.

She waved his concern away. 'I feel fine...' But as she said the words something tapped at her, another of those sensations of déjà vu she kept experiencing.

Condition...

The image of an oblong stick with a small window flashed through her mind. 'Have I been pregnant?'

His brows drew together. 'No. What makes you think that?'

'I don't know.' She blinked and shook her head in an attempt to clear the image.

He got to his feet and stepped over to her. He put a hand on her shoulder, peering at her intently. 'Anna? Are you feeling okay?'

She nodded then shook her head again. This was awful. There was something in her memories screaming to escape but she was helpless to find it. All she knew with any certainty was that this memory was bad and the only thing soothing her heightening fears was the sensation of Stefano's hand against her bare skin.

She took a shaky breath. 'Are you *sure* I've not been pregnant?' She didn't see how she could have been if she had used the injectable contraceptive.

'Very sure. I told you we said we would try for a baby one day in the future. Are you getting memories of that?'

'I don't know what I'm getting memories of.' She sighed, loosening the panic that had been trying to crawl up her throat. 'Nothing's clear.'

'It will come. Give it time.'

'You keep saying that. What if they never come back?'

'They will.' His fingers slipped lightly over the shoulders of her dress and rested in the arch of her neck. His gaze didn't leave hers.

Her chest filled with a feeling that was tight yet also fluid, moving through her veins and into her limbs; she was intensely aware of his closeness and the sensations shimmering through her at his touch.

One touch and she was a slave for more.

She looped her arms around his neck. 'What time have you booked the table for?'

The best way to shake off the dark uncertainty that kept trying to cloud her was by making love. Stefano's touch drove all her fears away.

He laughed huskily into her ear. 'We're already late.'

CHAPTER EIGHT

THE RESTAURANT STEFANO had booked them into was a short walk from their home in the Westside of Santa Cruz. Anna adored the clean, affluent neighbourhood. This was a district to soak up culture, enjoy the amusements and raise children.

Why did she keep thinking of children? And why did it feel like a blade in the chest whenever she did?

She pushed the thoughts aside. This was their last night in Santa Cruz and she wanted to enjoy every last minute of it, not have her unreliable mind take her in directions she couldn't understand.

The Thai Emerald was, as the name suggested, a Thai restaurant, located on the bustling beachfront.

She glimpsed a small room with a handful of tables before they were whisked up narrow stairs to a bright, spacious room with an open front overlooking the beach.

They were shown to a small square table near the front and menus were laid before them. Their drink order was taken and then they were alone.

Anna read her menu with a contentment in her heart she couldn't remember feeling since childhood.

'You look happy,' Stefano observed with a smile.

She beamed at him. 'Thai food is another favourite.'

'I know.'

'Do we ever cook?'

'No.'

He answered so firmly that she laughed. 'Melissa always did the cooking and I did the cleaning…' Her voice tailed off as she thought of her sister.

'You are most particular about tidiness,' he said with a grin.

'Melissa says I'm a control freak.'

'You like order. There's nothing wrong with that. I'm the same.'

The waiter came to their table with their wine and poured them each a glass.

'I've been thinking,' Anna said once their food order had been taken. 'I'm going to get in touch with Melissa when we get back to London.'

'I thought you were going to wait until she got home?'

'I'll drive myself crazy if I wait that long.' She sighed. 'I miss her. I can't wait another three weeks to speak to her. I'll borrow your phone if that's okay and call her.'

He nodded thoughtfully. 'If you're sure.'

'I am. I just feel…' She shook her head. 'Betrayed. I know it's selfish of me but I want to know why. After everything Mum did to us, to up and leave to celebrate a birthday with her? I mean, she left us. She left me in Melissa's care when I was fourteen years old and scarpered to the other side of the world to live with a man she'd known for only a few months. What kind of woman does that? What kind of *mother* does that?'

How many times had he heard all this? she wondered when he didn't answer.

Her mother wasn't a topic Anna liked to discuss. It was the judgement call she could read in people's eyes when they learned about it, as if they were wondering what kind of daughter she must have been if her own mother abandoned her so soon after her father had died.

It was something that ate at her. What kind of hateful child must she have been to elicit that desertion?

But Stefano was her husband so it was only natural that in the course of their marriage she had opened up to him. And all he was doing right then was listening to a story she must have shared however many times but couldn't stop relaying again now.

'I often wonder what would have happened if I hadn't put my foot down and refused to go with her. I don't see how our relationship would be any different other than the fact I would have been on the other side of the world to my sister. Melissa couldn't have gone. She'd just started university and was starting her adult life. I didn't want to leave her or my friends. I didn't want to leave my father.'

'Your father was dead,' he pointed out quietly. 'Didn't you want your mother to be happy?'

'Of *course* I did but it was so soon; his death was so sudden.' Her father had been killed when a wall had collapsed on him at the building site he was a manager of. 'All my life it had been the four of us, a tight family unit… How could she have loved Dad if she started seeing Mick so quickly after burying him? How can you visit a grave when you're on the other side of the world?' She rubbed her eyes, only slightly aware that they were wet. Where had those tears come from? She hadn't wasted tears on her mother in years. 'And how can you leave your fourteen-year-old daughter behind?'

'She knew Melissa would look after you.'

'Melissa was only eighteen. She shouldn't have been

put in that position.' She inhaled deeply, trying to keep her composure, but the tears leaking from her eyes seemed to have a life of their own. 'She was as devastated as I was at what Mum was doing. She didn't want either of us to go. I can't remember whose idea it was for me to stay with her, whether it was hers or mine...'

Anna took a large drink of her wine and carefully wiped more tears away. She didn't want Stefano seeing her with smudged mascara, not tonight. 'I didn't want to go and I didn't want my mum to go either. I wanted her to stay and be my mum. I really thought if I refused to go that she would stay. Even when she bought me and Melissa the flat with Dad's insurance money and set up a monthly allowance for us I thought she'd stay. Right up until the moment her plane took off, I thought she would stay.'

The pain she'd experienced when she'd realised her mum had gone—had really gone—had been indescribable. It had been like having her heart stabbed with a thousand knives.

There was a long period of silence before a warm hand covered hers and sympathetic green eyes held her gaze.

'When did you last see her?' he asked.

'She came to England for my sixteenth birthday. That was her first and last visit. All she could talk about was how brilliant Australia was and how good Mick was to her. We had a massive argument. She called me and Melissa selfish bitches and said she was glad to be rid of us.' The words almost stuck in her throat. 'She flew back early.'

From the shock resonating in Stefano's eyes, it appeared this wasn't a part of the story she had shared before.

'Have you had any contact with her since then?'

She shook her head. 'She sends us cards and gifts for birthdays and Christmas, and she's written a couple of letters, but that's it.'

'What did the letters say?'

'I don't know. We burned them without reading them.'

The waiter returned to their table with their starters. Anna sniffed her *kung sadung nga*, deep-fried prawns in sesame batter and glazed in honey, and felt guilty for lowering the mood.

After all her good intentions she was in danger of ruining their last night here.

Before she could apologise, Stefano said thoughtfully, 'You've been coping with this for a long time. Do you think it's time for you to deal with it and talk to your mother and see if things can be mended?'

'You don't want to mend things with *your* family,' she said, stung.

'That's different. I will never forgive them for how they treated me. I will never forget. I don't want reconciliation. All I want is for them to see me rich and successful; everything that they are not. But my family is not yours. They never cared for me but your mother cared for you.'

'She left me,' Anna said, coldness creeping through her. 'How could she have cared for me?'

'You said yourself you were a proper family before your father died. She loved you then. I would guess she told herself she was doing the right thing.'

'I was a minor. I'd lost my dad, puberty had just struck…my head and emotions were all over the place. I needed her. Mel should have spent her uni years living it up and behaving atrociously, not having to be guardian to her bratty younger sister without any support from the woman whose job it was to care for us. How can you make excuses for that?'

'I'm not,' he said steadily, 'But Melissa clearly thinks it's worth trying and you trust her.'

'But that's what I don't understand. What made Mel change her mind? She hates Mum as much as I do. We've always sworn we were better off without her.'

'You can't tell me you don't miss her.'

Suddenly terrified she would do more than leak tears, Anna bit into one of her prawns and concentrated on not crying.

Only when she was confident she could talk without choking did she say, 'I'm sorry. I didn't want to ruin the evening.'

'You haven't.' But his eyes had lost their sparkle.

'You're right that I've only been coping with it and not dealing with it,' she admitted. 'You're the first person I've trusted since she got on that plane. Other than Melissa.' Then, aware she was sinking the mood even lower, forced a bright smile on her face. 'Don't let me ruin the rest of the evening.'

'Anna...'

'No.' She put her hand on his and squeezed it. 'We can talk about this when we get back to London and reality, but our time here has been very special to me. We're making good memories and I don't want my mum spoiling them.'

A flicker of darkness crossed his features before he gave the dazzling smile she loved so much and leaned closer to her. 'We have a whole night to make even better memories.'

* * *

Night had fallen when they left the restaurant, lamps illuminating the streets, the sound of the Pacific clearer.

The longer the meal had gone on, the smaller the restaurant had seemed until it had shrunk to just the two of them. She hadn't seen anyone else. Her eyes had been only for Stefano. The restaurant had been busy but she couldn't describe a single diner or even remember the colour of their waiter's hair.

And Stefano's eyes had only ever been on her, seducing her, making her heart race so that she forgot she was eating possibly the best pad thai she'd ever tasted.

After the discussion about her mother he'd regaled her with gossip about the industry and his rivals, making her laugh aloud more than once.

But now, with the cool night air on her skin, her thoughts drifted back to her mother.

Her abandonment was a ten-year open wound.

Had her mum made a big deal during her one visit to England about how amazing Australia was in the hope her daughters would join her there? *Had* she missed them as much as they'd missed her?

She left you without a parent when you were only fourteen years old, Anna reminded herself.

It didn't change how much she missed her, even now. Stefano was right about *that*.

She'd been a loving mum, she remembered. Always busy, but always with a smile on her face. Quick to scold, but equally quick to forgive.

Her dad was gone from the earth. She carried an ache in her heart for him she knew would be there for the rest of her life, and accepted it. Welcomed it even, the pain a reminder of the father she had lost but would never forget. It was through no fault of his own that he'd missed the significant events in her life and she knew if he could be watching down on her then he would be.

Her mum was alive and well and missing all those moments by choice.

But she'd been there for Anna's sixteenth birthday.

Except she hadn't come back.

'You've gone quiet,' Stefano mused, his accented voice breaking through her reminiscences.

She squeezed her fingers tighter to his. 'Sorry.'

'Don't be. What are you thinking?'

'Nothing exciting,' she said, telling him the first untruth since she'd known him.

'I don't believe that what goes on in your brain is ever boring,' he teased.

'It's full of mundane trivia.'

'What is mundane?'

'Like boring.'

Without warning he dropped her hand and grabbed her shoulders, pulled her to him and kissed her fully and passionately.

And then just as quickly he broke away and took hold of her hand again. 'I bet your thoughts are not mundane now.'

He had that right.

By the time they returned to the beach house the only thing on her mind was making love to him.

When they stepped over the threshold, he gave her a long lingering kiss and said, 'Wait for me in the sunroom while I get us a drink.'

The lights of the sunroom were off, the only illumination coming from the night lights surrounding the swimming pool and bouncing through the wall of glass. It lent the room a romantic quality that perfectly suited her mood and her desire for one last perfect night here.

She looked out of the window and gazed at the dark ocean, only the distant flashes of foaming surf and the twinkling stars in the night sky differentiating one from the other.

Stefano came back into the room carrying two glasses of white wine. He joined her at the window, his arm brushing against her as he handed hers to her. 'Are your feet hurting yet?'

Startled at his question, Anna looked down at the fabulous shoes that, now she thought about it, were crippling her feet.

She must have been mad to wear such high heels on an evening that required walking. If she hadn't been so dazzled by their brilliance she would have worn flats and now her feet wouldn't ache so much.

'They're killing me.'

He tutted. 'I thought so. You always wear silly shoes.'

'They're not silly,' she said in mock outrage. 'I just happen to like nice shoes.'

'You have nice shoes that don't require you to cripple yourself wearing them.'

'If I wear heels it stops people tripping over me,' she said, deadpan.

He wiggled his left eyebrow in the way that always made her laugh, then took a large drink of his wine and put his glass on the low round table in the centre of the room. He took her hand and guided her to the rounded sofa that looked so much like a bed.

'Sit down,' he ordered.

'Bossy boots,' she said, deliberately taking a slow drink of her wine before obeying.

Stefano sat next to her, took hold of her ankles and put her feet on his lap.

'What are you doing?'

He unzipped the heel of her left shoe and gently tugged it off. 'Someone has to look after your feet if you won't,' he answered, a sparkle in his eyes. 'You are lucky you have married a man who gives fantastic foot massages.'

'And how do you know that?'

Her other shoe went the same way as the first. The relief to her poor feet was indescribable.

'*You* told me,' he said with a patient shake of his head, 'because you always insist on wearing silly shoes and then complain your feet hurt.'

The retort she had ready on her lips died away when he pressed his thumbs to the sole of her foot and slowly pushed up to her toes.

Stefano noted the way her eyes glazed as he began to massage her feet and experienced a thrill of satisfaction. Anna adored having her feet rubbed and right then he wanted to do nothing more than give her pleasure and wipe away the memories of her past he knew were suffusing her.

He would have given anything to stop her from talking earlier. He hadn't wanted to see her pain.

Dannazione, he shouldn't be aching to comfort her and wipe her demons away.

He could feel himself losing control of the situation and was determined to regain it.

'Put your head back and relax.'

A knowing smile playing on her lips, she placed her wine glass on the floor. Then she did as he'd suggested and lay with her head against the rounded softness of the sofa's back and her body in recline.

After massaging her left foot for a few minutes he switched to her right.

Anna sighed and finally closed her eyes. 'You really do give amazing foot massages.'

'I know.'

A snigger escaped her lips before she gave another deep sigh.

When he felt he'd worked enough on her foot, he moved his hand up to her ankle and then to her smooth calf, kneading the muscles with the pressure he knew she liked.

It occurred to him that he still knew far more about the responses of her body and what gave her pleasure than she did.

Up his hands went, over her knee, brushing the silk of her dress aside as he reached her thigh. This was where he had to be gentler, her inner thighs one of her most tender areas.

She kept perfectly still, only her deepening breaths indicating any response as his fingers inched ever upwards, his hand burrowing under her dress, deliberately keeping away from her most intimate area, teasing her, tormenting her.

Sliding his fingers back down her leg, he switched his attentions to her other leg and began the same sensuous trail.

Dio, but this was turning him on.

When he reached her thigh this time and kneaded his way to her hip, he hooked his finger into the side of her knickers.

Her breaths were now coming in ragged spurts, her cheeks flushed.

Taking hold of the elastic on her other hip, he gently

tugged her knickers down. When the soft dark hair between her legs was exposed, her eyes flew open.

There was such desire and trust in that stare. When she looked at him like that all he could think was that he wanted it to be like this between them always.

It was too late for thoughts like that. Too late to erase the past. Too much had gone on between them but he couldn't shake the thought that she'd said she trusted *him* unaware that, come tomorrow, he planned to destroy her.

This would be his last gift to her.

Stefano threw her knickers onto the floor then placed a hand on her ankle and gently pulled her legs apart. She writhed beneath him and he pressed a hand to her belly to steady her and placed a kiss on her inner thigh.

When he pressed his mouth into the heart of her she gasped and jolted as if she'd had a volt of electricity shot through her. A hand flailed out and touched his head.

He inhaled, breathing in her scent that he had never tired of, *could* never tire of.

Taking greater care than he had ever done in his life, checking his own ardour, which wanted nothing more than to rip both their clothes off and take her without ceremony, Stefano kissed and caressed the most intimate part of her to gradually open her up to him.

The fingertips on his head moved imperceptibly in tiny circular movements. Her breaths caught then deepened and tiny moans escaped her lips. The fingers on his scalp tightened and dug into him until finally, with the breathiest of gasps, her back arched and she shuddered.

Only when he was certain her climax was over did he haul himself up and put his hands either side of her head to stare down at her.

Anna had faced down everything life had thrown at

her before, never flinching or hiding away. Over the past few days they had made love countless times, done everything possible, but this... This felt different. *She* felt different and opening her eyes to meet Stefano's gaze was one of the hardest things she'd ever done. She was afraid of what she would find there.

As she forced them open she knew the thing she most feared was not finding what she suddenly realised she so desperately wanted to see. Love.

She swallowed and met his gaze.

Her breath came unstuck again. If not love, there was tenderness in the dark, swirling green depths and it filled her chest so completely that she hooked her arms around his neck and pulled him down for a long kiss.

'You've got too many clothes on,' he said gruffly into her mouth, his hands sliding down to her waist.

'So have you.'

He made deft work of the belt. As soon as it was unclasped, her dress unwrapped itself, only one small button holding the last of the material together, which he undid with no effort before sliding an arm behind her back to unclasp her bra.

Gathering her to him, he pulled her up so he could slide the sleeves of her dress and bra down her arms, leaving her naked before him.

'*Dio*, you're beautiful,' he muttered.

'Your turn,' she whispered, lying back down. She stretched her arms above her head, luxuriating in his dilated gaze.

He removed his shirt, then got off the improbably large sofa only long enough to shed his trousers and underwear.

And then he was back on top of her, his mouth covering hers, and with one long thrust he was inside her.

He took her with a feverish passion, raising her thighs to drive into her as deeply as he could, deeper and deeper, faster and faster, their bodies fusing together to become one pulsating being.

Anna's climax bubbled back into life and when he came with a groan she followed within moments, biting into his shoulder and pressing herself as tightly as she could to him as the pleasure exploded out of her.

For a long, long time, the only sound to be heard was their ragged breathing and the thundering of their hearts.

It was the most blissful state.

Eventually Stefano shifted his weight off her and she twisted onto her side to rest her head on his chest.

She kissed the taut skin beneath her. 'I'm so glad I married you. I would do it again in a moment.'

His response was to tighten his hold on her and kiss the top of her head.

CHAPTER NINE

ANNA CARRIED HER BOWL of cereal to Stefano's study, eating as she went. For once he'd woken before her, waking her to make love before saying he had a conference call to take and work to catch up on. When she'd asked if there was anything she needed to be getting on with herself, he'd kissed her and reminded her that she was technically still off sick.

She hadn't protested. Five days of sex, sand and sea had left work far removed from her life. She'd left school at eighteen and had worked constantly since. There had been no grand plan, just a determination to work hard and be self-sufficient. She hadn't known how wonderful it could be to kick back and relax and to let the cares of the world pass her by and here, in this bustling beach paradise, she'd been able to do just that. In a few hours they'd be heading up Route 17 to San Francisco and their mini holiday in Santa Cruz would be over.

She found Stefano rummaging through a filing cabinet and talking to himself. It took her a moment to realise he was in fact having a video call with someone on his laptop.

He raised a hand and winked to acknowledge her and carried on with his conversation in rapid Italian with a woman Anna couldn't see from the angle of his laptop but whose voice replied in equally rapid Italian.

Perching herself on his desk, Anna ate her breakfast while the two chatted. Although she couldn't understand a word of what they were saying, judging by Stefano's tone this was no business talk.

By the time he'd finished the conversation, she'd finished her breakfast and put her bowl on his desk. 'Who was that?' she asked.

'My sister.' He came over to her, took her face in his hands and gave her a kiss.

She looped her arms around his neck. 'Is she okay?'

'She doesn't like her neighbours. She has three male students living in the flat above hers and they make too much noise at night. They ignore her complaints.'

'Is she not scary like you?'

'I don't scare people.'

'You revel in it.'

He grinned and kissed her again. 'Only people who deserve it. And I have never scared you.'

'I've never scared easily. So what are you going to do about her neighbours? Kneecap them?' she joked, then pressed her lips to his.

'I think a threatening letter will do as a start,' he said into her mouth.

She nipped his bottom lip. 'Very wise.'

Laughing, Stefano unlooped her arms from round his neck. 'I have a conference call to make. Give me an hour and I'll come back to bed before we leave.'

'You don't need me here for it?' She had never missed a conference call in all the time she'd worked for him...

But then she remembered she had a new role, one she

only had patches of memories of. She would have to get a handle on it from scratch.

She wouldn't worry about that until they were back in London, she decided, sliding off the desk.

'No underwear?' he said with a lascivious gleam.

She turned, giving a hint of her bare bottom beneath her skirt. 'I can sit on your lap.'

'You can sit on my lap any time you like. Just not when I'm taking a conference call.' He pushed her playfully. 'Now go.'

'Okay, okay, I know when I'm not wanted.'

He gave her a stern look that only made her laugh harder.

She sashayed deliberately to the door, a thought striking her as she made to leave. 'How do I get on with Christina?'

His brow furrowed.

'I ask because…well, I'm ashamed to say this but when I saw her getting out of your car last week…it felt like a knife in my heart.'

'What do you mean?'

'I assumed she was your latest girlfriend.' She must have seen the darkening in his eyes he wasn't quick enough to hide for she hastened to add, 'Don't forget, I had no idea we were married. I was used to your rolling conveyor belt of girlfriends, it was an easy mistake for me to make. I couldn't understand why it hurt to see you with what I thought was another lover.'

Stefano made sure not to show any reaction. Lying to Anna had been easy when she'd first had the amnesia diagnosed. Now, every untruth felt rancid in his guts. She didn't yet have the memories to know that she'd only met his sister the one time, when she'd walked into their London flat early that morning and found Christina wearing her robe. Anna not being able to speak Italian and Christina not speaking English had given them a language barrier that had allowed Anna to assume the worst.

It came to him how Christina had later described the scene.

'She went white,' his sister had said. 'I thought she was going to be sick. I tried to speak to her but she couldn't understand me; she kept shaking her head as if she'd seen something horrifying, and then she walked out.'

Did that really sound like the actions of a woman calculating how to turn a situation to her advantage?

Now he allowed himself to think about it with some distance from the aftermath, did it not sound like the actions of a woman who'd received a terrible shock?

'You and Christina have a language barrier,' he said steadily. That wasn't a lie.

She eyed him with the look of someone who knew something was being held back. Then she shrugged her shoulders. 'Maybe that's my cue to start learning Italian.'

He was saved from further talk of his sister by the tone on his laptop ringing out to notify him his conference call was about to start.

Anna shrugged again, a wry smile playing on her lips. 'And that's my cue to leave. Have fun.'

After she'd closed the door behind her, Stefano took the seat at his desk and accepted the call. While waiting for the others joining to connect, he rubbed his forehead.

The game he'd been playing, the revenge he'd been savouring…it sat like a bad taste on his tongue.

He'd learned more about his wife in the last week than he had in their entire marriage. Before she'd stormed into his boardroom and humiliated him that day he would never have dreamt she could be a gold-digger or that his trust in her could be unfounded. Every instinct in his guts and in his head were shouting at him that somehow, in some way, everything was wrong.

This was *Anna*. The woman he'd desired and admired from their very first meeting. The woman he'd trusted enough to pledge his life to...

His head began to burn and his guts twisted with something worse than nausea. With his revenge only hours away, he came to the realisation that he couldn't go through with it.

When his conference call was over he would call Miranda, the journalist he'd entrusted into his confidence, and tell her the embargoed press statement he'd given to her a week ago was to be scrapped and buried.

He'd get tonight's awards over with and then he would sit down with Anna and tell her the truth about everything.

The moment Anna walked into Stefano's apartment in San Francisco, more memories returned. Throughout their days in Santa Cruz, more and more had appeared. Her memory was like a giant jigsaw puzzle and what had started as a mammoth hunt for the pieces was now coming together rapidly.

'When did we get a new sofa?' she asked, surprised to find the plump white one replaced with chocolate-brown leather.

'You remember it?'

'It was my favourite thing here.' This apartment was furnished along the same lines as the London one, with everything designed to show off wealth and great taste.

She already missed their Santa Cruz beach house. For all its opulence, it had felt like a home.

He strode to the kitchen. 'It got damaged a few weeks ago. Tea?'

She followed him in. 'Looks like the concierge service has been in,' she said, noting the freshly cleaned scent of the place.

'I called them to get everything ready for us. We're eating at the hotel tonight but there's plenty of snack food if you're hungry…' Suddenly he turned to face her. 'Do you remember the concierge service here?'

She nodded and grinned. 'Like the one in London but with extra "have a nice day."'

'Your memories are coming back quickly now,' he observed.

'There are still holes but they're filling.'

At that, judging by the gleam in his eyes, his mind had taken an entirely different route. She was glad. Tension had been etched on his face since his conference call that not even a long bout of lovemaking before they'd left had been able to erase. When she'd asked what was troubling him, he'd said only that it was to do with work and that he'd tell her about it after the awards. With work still feeling a lifetime away, she didn't bother to pursue it.

'You have a filthy mind, Stefano Moretti.'

He pulled her into his arms and nipped at her earlobe. 'And you love it.'

Yes, she thought, yes, she did. She loved him.

But hadn't she already known she loved him? That tight, painful feeling that had been in her chest since she'd seen Christina follow him out of his car; that had been a symptom of it. It was liberating to finally acknowledge the truth to herself.

She loved him.

With only flat shoes on, her face was flat against his chest. She inhaled his scent greedily and sighed into him before tugging at his shirt to loosen it and slip a hand up it and onto his back.

The words rolled on her tongue, so close to being spoken aloud, but she held them back.

The last time she remembered saying those words had been to her father in the minutes before they'd turned his life support off.

Stefano gathered her hair and gently tugged her head back. 'You don't want tea?'

'I'm not thirsty.' She moved her hands to the front of his shirt and began undoing the buttons. She might not yet be able to say the words to him but she could show him. 'But I *am* hungry.'

As was always the case, Stefano was showered, shaved and ready a good hour before Anna, who'd had a beautician provided by the apartment's concierge service in to help her.

He pressed Miranda's name on his phone again and tapped his foot while waiting for it to connect.

He hadn't been able to get hold of her. He'd left her three messages and sent two emails. Anna had disappeared for a couple of hours' 'retail therapy' that afternoon and he'd tried Miranda again, even calling her newsroom.

Miranda Appleton was editor-in-chief of the US's best-selling celebrity magazine that had an accompanying website with the highest daily click rate of any media in the world. Miranda had her finger on the pulse of all celebrity news and in today's instant world a billionaire such as himself was considered a celebrity.

He'd chosen Miranda for his scoop because, for all her unscrupulous dealings, she was a woman of her word and he'd known she wouldn't break the embargo.

And now she had gone off-grid. No one knew where she was. No one could reach her.

His call went yet again to her voicemail.

'It's Stefano,' he hissed quietly down the line. 'Miranda, I need you to kill that story. I retract my statement. You cannot publish it. Call me back as soon as you can.'

Feeling sick to his stomach, he waited for Anna in the living room, sitting on the new sofa that had been delivered to replace the one he'd ruined when he'd made his first trip to San Francisco after she'd left him. He'd remembered making love to her on it and the rage that had ripped through him, which had caused him to rip up the one item of furniture she'd loved, pulling chunks out of it as *she* had ripped chunks out of *him*.

He'd been as out of control as he'd been before prison had cured him of his temper.

Jail itself hadn't been too bad but the six months he'd served behind bars had dragged interminably. He'd grown to hate the confinement, the suffocation that came from spending all day every day in an enclosed space surrounded by people there wasn't a hell's chance of escaping from. He understood why prisoners might turn to drugs, just to relieve themselves of the brain-numbing boredom. As he'd already been hooked on nicotine at the time he'd known better than to take that route himself. But, still, the days had been so *long*.

His temper had been the reason he'd been incarcerated. He'd walked out of those prison gates with a determination to never let it get the better of him again and until Anna had left him, he never had.

He took a deep breath then got up to pour himself a large measure of bourbon. He downed it in one, then poured another.

The doubts that had been amassing in his head since their arrival in California had grown. Yet he always came back to the fact of that damned letter from Anna's solicitor demanding a massive slice of his fortune. Whatever had been going on in her head at the time, that demand had come from *her*. He should not allow fantastic sex and the old sparring easiness they'd shared to overturn the facts of the situation because in that respect nothing had changed.

His plan had worked perfectly. He'd seduced her. She'd even said she would marry him again. That should fill him with satisfaction, not make him feel as if he'd been punched a dozen times in the gut.

Never in his life had he felt such indecision. Since his imprisonment he'd learned to keep a cool head, analyse the facts and then make up his mind. Once it was made up, nothing deterred him from his chosen path.

He shouldn't let the past week cloud his judgement or deter him from his path now.

But he'd learned more about his wife in the past week than he had in almost a year of marriage and all his instincts were telling him he couldn't go through with it.

Where on earth was Miranda? Had she got his messages?

They'd planned the timings down to the minute. His statement was due to go online halfway through the awards ceremony.

He heard soft footsteps approaching and composed himself.

Anna entered the living room serenely, like a goddess emerging from an oyster shell.

All the breath left his body.

She wore a floor-length fitted red lace dress that pooled at her feet like a mermaid's tail. The front plunged in a V showing the tiniest hint of creamy cleavage. Her bare arms glimmered. Her face was subtly made up except for the lips, which she'd painted the same shade as her dress, and her dark hair shone, blow-dried to fall thickly around her shoulders.

She spread her arms out and made a slow twirl. 'Well?'

He cleared his throat. 'I think I'm going to be the envy of every red-blooded male in attendance.'

Her eyes sparkled, joy resounding from them. 'I couldn't believe it when I found this dress in my dressing room. Did I buy it for tonight?'

'I assume so. I've only been on one shopping trip with you.'

She grinned. 'I remember that. Was it that bad for you?'

'I've had better times watching envelopes being stuffed.'

'I'd never been shopping with an unlimited credit card. Can you blame me for getting carried away?'

He shook his head, remembering the glee with which she'd attacked the shopping district he'd taken her to. He'd often given old girlfriends a credit card to buy themselves something for a night out and they'd always played a game; pretending to resist, pretending to want their independence and not wanting to take from him. Anna had made no such pretence. She'd snatched the card out of his hand—a card he'd given her to keep and not just for the one occasion—and raced to the shops like a roadrunner, virtually leaving a trail of dust in her wake. Her chutzpah had made him laugh.

And then he remembered a time before they'd married, when he'd caught her making calculations with a pen and paper. She'd been trying to work out her finances to see if she could afford to pay for her and her sister to go on a five-star spa weekend in Dublin for Melissa's birthday. He'd offered to pay and she'd dismissed it out of hand. She wouldn't even discuss it. He'd noticed in the weeks leading up to that particular spa break that she had brought her own lunch into the office rather than eating in the subsidised staff restaurant, and he'd admired that she was prepared to economise when necessary and forego little treats if it meant having a bigger treat at the end of it.

She'd often spent her money on her sister, he remembered, and for the first time wondered if it was her way of making up for Melissa giving up her freedom to raise her. For all Anna's current happiness, he knew Melissa wasn't far from her thoughts. He knew Melissa being in Australia with their mother had wounded her in ways he couldn't understand.

Anna had only been happy to spend his money *after* they'd married and that had only been to feed her addiction to clothes shopping. She'd cheekily described it as *the* perk of being his wife.

Miranda, check your damn messages.

'Where did you say the awards were being held?' Anna asked, rifling through her small red clutch bag.

'At the Grand Palace Hotel.'

Her hand stilled and she looked at him. 'The Grand Palace Hotel?'

'*Sì*. It's been held there for the past five years. What are you looking for?'

'Double-checking I've put my lipstick in,' she replied, but her eyes had glazed over, her words mechanical and said without any thought, her mind clearly somewhere else.

'What's wrong?'

After a moment she blinked and shook her head. Her mouth pulled into a smile but there was a brittleness to it. 'Nothing. Shall we go?'

Aware that to leave it much longer would make them late, he took her hand and together they left his apartment.

Only the cramping in his guts acted as a warning sign that something was very wrong.

CHAPTER TEN

ANNA'S NAILS, MANICURED FABULOUSLY by the beautician, dug into the palm of her hand. Stefano sat beside her in the back of the stretched Mercedes, filling the silence with talk of a new super-secure Cloud-based system his employees were developing. She made all the appropriate noises and asked all the obvious questions she would always ask but her thoughts were far away. A year ago away.

When he'd said they were going to the Grand Palace Hotel, she'd had an instant image flash in her head of being at that hotel with Stefano before, but just as the memory had crystallised another, equally vivid image had come to her of throwing a jug of water over him in his London boardroom, in front of the entire board of directors.

By the time they arrived at the hotel fifteen minutes after setting off, she wanted to tell the driver to turn round and take them back. She felt sick. Memories had come back to her—flooded back—and she wanted to sit somewhere on her own and make sense of them all.

Because none of it made sense. She'd already remembered arguments between them and had accepted them without dissection. She would have been more surprised if they hadn't argued. She remembered missing him when he went away on business without her and, shaming as it was, remembered the fears and insecurities that had crept up on her.

What she hadn't remembered until only a few minutes ago, and which Stefano hadn't bothered to mention, was that she'd left him. More than that, she'd confronted him in his boardroom and lost total control of herself in front of everyone. What she still couldn't remember was why or what the aftermath had been.

She had almost the entire picture there before her but the biggest, most significant pieces were still missing. Her painfully thudding heart told her that she didn't want to remember.

The car door was opened and before either of them had moved from their seats, lights flashed around them.

The Tech Industry Awards, if one was to go by its name, promised nothing more than a bunch of eggheads crowded together in a room congratulating each other on their supreme eggheadedness. The truth was that these awards were prestigious and glamorous enough to rival the ceremony for any national film or music award. These were the awards the big players wanted and paid a fortune to sponsor. It was estimated the collective worth of the attendees this evening would make up the largest concentration of money in the world, and the press was out in force to cover it.

Above them, thick dark clouds had gathered. Anna gave an involuntary shiver. A storm was on its way and her foreboding only grew.

She made sure to keep her face inscrutable as she climbed out and took Stefano's hand. Ignoring the shouts from reporters throwing inane questions at them—she

distinguished at least three asking 'who' she was wearing—they went through the cordon opened for them.
Waving at the thick crowd of spectators, they walked up
the red carpet where only a select few journalists were
allowed to stand.

As they passed one reporter doing a piece for camera,
she caught some of what was being said.

'Rumours of the Moretti marriage being over have
been scotched by the couple's first public appearance
in six weeks.'

And then the reporter swung round and thrust the
microphone in Stefano's face.

'If you could choose one award to win tonight, which
would it be?'

'I couldn't choose just one,' Stefano answered with
the easy smile that made millions of women around the
world long to bed him. 'But whether we win anything
tonight or not makes no matter. Moretti's is the leading
software manufacturer and app developer in the world,
and the technology my dedicated staff are developing will
change the face of the world as we know it.'

'Fabulous!' The reporter gave the vacuous grin that
meant she hadn't listened to a word of his answer and immediately turned her microphone to Anna. 'What do you
have to say, Anna, about the reports on your marriage?'

Anna responded with an identical vacuous smile.
'What reports are you referring to?'

The reporter's composure wavered for only a second.
'The rumours that you had separated. Are we to believe
that you two are still together?'

Stefano put his arm around her waist and opened his
mouth to speak, but Anna couldn't bear to hear another
of his lies.

She smiled and made sure to inject sweetness in her voice. 'I think my presence here with my husband can speak for itself. Enjoy your evening.'

And with a gracious nod and another wave to the crowd, Anna and Stefano were taken inside by a couple of burly bouncers.

His arm stayed around her waist in that protective fashion she'd always so adored. Outwardly he appeared completely unfazed by the reporter's remarks. He'd buttered her up well for it, she thought cynically. Hadn't he remarked when she'd been in the hospital that the press were always speculating on the state of their marriage?

If only she could remember those last pieces of the scene, she would know what had come after she'd drenched him in water.

Knowing Stefano as well as she did, she didn't think it was something he would have easily forgiven her for.

If only she knew what had compelled her to do it in the first place...

Now was not the time to try and work it all out, not in a reception hall filled with industry bigwigs all wanting to shake hands, exchange stories and assert individual dominance. There was a convivial atmosphere, however, as rivalries were set aside for the night, at least superficially.

The Moretti table was situated directly before the main stage and thus in the glare of the majority of the video cameras. Anna kept her head held high as they joined the executives and company nominees who'd been invited to join them on this prestigious night, pretending not to see the curious glances being flashed her way.

Only one member of the UK board was in attendance, the rest from Sweden, Japan and America. She knew with one look that they all knew exactly what had happened in that boardroom. And they knew she had received her P45 for gross misconduct the very next day and had had no contact with any member of staff or with her husband...

Until the morning she'd woken with a bang on her head and her memories wiped.

And now, she remembered...

It explained everything. All the stares she'd received, Chloe's appropriation of her desk, Stefano's anger...

She remembered everything.

Everything.

Oh, how she wished she hadn't. Ignorance had been more than bliss; it had been an escape from the unbearable agony that had become her life.

Stefano put his hand on hers. Her veins turned to ice and she fought not to snatch it away. He whispered something in her ear and she fought not to flinch.

She made sure to keep a smile on her face and play the role of the happy wife. It was the greatest role she'd ever had to play.

When Moretti's was given its third award of the night and Stefano took to the stage with the innovative hipster who'd been the brains behind it, she clapped as hard as everyone else.

Her pride would not allow her to show publicly that her heart had been irreversibly broken.

But she couldn't keep it together for ever.

Not long after the halfway point of the evening she rose from the table.

Stefano grabbed her wrist. 'Where are you going?'

'To the Ladies'.'

'Can't you wait?' His nostrils were flared, his jaw clenched.

'*What?*' She snatched her hand away. 'Don't be ridiculous.'

As she hurried her way through the tables she became aware that shocked faces were staring at her. Voices at every table she approached dropped to a hushed whisper and there was a furious tapping of phone screens accompanied by more shocked faces.

Fortunately the ladies' room was empty. She wished there were a window she could crawl out of but if all she could have was a few moments to compose herself then she would take that.

Sucking in some deep breaths, she pressed powder to her white cheeks and fixed her eyeliner and lipstick, then took some more deep breaths for luck and left her brief sanctuary.

The stares and whispers were even more pronounced now. There was still a handful of awards left to be given but Stefano had risen from their table and was taking great strides towards her.

'We need to go,' he said, grabbing her hand and practically dragging her to the exit.

'It's not finished yet.' As much as she longed to escape the stares, protocol dictated that everyone should stay to the bitter end.

He didn't answer or slow his pace. If anything he moved faster.

If he could get her out of the hotel and into his car before the press noticed them, Stefano knew he had a chance. A chance to explain himself before Anna learned of the bomb he'd detonated.

The weather had taken a turn for the worse since their arrival. Thick droplets of rain were falling and the breeze had picked up.

They almost made their escape. The press were too busy huddled together in little clusters, staring at their phones, chattering frenziedly among themselves, to notice the couple slipping out half an hour early or the gathering storm around them.

But then a driver got out of a yellow cab and called out loudly, 'Anna Moretti?' and with a violent curse, Stefano knew he was too late.

He'd forgotten his instruction that Miranda book a cab for Anna and to make sure the driver arrived early with a picture of the passenger he was to collect. Stefano had planned to put her in it as his final flourish, to shut the door for her and never see her again.

His plan had worked perfectly.

Success had never tasted so bitter.

At the mention of Anna's name the press sprang into action.

Pounding feet rushed towards them, a babble of shouted words pouring out so thick and fast they should be incomprehensible. But judging by the pallor of Anna's face and the tiny stumble she made, she had heard them clearly enough.

His own driver pulled up. Stefano opened the back door himself and bundled Anna's rigid body inside.

It was only as he slammed the door behind them that he caught a glimpse of Miranda Appleton standing like a vulture next to her magazine's photographer, a smirk on her ugly, rancid face.

Anna sat like a mannequin pressed against the far door. She didn't look at him. She hardly seemed to be breathing.

The rain had turned into a deluge and the driver slowed to a crawl. With the silence stretching between them and an air of darkness swirling, it was a relief when they eventually came to a stop at the front of the apartment building. A crackle of lightning rent the sky, illuminating everything for a few brief seconds that were still long enough for him to see the shock carved on her frozen face.

She didn't notice they'd come to a stop.

'Anna,' he said tentatively. 'We're home.'

Still she sat there, immobile.

Only when he leaned over to take her hand—*Dio*, it was icy to the touch—did she show any animation.

Slowly her head turned to face him. 'Don't touch me.'

Then, with no care for any passing cars, she opened her door and stepped out into the deluge.

Stefano jolted after her and breathed a tiny sigh of relief that the road was empty of traffic.

Maybe it was the lashing rain that forced her hand but she walked sharply into his apartment building. She bypassed the elevator to take the stairs, her heels clip-clopping without pause all the way to the eighteenth floor.

There was no sign of her exertion when she shrank away from him as he punched in the entry code to their apartment.

She headed straight to their bar, snatched up the nearest bottle and took a huge gulp from it. Then she took another gulp, wiped her mouth with the back of her hand and put the lid back on.

Only then did she meet his eye.

She stared at him for an age before her face contorted into something unrecognisable and she smashed the bottle down on the bar with all her strength.

'*Bastard!*' she screamed as the bottle exploded around her, then reached for a bottle of brandy and smashed that too. The single malt went next, all accompanied by a hail of curses and profanities that seemed to be wrenched from her very soul.

The bourbon would have gone the same way had Stefano not sprung into motion—the destruction had happened within seconds—and wrapped his arms around her, trapping her back against his chest.

'Anna, stop,' he commanded loudly. 'You're going to hurt yourself.'

She thrashed wildly in his hold, kicking her legs backwards and forwards, catching his shin with the heel of her shoe, all the while screaming curses at him.

He winced at the lancing pain but didn't let her go.

In a way, the pain was welcome. He deserved it.

She caught his shin again and he gritted his teeth. 'Please, stop fighting me. I know you want to hurt me. I *know*. And I deserve it. Hit me, kick me, bite me, do whatever you want but please, *bellissima*, don't hurt yourself. There's glass everywhere.'

As if she could hurt herself after what he'd done to her. In the state she was in, he doubted she would feel any pain.

His words must have penetrated for gradually the fight went out of her and she went limp in his arms.

Cautiously he released his hold and braced himself for her to take him at his word and attack him.

Instead, she staggered to the centre of the living room and flopped to the floor. The mermaid tail of her dress made a perfect semi-circle around her. Her chest rose heavily and she lifted her head to stare at him. Misery and contempt pierced him.

Without saying a word, she removed each sparkling shoe in turn. There was a moment when he thought she was going to throw them at him but, after a small hesitation, she flung them to her side.

When she finally spoke there was a metallic edge to her tone that made his veins run cold.

'Did you enjoy your revenge?'

'I tried to stop it.' He knew it was a pathetic thing to say even before her face twisted.

He dragged a hand through his hair and took a deep breath before reaching carefully through the debris of glass for the saved bottle of bourbon.

'You couldn't have tried very hard.' She laughed, a robotic sound that made him flinch. 'I think your revenge worked. The ruthless Stefano Moretti shows the world that you mess with him at your peril, even if you're his wife. My humiliation will make front page news everywhere.'

He unscrewed the bottle and put it to his lips. The liquid burned his throat.

'It was too late to stop it. Miranda must have known I'd change my mind. She made it impossible for me to contact her.'

'Miranda Appleton? That witch?'

He nodded and drank some more.

'You're blaming *her*?'

'No. The only one to blame for tonight is me. I set it up.' After everything that had been said and done between them, the only thing they were left with was the truth. 'I called her last week, the day after I brought you home from hospital, and gave her a statement. I put an embargo on it that was to be lifted at nine thirty this evening.'

'And what did your statement say?' Though she was outwardly calmer, he could see she was clinging to her control by a whisker.

'That the rumours about our marriage were true and that I would be issuing you with divorce papers tomorrow morning.'

'Happy anniversary to me.'

'At the time I thought it fitting.'

'And all the times you made love to me? Treated me like a princess? Cared for me? Where did that all fit in? I suppose that was to humiliate me privately as well as publicly so that every time I thought of us together in Santa Cruz, the city I love, I would be reminded that I'd been a fool to think I could take you on and win?'

She knew him too well. Better than he knew himself.

Shame rolled through him like a dark cloud. He jerked a nod. There was nothing he could say to defend himself. He didn't want to even try.

'The cab? Where was that going to take me?' she asked.

'Out of my life.'

She laughed again. He had never heard such a pitiful sound.

'So, if I'm to believe you'd changed your mind—and in fairness I can see you got cold feet about the cab side of it, so let's give you the benefit of the doubt about that—what brought the change of heart about? You've played me like a violin all week to reach this point so why back out at the last minute?'

'I've been having doubts.'

She trembled but her voice remained steady. 'Doubts? That's a good one. Doubts about what?'

'About whether you really had set out to frame me for adultery and fleece me for as much money as you could get all along.'

Pain lashed her features. 'That's what you believed?'

He gripped the bottle tightly. He'd been so caught up with all that had just happened that he'd lost sight of what had driven him to these actions in the first place.

He'd done wrong—he knew that—but she had too.

'You're the one who found a strange woman in our apartment and immediately decided I was having an affair.'

She shook her head with incredulity. 'If you'd come back early from a trip abroad and found a strange semi-naked man in the apartment, what would you have thought?'

Stefano's heart was thumping violently against his ribs. 'I do not say I wouldn't have been a little suspicious but I wouldn't have made assumptions as you did.'

No, if he'd found a strange man in his apartment wearing his robe, his fist would probably have connected with the man's face before he'd had time to think.

'I would have asked you to explain,' he continued, pushing the thought away. 'I would have listened to your answer. You didn't ask for my side. *You* decided the facts to suit yourself. You swore at me and threw water over me in front of my most senior members of staff. You humiliated me.'

'You were ignoring me.'

'When?'

'That night. I called. It went to voicemail...'

'My sister who I didn't know existed had suddenly appeared in my life,' he interrupted. 'I had just been told the father I thought had died when I was a child had been alive all these years and had a new family but that there was no chance of me meeting him because he had died a few weeks before. Forgive me if I was too busy trying to make sense of my life to answer my phone.'

He hadn't even noticed it ring. Christina had sent a courier to his apartment with a letter and some photos—photos of *him* as a child—ending her note with a number for him to call.

She'd been waiting outside the apartment building.

'Too busy to answer the phone for your *wife*? Too busy to call when I left a message *and* texted you asking you to call me?'

'I didn't get the messages until four in the morning when it was too late to call you back, but I did text you. I told you I would call you later in the day, which I would have done after the meeting you interrupted, but you jumped to the conclusion that I was with another woman. You stormed into my boardroom and accused me of having an affair in front of my most senior members of staff. You threw water over me.' As the humiliation flooded back over him, his temper rose. 'You broke your word. You said you would trust me. You lied to me!'

Anna stared at him for the longest time, her lips parted but with no sound coming out. But then the colour rushed back across her cheeks and she got to her knees to thump the floor.

'You selfish, selfish *bastard*. Twisting this all round to hide what you've done. I've made mistakes and done things I'm ashamed of but you took advantage of my amnesia just so you could have your revenge. You let me think I still worked for you! No wonder you didn't want me calling Melissa—that wasn't for my sake, it was to protect your lie! You've been lying to me for over a week!'

'You hit me with a demand for a hundred million pounds!' he shot back. 'You knew I wouldn't take that lying down.'

'Of course I knew that! Why do you think I issued it?'

'You *wanted* me to react?'

'I wanted you to speak to me and I was crazy enough to think that demanding a hundred million and a load of your assets would force you to communicate. You'd cut me off. You fired me and blocked my number. You served me with formal separation papers. You changed the security number for the apartment so I couldn't get in. It was like I'd never existed for you. I wanted to hurt you as much as you were hurting me. I knew the only way I'd be able to get your attention was by hitting you where I knew it would hurt the most—your wallet.'

'You walked out on *me*,' he reminded her harshly. 'Did you think I would beg you to come back?'

'I came back the next day and couldn't get into the apartment. You didn't even give me twenty-four hours before locking me out.'

The cold mist in his head had thickened, nausea roiling in his guts as he thought of his own contribution to the mess that was the end of their marriage. He *had* cut her off. His pride and ego had been dented so greatly that he'd struck back before she could do any more damage.

'Why did you want to get my attention so badly?'

'Because I needed you and because, despite everything, I couldn't accept we were over.' She pinched the bridge of her nose and held out her other hand for the bottle. He took a nip himself before passing it to her.

She took a long slug.

'Don't you think you've had enough?'

Her hair swished as she shook her head. 'Nowhere near enough.'

The trembling anguish in her voice sent a fresh roll of dread through him.

Her hands were shaking so much the bottle slipped

from her hand and onto her lap, then rolled onto the floor.

In silence they watched the transparent fiery liquid spill onto the dark carpet.

'Anna,' he said quietly, 'why did you say you needed me?'

Her face rose to meet his gaze. Her eyes were stark, her bottom lip trembling.

All these weeks he'd been determined to think the worst. Anna had made assumptions but he had too. He could admit that.

She swallowed a number of times before saying in a voice so small he had to strain to hear, 'I lost our baby.'

'What...?' The question died on his lips as the cold mist in his head froze to ice.

The devastation on her face was so complete that he knew with gut-wrenching certainty that he hadn't misheard her.

He could no longer speak. His tongue felt alien in his mouth.

He gazed at his wife's white face and huge pain-filled eyes and the room began to spin around them. His heart roaring in his ears, he reached out blindly for her but then his knees buckled beneath him and he groped the arm of the nearest chair before they gave way completely.

Dio, what had he done?

CHAPTER ELEVEN

ANNA, HER STOMACH CHURNING, bile rising inside her, clenched her hand into a fist and shoved it against her mouth to stop herself from screaming.

How she'd prevented the screams from ripping out of her when it had all come back to her that evening she didn't know, could only guess it had been iron determination not to let the liar she'd married see her misery or the avid curious faces of their peers that had made her succeed. But now the words were out and there was no putting them back and it hit her like a tsunami that had been gathering into a peak and now came crashing down on her.

That last piece of her memory had come when she'd glanced at the menu in the hotel and read that their first course was smoked duck.

She'd been eating smoked duck in their Parisian hotel when she'd confessed to Melissa that her period was three days late.

She'd never seen Stefano lost for words before, never seen him be anything but arrogantly self-possessed. Seeing the colour drain from his horror-struck face sliced through the protective shield she'd been clinging to and her whole frame collapsed.

She fell onto her side and brought her knees up to her chin, wrapping her arms around them, and wept as she hadn't done since she was fourteen years old and she'd woken to the realisation that she would never see her father again.

The pain was unbearable, carving through her like a white-hot knife.

Through the sobs racking her body, she was aware of movement. Stefano had shifted to sit beside her on the floor.

It only made her sob harder. It was as if she were purging herself of all the pain in one huge tidal wave of grief. The loss of her father, her mother's desertion, her sister's betrayal and, fresher and more acute than all this, the loss of the man she loved and the child she'd so badly wanted.

That was something else her amnesia had anaesthetised her against: her increasingly desperate need for a child. Stefano's child. She'd sensed her marriage fragmenting around her and had tried to push the need aside, knowing theirs wasn't the stable marriage one should bring a child into. It hadn't stopped her craving one and when she'd discovered she was pregnant her joy had been so pure and true that for a few magical hours she'd allowed herself to believe that everything would work out between them and that Stefano would stop pushing her away and let her into his heart.

Now, with her memories acutely fresh, she had to accept what she'd been unable to accept in the month before she'd hit her head and slipped into blissful ignorance: that their relationship was over and all her dreams were dead.

It was a long time before the tears stopped flowing and her shuddering frame stilled enough for her to think clearly again. Her chest and throat sore, she dried her eyes with the hem of her dress and hauled herself into a sitting position with her legs crossed as she'd sat when she had been a child.

Stefano, who hadn't said a word, stretched his legs out beside her and gave a long sigh. 'You were pregnant?' he asked in a tone of voice she'd never heard before. He sounded…defeated.

She gulped for air, wishing with all her might that she could lapse back into ignorant bliss. 'Do you remember I switched the contraceptive injection I was using?'

He nodded jerkily.

'I forgot it was an eight-week course and not a twelve-week like the old one.' She sucked in more air, remembering how all over the place she'd been emotionally at that time, how her fears about her marriage had come to cloud everything. 'When I told Melissa I was three days late she couldn't believe I hadn't done a pregnancy test. She dragged me around Paris looking for a chemist so we could buy one.' She almost smiled at the memory. It was pretty much the first time in a long while that she had been happy and the last time she and Melissa had been comfortable with each other. 'I didn't think I was. I thought it was the kind of thing women knew instinctively.'

'But you were?'

She nodded and swallowed back the choking feeling in her throat. 'I was going to wait until the morning before I did the test but I couldn't resist doing it when we got back to the hotel. I was so distrustful of the result that I dragged Melissa back out to get another one and that came out positive too. That's why I called you. I was so happy I couldn't wait to tell you.' She cast him a rueful stare. 'And I was feeling a bit guilty for not taking the test with you.'

He raised a weary shoulder. 'It doesn't matter. You do everything with your sister. I'm used to it.'

'You think that but Melissa didn't see it that way,' she whispered. 'We *used* to do everything together, until I married you. I didn't realise how lonely she was without me. After I left that message for you to call me back she sat me down and told me she was going to Australia.'

Stefano whistled quietly.

'She'd been planning it for months. She'd been secretly speaking to Mum and arranging it all. She'd booked her flights, booked the time off work… All she'd been waiting for was the right time to tell me. She picked her moment perfectly, when I was on top of the world with news of the pregnancy to dull the impact of it.'

'And did it?'

'Nope.' She wiped away a tear. 'We had a huge fight. We said some *horrible* things to each other. She called me a selfish bitch and she was right—I was. It was all about *me* and how I felt. See? Selfish. I left her in the hotel and went to the airport and stayed there until I could get a flight back to London in the morning. I didn't sleep at all. I kept hugging my phone waiting for you to call me back. I was desperate to speak to you. I can't describe how I felt—on the one hand thrilled and elated that we were going to be parents, a little scared of how you'd react, and devastated at what I perceived as Melissa's betrayal.'

'Why were you scared of my reaction?' he asked hollowly.

She wiped away fresh tears, struggling to keep her

voice audible. 'You'd become so distant. I knew you were angry that I suspected there were other women but I *didn't* believe it. I *did* believe you but when you gave me that promotion and started travelling abroad without me…I thought you were bored of me.'

Stefano's voice cracked as he said, 'I promoted you because you were the best person for the job and I knew I could travel abroad leaving my company in the best hands.'

Promoting Anna had been a business decision. Anyone lucky enough to employ her would have done the same. And the time apart had done them good. Had done *him* good. Being together day and night hadn't been healthy. He'd expected their marriage to be eventful and fun. He hadn't expected to want to strip the skin from Anna's body to discover the secrets of her heart.

That had been dangerous. Unhealthy.

He'd thought some distance was necessary. He hadn't realised it would feed into her insecurities.

'I became paranoid. I couldn't sleep for thinking of all the women who would be flaunting themselves before you, lining themselves up to replace me.' Her red eyes were huge on his. 'I was terrified one of them would catch your eye and then the press published those pictures of you. I knew you were telling me the truth but by then I thought it was only a matter of when. I would wake every day wondering if it would be our last, always thinking, *Is this the day he meets someone else? Is this the day he tells me we're over?'*

'Anna, I made a promise to be faithful to you.'

'No, you promised to tell me if you met someone you wanted to sleep with so I could walk away with my dignity intact.'

'I kept that promise. I never cheated on you. I never wanted anyone else. I never gave you reason to doubt me.'

'Stefano, our marriage was based on two things. Sex and work. When you started pulling away from me and leaving me behind it was like you didn't need me any more. I knew you would never love me but I didn't think it mattered. I thought it was a good thing, better than having someone say they would love me for ever and then cheat and break my heart.' She shrugged and gave a choking laugh, then put her hand under her nose and closed her eyes. 'Oh, the lies we tell ourselves,' she whispered. 'I was already in love with you when we married but in total denial about it. What I really wanted was for you to tell me you didn't need to make that promise. I wanted you to say there would never be anyone else for you but me.'

The spinning in the room had turned into a whirlpool.

How could he have been so blind? So busy running from his own feelings that he'd dismissed Anna's fears thinking his word alone should be good enough for her.

He was feeling now. Feeling more than he had ever wanted, feelings he'd spent his life escaping from.

'And then you found Christina in the apartment,' he stated quietly.

She lifted her knees to wrap her arms around them and rocked forward. 'I lost my mind. Seeing a beautiful woman in our apartment dressed in my robe; it was my worst nightmare come to life. I wanted to hurt you. I was out of my mind. Truly, I wasn't thinking straight. What I did in your boardroom… I am so ashamed. I don't blame you for cutting me off as you did. I brought it on myself.'

Every word that Anna said plunged like a knife into Stefano's heart. How could she blame herself? This was all on him. If he hadn't been so full of outraged wounded pride he would have seen something had been seriously wrong with his wife.

But he hadn't thought of her. He'd thought of only himself.

Eventually he was able to drag out of his frozen throat the question he most feared hearing the answer to. 'What happened to the baby?'

'I lost it two days later.' A huge shudder ran through her and she buried her face in her knees, fresh sobs pouring out of her.

Feeling as if he'd been kicked in the stomach, Stefano pulled her to him. This time he allowed his instincts to take over, wrapping his arms tightly around her, pressing his mouth into her hair, wishing he knew the words that would make everything better and stop the cold agony he knew was consuming them both.

She clutched at his jacket, her tears soaking into his shirt. 'It was the only thing keeping me going. I know it must sound stupid but I'd pictured our baby. I'd planned its whole life out in my head…'

'It doesn't sound stupid at all,' he cut in. In his mind's eye he could picture their baby too…

Fresh bile rose swiftly inside him and grabbed at his throat, making his head spin.

'Where were you when you…?' He couldn't bring himself to say it.

'In my hotel room.' She took a gulp of air. 'I'd checked into a hotel because I couldn't face Melissa after our row and you wouldn't let me anywhere near you.'

'You were alone?'

She nodded into his chest. 'So, selfish creature that I am, I went back to my sister.'

'You are *not* selfish,' he stated fiercely.

Anna had had to go through that trauma on her own? The only selfish one here had been him.

'Aren't I? I hated the thought of her seeing our mum.'

'No,' he contradicted, 'you were scared you would lose her too. You lost both your parents when you were at an age when you needed them most. Your father, rest his soul, did not leave by choice but your mother did. Is no wonder you find it hard to trust people—the woman who should have been there for you left you behind.'

And if he'd ever allowed Anna to open up to him during their marriage instead of avoiding any kind of intimate talk he would have known how shattered her mother's emigration had left her. He would have known just how vulnerable she was and would have made that damned call to her instead of telling himself she would be fast asleep and wouldn't mind waiting.

You did know she'd mind but you were running scared. Anna got too close, didn't she? You were waiting for an excuse to push her away before she rejected you like everyone else you ever knew did.

She hadn't been asleep. She'd been in an airport waiting to return home to him with the best news of their lives and some shattering news of her own. She'd needed him.

He squeezed her even tighter to him. 'Melissa looked after you?'

'Melissa always looks after me.' Anna tilted her head to look at him. 'She's always been my lifeline, and you're right, I was scared I'd lose her. We muddled along as well as we could but it was hard. We'd both said things we couldn't take back. When she left for Australia it was without my blessing. She even left me a note asking for my forgiveness when it should have been me down on my knees begging for hers.'

'Anna…'

'No, please don't make excuses for me. I'm not fourteen any more. I've always known how much Melissa missed our mum but ignored it under my own self-righteousness.'

'Or did you ignore it because it meant you would have to confront how much you missed your mum too?'

'Don't say that,' she protested.

'You must have missed her. I always missed my mother and I never even knew her.'

'Did you?'

She sounded so surprised that he couldn't help but give a grimace of a smile. 'All my life. And I missed my father. I look now on all the years we missed out on when I could have known him and I think what a waste those years were.'

'But do you regret cutting the rest of your family out of your life?'

'Not at all. I will never have them in my life again but my situation with them is different from yours. I never loved them and they never loved me.'

Since his *nonno* had died, Anna was the only person who had loved him. Lots of women had claimed to love him but he'd always known their words to be a pack of lies. Anna was…

She was the only one.

'You still think I should see my mother?'

'You will never find peace until you do, that much I do know. Speak to her. Hear her side. Admit to yourself that you need her in your life. See if you can build a relationship.'

She fell silent.

'I can come with you.'

'Where?'

'To see your mother. I can come as support.'

Her laugh sounded genuine but as she disentangled herself from his hold he saw fresh tears were streaming down her face.

'I needed your support five weeks ago.' She shook her head and wiped the tears away then straightened.

'Let me give it to you now,' he urged. 'I wasn't there for you...'

'No, you weren't.' Her shining eyes bored into his. 'And I don't blame you. I understand what a shock it must have been for you having your sister turn up out of the blue and learning about your father.'

'I should never have cut you off.'

'No, you shouldn't, but I knew the type of man you were when I married you. I knew you didn't do forgiveness. One strike and the person's out—humiliating you was my strike and I accept that...'

'No, don't accept it. I was a *fool* to behave like that.' A fool and a cruel, selfish bastard. 'If I'd any idea what you were going through I would never have...'

'It doesn't matter!' She took a deep breath and got unsteadily to her feet. 'None of it matters any more, don't you see that? Our marriage is over and it's time I learned to stand on my own two feet.'

The freezing fog in his brain thickened, making his ears ring. 'It doesn't have to be over. We can start again.'

'It does.' She folded her arms across her chest. There was something in her stance that made her appear taller.

'We could forgive each other everything that happened, draw a line in the sand and start again, but I'll never forgive you for what you did to get your revenge.' She shrugged her shoulders but the whiteness of her face belied the nonchalance she was trying to portray. 'That was despicable and I hate you for it.'

On legs that were surprisingly weak, he got up to stand before her. Something was scratching at him, clawing at his chest, making it painful to breathe. 'You said that you loved me.'

'And I did love you. With all my heart. All through my amnesia I kept thinking you were holding back from telling me you loved me to keep the pressure off my recovery but the truth was you never loved me, did you?'

The pain in his chest increased. He couldn't form any words. Not one.

'You killed my love and all my trust in you,' she spat. 'If I ever marry again it will be to someone who wants more than just my body and my business brain.' Her voice caught but when she continued her tone didn't falter. 'It will be with someone who can love me too and trust me with their heart. I have to hope for that.'

And with that she turned her back on him, picked up her clutch bag from the table and headed for the front door.

'Where are you going?' Things were moving too quickly. She couldn't just *leave* like this. 'Look at the weather out there.'

The rain was lashing so hard it fell like hail against the windows.

She didn't turn around. 'I'm going to check into a hotel and in the morning I'm going to go home. *My* home. Mine and Melissa's flat. After that, all I know for certain is that I have to stop relying on other people to hold me up and learn to hold myself up. If Melissa stays in Australia then I will give her my blessing.' Then she did turn and gave the smallest, saddest of smiles. 'Maybe I will fly out there too. I don't know.'

There was nothing left to say. He could see it in her eyes. Anna was going to walk out of the door and this time it would be for good.

She didn't say goodbye.

She closed the door with the softest of clicks but the sound echoed like a ricocheting bullet.

Stefano stood on the same spot for an age, too numb and dazed about everything that had just happened to take it all in. A part of him expected—hoped—that the door would swing back open and she'd walk back in and tell him she'd changed her mind.

It didn't happen.

Her discarded shoes lay on their sides where she'd thrown them. Her feet were bare…

His legs suddenly propelled themselves to the window that overlooked the street below. He pushed it open and stuck his head out, uncaring that the storm soaked him in seconds and blinded his eyes.

Through the sheet of water running over his face he caught a glimpse of a red dress disappearing into a cab. Seconds later the cab pulled away from the kerb and soon he lost sight of it.

Anna had gone.

A week later Stefano strolled through the entrance foyer of his London apartment building. The two receptionists on duty greeted him warmly but with the same subtle wariness he'd been receiving at work that had become more marked since his return from San Francisco. He was used to fear but this felt different. Now people treated him as they would when confronted with a dangerous dog they didn't want to provoke.

Anna had treated him like that before she'd collapsed at his feet with her concussion.

He blinked her image from his mind.

It mattered nothing to him how his staff behaved towards him. He preferred everyone to keep their distance. He didn't need their chatter. If someone wanted to speak to him, he was all for getting to the point, cut the chit-chat and get on. Small talk was discouraged.

Anna had taught him the term 'cut the chit-chat'. It had made a sharp but smooth sound in his mouth that amused him. *Had* amused him. It had been a long time since he'd found anything funny.

He took the bundle of letters one of the receptionists held out for him with a nod and was about to continue to the elevator when he remembered Anna's not so subtle way of pulling him up on his manners those two and a half years ago.

With two short sarcastic words, *you're welcome*, she'd reminded him that being Europe's top technology magnate didn't stop you or the others around you being human and that humans needed to feel appreciated.

He paused, looked the receptionist in the eyes and said, 'Thank you,' then wished them both a good evening and carried on up to his apartment.

Only after he'd dumped his briefcase and poured himself a bourbon did he sit on the sofa and go through his mail.

He put his thumb and middle finger to the bridge of

his nose and squeezed to keep himself alert but, *Dio*, he was ready for bed.

It was all rubbish. Rubbish, rubbish, rubbish… He should employ someone to take care of his personal life as he did his business life. Then he wouldn't have to deal with bills and the other necessary parts of life. Considering he'd abandoned running a household within weeks of having one, that thought would be funny if he hadn't lost his funny bone. Or would it be ironic? Anna had been a great one for finding irony funny. She'd found a lot of things funny. His life was a much less cheerful place without her. He hadn't noticed that when she'd left him the first time as he'd been too busy wallowing in his own sense of… What had she called it? Self-righteousness? She'd been describing herself when she'd said it but it applied to him too.

It had only been since his return from San Francisco when he'd refused himself the luxury of self-righteousness that he'd really noticed how the colour had gone from his life. Maybe it had been because she'd come back to him for that one week and they'd learned more about each other then than they had in the whole of the two and a half years they'd known each other.

Why couldn't he stop thinking of her?

He took a healthy slug of his bourbon and opened the last item of mail, a thick padded envelope with a San Francisco postmark.

This must be the gift the concierge in his apartment there had messaged him about. It had been delivered shortly after he'd left for London on the day that was his and Anna's first wedding anniversary. Not caring what was in it—not caring about anything—Stefano had told the man to forward it to his London address.

And now it was here.

Inside the packaging was a small square gift-wrapped box.

He twisted it in his hands, his heart racing as his mind drifted back to Anna's insistence on some solo 'retail therapy' that afternoon before the awards ceremony.

He'd thought it strange when she'd returned empty-handed.

He could not credit how much he missed her. It hadn't been this bad before.

No, it *had* been this bad before but he'd masked it from himself. And it had been more than self-righteousness that had masked it but a mad fury like nothing he'd ever known...

She'd made assumptions about Christina, but hadn't he made assumptions about Anna being a gold-digger? Hadn't he been as determined to see the worst in her as Anna had been to see the worst in him?

He sat bolt upright, his brain racing almost as madly as his heart.

Dio, he could see the truth.

Somewhere along the line he had fallen in love with her. The man who had spent his life avoiding serious relationships for terror of being hurt and rejected had fallen in love.

Because he *had* been terrified. For all his disdain at people who refused to let go of their childhood he could see he'd done the opposite and buried his under a 'don't care' bravado when all the time he'd been running, trying to stop it ever happening again.

He bent his head forward and dug his fingers into the back of his head as he strove to suck in air.

How could he have been so blind and stupid?

He'd blown it.

He loved his wife but the joke was on him because she didn't love him any more.

Breathing deeply, he looked again at the gift-wrapped box.

Feeling as if he were opening something that could bite him, he ripped the wrapping off and snapped the lid of the black square box open.

Nestled inside it were two gold wedding bands.

CHAPTER TWELVE

ANNA ACCEPTED THE bottle of water from Melissa with a grateful smile of thanks.

The sand on Bondi beach was fine and deliciously warm between her toes, the sun blazing down and baking her skin. As it was a work day and the schools were open, the beach was busy but not packed. While there wasn't the privacy she'd found at hers and Stefano's Santa Cruz beach house, there was an easy vibe that almost, *almost* gave her the peace she so longed for.

The rate she was going she would never find peace. Not in herself.

Melissa stretched out on the sun-lounger beside her and they sat there amiably, sunglasses on, soaking up the rays.

'What do you want to do later?' Melissa said after a while.

'I haven't got anything in mind. You?'

'Shall we borrow Mick's Jeep and go for a drive and explore the suburbs?'

'You'll have to drive. I haven't been behind a wheel in years.'

'All the more reason you should drive. Use it or lose it.'

Anna laughed but it was a muted sound compared to the way she used to laugh.

'Shall we invite Mum with us?' Melissa asked carefully.

'If you want.'

When Anna had flown out to Australia it hadn't been to make her peace with her mother but to make her peace with Melissa. She had been determined to do what Stefano had suggested though, and sit down and talk to her mother, if only just so she could move on.

Her mum hadn't quite seen it like that. Anna had arrived at the house to find the whole ground floor covered in balloons and banners to welcome her. All the neighbours and Mick's family had been invited round to meet her. Melissa had stood there, eyes pleading for Anna to go along with it—Anna could almost read her mind, realising her sister was begging her not to make a scene.

Making a scene was the last thing she'd wanted to do.

She'd looked at her mum, flanked by her husband and stepkids, and seen the desperate excitement in her eyes, and the fear.

Too much water had passed under the bridge for Anna to throw herself into her mother's arms as if nothing had happened but she'd returned her embrace coolly.

It had been almost a decade since she'd last seen her and she'd taken in the marked changes time had wrought. Her mother had done the same in return. They'd stared at each other for so long that Anna's eyes had blurred, her heart so full that it pushed up into her throat and then she really had fallen into her mother's arms.

As the evening had progressed and she couldn't make a move without tripping over her mother, Anna had come to understand exactly what it meant for her mum to have her youngest child under her roof and had cancelled her hotel reservation and agreed to stay there, sharing the guest room with Melissa.

That had been two weeks ago.

They had spent a long time talking. They'd been honest with each other. Many tears had been shed. A bucketful of them.

Her mother had apologised over and over for leaving her behind and for the cruel words she'd spoken the last time they'd been together. She hadn't made any excuses. She knew she'd been selfish and had effectively abandoned her daughters for the sake of a man. Her bone-deep guilt had been her punishment.

If Anna were being cynical she could say that if the guilt had been that bad, she could always have come home to them.

She didn't want to be cynical any more.

Things were still awkward at times but slowly they were forging a rapport. Perhaps they would never regain their old mother-daughter relationship but Anna was confident that when she returned to London they would retain some semblance of one. It was entirely in her hands. Whatever wrongs her mother had done, Stefano had been correct in his assessment that she had missed her. She needed her mother in her life.

She hadn't known how badly she'd needed her until she'd found her again and found the courage to let go of her anger and forgive.

She just wished the pain in her heart would ease. Not even the peace she'd made with her sister and the forgiveness she'd found for her mother had eased it. And it was getting worse, especially since Melissa had given her the pin code for her phone—it turned out she'd used Stefano's birthday—and she'd gone through all her photos and videos. There was one video where she'd sneakily filmed Stefano taking a shower. The footage showed his start of surprise when he'd spotted her, then his wolfish grin as he'd opened the glass shower door. The footage went dark when he grabbed her phone and threw it onto the floor.

He'd then grabbed *her*, she remembered, and dragged her fully clothed into the shower with him. Her clothes hadn't stayed on for much longer.

Her heart ached to think of him and when she closed her eyes all she could see was the despair on his face when she'd walked away.

She had never seen him like that before, not her strong, powerful husband. She'd seen him in passion and in anger but never in wretched defeat.

A fresh wave of pain hit her as she imagined him now and all he was having to cope with.

He'd been coping with it ever since she'd burst into his boardroom.

He was dealing with a father who'd been alive his whole life while he'd thought him dead. A father who *had* wanted him when no one else in his family had cared enough to even buy him shoes that fitted. He was dealing with a sister he hadn't known existed until a few months ago, his first true familial relationship since he'd been seven.

And now he was having to deal with the knowledge that he and Anna had conceived a child together but that its tiny life had died before he could even celebrate its conception.

She knew too that he carried guilt over his treatment of her.

It was a heavy burden for him to carry and he was having to carry it on his own.

But he probably wasn't alone, she scolded herself. This was Stefano she was thinking of; his bed was never empty for more than a week.

Immediately she castigated herself. He'd been faithful to her throughout their marriage and it was wrong of her to make assumptions now. She'd leapt to conclusions when she'd found Christina in their apartment and had been paying the price for it ever since. For all the horrendous wrongs he'd done, the only solid image in her mind was Stefano watching her leave his apartment, as haunted and haggard as she had ever seen him.

He'd asked her if they could start again…

But she'd dismissed him.

He hadn't wanted her to go.

She shook her head to clear it. She would have to see him in person soon. She needed to be strong, not let doubts creep in.

He'd had doubts. He'd tried to stop the revenge he'd plotted down to the smallest detail from being carried out.

He'd asked her if they could start again…

Discovering the truth that night in San Francisco had been the most soul-destroying thing she had ever lived through. Learning that he'd seduced her and made her fall in love with him for revenge… She'd understood all this at the same moment the awful memories of their parting and the miscarriage had come back to her. The two had become a singular issue in her mind and the pain it all had unleashed had been too much to bear.

Time apart had given her some perspective.

He'd told her he wanted to start their marriage afresh

and she'd dismissed it without properly listening to what he was saying. He'd told her he wanted to start their marriage again *after* she'd told him she loved him. This from the man who didn't do forgiveness or love.

Melissa's voice cut through her rambling thoughts. 'You okay, chook?'

'Sorry? *Chook?*'

'Mum says it's an Aussie term of endearment.'

Anna's lips twitched but that was the nearest thing to a smile she could muster.

'Anna? You okay?'

She blinked herself back into focus and shook her head. 'I don't think I am.'

'What? You're not okay?' Alarm spread across Melissa's face. 'Are you feeling unwell? Are you going to be sick again?'

'No, nothing like that. No. Mel…I think…'

'What?'

Her mind running this way and that, Anna got to her feet and started throwing her stuff into her beach bag. 'I need to go back.'

Melissa hastily slid off her sun-lounger. 'I'll come with you.'

In less than a minute they'd gathered all their stuff together and thrown their shorts and T-shirts back on and Anna was steaming along the beach, unwittingly spraying sand in sunbathers' faces, while Melissa struggled to keep up.

'Slow down,' she pleaded. 'The house isn't going anywhere.'

This time Anna did find a proper smile. 'I'm not going back to the house, I'm going to the airport.'

'What?'

'I'm going home.'

'You can't.'

'Watch me.'

'No, you idiot, I mean you can't go to the airport—your passport's at Mum's.'

'Oh. Yes. Right.' But it only slowed her for a moment and then she walked even faster, mentally calculating how quickly she could get to the airport. Her return flight was booked for a week from now. She was sure the airline had fixed flights so that would mean a plane would be leaving for London that evening. She needed to be on it.

'What do you want to go home for?'

'I need to see Stefano.'

'Anna, *no...*'

'Yes.'

'You were going to wait. Let things settle a bit more before telling him.'

'It's nothing to do with that.'

Melissa grabbed her arm and forced her to stop. 'Anna, will you listen to me? Please? Whatever you're thinking, don't do it.'

'Mel...I love him.' Totally. Utterly. Irreversibly.

'That man *destroyed* you.'

'No,' she contradicted. 'I think we've destroyed each other. And maybe we can fix each other.'

It was a fifteen-minute fast walk back to the house. Melissa was puffing behind her as Anna rushed through the front door, her adrenaline levels too high to need to catch a breath.

She hurried up the hallway to the stairs, about to go to her room and get her flight details so she could get straight on the phone to the airline...

'Anna, is that you?' came her mother's voice.

'Yes, sorry, give me a minute.'

Her mother appeared at the kitchen doorway, her face flushed. 'You've got a visitor.'

'Me?' Who would be visiting *her*? She didn't know anyone here apart from her mum's friends and family.

She stepped into the kitchen, turned her head to the large table and froze.

After several long, long moments she closed her eyes then slowly opened them again.

Stefano was sitting at the kitchen table. Her mum's golden retriever, George, had his head on his lap.

'What are you doing here?' she whispered, placing a hand to her chest to stop her heart from jumping out of it.

'Visiting you.' Slowly he rose to his feet.

She inched closer and drank in the face she hadn't seen in what felt like for ever until she was only a foot away.

A mere two weeks apart had left marked changes in him. He was paler than she remembered. His hair needed cutting. He looked as if he'd slept in his canvas shorts and crumpled shirt.

As if he could read her mind, one side of his mouth curved up and he said, 'It was a long flight.'

She couldn't think clearly. The joy bursting into life inside her was marred with caution.

He'd flown across the world to see her just as she'd been gearing up to fly across the world to see him and to find out if there was any chance of a future together for them.

But what if he was here for a different reason? What if he only wanted to discuss their divorce?

Every morning since she'd left San Francisco she'd promised herself that today would be the day she would call her lawyer in England and start proper divorce proceedings. After all, they'd been married for a full year. There was nothing to stop them.

And yet, for all her anger and misery, she hadn't been able to bring herself to do it.

Had the time apart that had been so painful to her only been a healer for him?

Until he told her his reasons for being there she would not allow the screaming excitement running through her to take control.

'Is there somewhere private we can talk?' he asked, breaking the silence that had formed while she stood there trying to catch a coherent thought.

Her mum and sister quickly shuffled out of sight but Anna didn't trust that they wouldn't listen in to what was going on.

'The garden?'

He nodded and, on legs that had gone from having bones supporting them to what felt like overcooked noodles, she led him outside. George slipped out with them before she could close the door.

Her mum's garden was a lovingly tended spot with a good-sized swimming pool. They sat carefully on the large swing chair with a canopy to shade them from the blazing sun, both making sure not to sit too close to the other. They were still close enough that Anna's body vibrated at his nearness and she had to fold her hands tightly together to stop them stretching out to touch him and feel for herself that she wasn't dreaming this.

George sat himself at Stefano's feet and he leaned down to rub the dog's head.

'I think you've made a friend,' Anna commented softly.

'I like dogs.'

She hadn't known that. 'You should get one.'

'One day. He's your mother's?'

'Yes.'

'How are things with her?'

'Better than I thought they'd be.'

'You've forgiven her?'

'Just about.' She would never be less than honest with him. 'It's so hard to let the past go but I have to. If I've learnt anything in recent months it's that holding onto anger destroys you as much as the other. She's made mistakes—massive ones—but I have too and I know she's genuinely sorry. I am too. I just want her back in my life.'

They lapsed into silence that stretched so unbearably tight that Anna couldn't endure it a moment longer. 'Why are you here?'

'Because I'm falling apart without you.' His shoulders rose and he turned his head to look at her. 'I want you to think about coming back. Not to me, I know you won't do that, but back to Moretti's. The staff are on the verge of mutiny because without you there I have lost my conscience. You can have your own office so you don't have to see me if you don't want to. You can boss me around just as well by email as in person. Name your terms and your price.'

Stefano didn't take his gaze off her. He sought every tiny flicker of reaction on her face.

Her forehead furrowed. 'You want me to come back to *work*?'

'I know I'm asking a lot of you.'

'You're not wrong.'

'Please. Hear me out. Anna, it's not just Moretti's that's falling apart, is me. *I'm* falling apart. I know you won't come back as my wife but I miss having you in my life. You keep me sane. You help me see things clearly. I need you.'

He'd never said that before to anyone. He'd learned at too young an age that people were too often faithless and cruel to each other to allow himself to ever need someone. The only person he'd ever needed was himself.

Much of the colour had left her face.

'If you come back then it will be on whatever terms you choose. Having you close by will be enough for me.' He ran his fingers through his hair to stop them from touching her. 'I know it's over for us. How I took advantage of your amnesia was unforgivable. I was furious about your assumptions that I was having an affair but I made assumptions of my own. I swore you had to be a gold-digger because I couldn't face the truth that you were in love with me and I was in love with you.'

She sucked in a breath and he grimaced. 'I know it's too late for you to hear that but, please, allow me to explain. I know I won't have your forgiveness but I would like your understanding.

'Your instincts about your promotion were right—I did give it to you so I could be rid of you—you *were* the best person for the job but that was secondary—but it wasn't because I was bored with you. You were scared I would leave you but I was already scared you would leave me. I've never been wanted for myself before, not since Nonno died. The rest of my family didn't want me and you know as well as I do that they treated me like dirt. When I left them to fend for myself, people didn't want *me*, they wanted to use me; bosses exploiting my age to try and underpay me, drunk women seeing me as nothing but a handsome face to have sex with. When I finally made my fortune people didn't want me for myself, they wanted my fame and money. You were the first person to see through the expensive suits and see the man inside. How could you like that man when no one else had ever liked or wanted him? I deliberately pushed you away because I was too much of a coward to acknowledge that I loved you. I pushed you away before you could push me.'

His soul laid bare, Stefano took a long breath and covered her hands. A glimmer of hope fluttered in him when she didn't resist, her eyes still on his face, wide and glistening.

'I can't be without you,' he said, willing for her to believe him. 'I can't even breathe normally. Days without you are an eternity. Please come back. If all you can offer is to take your place in Moretti's again then that's enough.'

Time itself seemed to morph into eternity while he waited for her to respond.

When she moved her hands out of his hold his heart sank so sharply it caused physical pain.

But then she placed one on his cheek and moved her face a little closer and his heart dared to rise back up.

'After all you've just said are you only offering me my job back?'

He trapped the hand palmed against his cheek. 'Anna, you have my heart. Whatever you can give I will accept. I need you and I will take whatever you can give.'

'But what do you *want*?'

Something in her expression sent warmth into blood that had been cold for weeks. 'I want you to ask me to make that promise I made to you again so that I can tell you I don't need to make it because there will never be anyone else but you for me.'

Slowly her face moved to his and then her eyes closed and her lips pressed gently against his.

He hardly dared to breathe. He'd flown out here knowing he needed to make that one last move and strip himself bare for her. He'd reconciled himself to them being over but had been unable to reconcile with Anna being out of his life for good. She was so much a part of him that her not being there had been like living with a piece of himself missing.

'I don't want to come back to London as your employee,' she whispered into his mouth. 'I want to come back as your wife.'

This was more than he had dared hope for. Far more. 'You do?'

Her nose brushed his as she nodded. 'I love you.'

A boulder settled in his throat and he swallowed it away. 'But can you forgive me?'

'We've both made mistakes. If we can't draw a line under them and make a fresh start then we'll both suffer for it.' She smiled, though her chin wobbled. 'It's been agony for me without you. I'd already decided to come home and see if there was any chance for us.'

'Really?'

She nodded. 'That's why I came back early from the beach. It had all suddenly become clear for me. I thought my love for you had died but that was my hurt and pride talking, not my heart.'

'I swear I will never do anything to hurt you again.'

'We're both stubborn and fiery. We'll probably spend the rest of our lives arguing with each other.'

'As long as we spend the rest of it making up then I can live with that.' And to prove his point he put a hand round the back of her head and pulled her in for another kiss, this one deep and full of all the love and desire he felt for this beautiful woman without whom he was nothing but a shell of himself.

She was everything to him, his lover, his confidante and his sparring partner. It would be easier to live without a limb than without her.

'How do you feel about us becoming parents?' she asked him between kisses.

He put his finger under her chin.

For all that they'd forgiven each other everything, Anna being alone when she miscarried their child was something he would never forgive himself for.

'When the time is right we can try for a child. I want us to have a football team of *bambinos* and a couple of dogs for them to play with but not until you're ready for it.'

He thought he would see sadness in her eyes but they were bright and…knowing.

'Anna?'

Suddenly the most enormous grin beamed from her face.

'You're not?'

'I am.' She snuggled into him, her head on his chest. 'I took the test last week.'

'With Melissa?' he asked drily. This was unbelievable. He'd left London feeling as if he were drowning, seeking Anna as a life raft, and now felt as if the sun were shining especially for them.

'Yes.'

'And one for luck?'

'Yes.' She pressed herself even tighter to him. 'Neither of us knew it at the time but I wasn't protected when we were in Santa Cruz—I never had another injection after

I lost…' The kiss on her head and the tightening of the arms around her showed that Stefano understood what she was struggling to vocalise. 'I'm sorry for not telling you sooner,' she whispered into his chest. 'I was trying to get my head around it and I knew it was something I had to tell you to your face. But I was going to tell you as soon as I got back to London. I swear.'

He ran his fingers through her hair. 'Don't apologise. I know you would have told me. How are you feeling?'

'A little sick at times but nothing to complain about.' Her face shone as she gazed up at him. 'And you?'

He kissed her. 'I feel that you've given me all my birthday and Christmas presents in one go.'

And speaking of presents…

He disentangled himself just enough to pull out the small black square box he'd carried on his person since he'd opened it a week ago.

She recognised it at once, her eyes widening and somehow brightening further. 'I was going to give you that…'

'On our wedding anniversary,' he finished for her.

She held out her left hand for him and he slid the smaller ring onto her wedding finger then kissed it. 'I love you.'

'I love you too,' she whispered before taking the larger ring and sliding it onto his finger and kissing it in turn.

It took a long time for Stefano to comprehend the magnitude of all that had happened, how his last throw of the dice had brought him rewards he'd not allowed himself to dream of.

He had his wife back and this time he would honour and cherish her until his dying breath.

EPILOGUE

ANNA SAT ON the side of the bath watching Stefano, who was leaning against the wall looking at his watch, light bouncing off his gold wedding band, a white oblong stick in his hand.

The bathroom door was shoved open and Cecily, their three-year-old daughter, came flying in followed in quick succession by her four-year-old brother and their slower, sappy King Charles spaniel, Alfie.

Cecily threw her arms around Anna's legs. 'Mario hit me,' she wailed.

'She threw my ice cream on the floor!' he hollered indignantly.

'Behave, the pair of you,' Stefano scolded, amusement lurking in his eyes. 'And no hitting.'

'But…!'

'If you can't play nicely together we won't go to the beach,' Anna cut in. With Mario due to start school in England that September, they'd decided to spend the summer in their Santa Cruz beach house, the unanimous family favourite of all their homes.

Two months before Mario had been born, they'd left their London apartment and moved into a rambling manor house in Oxfordshire surrounded by acres of land for their football team of children to play in. It was an idyllic existence. Picture perfect. Apart from having two children who liked nothing more than fighting furiously, of course.

'No fair!' they both shouted together. Still bickering, the pair of them toddled off to their playroom, no doubt leaving a trail of chaos and destruction in their wake. She found it remarkable that their mess didn't bother her at all.

'Are you sure you want another one?' Stefano asked, laughing.

She grinned. Their football team hadn't quite materialised. After having two children with a gap of less than a year between them, they'd decided to wait and enjoy them before having any more.

She'd come off the pill a month ago.

'I think we can cope.'

'That's a relief.' He passed the stick to her, his grin now as wide as his face. 'Because according to this, we're having another one.'

Anna read the blue plus sign, her own grin widening to match her husband's.

With a whoop of delight, Stefano picked her up and planted kisses all over her face.

Wrapping her legs around his waist and her arms around his neck, Anna returned the kisses. Even with two children and another on the way, their desire and love for each other remained undiminished. There wasn't a single aspect of her life she would change. Together they'd created a family filled with love and laughter, arguments and *lots* of making up.

'Daddy! What are you doing to my mummy?' Cecily was standing in the bathroom doorway, her arms folded and the same expression on her face that Stefano always used when he wasn't amused by something. 'Put her down at once!'

Stefano put Anna down, gave her one last kiss for luck, then scooped his daughter up and carried her, screaming with laughter, upside down to the playroom.

* * * * *

A DANGEROUS
SOLACE

LUCY ELLIS

CHAPTER ONE

GIANLUCA BENEDETTI APPRAISED the shapeless suit and then the woman in it. She had potential, if she ditched the floppy large-brimmed hat, took down her hair, stepped out of the suit and started all over again from scratch. She had the essentials. She was tall, her legs were good from what he could tell, and there was a liveliness to her that she seemed to be repressing as she went to stamp her foot but then arrested the gesture.

Which drew his attention to her shoes. They didn't quite fit the image of the woman wearing them. Elegant low heels, graceful arch, red leather slingback, with a complicated knot of red silk flowers running over the toes. The shoes were fussy and feminine. The woman in them was not.

'Give me back my money!' Her voice was clear, crisp and no-nonsense, for all she was obviously angry. Gianluca could tell by her accent she was Australian, which accounted for the plain speaking.

The guy was giving her the runaround. In the crowded domain of the arcade people were making a detour around the brunette standing in front of the kiosk. She looked like a ticking time bomb ready to go off.

The foot trembling with indecision above the pavement came down with a decided stamp.

'I am not going anywhere until you refund me that money. I gave your company forty-eight hours' notice. It says clearly on your website that refunds are possible with *twenty-four* hours' notice.'

Gianluca shut down the European markets, pocketed his personal device, and strolled away from the doorway of the coffee bar he'd been frequenting all his adult life in Rome.

Impeccable manners towards women instilled in him by a Sicilian grandmother had him approach her.

'*Signora*, may I be of some service to you?'

She didn't even bother to turn around. 'I am not a *signora*, I am a *signorina*. And no, you may not *help me*. I'm perfectly capable of helping myself. Go and ply your trade with some other idiot tourist.'

Gianluca leaned closer. She emitted a light fragrance, something floral, definitely too feminine for this dragon of a woman.

'My trade?'

'Gigolo. Escort. Servicer of women. Go away. I don't want you.'

Gianluca stilled. This dragon thought he was a male prostitute?

He looked her up and down. She hadn't even bothered to turn around. Common sense told him to shrug and walk away.

'So, *signorina*…' he laid on the emphasis '…maybe you're hard up, yes? You need to remember what it is to be a woman?'

'Excuse me?' She turned around, angling up her face, and in a single stroke Gianluca lost every preconception he had built around her.

The shapeless clothes, her tone—he'd taken her to be older, harder…certainly less attractive than—*this.* She had creamy skin, wide brows, amazing cheekbones and—what was most intriguing—soft, lush lips. A veritable ripe strawberry of a mouth. But her face was dominated by a pair of ugly white-rimmed sunglasses, and he had to resist the urge to tug them away and get the full effect.

Although he definitely got a sense of her eyes widening.

'It's you!' she said.

He raised a brow. 'Have we met?'

This wasn't an unknown scenario over the years. His past football career—two years of kicking a ball around professionally for Italy—combined with his title had given him something of a public profile beyond the usual roaming grounds of Roman society. He made sure his tone offered no encouragement.

The dragon-who-wasn't took a step back.

'No,' she said fast, as if warding him off.

He became aware that she was looking around as if searching for an escape route, and for some reason his own body tensed. He recognised he was readying himself to give chase.

Madre di Dio, what was going on?

A pulse pounded like a tiny drum at the base of her throat, and he couldn't have said why but it held his attention. She made a soft sound of panic. His eyes flicked up to catch hers and sexual awareness erupted between them. It was so fast, so strong, it took him entirely off guard.

He stepped towards her, but she didn't shift an inch. Her chin tipped up and her eyes flared wide, as if she was waiting for something.

Something from *him*.

Something he couldn't quite put his finger on.

Basta! This was getting him nowhere.

Irritated by his own unprecedented behaviour—getting involved with a strange woman on the street, allowing his libido to get away from him, lingering as if he had the day to while away when he had a meeting lined up across town—he did what he should have done when he'd emerged from the coffee bar five minutes ago.

'In that case, enjoy your stay in Rome, *signorina*.'

He'd only gone a few steps when he found himself turning around.

She was still standing there, swamped by that god-awful jacket and wearing those trousers which did nothing for her, and yet...

He was noticing other things about her—the pink of her

nose, the slightly hectic expression on her face. She'd been crying.

It stirred something in him. A memory.

A weeping woman usually left him cold. He knew all about female manipulation. He'd grown up observing it with his mother and sisters. Tears were usually a woman's go-to device for getting her own way. It never ceased to amaze him how a pretty bauble or a promise could dry them up.

But instead of walking away he strode over to the kiosk, read the sign that told him this was Fenice Tours, which was run by a subsidiary of the travel conglomerate Benedetti International had business with, and took out his phone. As he thumbed in the number he told the guy he had sixty seconds to refund the *turista* for her ticket or he'd close the place down.

With a few more well-placed instructions he handed over his phone. The man took it with a sceptical look that faded as his employer's angry voice buzzed like a blowfly on the other end.

'*Mi scusi, Principe.* It was a—a misunderstanding,' the guy stammered.

Gianluca shrugged. 'Apologise to the lady, not to me.'

'*Si, si—scusa tanto, signora.*'

With gritted teeth she accepted the euros. For all the fuss she had made, Gianluca noticed she didn't bother to check them, just folded them silently into her bag—a large leather affair that, like her clothes, seemed to be part of an attempt to weigh herself down.

'*Grazie,*' she said, as if it were torn from her.

There was no reason to linger. Gianluca was at the kerb opening up his low-slung Lamborghini Jota when he looked back.

She had followed him and was watching him, her expression almost comical in its war between curiosity and resentment—and something else...

It was the *something else* that kept him from jumping into the car.

She seemed to gird herself before walking over.

'Excuse me.' Her voice was as stiff as her manner, but it didn't take away from the rather lovely combination of her full mouth and dramatic cheekbones, or the way her caution made her seem oddly prim. It was the stiff formality that had his eyes locked to hers.

'I'm curious,' she said.

He could feel her gaze searching his face as if hunting for something. Curious, but not thankful, he noted, amused despite the wariness that told him something about this wasn't right.

'Could you really have shut it down?'

She angled up a stubborn chin made somewhat less forth-right by the soft press of a dimple and hard suspicion narrowed his gaze.

Where had he seen that gesture before?

Yet he gave her a tight smile, a smile that didn't reach his eyes—the one he handed out to women as a courtesy, telling them he recognised that they were female, and as a man he appreciated it, but alas it could go no further.

'*Signorina,*' he drawled, 'this is Rome. I'm a Benedetti. Anything's possible.'

He was pushing through the mess that was Rome's mid-morning traffic when her reaction registered. She hadn't looked flattered. She hadn't even looked shocked. She had looked furiously angry.

And against his better judgement it had him turning the car around.

CHAPTER TWO

AVA STOOD AT the kerb as the low-slung sports machine vanished into the traffic and let shock reverberate through her body until the only thing left was the burn.

Benedetti.

All she could think was that this wasn't how it was supposed to happen.

Over the years she'd had a few false alarms—moments when a deep voice, an Italian accent, a pair of broad shoulders had brought her head snapping around, her senses suddenly firing. But reality would always intervene.

Clearly reality had decided to slap her in the face.

It came over her in a rush. The flick of a broad tanned wrist at the ignition of a growling Ducati motorcycle. The tightening of her arms around his muscle-packed waist as they made their getaway from a wedding he'd had no interest in and she'd been cut up about. The memory of a flight into a summer's night seven long years ago that she still couldn't shake.

It was all Ava could do as she stood in the street to keep the images—those highly sexual images—at bay.

Finding herself in the early hours of a summer morning lying in the grass on the Palatine Hill, her dress rucked up around her waist, under the lean, muscular weight of a young Roman god come to life was *not* something a woman forgot in a hurry.

Finding herself repeating it an hour later, in a bed that had once belonged to a king, in a *palazzo* built literally for a princess, on a beautiful *piazza* in the centre of the city, and again and again into the first flush of dawn, was also something that had stayed with her. And all the while he had lavished her with praise in broken English, making her feel like a goddess he had every right to plunder.

In the glare of a new morning she had slipped from the palace unnoticed and, Cinderella-fashion, left her shoes behind in her haste to flee what had promised to be an awkward aftermath.

Her feet bare, her frothy blue dress hiked up around her knees to allow her to run, she had been in equal measure elated and a little *triste*, her body pleasurably aching from all the unfamiliar clenching of muscles she hadn't known she had.

She'd flagged down a taxi and driven away, and if she had looked back it had been only to fix the memory, because she'd known it would never happen again.

It had been a moment out of time.

She'd flown back to Sydney the next day, resumed her climb up the corporate ladder and assumed she would never see him again.

Clearly she had assumed wrongly.

Pulling herself together, Ava stepped away from the kerb and told herself she most definitely wasn't going to allow the memory of one night with a Ducati-straddling, over-sexed soccer player to wreak havoc with her plans. She'd been handling everything so well up until this point.

Perhaps too well, niggled her conscience as she battled her way along the pavement. Wasn't she supposed to be heartbroken?

Most women would be. Being dumped on the eve of expecting a proposal from your long-time boyfriend in a foreign city and then travelling on in that city on your own would unsettle anybody.

Fortunately she was made of sterner stuff.

Which was why she was on her way to the Spanish Steps, to join a tour of literary sites in Rome.

Ava pulled her hat down hard on top of her head. She certainly wasn't going to allow a freak sighting of one of Italy's natural wonders in a city street to derail her from her purpose.

So what if that puffy pale blue bridesmaid's dress was buried deep in the back of her closet at home? So she'd kept the dress? So she was in Rome?

It had nothing to do with that long-ago night when everything she'd believed about herself had been turned on its head.

Well, not this time. Nowadays she had it all under control—when she wasn't careering hot-headedly around the streets of Rome looking for the...what was it...? She consulted her map. The Piazza di Spagna.

She ignored the racing of her heart, told herself there was *no way* she was going to fumble through an Italian phone directory searching for the address of the Palazzo Benedetti. She mustn't even *think* that! Rome had definitely been a mistake. The sooner she picked up that hire car tomorrow and headed north the better.

Now—Ava looked around in confusion, discovering she had walked into a square she didn't recognise—where on earth was she?

'This is *pazzo*,' Gianluca muttered under his breath as he idled his car across from the little *piazza*. He'd followed her. He'd put the Jota into a screaming U-turn and cruised after that flapping hat, those flashing red shoes.

Inferno, what was he doing? He was Gianluca Benedetti. He didn't kerb-crawl a woman. And not *this* kind of female—one who wore men's trousers and a silk shirt buttoned up to her chin and seemed to have no conception of what it was to be a woman.

Many women had creamy skin, long legs, and if they did not have quite the drama of her bone structure they certainly did a lot more with it.

She wasn't his type. Yet here he was.

He could see her pacing backwards and forwards over the cobblestones, holding something aloft. He got the impression it was a map from the way she was positioning it.

His phone vibrated. He palmed it.

'Where are you?' Gemma's voice was faintly exasperated. *Stalking a turista.*

'Stuck in traffic.'

He glanced at the piece of Swiss design on his arm. He was extremely late. *What in the hell was he doing?*

'What do I tell the clients?'

'Let them cool their heels. I'm on my way.'

He pocketed the phone and made up his mind. As he strode across the *piazza* he wondered at the complication he was inviting into his life.

She was walking slowly backwards, clearly trying to get the name of the square from a plaque on the wall above her. He could have saved her the effort and told her she'd have no luck there. It was the name of the building.

She careened into him.

'Oh, I do beg your pardon,' she trotted out politely, reeling around.

The good manners, he noted, were for other people.

It was his last half-amused thought as he collided with her eyes. One part of his brain wondered if they were coloured contact lenses—except judging by the rest of her attire he doubted she'd go to the trouble.

No, the eye colour was hers, all right. An extraordinary sea-green. One of those colours that changed with the light or her mood. Eyes that shoved the rock out of the mouth of the cave inside him he'd had sealed up for many years. Eyes and a mouth, and a soft, yielding body which she had taken away from him when he had needed it most.

Her features coalesced around those unusual eyes and the impact fairly slammed into him. The other part of his brain was free-falling.

'*You!*'

His sentiments exactly.

The softer note in her voice long gone, she leapt back in horror. But he noticed at the same time that she wrapped her hand around his arm, as if anchoring herself to him. Which struck him as entirely ironic, given the last time he'd laid eyes on this girl she'd been so anxious to escape from his bed she'd left her shoes behind in her rush.

From nowhere a resentment he hadn't known he was carrying ricocheted like a stray bullet around his body.

What in the hell was she doing back in Rome? Back in his life?

His eyes narrowed on her.

'Are you following me?' she accused swiftly.

'*Si.*' He was not going to deny it. Why would he?

The look on her face was priceless.

'You appear to be lost, *signorina*,' he observed smoothly, raking his gaze over her eyes, her mouth, the amazing clarity of her skin. 'And as we already know one another—'

If anything the rapt horror on her face only increased, heightening his sense of satisfaction.

'Allow me to offer some more assistance.'

She tugged self-consciously at the atrocious silk shirt and stood a little straighter, sticking out that chin.

He was going to enjoy making her squirm, and then he would let her go.

'Is this a profession for you? Following women around the city, pushing help on them whether they want it or not?'

'You appear to be the exception to my rule to let a woman struggle on alone.'

'Do I appear to be struggling to you?'

'No, you appear to be lost.'

She pursed her lips, staring rather pointedly at the map. She was torn—it was all over her expressive face. The indecision and—more satisfying to his ego—anxiety.

Gianluca told himself a sensible man would walk away.

Anything between them now was beneath him. He'd made the identification. He knew exactly who this woman was—or who she purported to be. Seven years ago he'd entwined all kinds of ridiculous romantic imaginings around this girl, none of them bearing scrutiny in the harsh light of day.

Besides, on *this* day she was proving entirely ordinary—a little frumpy, in fact. Certainly not a woman he would glance at twice. Which didn't explain why he'd turned the Jota around and right now was unable to take his eyes off her.

'It's too late now anyhow,' she muttered to herself.

Si, far too late. Although unexpectedly he was fighting a very Italian male need to assert himself with this woman.

'I've missed the start of the tour,' she said, as if it was somehow his fault.

Gianluca waited.

She stared holes in the map.

'We're supposed to be meeting at the Spanish Steps,' she added grudgingly.

'I see.' Not that he did see.

He decided to cut to the chase and draw down the time this was taking.

'The Spanish Steps are straight down here.' He pointed it out. 'Make a left and then a second right.'

She was trying to follow his directions, which meant she was forced to look at him, and at the same time she was fumbling to put on her ugly sunglasses. Seeing as the sky was overcast, it was clearly a clumsy attempt at disguise.

Something about her hasty and long overdue attempt to hide irritated him. She clearly wasn't very good at subterfuge, and yet she had been a true genius at escape seven years ago. Gianluca found he was tempted to confiscate the glasses.

Safe behind the shaded lenses, she tipped up her glorious cheekbones. 'I suppose I should thank you.'

'Don't feel obligated, *signorina*,' he inserted softly.

Those lips pursed, but nothing could destroy their luscious shape.

Pushing aside the knowledge that this promised endless complications, he reached into his jacket and took out a card, took hold of her resistant hand and closed her fingers over it. They felt warm, smooth and surprisingly delicate.

She snatched her hand back and glared at him as if he'd touched her inappropriately.

A far cry from the last time he'd had his hands on her.

'If you change your mind about thanking me, *signorina*, I'll be at Rico's Bar tonight around eleven,' he said, wondering what the hell he thought he was doing. 'It's a private party but I'll leave your name at the door. Enjoy your tour.'

'You don't even know my name,' she called after him, and it sounded almost like an accusation.

His gut knotted.

Exactly. If he'd known her name seven years ago this little piece of unfinished business would have been forgotten.

Just another girl on another night.

But it hadn't been just another night.

It was a night scored on his soul, and the woman standing in the square was a major part of that. *Si*, it explained why his chest felt tight and his hands were clenched into fists by his sides.

Ruthlessness was in his blood, and Gianluca never forgot he was a Benedetti. In this fabled city it was impossible to forget. His ancestors had led Roman legions, lent money to Popes and financed wars down the ages. There was enough blood flowing through the family annals to turn the Tyrrhenian Sea red.

It enabled him to look at her with detachment.

'How about Strawberries?' he drawled. The quiet menace in his tone was usually enough to send CEOs of multinational corporations pale as milk.

She lowered the sunglasses and those green eyes skewered him.

A dark admiration stirred. This woman had the makings of a formidable opponent.

He could enjoy this.

Basta! This was no *vendetta*. She was, after all, a woman, and he—naturally—wasn't that kind of man. He was a chivalrous, civilised, honourable member of Roman society. This was merely an exercise in curiosity, in putting a footnote to a certain episode in his life. The first and only time a woman had run from him.

He slid into the Jota and gunned the engine.

The fact his knuckles showed white on the wheel proved nothing.

But as he merged with the chaotic traffic again he recognised it was not his Benedetti side that was in the ascendant here. It was the Sicilian blood from his mother's people, and it responded instinctively to the knowledge that this little piece of unfinished business was at last in his sights once more.

CHAPTER THREE

Ava forced herself to block the encounter out of her head as she followed his directions and caught her first glimpse in seven years of the Spanish Steps. Despite the crowd she found her tour group and fastened on, all too aware she was already hot and tired and flustered.

He'd followed her.

Yes, but he likes women. That's his modus operandi. He sees a girl. He takes her.

He saw you, he wants you.

Ava tried to focus on what the guide was saying about Keats's death, but all she could think about was her own small death of pride, which had her desperately wanting to go to this club tonight, to see him again…

She shut her eyes and screwed up her resolve. She wasn't the kind of woman who slept with random men—and that was all it ever could be with a guy like Benedetti. A night, a handful of hours—entertainment for him.

You liked it. He saw you. He wants you.

It wasn't any kind of reason for offering herself up to be hurt again.

It's not as if you've got anything to lose. You're a single woman and this is Rome.

For a moment her resolve slipped and her surroundings rushed in. For beyond the hurried crowd and the noise of traffic was the city itself, imprinted on her mind by countless Hollywood films. *Bella Italia*, where magical things were supposed to happen to single girls if they threw coins in fountains. And sometimes those things *did* happen—but this girl had misread the signs.

Every time she got it wrong. She wasn't going to get it wrong again.

Emotions welled up unexpectedly, filling her throat, making it difficult to breathe. She'd been crying again this morning and she *never* cried! Not even when Bernard had rung her three days ago, at the terminal in Sydney International an hour before take-off, to tell her he wouldn't be coming to Rome.

Just as her realisation had begun to take shape that there would be no romantic proposal in front of the Trevi Fountain, and before she could examine the overwhelming feeling of *relief* that had washed over her, he'd broken the news that he had found another woman—and that with *her* he had passion.

It had been a low blow, even for Bernard. He'd never been particularly sensitive to her feelings, but she had assumed up until that moment that half the blame for their lacklustre sex life was shared by him.

Apparently not. Apparently it was all down to her.

'Passion?' she had shouted down the phone. 'We could have had passion. In *Rome*!'

Yet ever since—on the long-haul flight, on the taxi ride from Fiumicino Airport to her historic hotel, over the two nights she'd spent staring at the walls as she listlessly ate her room-service dinner in front of the Italian melodrama she was just starting to get hooked on—Ava had nursed a suspicion that she had chosen Rome as the site of her proposal for entirely *romantic* reasons that clearly had nothing to do with Bernard.

She was beginning to suspect there were unplumbed depths of longing inside of her for a different life.

A romantic life.

But it was no use. Romance belonged in the movies, not in real life. Certainly not in *her* life. She'd learned that young, from watching the break-up of her parents' marriage, seeing her mentally ill mother struggle to support them on a pension, that the only way to survive as a woman was to become financially independent.

So she had worked hard to get where she was, but it meant she had never had time for a social life, had never gone through the rites of passage her peers had taken for granted.

As a consequence she had done a very silly thing seven years ago, and another silly thing when she'd convinced herself to marry a man she didn't love.

No, Bernard was not the right man for her. But neither was an oversexed soccer player who thought he could just pick up a woman like a coin in the gutter and put her in his pocket.

Her fist opened to reveal the embossed card she'd been carrying around for the last half hour. She held it up and read the simply inscribed name and several contact numbers. A memory slid like a stiletto knife between her ribs. All those numbers—but she'd rung his numbers before, hadn't she? None of them led to him.

Giving herself a shake, Ava slipped away from the group. She was going back to the hotel.

Everything was a mess and it was *his* fault.

Not Bernard's. What had she been thinking, being with Bernard for two long years? Going so far as to orchestrate a romantic proposal? Booking the plane fares, a luxury hotel, a driving tour of Tuscany…?

What had possessed her to set up such a ridiculous romantic scenario with a man she didn't love, in this city of all cities…?

Ava's heart began to pound, because she had the answer in her hot little hand.

What was she doing back in Rome?

It was the million-dollar question and it had Gianluca entertaining scenarios that, frankly, were beneath him.

Behind him the private party was in full swing—a welcome back to Rome for his cousin Marco and his new wife—

but Gianluca found himself constantly scanning the *piazza* below for a certain dressed-down brunette.

He hadn't been able to get her out of his head all day. It wasn't the fresh-faced girl who had lain down with him in the grass on the Palatino who was rifling through his thoughts, though, but the tense, angry woman who looked as if she hadn't had a man between her thighs in a good many years. The sort of woman who, for whatever reason, had forgotten how to *be* a woman—although in this lady's case he suspected it might be a wilful act.

He smiled slightly, wondered how hard it would be to perform that miracle.

Given the sexual attraction that had flared between them in the street today, not hard. Anger, he acknowledged, could be a powerful aphrodisiac.

His smile faded. His parents had conducted that kind of relationship. Volatile, glass-breaking performances on his Sicilian mother's side, and passive-aggressive acts of sabotage from his father as he withheld money, access to the family jewellery, use of the Benedetti *palazzi* dotted around the country. Yes, the married state had a great deal to recommend it.

The irony was that he was here celebrating a wedding. The advent of a baby. The things that made up happiness in other people's lives. Just not if you had Benedetti attached to your name.

It was a lonely thought and he pushed it aside. Life was good. He was young, fit and obscenely successful. Women fell at his feet. Men scrambled to get out of his way. Everything he touched turned to gold these days. Forget the dragon. Forget the past. Take those lessons and apply them to what was to come now.

He turned away from his contemplation of the famous square below and strolled across the terrace to join the party.

'*Signorina*, we sit here all night or I take you somewhere else? Give me something to work with!'

Across the road Ava could see women in tiny scraps of nothing much going happily into the popular nightspot. She shoved money at the driver, took a breath and launched herself out of the cab. The cool air licked around her legs and she almost dived back in.

She knew she was being silly. The burgundy red cocktail dress came to her knees and covered her shoulders and arms. It was perfectly acceptable. Perhaps it clung to her long thighs as she moved, and her calves in black stockings felt exposed as she made her way across the road, heels clicking on the pavement, but nobody was going to laugh at her and point.

As she approached the glass front of the upmarket nightclub she began to feel a little differently. The pulsing blue and gold neon lights gave a dreamlike quality to the atmosphere, and far from feeling on show she realised for once that with her hair and her dress and her heels she fitted right in. There was nothing show-offish about her appearance.

She had a very real fear of making a spectacle of herself in public. Growing up, she had seen her mum's illness provide far too many opportunities for that to happen. She had set up her life to avoid social situations as much as possible, but tonight she didn't have much choice.

The doorman said something pleasant to her in Italian and Ava found herself inside, waiting behind the other patrons, relieved she had dressed up. For the umpteenth time her fingers went to the ends of her hair.

This afternoon she'd taken her long brown plait to the hairdresser, and after a process of a great deal of pointing and gesturing her hair was now swinging with more bounce and life than it had ever had around her shoulders. She'd left that hairdresser feeling as chic as any Roman woman, very modern, and in control of her own destiny once more.

As with cutting several inches off her hair, it had been her choice to wear a cocktail dress. That it was brand-new, bought today, and she couldn't remember the last time she'd worn a frock had absolutely nothing to do with a man this morning telling her she had *forgotten how to be a woman.*

She couldn't see him anyhow as she came down the steps and made her way slowly through the crowded bar. Confusion assailed her. Should she wait? Should she ask for his table? Worryingly, the place seemed to be full of beautiful women not wearing very much clothing. She couldn't possibly compete.

As if to hammer this home a glamorous blonde slunk past her on stab-your-heart-out heels, scantily clad in a dress that looked sewn on. Ava followed her progress, along with every man in the vicinity, although her thoughts—*She must be cold*—probably didn't align with theirs.

Perhaps she'd over-estimated the transformative powers of a new hairstyle?

Feeling her confidence slipping away, Ava scanned the room, spotted the winding stairs at either end. There was another level. She caught sight of the blonde making her wiggly way up and up. Should she go upstairs? Should she ask for his table?

For the first time it occurred to Ava with a stab of unease that the invitation had been general, more along the lines of *come along—enjoy yourself.* Not specific—not *I find you attractive, perhaps even on some subliminal level remember you, and I want to spend some time with you.* It was entirely possible she had misinterpreted him.

Yes, Ava, you've got it wrong again...

But in that moment she caught sight of a dark-haired woman in a burgundy dress staring back at her across the room. Her eyes were made up with kohl and lashings of mascara, dark and mysterious, her mouth was a vivid splash of red colour like a full-blown rose, explosive and passionate. She was something other than beautiful. She was *dramatic.*

It wasn't until she lifted her fingertips once more to her hair that Ava experienced the little shock of recognition. It was a mirrored wall. The woman staring back at her was—well, *her.*

She ignored the thundering voices that told her she was lining herself up for a fall and made her way upstairs.

Marco handed him a fresh beer. 'To the future.'

This was the first time Gianluca had been able to catch up with his cousin since the massive wedding back in Ragusa. They'd played professional football together in their early twenties. Marco had been dropped due to injury; Gianluca had cut his contract at the height of his career and fame to perform the military service expected of a Benedetti male.

He was still feeling the reverberations of that early shot at sporting immortality. Soccer was his country's religion, and for two short years he had been its idol—Rome's favourite son—and nobody let him forget it.

'*Your* future,' he amended, and scanned the room for the bride. Sure enough she was nearby, deep in a huddle with her girlfriends. She was also noticeably pregnant. She saw them and made her way over.

'We were just toasting the Benedetti heir,' Gianluca informed her, kissing each warm cheek she proffered gently.

'That's your son, not mine,' Marco reminded him.

'There aren't going to be any, my friend. So drink up.'

'According to Valentina there will be.'

'You'll fall in love, Gianluca,' said Tina Trigoni, fitting herself into the curve of her husband's arm. She barely came up to his shoulder. 'And before you know it you'll have six sons and six daughters. You'd better,' she added. 'I have no intention of sacrificing my children to the Benedetti legacy.'

'Valentina—' began Marco, but Gianluca gave her a faint smile.

'Glad you've been paying attention, Tina.'

'Although you'll never settle down while you date these bubbleheads.'

He lifted a brow.

'Women with bubbles over their heads—like in the cartoons,' said Tina, making an illustrative gesture. 'Blank bubbles for other people to fill the words in.'

Gianluca privately acknowledged she wasn't far off the mark. But then he wasn't looking for a mother for his children.

'You've been talking to my mother.'

'God, no. I'm not that brave. You *do* know she thinks a twenty-year-old Sicilian virgin would fill the nursery? I heard her talking to your sisters about it.'

Marco snorted. 'Does your mother know you at all?'

Did his mother know him? Hardly. And that was the point. The Benedettis threw their boys out to be raised like Romulus and Remus in Rome's foundation myth, to be suckled by the she-wolf of the military until they came of age.

His mother had conformed to the Benedetti traditions like all the women who came before her and expected him to do the same.

No, his mother didn't know him—at all.

'Find me a wife then, Tina,' he said derisively. 'A good, plump Sicilian virgin and I'll follow all the customs.'

'Find you a wife and thousands of hopeful women will weep,' Marco observed, swigging his beer.

But Valentina looked interested. 'I don't know about virgins—are there any left over the age of twenty-one?'

Completely out of nowhere his mind reverted to a pair of unusual green eyes. There were some, he thought. Once. A long time ago.

'But frankly, Gianluca, I don't know if I should introduce any of my friends to you. It's not as if you're ever serious about a woman.'

'Her friends are queuing up to be introduced,' inserted Marco. 'I'm glad I don't make the kind of money you do.'

'Yes, because then I would have married you for your money,' said Valentina lightly, 'instead of for your charm.' She gave her husband a smart look. 'Besides, I don't think they're entirely after his money, *caro*.'

Gianluca listened to Marco and his wife banter and for a

moment acknowledged that this was what he would miss. All going well, Marco and Tina would grow old together, nurse grandchildren on their laps, reminisce about a life well lived.

In forty years' time… He came to a dead stop. The way he was going he'd be a rich man in an empty castle. He looked past the happy couple and saw only his parents' screaming matches, their empty lives performed on the stage set that was the Palazzo Benedetti. One of the most admired pieces of private real estate in Rome. If only people knew the generations of unhappy women who haunted its corridors.

His own mother had been a stunningly beautiful hot-blooded girl from the hills outside Ragusa. Maria Trigoni had married into the social stratosphere and contorted herself into the role of Roman *principessa*. She had played fitfully at being wife and mother when she hadn't been completely taken up with her lovers or her much-desired role in society.

Her only real loyalty was to her family in the south—the Trigonis. Marco's father was her brother. She would vanish down there for long periods of time. He remembered each one of those disappearances like cuts to his back. The first time it had happened he'd been three and had cried for a week. The second time he'd been six and had been beaten for his tears. When he was ten he'd tried to telephone his mother in Ragusa but she'd refused to take his call.

Privately Gianluca suspected the moment a woman put on the Benedetti wedding tiara she lost a bit of her soul. So sue him—he wouldn't be passing on *that* little tradition.

He swigged his beer, barely tasting it as it went down. He had no intention of settling down, providing an heir to the Benedetti name. It was enough that he'd restored its honour.

Besides, after two years on active service he knew better than most that life was lived in the moment, and at this particular moment he was enjoying a little variety in his life. He knew it irritated his mother, disappointed his grandmother, but as a Benedetti male it was almost expected that he would pursue women in numbers.

The old cliché that there was safety in numbers was true. He had a reputation now for being a bachelor who couldn't be hooked. He played up to it.

As if conjured by the direction of his thoughts a woman stepped out onto the terrace.

She was slender and curvy all at once, and the lights turned her hair platinum.

'There's my cue,' said Gianluca.

'Fast cars and fast women—this is why I refuse to introduce you to my girlfriends,' Tina called mischievously after him.

As he approached, the blonde turned up a flawless face and batted long lashes over her Bambi eyes.

'Come and dance with me, Gianluca.'

'I've got a better idea,' he said, shouldering past her. 'Let's get a drink...' For the life of him he couldn't remember her name.

'Donatella,' she said coldly, in that moment losing the little-girl act.

'Donatella—*si*.' He suspected from her tone that he'd forgotten her name more than once tonight. It wasn't important. She'd only latched on to him because of his name, his reputation.

He slid a hand into his jacket, dragged out his PDA. He'd have a drink, do some work, lose the blonde. But she was a good excuse to put his head back into what mattered—making a deal, setting up the next one, keeping an eye on what the Asia-Pacific markets were doing overnight. Not contemplating what Marco had found seemingly so effortlessly: a good woman. While he, Rome's pre-eminent bachelor, had been stood up by a sexless Australian dragon who clearly didn't know her loss was what's-her-name's gain...

He rifled through his mind for the blonde's name again, gave up, and hit the bar for another drink.

Ava gave her name to the hostess and naturally only drew a blank. Part of her had hoped she would just be waved on in.

'Strawberries,' she whispered.

'Scusi, signorina?'

Ava cleared her throat. 'I believe I'm listed under the name "Strawberries".'

Her mouth felt dry, her skin prickled, and she was sure the couple behind her were finding this hilarious. She closed her eyes briefly to fortify herself. Public humiliation suddenly felt all too close. 'I'm Signor Benedetti's guest.'

Just saying it made this all real, and Ava felt her Dutch courage—a glass of white wine before she left the hotel and two reds downstairs—curdle in her stomach like milk left in the sun.

'Ah, *si.'*

The hostess seemed to find nothing unusual in a woman being listed as a fruit on Gianluca Benedetti's guest list, and the thought made Ava's belly clench a little tighter.

She made her way through a crowd of women in slips and heels and men in Armani before coming to a standstill.

Gianluca Benedetti was lounging like some kind of broad-shouldered Caesar, with his arms thrown across the back of a black leather settee, his powerful shoulders and chest delineated in a form-fitting dark shirt. His high cheekbones, sensuous mouth and uncompromisingly firm jaw gave him the look of one of Michelangelo's marble carvings of male beauty.

Genetics had been so good to him there had to be a price. Spitefully Ava wished she could be around to see it exacted from him. He wasn't alone—as if she had *ever* expected him to be alone. What had she thought? He'd be waiting for her? This was some sort of *date*?

His head was angled negligently to one side for a scantily clad blonde to whisper sweet nothings in his ear.

The blonde, naturally. The stab-your-heart-out heels blonde.

A sick feeling invaded her insides.

She was never going to be that woman.

For a teetering instant Ava was transported to that long-ago reception for her brother's wedding. She had been a socially awkward young woman who just hadn't fitted in with the glamorous, international crowd, watching from the sidelines as Gianluca Benedetti—Italian soccer star and possibly the most desired man on the planet—reclined on a banquette, gesticulating as he talked football with another guy. He'd had two girls wrapped around him like climbing vines, blonde and brunette. The equivalent of gelato flavours for grown men. He hadn't even been paying attention to them.

At the time she had christened them *vines*, but, oh, how she had wanted to be like them. Just for one night to be a sexy, no-consequences girl, in slip and heels, hanging off the hottest guy at the party.

Even as she had struggled to come to terms with the odds of her ever being that kind of girl her eyes had moved over the object of their attention and for the first time in her life she'd been hit by something and hadn't been able to hit back.

The tsunami of feeling that night had carried her past her inhibitions—past the little voice of caution that always asked if this was the right thing to do, if there would be consequences for her actions, the voice of a girl who'd had to look after herself from a very young age. That night she hadn't cared about the consequences.

She had only cared about him.

Having him.

Feeling sick now, she was unable to credit that she had stepped so easily back into the same shoes, that she had learned nothing from her experiences.

Before she could even formulate her next move he was getting up, throwing back those broad shoulders and unexpectedly moving her way. It was so sudden her first instinct was to turn tail and flee, but she wasn't an uncertain girl any more. She could handle this.

Sucking in her tummy, adjusting the line of her dress, she prepared herself for what she would say.

I came but I wish I hadn't. You're a womaniser, a cad and a bounder, and I wish I'd never met you.

He was less than a metre away when she realised he wasn't coming over to her. His hard gaze moved unseeingly over her, as if she were one of the faceless crowd, and Ava realised she wasn't going to have her moment.

He'd issued the invitation but he'd already forgotten about her. She hadn't even made enough impact this morning for her face to register with him.

Her stomach buckled.

She watched him moving easily but inexorably towards the exit, the doors opening and swallowing him up.

Ava only became aware that she was struggling to push her way through the crowd when someone stepped on her foot and she lost a shoe. Pausing to scoop it up, she pushed through the exit doors, then virtually ran outside. She hesitated on the steps leading down into the square, but only to scan desperately for the direction he'd taken.

She gave a start as she caught sight of him, moving out of the darkness across the square.

Shoving it all aside—a lifetime of prudence, plans and protecting herself from men like this one…well, any man really… not to mention leaving her perfectly good A-line coat behind— Ava began to run after him.

CHAPTER FOUR

GIANLUCA HEARD THE FOOTSTEPS, light, fleet heels striking notes on the cobblestones.

He turned around and for a moment they simply looked at one another.

As she began to walk slowly up to him he wondered what had become of his determination never to let life take him by surprise again. His mouth ran dry, his body did what was natural when faced with this much woman. Because, *Dio mio*, she was a sight to make a man glad Adam had had a rib.

She'd obviously gone to some trouble in the transformation department.

It wasn't a stretch to assume it was all for him.

He ran his eye from the erotic promise of her mouth to her decadent bosom and then to the dainty ultra-feminine shoes clasping her feet. No wonder.

The shirt and trousers she'd been hiding beneath this morning hadn't advertised a shape that could only be fully appreciated by an Italian male—generous curves thrown into relief by the accent of her narrow waist.

This was the shape he'd discovered when he'd finally parted her from the puffy blue dress.

She was a walking fantasy if your tastes ran to Gina Lollobrigida.

His did. He'd had a poster of her on the wall of the room he'd kept at his grandparents' villa outside Positano. Part of the pleasure of summer breaks from the military academy he'd been bricked up in by his indifferent parents had been getting back to that house, to his kind old grandparents, but also to Gina.

Almost at once the full force of the past swung in. She wasn't the girl who had lain with him in the grass on the Palatino. That girl had never really existed. And now any trace of her was gone.

As she approached, the low lights of the square illumined her eyes and he glimpsed uncertainty and something else— hopefulness.

But it must have been a trick of the light, because she lifted her chin and her green eyes clashed like an army of the night with his.

There was a dark sort of satisfaction in the knowledge that she had come after him, and it cautioned him to wait and see what she would do.

At the same time he saw what else he'd missed. A huddle of paparazzo across the square. In a second they'd focus in on him, and in this mood the last thing he wanted was a mob of jackals around him.

As excuses went, it wasn't a bad one.

Asserting the cool, dominant masculinity which got him what he wanted in most situations, he stepped up to her, hooked his arm around her waist and told himself this had nothing to do with what he wanted but rather was necessity.

'Scusi, signora,' he murmured, as if apologising for blocking her path, and in the next instant he was kissing her.

He spread his hand at the base of her neck and held her in place, aware this was incredibly intrusive…and undeniably very erotic as she wriggled frantically against him. He clamped his other hand on her wide shifting bottom.

It was still thumping through him exactly who this girl was when he began to enjoy her struggle. He wanted her fists to thump against his chest, her fury at being restrained to come out. *Come on, cara, let's see if you can get away this time.*

He was fiercely turned on, not only by his thoughts but by the feel of her. Her body was so blatantly female every movement of it against his was virtually X-rated. The scent of night-blooming jasmine seemed to be everywhere. His mouth took hers again and then again, until hard and aching he forced himself to release her. All he could see were those bright, astonished green eyes, the curve of her upper lip pinpricked with tiny beads of perspiration, and lower the heaving of her bosom. Instantly he wanted to pull her in tight again, for the press of her warm curvy body that fitted him so perfectly.

In a world of women for whom high heels merely put them on stilts, failing to give them the length in their bodies he needed, he had one in his arms who was built to the perfect scale for a man like him—a little over six feet, with generous hips pressed to cradle his, her breasts soft and full against his chest.

He knew they'd been seen. So he bent his head close to hers. From any sort of distance it was an intimate gesture.

Her green eyes flew to his. Astonishment had given way to fury. It wasn't just in her expression, it was in the aggressive tilt of her body. She was literally seething, and the female pheromones hit him hard and fast, tightening his body into the kind of surging lust he had been careful to keep in check on that long-ago night.

She had been so uncertain. He hadn't wanted to overwhelm her…

But she wasn't that girl any more. She was the woman who had run out on him… And he wanted her any way he could get her right now. Down a dark alley, working up her skirt, tearing her tights, teaching her who was in charge. She didn't run from him. *Ever.*

Gianluca could hear his own harsh breathing.

Why was she pretending not to know him? What had she been doing, walking into the bar dressed like this? What kind of woman was she? The kind who indulged in anonymous cou-

plings with strangers and never looked back? Why in the hell
was she back in his life now? What exactly had he walked into?

He glanced in the direction of the paparazzi.

Lust and anger mingled in a disturbing cocktail. What had
happened to the cool pragmatic man of his reputation?

He looked down at her, reclaimed the higher ground.

'*Scusi, signorina.*' The irony in his scraped-down voice was
clear, but his code of honour meant he must say it. '*Mi volevi
dire nulla di male.*'

He meant her no harm.

No, no harm. He wanted to *kill* her.

Overwhelmed, shocked by the sudden proximity of a big, im-
measurably strong male bearing down on her, Ava struggled
to make sense of what had just happened even as she instinctively cleaved her body to his.

She should back away now. This was highly imprudent
and anything between them couldn't possibly end well. Now
was her chance. He wouldn't ask any questions. She was still
a stranger to him.

But she hadn't over-exaggerated the memory of the effect
of this man on her senses. There had to have been something
on that night so long ago that had made her throw all caution
to the wind, and now she knew.

She suspected it had something to do with his dark adaman-
tine voice, with that sexy, drawling Italian accent running so
softly through everything he said, making her a little bit wild.
If she closed her eyes she could feel his mouth trailing the softest butterfly kisses down the centre of her body as if anointing
her. Nobody had ever touched her that way before or since.

'*Signora?*'

Her eyes fluttered open. He was looking down at her with
a hot intensity that liquefied her very bones and with something else—something dark and terrifying.

'*Signorina,*' she answered in a strangled voice. 'Remember, I'm not married.'

He actually reared back slightly, before his eyes narrowed thoughtfully on her.

For a moment neither spoke, and then his half-lidded golden gaze flared out of the darkness at her.

'Can you run in those shoes?'

'S-sorry?' That wasn't what she had expected to hear.

'Those men over there are paparazzo. If they recognise me your photograph will be in all kinds of places you don't want it to be. Can you run in those shoes?'

He didn't wait for her response. He pulled her in against him, one hand on the small of her back, and began walking her fast across the square, back the way they'd come.

Ava knew she should be protesting, or at least asking more questions, but she felt oddly buoyant—furious with him one moment, swept up in excitement the next. And, really, what was she supposed to do when he was just whisking her along with him?

She thought fleetingly of the nearby Trevi Fountain and how in another life she should be there with Bernard right now, pretending to be in an old Hollywood film as he slid the ring she had chosen onto her finger. The thought of how wrong that scenario was on every level floored her. What *had* she been thinking?

Ava glanced up at this man's profile, at the hard lines speaking of an aggressive masculinity that took what it wanted.

Something fierce ripped through her in response and she quickened her pace.

He turned that hard gaze on her. 'You came.'

Ava pushed aside the shiver of premonition, the suspicion he was not just talking about this evening, because all of a sudden he had her hand and they were running.

Too soon they turned a corner and a shiny black limousine glided across the road towards them.

'This is my ride,' he said. 'I prefer to walk on a fine night, but it looks as if we're not in luck, *signorina*.'

He let go of her hand to get the door.

She hung back, hugging herself in the cool spring evening.

'Let me take you where you want to go,' he offered, with an expressive turn of a well-shaped hand, holding the door for her.

And Ava felt herself tumbling through time until she was once more that unhappy girl in a frothy pale blue dress, standing on the steps of a grand *palazzo*, looking in vain for a taxi cab. And he was the beautiful boy with the super-charged ego and five hundred pounds of Ducati growling between his legs, offering her a ride with an attitude of complete confidence.

The confidence had clearly solidified with the years as the dark drawl barely held an enquiry at the end of it. She was a woman. Of course she would dive into his car—no questions asked. Given she had chased after him across the square, joined in when he kissed her, and would still be holding on to his hand like a teenage girl with her first crush if he hadn't released her...he probably had a point.

She had been in limousines before, ferried to and from corporate events that required her to walk the walk. But as she slid across the dark leather seating she recognised this was pure luxury—beyond the expense account of even the multi-million-dollar turnover of her business.

In the street he had been magnetic. Up close in the intimate, quiet confines of the car Ava felt a little overwhelmed by his physicality.

She wished once more she had her coat, aware that her body was on display in this dress, the hem pulling up over her knees. She tugged at it without making much difference.

'I apologise for all the subterfuge.' He sounded so Italian, so *formal*—as if he hadn't kissed her and swept her into his car.

He had pushed back his coat, revealing the hard contours of a supremely fit body. Everything about his clothes screamed money and good taste, and they fitted him with a fidelity that made it impossible for her not to look at him.

Those golden eyes flickered lightly for just a moment over her body, as intimate as any touch, and Ava felt her nipples tightening as heat curled responsively in her pelvis.

It was a shock, wanting him like this. She hadn't expected the pull between them to be this strong. But perhaps it explained one or two things…

'If you give me the name of your hotel I will take you there.'

All of her fears of being exposed, of being disappointed, of losing the specialness of her memory of this man coalesced into one defining moment: *he was going to get rid of her.*

'Or,' he said in a quiet undertone, filling the tense silence, 'we could go on to a quiet place I know first, have a drink, and you can tell me what brings you to Rome.'

He'd said *first*. What came second? Ava tried to ignore the tingling behind her knees, the way it seemed to creep into her thighs. Was he propositioning her? Did he want them to go to her hotel, take their clothes off and…?

Up until this moment she'd agreed with Bernard when he'd told her she just wasn't a passionate woman, and yet here she was, starting up some kind of a sexual fantasy activated by nothing more than a single word: *first*.

'I don't—' she began. *I don't know*, she finished silently. *I don't know how to do this.*

'A drink in a public place. Two civilised people.'

Had he put a faint emphasis on *civilised*?

'Isn't that why you are here…?'

Ava wondered with a sort of horrified fascination if he'd just read her mind…

'To have a drink with me?'

To her continued amazement she felt desire like honey slide through her body. This didn't happen to her. It *never* happened to her. Sexual desire was something she had to *work* on. It never ambushed her like this.

It was a timely reminder that he was a man used to being pursued by women, and she was a woman who had never inspired pursuit in a man.

Most memorably in *this* man.

The heat in her blood suddenly knifed her.

'I won't be sleeping with you tonight.'

He gave her an amused look. 'I wasn't aware I had asked.'

Real embarrassment crawled through her. *She* was the one thinking about sex.

'I wanted to be clear,' she said uncomfortably.

'What if we just have that drink?' He'd leaned forward, clearly to instruct his driver, when something occurred to him. 'Are you hungry?'

Ava shook her head. She didn't think she could stomach a bite.

As he gave instructions to his driver Ava wondered what exactly she thought she was going to accomplish here tonight. She eyed him uncertainly. This entire situation felt illicit and fraught with danger. This was not what a sensible woman did, and beneath the glamorous dress and styled hair she was still at heart a conventional girl in her relationships with men, stand-offish at the best of times. In the hare and the tortoise race she was the tortoise, steadily persevering with a man—specifically with Bernard—until inevitably it all fell apart.

She imagined Gianluca Benedetti's private life moved at supersonic speed, and if anyone ended anything it would be him.

'I apologise,' he said, sitting back, that deep voice made far too seductive by the upper-class Italian accent. 'It wasn't my intention to ignore you tonight.'

No?

'My mind was somewhat preoccupied.'

Snap! 'Yes,' she said, also sitting back, unable to keep some of the derision out of her voice. 'I saw what was occupying it.'

A frown touched his brow.

'The blonde woman who forgot her clothes?' she reminded him.

His expression eased. 'Ah, Donatella, *si.*'

She noticed he made no effort to deny she'd been the source of his preoccupation. Ava tried not to grit her teeth. They weren't on a date. He owed her nothing. She still wanted to hit him.

She didn't really know what she'd been expecting. She suspected it went along the lines of *I remember you. I've never forgotten you. I never got your message...*

'There's something I should tell you.'

'*Si?*'

'This isn't the first time we've met.'

'Is that so?'

'I don't seem...familiar to you?'

He shrugged.

Ava knew right then that any chance of her making a little joke of it, or him being enchanted or curious, or even maybe a little regretful had evaporated.

'I meet many people. Forgive me if I don't recall your face.'

His tone was reasonable, his words polite—too polite. But the sentiments...they stung...

I don't recall your face. I don't remember lying in the grass on Palatine Hill, cradling you in my arms. I don't remember a single one of the personal confessions you made because, really, it meant nothing to me.

'You really don't remember?' she persevered.

A look of irritation flashed across those hooded eyes.

'No doubt you will tell me.'

Ava knew it was irrational. She knew she had no right to expect something so fleeting, so long ago, to have stayed with him as it had with her. She hadn't realised until that moment how deep she'd been into this fantasy. She really had to stop it now—unless she was keen on full shake-down humiliation.

She stared blindly at the dark window, wishing she hadn't locked herself in such a confined space with him.

'I'm waiting,' he said coldly.

Her gaze was dragged back to his. Why was he looking at her like that? Was she about to break some sort of rule against mentioning illicit encounters in Roman parks? It wasn't as if she'd been stalking him for seven years. She hadn't made a pest of herself. Good grief, she'd done everything possible to avoid thinking about him!

'It's not important,' she said, sounding stiff when what she felt was awkward. 'Let's just forget it.'

He spread those big hands expressively, as if he was actually encouraging her to put him straight. But she wasn't fooled. She had negotiated with sharks before in her professional life.

'Have I read this wrong? You stalk me, pursue me across a public square, and now you hit me with this little confession. What's the angle here, *signorina*?'

The angle? For a moment she struggled to make the connection. She understood the tone. But why was he speaking to her like this?

Ava could feel perspiration prickling along the nape of her neck. She hadn't expected him to be this…intimidating. Where was the sensitive, caring boy she'd found under the swaggering, oh-so-sure-of-himself exterior she'd initially been drawn to? She might have only spent a night with him, but they had *talked*—really talked. She'd said things to him she'd never told another living soul, and at the time it had felt mutual. How had he evolved into this hardened, suspicious man, ready to believe the worst of her at the drop of a hat?

What had happened to him?

'I did not stalk you,' she said woodenly, determined not to show how truly dismayed she was. 'I did not pursue you. Those are not the facts.'

'Come on.' He sat back, looking her over. 'You come to Rico's, dressed like this—'

He gestured at her beautiful frock as if her clothing was an incitement, instead of a fraught choice she had made that afternoon in front of a mirror in a boutique. If the lady assisting hadn't been so genuinely helpful she'd probably be sitting here in a trouser suit.

She was tempted to tell him that far from being a *femme fatale* she was so inept at rolling on stockings she'd ruined two pairs before she'd finished getting ready tonight, and those stockings weren't cheap…

'—on the strength of a flimsy invitation a woman with any common sense and self-esteem would ignore.'

Ava was so busy thinking about the four pieces of cobweb silk she'd left strewn on the bed and the wastage they entailed that she almost missed the impact of the rest of his statement.

The sentiment found its home.

She didn't know where to look. She'd been spot-on back in the bar, when it had occurred to her that he hadn't been serious at all…but she'd taken him very seriously—*too* seriously—and now it was too late to avoid disaster. She'd mistaken the kiss as proof of something. Oh, what was wrong with her? She *always* got social interaction between men and women wrong. Every time.

This was why she'd stuck with Bernard for so long, terrified of what would happen to her out there on the singles scene. She'd been out there once before…when she came back from Rome seven years ago, looking for something approaching what she'd found that night with this man. What she'd got was a guy called Patrick whose sports car and good looks had been her fledgling attempt to put herself out there, to run in the fast lane, and his dating her had been an attempt to slow himself down. She'd discovered a few months into the relationship that he hadn't slowed down at all.

Right now she just wanted out of this car. She needed to run and hide and make sense of this—and then kick herself for being such a fool.

'I didn't issue that invitation. If it was flimsy that's down to you,' she mumbled. 'And you don't need to question my common sense. Right now I'm doing enough of that for the both of us!'

She saw his eyes narrow on her, as if something about this wasn't playing out as he'd expected it to.

When he did speak again it was in a low, silky tone. 'So, where have I gone wrong, *signorina*?'

Just about everywhere! She should be able to laugh about this, but the joke fell flat because it was on her. Right now she knew she was in serious danger of losing it in a major way if she didn't stick to the facts. Cold, hard logic had always been her anchor, her guiding light, and she grasped it now.

'Flimsy invitation or not—' she kept her voice steady '—you *invited* me!' When he didn't react she repeated stubbornly, 'You *invited* me.'

He took out his phone and she watched his thumb move idly over the keypad. He looked so relaxed, as if this entire argument were nothing, and yet his words had been wielded with scalpel-like precision as he took her apart.

'Did you set up the paparazzo?' He didn't even look up.

Ava snorted—she couldn't help it—and his eyes lifted from his phone as if no woman should make such a sound in his vicinity.

Good. She didn't want to be his kind of woman anyhow. 'Do you know what you are? A bully, and a—a playboy, and none of this is fair.'

'Is that so?' His attention had returned to the phone.

'Right now all I'm thinking about is the *hours* I spent getting ready for tonight,' she admitted, wondering why she was even bothering to tell him this—he was much more interested in his phone. 'And I don't have a clue why I did it.'

'To impress me,' he said, as if it were obvious.

Ava's jaw dropped. 'Your ego is astounding!' A blast of anger that demanded she call in a little justice fired up her temper. 'Just you put down that phone and listen to me.'

He lifted his eyes slowly and Ava wished he hadn't. She swallowed—hard—but she'd come a long way in life and she didn't let anyone intimidate her any more.

'I'm not one of those floozies climbing all over you at that bar. Let me give you some facts. Last month I was listed in the top fifty women in business in Australia. It may not mean much to you, *Prince* Benedetti, but it does mean I don't *bar-crawl*, I don't milk men for profit, and I certainly have no idea how you contact a paparazzo.'

'And you are giving me this fascinating glimpse into your life…why?'

With that a great deal of the fight went out of her.

What was she doing? She had a single memory of something wonderful and it was falling apart in front of her eyes. She couldn't even really blame him, because although this man had ripped her blinders off seven years ago the truth was she had sent herself off to live a life devoid of colour, of passion, of sex.

It was a startling realisation, and as if reality had decided to tear down *all* her supports, tension combined with one glass of white wine and three glasses of red on an empty stomach began to swirl and shift in her belly. Everything else was wiped out by the very real knowledge she was probably going to be sick.

'Time to wind this up,' he said, shooting the sleeve on his left arm.

He wanted her to get out. This wasn't his problem. He was just a man to whom everything came easily, and she was a woman for whom nothing had come without hard work. She gathered up her handbag.

'Come,' he said brusquely. 'Give me the address of your hotel and I will see you home.'

Ava ignored him and grappled with the door. The flash of impatience she'd heard in his voice had her retaliating as she struggled out, 'Why bother? You didn't last time.'

It was an unfair thing to say, but she was past being fair, and it would have made for a great exit line—but she ruined it by toppling straight onto her hands and knees in the gutter.

Could it possibly get worse? Swearing under her breath, she clambered to her feet, hopping about as she whisked off her heels. She'd walk in her stockinged feet. She might as well—she'd just laddered her last pair anyway.

She was plodding down the street, not sure where she was going, when she heard him call out in that deep, resonant voice.

'Evie!'

She didn't even turn around, wondering who the hell Evie

was. Right now she just wanted to put as many blocks as she could between them.

Oh, why was everything so hard for her? Other women went on dates, were romanced, kissed, cuddled and adored. Other women came to Rome and had adventures. She felt pretty sure all of those women didn't end the night walking the streets in their stockinged feet.

Blearily she rummaged in her bag for the hotel's card she'd picked up on her way out this morning. All she needed to do was find someone and present it, and get some directions. How hard could it be?

She gave an *oomph* as she almost toppled over a stone bench that had somehow leapt into her path, but an unyielding male hand closed around her elbow and fluidly turned her into his arms.

'Stop it—let me go!' she huffed, pushing against his chest, aware mostly of the heat of his body, the delicious scent of him, and her own giddy reaction as she tried to free herself. She turned this way and that until she realised he wasn't holding on to her, just trying to steady her. Why did she need steadying?

She heard him say, '*Dio*, you're drunk.'

It wasn't an accusation…more an observation.

She lifted her chin to sling back a clever reply—something along the lines of, *I'd have to be to go anywhere with you…*

Instead she gazed owlishly up at him.

'I will drive you back to your hotel,' he informed her in a tight voice, but somehow he didn't seem angry any more.

Ava wanted to argue, but she already knew she was in no condition to make a fuss.

'Where to, *Principe*?'

His driver, Bruno, addressed Gianluca calmly over the roof of the limo, as if ferrying drunken sick women around the city nightspots was a regular occurrence.

Good question.

A sensible man would find out where she was staying, do the right thing and not look back.

Si, a sensible man… He'd just bounded out of the car and charged after her, so clearly he didn't qualify.

He had not behaved sensibly from the moment he'd put the Jota into a screaming U-turn this morning. No, it was long past time to assert his much-vaunted judgement.

He leaned down to find out where she was staying.

To his surprise she appeared to be asleep. He gave her a gentle shake. Her head fell forward.

Bene! Drunk. Blind drunk.

Swearing under his breath, he noticed her right hand was clutching something. When he prised open her fingers he found some crumpled euros and an embossed white card.

She was offering him money?

A cab—of course… It all clicked into place. She'd thought he would just bundle her into a cab? In her condition?

Pulling back on his first thought to wake her up and get this sorted out, he retrieved the card.

The Excelsior.

Nice hotel. Not far from here.

Being as careful as he could, he gently shifted her into a more comfortable position. Her mouth hung slightly open and she was breathing softly. For the first time the tension had left her face. She looked as if butter wouldn't melt in her mouth. She looked like a woman who *didn't* go to bars to pick up men and drink so much she passed out. She looked, in short, like the kind of woman who needed looking after.

He pitied the poor *bastardo* who ended up with that job.

Then he noticed other things. There were holes in the knees of her stockings. Her dress was thin. She must have been cold out on the street. Not questioning his actions, he shrugged out of his coat and laid the heavy silk-lined jacket over her.

Unexpectedly she pulled her head back and opened her eyes, green and swimming. She seemed to try and focus. For a moment neither of them spoke, and then she dropped her head again and made a sound that reminded him a little of a hog rooting for truffles. He was so astonished he smiled.

Straightening up, Gianluca slid the hotel card into his back pocket.

'Casa mia,' he said to Bruno. Home.

CHAPTER FIVE

'WAKE UP, SLEEPING BEAUTY.'

A deep, sexy male voice nudged her out of her dream.

Who says I'm not a passionate woman? Ava thought happily as the landscape of his face enlarged, each delicious detail communicating itself to her—the olive perfection of his skin, the line of his sensuous lips, eyes so golden they blistered like a flame over black heat until all she could see was the darker rim of his iris, like an eclipse of the sun. Everything was dark and warm and...*real*.

He was kissing her. The feel of his lips coaxing hers so confidently had all the hormones in her body popping like seeds coming to the surface of the earth after a long winter. She strained towards him and long fingers tangled in her hair as he murmured against her lips, *'Cosi dolce, cosi dolce, mi baci bella.'*

So romantic...so enticing...so real...

She lurched to full consciousness. Her eyes flew open and fixed on the living, breathing version of the dream she had entertained too many times over the years. All two hundred pounds of prime female fantasy.

'You!'

'Yes, me, *bella*. Who did you think you were kissing? Or do we all blur after a while?'

What on earth was he talking about?

Lifting her hands to his chest, she gave him an almighty

shove. But he was fixed over her, his expression nowhere near as friendly as his mouth had been.

'Get off me, you—'

Ava wasn't sure what to call him, but the solid weight of all that hard muscle under the flat of her hands, the appealing masculine scent of him curling around her, and her mouth still tingling like an electrical storm after his kiss made her protests sound a little feeble to her ears.

He clearly thought so too. He gave her an intriguing appraisal from her bed-head hair, to her raccoon eyes, to her bare shoulders.

Bare shoulders.

Ava clapped a hand to her chest. She was naked. Holy hell! She was too well-endowed to be going around without a little stitching and support. She wriggled. No, not naked. She definitely had her knickers on. Vaguely she remembered flinging her clothes off. She was pretty sure no one else had been involved.

'Get off,' she slung at him again.

'I like you better when you're unconscious,' he commented. But before she could process that he had sprung up with a lithe, muscular grace she could only envy and was heading for the door.

Ava struggled to sit up and keep the sheet gathered modestly under her arms. Her eyes widened slightly, because for a moment there she thought she'd glimpsed a distinct bulge in those jeans.

A band tightened around her skull and she winced.

'Where are you going?' she groaned.

'It's a new day, Ava. Get dressed.'

And with that smooth-as-silk instruction he was gone.

Ava stared at the door he'd shut behind him and then down at her own long shape, wrapped in a white sheet like a mermaid. Instinctively her fingertips caressed the fabric—a thread count so high it felt like water on her bare skin. For a moment her mind went fuzzy again, and she felt the softness of his breath mingling with hers, the solid weight of him under the press of her hands and the new knowledge that he was every bit as susceptible as she.

Come back, her libido pleaded.

She slapped a hand to her head. What had got into her? Her hormones had led her into all this trouble and she was still letting them run riot!

The pulsing behind her eyes gave an extra punch, as if to remind her of the evils of giving in to rogue impulses, and she lowered her head carefully back down onto the pillow. It felt like a brick.

Get dressed, Ava... He could go to hell...

Ava... Get dressed Ava.

Ava.

She almost fell out of bed. He knew.

He needed a cold shower.

Gianluca stood under the pulsing jets in the wet room, massaging out the tension bunching in the tendons behind his neck.

Ava Lord.

Not *Evie*—Ava.

For seven years when he'd thought of her—and it was about time he acknowledged he *had* thought of her—it had been as Evie.

It had been one night, years ago. How could he be expected to get her name right? But he had never known her real name. Somehow he'd misheard, and she hadn't corrected him, and right now *that* was the sticking point for him. Had it been so anonymous for her she didn't need names? And why was that little detail bothering him? A better question was why did his gut muscles clench when he remembered rolling over and finding her gone?

He'd been twenty-two at the time, had what he'd imagined was success, in the form of a media frenzy around his soccer career, and girls had been climbing down drainpipes to perform for him. He'd been an *idiota* plenty of times in those early years when it came to women, and he'd been pretty jaded by the time Evie…*Ava* dropped into his lap.

It had been different, though. *She* had been different. She'd had attitude even then—giving him directions when he was cruising the Ducati downtown, fussing and complaining. He'd humoured her and pretended to get lost. He'd thought he'd enjoy watching her lose it…but she hadn't.

Instead she'd lost her edge and grown curious about his city, and then excited when he took her to the Forum, where she'd wanted to know the entire history of the place. He'd found himself having to compete with monuments and long-dead historical figures for her attention.

She'd made him compete. She'd forced from him what other girls had never demanded—to be entertained. By the time they'd reached the top of Palatine Hill she'd had him in the palm of her hand.

He actually hadn't planned anything when they'd sunk down into the grass. She'd talked a lot, he remembered, and he'd found he didn't mind listening. He might have said a few things himself, and when she'd begun to cry he had kissed her, because her tears had felt real. It probably wouldn't have gone beyond that…but she had smelled incredible, and tasted so sweet, felt warm and soft. The minute he'd slid his hands under the boned bodice of her fairy-tale dress and felt the warm satin weight of her breasts, her nipples pushing up against his palms, there had been no going back.

He had known she wasn't like any girl he'd ever met. He had known there would be a messy aftermath. He had known he was inviting a thousand complications into his clear-cut life but he'd dived in anyway.

Evie, Evie, Evie. *Ava.*

What he hadn't known was that she'd cut and run before he could learn another detail, and within minutes of waking to an empty bed he'd received the phone call that had changed his life.

He was still shouldering those changes.

What he also hadn't known then was that seven years later he'd be woken at 6:00 a.m. by another phone call, this time from his cousin Alessia, to tell him her husband's sister was in Rome. She was refusing point-blank to come to them. He was to bring her with him this weekend.

'Her name is Ava Lord and she's staying at the Excelsior. Josh has been ringing and ringing, but her phone's switched off.'

This had been followed by another phone call from his mother. 'You *must* pick up this girl, Gianluca. Alessia tells me she refuses to come to us. We were not kind to her at Alessia's wedding, and I'm afraid it's influencing her decision-making. I feel it's my fault.'

Gianluca killed the water jets and, shaking his cropped dark hair free of water, padded from the wet room, dragging a towel over his shoulders.

Ava Lord.

Alessia only had to say her name and he knew what he'd done.

He'd gone and slept with the groom's sister!

He shaved and dressed rapidly, punching his arms into his shirt, swearing under his breath. Going into his room earlier this morning he'd intended to confront her. But that had been his first mistake.

He'd found her lying in the middle of his bed, twisted in a sheet that did nothing *not* to remind him of how lush her curves were, making it pretty obvious that she was naked under the sheet.

Her thick, lustrous hair had been spread about and one arm flung out, as if to showcase the curve of shoulder, breast and hip. It was a ratio of numbers that would make a mathematician weep.

She had shifted, and the full impact of her made-for-sin body had been outlined in fine white Egyptian cotton. All the blood in his body that hadn't already headed that way had surged to his groin.

Madre di Dio.

How was he supposed to conduct any sort of conversation with her and not think about sex?

Irritated, he'd hit the controls for the window shutters and a wave of morning light had splashed over the bed. He'd intended the harsh light of day to take the edge off her sensual display.

'Come on—wake up.'

He had reached down to shake her but his hand had hovered over her bare shoulder. He'd tried to find a portion of her body he could touch with impunity, but she seemed to be made up entirely of erogenous zones. He had known if he touched any part of her it would be soft and pliant and far too female, and his self-control would be history...

Cursing under his breath, he had struggled to peel his mind off the rise and fall of her chest.

'Wake up, Sleeping Beauty.'

She'd murmured something and his gaze had been drawn away from the sheet and due north, like a compass, to that strawberry of a mouth, as luscious as any of her curves. Sultry green eyes had gleamed behind slowly lifting lashes.

She'd absolutely killed him.

God help him, he'd wanted another taste of the soft pink fullness of her lips, the heat of her mouth, the explosive re-action in the kiss they had shared last night. His ungoverned imagination had moved on, taking the sheet down slowly. He would shape the heaviness of her breasts with his hands and feast on nipples he remembered amazingly clearly as being the same strawberry colour as her mouth...and when she was wet and wanting, begging him to come into her, he would push himself deep inside her, fill her hard and...

She'd given a sigh, gazing dreamily up at him as if await-ing his pleasure. There had been only one thing for it under the circumstances.

He'd leant down and found her lips with his, and that kiss in the *piazza* last night had been pushed aside by the sweetness of this one. Her mouth had been as luscious as he'd remembered, and just like last night she had responded. This time there had been no fury in her—just sleepy, soft sensuality.

Even half asleep she had kissed a man as if her heart and soul were involved, and he had found himself tangling his hands in her thick, silky hair until…

'You!'

He had drawn back and seen the shock and accusation in her eyes. As if she'd had no idea who she was kissing. As if she responded to every man who put his arms around her, drew her close, put his mouth on hers with the same *incredible* abandon.

Dio mio, he told himself now, as he put his hand to the door. It wasn't jealousy of other men that had driven him from that room this morning into a cold, cold shower. It was a matter of good taste.

This was not some woman he'd just picked up last night. There would be no indiscriminate coupling. Not now that he knew her identity.

She was his guest. She was Alessia's sister-in-law. She was the one woman in Rome he definitely *wouldn't* be sleeping with.

This time he made sure he knocked before shoving open the door. He didn't know what he expected—at the very least a woman dressed. Her hair would be better neatly combed away into that ugly knot she'd been wearing yesterday—before all of this got out of hand.

Instead she was sitting in the middle of the bed, legs tucked under her, wearing the sheet.

Still wearing the sheet.

Naked.

'*Santa Maria,*' he snarled. 'For the sake of decency, will you put some clothes on?'

Her head jerked around and for a moment she looked almost shocked. But it must have been a trick of the light because those green eyes instantly narrowed and she yanked at the sheet, winding it more securely under her soft, pale arms.

Bene. That was exactly what he wanted. Her covered up. Except if anything the gesture only exaggerated the spill of flesh beneath her fine collarbones and made her more of a feast for his male senses.

He hadn't realised until this moment how incredibly appealing a voluptuous woman could look in nothing but a bedsheet. He'd clearly been sleeping with far too many skinny girls. She was every inch Venus emerging from the foam. A goddess of love and sex and the secrets of the flesh. If she went about in nothing else but a sheet there would be riots on the streets of Rome...

'*That's* what you've got to say to me?' She sounded incredulous.

He tore his thoughts away from her bountiful cleavage and told himself he needed to tackle this rationally—and for that to happen ideally certain things needed to occur. He needed another cold shower and she would need to be dressed. But, frankly, he didn't have time.

He folded his arms. 'I've got plenty to say to you, Signorina Lord,' he said heavily. 'Given your lack of modesty, we'll get started now. Does your brother know you're here?'

She blinked at him. Clearly it wasn't what she'd expected him to say.

'My brother?'

'*Si*—the brother you so cleverly omitted to mention.'

She shook her head. 'Why are you interested in my brother?'

'I suspect he would have been interested in me seven years ago, when I deflowered his sister in a public park.'

The look on her face was priceless.

She clearly understood nothing. His position, hers, how everything had now taken on a different complexion.

'I am the head of the Benedetti family. You are a de facto member of that family by marriage. I hold responsibility for your safety while you're here in my city.'

It was a perfectly reasonable thing to say. Gianluca waited for her response. A little feminine reserve would go a long way at this moment. She would ask for his assistance and he would give it.

She gave him an incredulous look. 'You are *kidding*?'

Gianluca knew in that moment this was going to be a long morning.

'I rarely...*kid*.'

'Then I'd kindly ask you to keep your nose out of my private business. You most certainly are not responsible for me—and nor, may I add, is my brother.'

'In point of fact,' he responded with bite, 'I *am* responsible for your brother. I employ him.'

'You do not,' she asserted confidently. 'Josh runs a vineyard in Ragusa.'

'*Si*—on my land in Sicily.'

Ava frowned. This wasn't the picture Josh had painted in their rare phone calls. She had thought he was doing well, that he was his own man and the vineyard he owned was thriving. In point of fact when she'd last talked to him a few days ago he'd used the start of the harvest as an excuse not to see her.

'I'm not any happier about this than you, Signora Lord. A day never starts well when my mother feels the need to phone me.'

'*Signorina,*' she reminded him—then wished she hadn't, given the now speculative look on his face.

'*Signorina,*' he said, disturbingly softly.

'Yes, well...I've heard about how close Italian men are to their mothers,' she bustled on crisply.

'We speak three times a year: Easter, Christmas and her birthday.'

His eyes moved lazily over her and Ava shifted a little.

'This morning will make it four—because of *you, signorina.*'

'I'm bringing mother and son together,' she responded dryly. 'I'm doing you a service.'

He ignored her. 'According to the women of my family, with whom I make it my practice not to get involved,' he added with wry emphasis, 'you refuse to see your brother because you feel they have offended you in some way.'

She didn't miss the way he made it sound doubtful that anyone had offended her, as if his precious family couldn't possibly have done anything to hurt her…

Ava's temper was rekindled. 'What's it got to do with them?'

'Apparently they feel responsible for some unhappiness you experienced at your brother's wedding all those years ago.'

You. You are responsible for my unhappiness!

Ava sucked in a breath, aware she had been far too close to blurting that sentiment out. Where on earth had it come from? Surely she didn't believe that? But she was very afraid she did, and it was motivating her frustration with him.

Almost helplessly she silently willed him to mention the real issue, which was their long-ago night together, so she could dismiss it out loud as unimportant and all in the past.

'It's not their business,' she said mulishly when she realised that—just like a man—he had said all he was going to say.

'You can discuss it with them,' he said.

'I'm certainly not discussing it with *you*!'

'*Bene.* I have no interest in your varied sex life. I am, however, the man who will be sending you south this afternoon.'

What varied sex life? He'd clearly confused her with one of his bimbos.

She watched him scoop up her dress, which she'd so embarrassingly thrown onto the floor in her drunken state last night. He shook it out and tossed it to her.

Ava watched in horror as he picked up her bra—all pretty black lace filigree, but substantial enough to support her—and dangled it in front of her.

She snatched it from him, narrowing her eyes at him. He probably had a pile of these—souvenirs from all the other women who had passed through this room. Oh, if only the walls could talk—if only she could find that pile, wrench open the door and point out his stash and confront him with his rampant promiscuity…

Gianluca said calmly, 'Once you are dressed we will talk about this.'

What? No suggestive comments? No questions as to why she'd seen fit to strip herself in the middle of the night…? No interest on his part in her being naked…?

Ava was suddenly aware that what she was feeling was fast approaching disappointment. It was completely inappropriate and she veered her thoughts in the other direction. She really should have got dressed some time ago, instead of sitting here mulling over what he knew and didn't know.

It was clear he knew *everything*.

CHAPTER SIX

'DID YOU HEAR ME?' he repeated impatiently. 'Dress yourself and we will talk.'

'Just a minute.' She gathered the sheet around her, as if another layer might give her the requisite dignity she felt she was presently lacking. 'What have you said to your mother about me?'

'My mother?' He rubbed the back of his neck, drawing into prominence an impressive bicep.

'Yes—the woman who gave birth to you,' she snapped impatiently, convinced he was just showing off his incredible body to taunt her. 'Or did you spring fully formed from the head of Zeus? I wouldn't be surprised…' She muttered the last.

'You really want to discuss my mother?'

No, she wanted to run a hundred miles in the other direction from his mother!

She had experience in facing down corporate sharks in boardrooms when a lesser woman would be knock-kneed to enter, but Maria Benedetti—La Principessa—had looked down her patrician nose at Ava seven years ago, as if the Lord family were somehow not good enough for the Benedettis.

God knew what she would say about this situation—her precious firstborn son standing over her, fully dressed, groomed, every inch the cool upper-class Italian male, and she in her knickers, wrapped in a sheet, at a complete disadvantage after a drunken night on the tiles.

If only she hadn't rung Josh. But she'd been so unhappy when she had first landed in Rome she'd been desperate to hear a familiar voice. He'd been so standoffish she'd turned off her phone, and now his wife wanted to stick her nose in…

'Signorina Lord?' he rapped out impatiently.

'What?'

'Get dressed.'

'No. I want to know what you said to her!' Ava was aware her voice had risen rather shrilly and knew it could be ascribed to panic.

He scrubbed his jaw with the heel of his hand. 'I won't be mentioning our little encounter, if that's what concerns you.'

'I didn't mean that.'

Unaccountably she wondered why he wouldn't mention it. What exactly was wrong with her?

'Anyway, there was no "encounter", as you call it,' she grumbled. 'Unless you had your way with me while I was unconscious.'

An electric silence greeted her suggestion.

'Not that I'm accusing you of anything,' she amended, beginning to feel a little uncomfortable.

The silence lengthened.

'All right—forget it,' she muttered, not sure where to look.

'I can assure you that did *not* happen,' he breathed, as if she had been offensive.

'I was joking.'

'You are naked in my bed,' he said with precision. 'I call that an encounter.'

'You must be slipping.'

He gave her such a long look she began to feel a little flushed.

'Indeed I must be,' he said at last. Restlessly Ava tucked the sheet a little more firmly under her arms.

'What do you call last night?' he asked, still watching her closely. 'A typical Friday night?'

A typical Friday night for her was working after everyone

else had gone home, a glass of her favourite wine and an episode of *Poirot*.

She would just *die* if he knew that.

'I call it being drunk and heartsick,' she said haughtily.

'Drunk, yes. But, flattering as I may find it, I doubt you are still holding a candle for me, *cara*.'

Once you've ridden a giant rollercoaster, the small ones for ever after seem tame.

Longing welled up at that thought and flooded her.

'And if you are,' he said, in the same stroking voice, 'you need to let it go.'

From nowhere, resentment went off in her body like a rocket.

'Heartsick over my boyfriend, you pig—not you!'

His expression grew taut again. 'You will refrain from calling me names.'

Ava felt the heat rush to her face and knew she was revealing too much about her feelings.

'I apologise,' she said stiffly, before adding, 'But you provoked me.'

One dark eyebrow lifted, as if this couldn't possibly be the case. 'Where is this boyfriend?' he said, clearly sceptical.

'None of your business.'

'He lets you out at night on your own? To sit at bars and drink?'

'I do *not* sit at bars and drink! And what do you mean—*lets* me? I'm a grown woman. I can do what I like.'

'He is not Italian, then?'

'Who?'

'The *boyfriend*.' He said it as if she'd just made Bernard up.

Hitching up the sheet, she strode off the bed like a ship in full sail and headed for her handbag, sitting on the armchair under the window.

Furiously she rummaged in it with one hand.

'What are you doing now?'

The low rumble of amusement in his voice was not helping

her temper. She wrenched open her bag and dug around until she located her phone.

'Here. This. Look.'

She held up a recent image of Bernard's pleasant settled face as he'd sat opposite her in a famous Sydney harbourside restaurant. She liked this picture because in it he looked like everything she'd needed him to be but often was not: solid, reliable, dependable.

'My boyfriend,' she said, as if producing a rabbit out of a hat.

Gianluca glanced seemingly without interest at the image.

'You could do better.'

'Pardon me?'

'He has no love for you or you would not be here on your own. If you were *my* woman you would know better than to behave as you did last night.'

Ava tried not to imagine exactly what being his woman would involve, but her instinctive, *completely un-PC* response must have shown, because there was something all too like a male lion surveying his pride of females about the way he was looking at her.

That did it.

She wasn't having this. She really wasn't. Not from him.

'Are you *serious*?' Her voice rose to an unbecoming level 'Your woman? What does that even mean? And you know nothing—*nothing*—about my relationship with Bernard!'

'Bernard?' he repeated. The amusement lurking in those golden eyes almost undid her completely.

'Yes, Bernard.' To her horror tears sprang up behind her eyes. She couldn't bear it if this man made fun of her—of her sad, mixed-up reasons for that particular relationship. It was all such a mess. 'For your information we came to Rome to get engaged, but we broke up! Oh, what would *you* know about relationships anyway? You use women and throw them away.'

'*Cosa?*'

'You heard me. You're a—a rake.'

'My English is usually very good,' he said smoothly, 'but are you comparing me to a garden implement?'

And just like that the fight went out of her. He wasn't taking any of this seriously and she was making an idiot of herself—again. Ava shook her head and quietly put Bernard back in her bag. She scanned the floor for her shoes.

'I need to go,' she said. 'Just forget all of this even happened.'

Gianluca didn't respond, and when she glanced up she realised why. He had taken his phone out.

Nice.

Thoroughly disillusioned and miserable with herself, Ava dropped to her knees and reached under the bed, feeling for her shoes. Belatedly she realised she was sticking her most ample asset into prominence—but really what did it matter at this late stage?

Gianluca Benedetti was a gorgeous man with a habit of beautiful women, and she wasn't his type...at all. And, frankly, when it came down to it he wasn't very nice...

'Ava.'

The way he said her name sent shivers through her. It was really inconvenient. Still, it wasn't as if she'd be hearing her name on his lips for much longer.

'What?' she asked ungraciously, hooking her head out from under the bed.

He was looking at her bottom.

Ava almost hit her head on the bedframe in her haste to get herself vertical.

'*Bella*, what are you doing?'

Was it her imagination or was his voice pitched lower than earlier? And why was he calling her beautiful?

'My shoes—they're missing.'

'You don't say? Come here.' He beckoned to her with that well-shaped hand.

When she hesitated he looked faintly exasperated, as if waiting around wasn't something he was used to.

'*Adesso, cara.* I have something to show you.'

He was clearly not used to waiting around. Most women probably leapt to attention when they heard His Master's Voice, she thought witheringly.

He extended his phone to her.

It was one of those ultra-sleek not long on the market models. Under normal circumstances Ava would have practically salivated.

Instead she almost dropped it.

Her stomach bottomed out.

A man and a woman engaged in a clinch on a cobblestoned square at night.

It would have been romantic but for the identity of the couple.

'It's too far away. You can't see the faces,' she said hopefully, her voice airless.

Gianluca scrolled to the next image.

Himself—amazingly photogenic—it seemed, along with everything else—up close in a smooch with a woman whose eyes were closed and who had a look on her face Ava hadn't even known she could produce. She looked as if she was swooning, and perhaps she was. She looked like everything her ex Bernard had accused her of not being.

A woman carried away by passion.

'Is that me?' She lightly touched the screen with her index finger.

The image didn't dissolve. It was real.

'Welcome to my life,' he informed her tightly.

For some reason she could feel him regarding her closely.

'Public property.'

Ava snatched the phone off him and began to scroll frantically through the shots. In two of them it was clearly her. Then she shrieked, 'Oh, God—I look so fat!'

'That's all you have to say?'

'It's all right for you.' She eyed him mutinously. 'You're not wearing shiny fabric and being shot at an unfortunate angle.'

Gianluca retrieved the phone. 'You look fine. And that's not the issue.'

She looked *fine*?

Last night was the best she'd ever looked…and he thought she'd looked fine. That didn't leave her with far to go this morning, with her bed hair and smudged make-up.

'You need to leave Rome—now—and I'll need to know where you are.'

Still contemplating the fact that her round behind looked at least a size bigger in that photograph, and that the entire world was going to be looking at it and making comparisons with every skinny-minnie model he'd ever dated, she was a little slow to pick up on what he was saying.

'Leave Rome?' she repeated, then focussed. 'Leave Rome! Why?'

'Because more photographs will be taken of you. Information will be sourced. You will be a five-minute wonder.'

'Information? What information?'

'Your name, your origin, what you do, who you are. Run-of-the-mill for me, but not so much for you, *si*? So you go to Ragusa for a few days and this dies down.'

'Like hell!'

'There is also the small issue of my future wife,' he said under his breath as he scrolled through the messages on his phone.

Ava's head whipped around.

He glanced up and had the grace to look marginally uncomfortable.

'It's a joke, Ava.' He made a gesture. *'Non e importante.'*

Ava forgot all about her behind being shown around the globe for the world's media to lampoon as she felt something fragile and new sprouting inside her wither and collapse.

'You're engaged and you *cracked onto me*?' She couldn't keep the feeling out of her voice.

'Cracked?' He pocketed the phone and made one of those extravagant Latin gestures of incomprehension with his hand.

'Tried it on…made overtures…you know—*cracked*.'

'I'm not engaged yet,' was his cool response.

'Semantics,' she shot back, her entire stomach free-falling. 'Oh, what a piece of work you are. Well, you can stuff it.' She began looking for her shoes again, this time throwing things around—cushions, the throw on the armchair. She would have liked to have flung the chair at him.

His voice wrapped round her like a strong arm. 'I wasn't the one trawling for sex, *cara*.'

Ava stopped thrashing about. In point of fact her arms went spaghetti limp and her head jerked round. 'Excuse me?'

He was watching her with that cool, Italian sex appeal some women probably found irresistible.

'Look, I understand you're broken-hearted or whatever—'

Again with the scepticism. 'Let's go with whatever,' she retorted.

'But you weren't looking for Prince Charming last night,' he finished with brutal candour.

'And guess what?' she snapped back. 'I didn't find him!'

In that moment she hated him so much that if she'd had something to hand she really would have thrown it at him.

He was *engaged*—and who knew how many women had been under his bridge in the last seven years?

Whereas she'd had exactly three. *Three!* Three men under her bridge. She'd kept her bridge nice. He probably had a toll on his. Thousandth woman through gets a bottle of Bollinger and an engagement ring. How dared he call her morality into question?

'I'm not going anywhere, bud. This is your problem. You caused this. You were the one who kissed *me*.'

'I will remind you that it was you who chased after me like a demented banshee across that square. I wasn't given much choice after that little performance.'

Great—so now he'd kissed her because he'd had to.

'And now, *signorina*, because of your activities last night we're front page on Rome's leading gossip sheet. Which means my PR people will be spinning this because you're family, and so, like a good member of the extended Benedetti family, you're going to be where the rest of us are this weekend.'

'What do you mean? I'm not a member of the Benedetti family!'

'You, madam, are going to Ragusa.'

'I bloody well am not! I've booked a driving tour of Tuscany.'

A romantic trip she was now doing all on her own.

He laughed. He actually laughed.

She didn't think. She reacted. Overcome by a surge of feeling far beyond what his reaction warranted, she lunged at him.

He caught her arm easily and dislodged the sheet. Ava gasped and, unable to stop the slippage, jammed her breasts up against his chest, effectively imprisoning the sheet but giving him a full body imprint. Outrage dissolved as she suddenly found herself in a very precarious position.

He felt hard and hot and…interested. Yes, definitely considerable interest on his part. A lightning flash of sexual heat shot up her body in response and her nipples sprang out like little pink missile launchers. If she'd wanted his attention she now had it.

She was appalled by how quickly this entire situation had got out of hand. She couldn't believe she'd physically attacked him. Couldn't believe anything about this mess and drama was turning her on—and, unexpectedly, him. Oh, yes, his arousal was unambiguous against her belly and she could feel the tremor in his body.

'Let me go!' she squeaked, unable to look up because they were so close. She didn't trust him or herself. She'd been forced to address the base of his throat, where the skin was golden and dark hairs curled invitingly, and she fought the urge to touch him there too.

To her surprise he did as she asked and let her go. Ava grabbed at the sheet, hauling it into place and sitting down heavily on the bed, feeling very much at a disadvantage. She couldn't fight her corner like this. Where was her dignity?

She pulled clumsily at the bedsheet toga, making sure everything was securely in place.

'I'm not a member of your family,' she reiterated. 'You can't force me to go anywhere.'

She glanced warily at him and discovered he was watching her broodingly. For a moment she thought he was actually considering that she might be right. Instead of feeling triumphant, Ava experienced a trickle of uneasiness as she realised after this morning she would probably never see him again.

'Besides,' she said, trying to ignore that feeling, 'how will you explain kissing a member of your sainted family, Mr Spin Doctor?'

'It was a friendly peck, blown up as something else by the nature of photography,' he said with amazing cool, his golden eyes screened by dense black lashes. 'We had both dined with friends and I was escorting you back to the *palazzo*.'

Her mouth fell open slightly. Damn, he was good. It must be practice. Her eyes narrowed like a cat's.

'You are, naturally, staying with me, and today we travel south and join the rest of the family for my mother's birthday celebration at the weekend.'

Ava swallowed. Another Benedetti clan gathering. Another opportunity for her to feel like a spare wheel. She really, *really* didn't want to go.

'Is your fiancée going to be there?'

He actually looked discomfited. 'There is no fiancée,' he said, with the air of a man being made to suffer.

To Ava's amazement colour scored those ridiculously high cheekbones.

'There will be a lot of people at Ragusa next weekend. Those photographs will be discussed. Nobody who knows me is going to believe the story. We will be the object of some speculation.'

'That bothers you, does it?' she said stiffly, thinking of the blonde with almost no clothes on last night. He might as well have said, *I don't want my friends and family to meet you and think we're a couple.*

He pushed his fingers restlessly through his thick hair. '*Dio*, it is the custom in my family for the eldest son to marry and produce the next generation. It is the reason I never—*never*—bring a woman with me to Ragusa. This—' he indicated her and the rumpled bed '—and me arriving with you in tow is going to cause trouble.'

'Don't worry,' she said stonily, staring past him, her heart pounding, because she'd thought she was long past being the girl who didn't make the grade, 'your mother *hates* me. She'll probably put strychnine in my water and then all the speculation will stop.'

There was a loaded silence.

'Besides, I'm not coming. If I don't turn up there won't be a problem, will there?'

Ava told herself the petulance in her voice was merely the end effect of a week in which she'd been on the wrong end of the stick with not one man but two. Two men who were clearly happy to put their own comfort before her own. As if her feelings weren't worth even a little consideration. As if she didn't have feelings at all.

Was that why Bernard had thought it fine to break up with her over the phone?

As for Italy's Natural Wonder here—she'd seen him in action last night and was under no illusions as to the kind of women he dated or how he treated them. She should be glad she knew how he saw her—a mistake from the past, one he'd been lumbered with and was now doing the best he could to limit damage to his reputation, to his comfort. She knew all about that. Her father had given her early lessons in just how disposable she could be, always putting his needs first, constantly cancelling access visits, until eventually he didn't bother to show up at all.

She needed to keep that in mind. That way she wouldn't be

doing anything silly—as she had last night, when she'd kissed him, or this morning, when she'd kissed him again… Really, she had to stop the kissing!

But none of it explained why this man putting himself first should actually *hurt* her, when Bernard's actions had done nothing more than upset her travel plans. It was baffling.

He was nothing to her.

CHAPTER SEVEN

GIANLUCA STOOD AT THE open window, watching as Ava climbed into a taxi. She was sneaking out again—after he'd given her specific instructions to get herself dressed and join him downstairs.

Very few people defied him, and despite the trouble she had caused he couldn't help admiring her determination.

She'd pinched his coat, which was far too big for her, and with her hair standing up on end and without her shoes she looked like a woman fleeing a morning-after gone awry. It briefly crossed his mind that this was how it must have been all those years ago, when he'd been oblivious upstairs in his bed. His smile deserted him.

He remembered waking and reaching for something—someone—who was no longer there. When he'd realised she was gone, leaving nothing—no note, no contact, no name, just shoes—instead of the relief which had been his usual reaction at that age, when a girl from the night before vanished back into the ether from which she came, possessive instincts he hadn't known he harboured had ramped up and he'd been out of that bed, pulling on his clothes, determined to track her down.

Then the phone call had come...

His father's body had been discovered and taken to the hospital. He had driven there instead, and by the time he'd got around to looking there had been no trace of Cinderella...

Just the shoes she'd left behind.

Those shoes.

Red, with complicated straps.

Si. His expression grew taut and some of the volatility he worked hard to contain tightened his hands on the window frame. It was the shoes he had recognised yesterday on some subliminal level. Not the girl. She had been hidden under layers no self-respecting Roman woman would venture outside in. So completely without style, without manners, and with her femininity clearly of no interest to her. No man would have looked twice at her.

Yet he had.

Which made him suspect something else was at work here.

The cold, rational diagnostics he'd relied on to build one of the most successful trading firms in the world were clearly not standing up to the bone-deep traditions he'd been raised with.

Benedettis didn't show emotion. They put duty above personal desire, gave service to the state. But the customs and currency of his mother's volatile Sicilian family—peasants from the mountains, bandits and priests—meant that when you took a woman's virginity it meant something. Deep down at some primal male level where it was probably best to keep it buried, it had created a bond. In former days he would probably have married her.

Gianluca cleared his throat. Fortunately they were not living in former days. Besides, he was Rome's pre-eminent bachelor. He'd once made the throwaway comment that he'd marry when George Clooney cashed in his single days and it had appeared in print a few days later, out of context, cementing his desirability for a certain ambitious class of woman.

Although Ava seemed not to realise he was a catch. She seemed to find it imperative to run away from him whenever the opportunity afforded itself. He found a growl had risen in the back of his throat as he watched her taxi drive away.

There was no other woman who had left his bed so fast or so anonymously.

Run from him.

Even now something almost primitive drummed inside his skull. She would leave when he told her she could leave. It was a feudal notion, but he wasn't going to step away from his very strong masculine instinct to hold what was his.

In the back of the taxi cab Ava stopped fuming and began rummaging in her bag for her phone.

It was just a bit of harmless research, she told herself, as she tapped his name into a search engine. She wasn't exactly being nosy—just protecting her interests.

She scanned his many entries, wondering where the football-playing career had gone. It seemed to have been swallowed up by venture capital projects, leveraged buyouts, takeovers, private equity deals. All of it involving the kind of financial acumen and strategic planning she hadn't factored in to her admittedly somewhat dated picture of this man.

The family business, she told herself sternly. That was all. He was a Benedetti. Finance was in his blood. The family had always owned banks. Benedetti International, however, was a relatively new entity, and it already dominated the markets. Which meant he must be doing something right.

A little thrown by her discoveries, she pressed on images and the small screen flickered to life with pictures. Her thumb only trembling slightly, she clicked her way through Gianluca Benedetti at film premieres, parties, the FIFA World Cup, a polo match in Bahrain, as a guest at a royal wedding. In nearly every single photo a beautiful girl in a slinky dress was glued to his side.

He certainly didn't seem to have a type. Tall, short, reed-slim, curvy... Her mouth tightened. True to form, *female* seemed to cover it for him. And in numbers.

True, he didn't seem to be serious about any of them—not that it mattered. She would guess that when he finally got around to it, Gianluca Benedetti would do the whole roman-tic proposal/engagement thing properly—if only because he liked to be the best at everything.

The woman would get the full package. He wouldn't need pointers. He'd probably fly one of those leggy heiresses to the Bahamas, whip out a diamond the size of a rock and serenade her with a string orchestra.

Whatever...

Ava snapped her phone shut. What a woman *wouldn't* get from him was an assurance that he wouldn't follow the next fast-moving skirt in the other direction...

Although dullness hadn't stopped Bernard from doing exactly that!

Nice, safe Bernard. Her go-to boyfriend. When people asked *How is your life going?* they didn't mean your business being listed on the stock market—well done. Your employees have reported high enjoyment stats from their job—good on you. You own a place with a harbourside view outright, on your own—fabulous! What people really meant when they talked about 'your life' were your relationships. Everyone wanted you to be in a couple of sorts. To have what they had. Otherwise you stood out too much, you attracted attention, you were *different*. Ava had had enough of being different growing up to last her a lifetime.

Socially, a partner was important, too. You couldn't just turn up to functions on your own.

Meeting Bernard at twenty-nine had been a huge release from those demands. Instead of turning up with a different man on her arm every time—or, worse, alone—she'd had Bernard. People had begun to remember his name. They'd been invited to more intimate functions. People had referred to them as a couple, and gradually they'd become one.

It had suited them both—professionally and personally. If the initial spark between them had never been anything more than a fizzle, they still had a working friendship to fall back on.

But deep down she'd always known that if he left her—unlike when her father had walked out—she wouldn't be heartbroken.

Perhaps the proposal in Rome had been her get-out-of-jail-free card. Perhaps deep down she had known it would push Bernard to make the decision they both knew had been on the cards. It wasn't as if their intimate life had even existed for the last six months. Now she knew why. He'd been going elsewhere, to another woman for *passion*. But she'd hardly noticed—and what on earth did *that* say about her?

The same thing Bernard had said. She just wasn't a passionate woman.

But she did want a little romance. In her longing for that she'd forgotten what her relationship with Bernard had been all about. Practicalities. Practicalities *she* had put in place.

So for five minutes she'd imagined herself into a relationship that didn't exist. A proposal by the Trevi Fountain. A driving tour of Tuscany. Perhaps they'd find an old villa, come back to Italy every summer and restore it... She might even wear a button-front cotton dress and forget to put on her shoes, stomp grapes between her toes... All clichés she'd gathered from films and books about finding oneself in *bella Italia*.

With Bernard?

He had never liked her in a skirt—said a woman with her hips was better off in trousers. She'd been forever buttoning up her shirts for him when he'd said her cleavage made her look like a barmaid. Moreover, *he* wouldn't have been able to restore anything—not with his dust allergy—and as for stomping grapes with his bare feet...well, she couldn't actually remember a time when she had seen him without shoes and socks outside of bed. No, he *did* wear his socks to bed...

The thought depressed her so much Ava sat up a little straighter. Unexpectedly she thought of Gianluca Benedetti's long, well-shaped feet, their smooth olive skin, the way her smaller feet had tangled with his in the white silk sheets.

No, no, *no.*

Grappling with the window, she wound it down and cool air hit her hot face.

She looked out into the busy morning traffic and told herself to do what her deadbeat dad, on the scant occasions she had spent with him as a small girl, had always told her to do when she asked why he didn't live with them anymore and whether it was her fault: toughen up, not ask stupid questions and then she wouldn't get a stupid answer.

Ava closed her eyes. No. No more stupid questions. The sooner she put mileage between herself and His Highness the better.

Safe in her hotel suite, Ava showered and, still slightly damp in her robe, began transferring her clothes into her suitcase, aware she had a scarce half hour before she was expected to be out of there. She was convinced she was doing the right thing. So why was her conscience niggling? Josh didn't really want to see her. He didn't need her. He'd made that plain enough seven years ago and followed it up with such limited contact she no longer phoned him even on his birthday, only sent cards.

Seven years ago in this very city she'd told him she thought he was making a mistake, marrying so young when he had his whole life before him. He in turn had told her the reason he'd fled Australia at the age of eighteen was to get out from under her thumb, and that he had no intention of taking her advice. Furthermore, she knew nothing about love, because the only thing she cared about was her bank balance. If she ever found a man who stuck around it would probably be for her money. She was going to end up rich, disappointed and alone.

Ava noisily zipped up her suitcase. There was a sharp rap on her door. Room Service with her late breakfast.

'It's open!' she called out, her voice a little shaky as she pushed aside the painful memory.

'You should be more careful, *bella*. This is not a safe city for a woman on her own.'

Gianluca strolled in before she could so much as move to slam the door in his face.

'Good to see you've packed—but you need to put some clothes on.'

Ava squeaked her dismay.

'How much luggage do you have? There's not much room in the Jota.'

'I am not going anywhere with you,' she protested, even as she drank in the scent of him so close to her, absorbed the strength of those shoulders clad simply in an open-necked shirt and a sports jacket. How did he manage to look so stylish and at the same time supremely masculine? What was wrong with her that everything female in her leapt at the sight of him? She folded her arms across her traitorous breasts, well aware, given how sensitive they were to him, that everything would be on display.

'Come now.' He smiled down at her, pinched her chin. 'No more games, Ava. We go now.'

She wrenched her chin free, shocked by the intimacy the gesture implied. It made her shriller than she needed to be. 'This isn't a game, Benedetti. I have a car booked. I intend to see Tuscany.'

'Monday.'

'Sorry?'

'I will fly you there myself. Next Monday. But first you must do the right thing, *si*? Join the family.'

'Your family. Not mine.' Something lurched in her chest, because she'd met the Benedettis and they had looked down their noses at her.

'It depends,' he said, brushing the tangle of damp hair out of her eyes as if he had every right to touch her.

Ava tried to avoid his hand but he hooked an unruly lock over her ear.

'Your brother is in some financial difficulty with the vineyard.'

Ava stopped dodging his hand. Now he had her attention. 'What are you talking about?'

'Perhaps his marriage is not in good shape because of this?'

Ava frowned, trying not to enjoy his fingers tangling in her hair, trying to focus on what he was saying about Josh.

She really ought to make him stop.

'Your presence might be—what is it called?—the elixir they need.'

'His marriage is in trouble?'

His hand dropped away from her hair and he picked up her suitcase.

Ava digested this startling news and told herself she wasn't thinking *I told him so. I warned him. I was right.* Josh needed her.

She touched her hair where Gianluca's fingers had played so intrusively.

Suddenly Tuscany didn't seem at all important.

'Why should I believe you?'

He merely hefted her suitcase off the bed.

'Go and put some clothes on, *cara*. We leave in ten minutes.'

He was waiting outside, leaning against the same low-slung machine she'd seen him in the other day.

He looked as if he'd stepped out of the pages of *GQ*—six and a half feet of Italian cool.

Swinging her handbag over her shoulder, she told herself to get moving and to stop ogling him. He was a gorgeous man, but if he knew the power he had over her he was sure to use it against her.

'Well, let's get this over with,' she said.

Gianluca simply stared.

In receipt of his loaded silence, Ava lifted a hand uneasily to her hair, neatly pulled back into what she'd thought was a fetching ponytail.

'What are you staring at?'

'Why are you dressed as a man?'

Convinced she hadn't heard him right, Ava repeated, 'Dressed as—?'

A man?

He was frowning at her. She'd heard him right. Her skin began to feel tight all over and then to prickle.

He thought she looked like a man?

Gianluca Benedetti's expression was a study in masculine perplexity even as Ava wished the ground would swallow her up.

Not looked like a man, she reminded herself. *Dressed as a man. It's not the same thing.*

'It cannot be that you are now a lesbian?'

In any other situation Ava would have reminded herself that she celebrated human sexuality in all its richness and diversity. Right now, under the scrutiny of the most aggressively heterosexual man she had ever known—moreover a man who had kissed her last night and this morning with such a devastating effect on her senses she was still under its influence—she felt as if he'd slapped her.

With a handful of words he'd scraped off the layers of confidence she'd painted on over the years and exposed the sensitive young girl who'd never known her place in the world until she'd toughened up and gone out and made a place for herself. This man had been born gorgeous, entitled and rich. A man who never doubted his place in the world.

'Yes,' she said, tilting up her chin, 'that's exactly what I am. A card-carrying, definitely-no-men-on-board lesbian. Can we go now? The sooner we start out the quicker this will be over.'

He opened her door.

'I can do that myself, you know,' she snapped, and slid inside.

He shut the door with a click.

'I can do that too,' she muttered, stuffing her bag down at her feet and adjusting the seatbelt.

He was beside her but made no move to start the car.

'I thought we were in a hurry,' she said stiffly. She hated that she now felt self-conscious in her tailored black pants and high-necked white silk blouse. There was nothing wrong with her clothes. They were practical.

She eyed his bespoke jacket, the crisp pale green shirt that somehow clung to his broad chest and muscle-packed waist and abdomen as if it had been ironed on, the faithful fit of those dark jeans to his long, powerful legs. He looked as if he'd stepped off the catwalk at Milan, and she had a flash of the sort of woman who would stride off that catwalk with him. Elegant, racehorse-thin, not afraid of colour.

Ava plucked at her sleeve. At least her silk blouse wouldn't crease, and there was absolutely nothing wrong with the black trousers. They gave the illusion of a flat tummy and reduced the impact of her round derrière. She had twelve pairs hanging up in her closet at home. A woman who wasn't reed-thin needed to downplay her lumps and bumps.

He had the body of a Roman athlete, fresh from killing something in the arena. Whatever he wore was going to look good.

Not that she was paying particular attention to how good he looked. No, she was just settling accounts in her head. There were all sorts of reasons she preferred black and white to… Why weren't they going anywhere?

'Why aren't we going anywhere?' she demanded, refusing to look at him.

'I have offended you,' he said unexpectedly.

'Don't be ridiculous,' she muttered.

'I am not accustomed to women wearing trousers.' He spoke carefully, as if choosing his words. 'I shouldn't have implied you lack femininity because of your wardrobe choices.'

Ava felt her stomach hollow out.

'You presuppose I care what you think.'

But she did care. She suddenly wished she'd put on a skirt. But she didn't own a skirt.

She turned her head and immediately wished she hadn't, because he was so close. Too close. She could see where he'd shaved this morning, see the indent of his upper lip, and had a sudden, shocking longing to press her mouth to it.

'I know you were trying to insult me, but it's water off a duck's back,' she informed him, wrenching her attention off his ridiculously sensuous lips. 'What I am about to say will come as a shock to you, as I suspect no woman has ever told you the truth.'

'You could be right.'

'But I'm not afraid of the truth. I like to face things head-on.'

'Go on,' he encouraged, almost gently.

A little thrown, Ava gathered herself together. He wasn't being nice to her. He was just lying low to get her to attack him and then he'd swing in with something insulting that made her feel…made her feel…

'The truth is you're just a handsome face with a lot of money and a habit of control, so women let you get away with murder. I haven't and you don't like that.'

'Is that so?' He was smiling at her as if he saw right through her.

Ava looked away, folding her arms. 'That's so,' she said, and wondered why she didn't sound sure.

CHAPTER EIGHT

GIANLUCA SLOTTED THE Jota in at the circular entrance and leapt out with an energy and purpose that mocked her indecision.

Ava trembled, frustrated by her own complicated desires as she climbed out of the car.

'Why have you brought me back here?'

'It is my home.'

'I understand that,' she said with exaggerated patience, but he was already taking the steps, leaving her standing by the car.

He wasn't giving her any time to think. Ava said something rude under her breath and took off after him.

In the vast entrance hall she was vaguely conscious of the black and white parquet underfoot, the grand shallow staircase ahead. But only because Gianluca was on his way up it.

'Benedetti!'

He didn't respond.

'I demand you answer me!' she shouted, and her voice echoed around them. She jumped, startled.

He lifted his hands in a gesture of male impatience.

'Must we have theatrics every time you fail to notice the obvious?'

Ava was on the verge of informing him that she'd never indulged in theatrics in her life. She was a calm, measured woman and she never shouted... She was only shouting now because he was—which was when she realised he was on the move again. She hurried upstairs after him. Why were they going upstairs? His bedroom was upstairs. *Lots* of bedrooms were upstairs.

'What is obvious?' she demanded, her voice only quavering slightly. 'This is *not* the airport.'

'No, it is my home.'

Ava narrowed her eyes on him. 'At the risk of pointing out more of the obvious, your home is *not* an airport! How do we get from here to Ragusa?'

He stopped so suddenly she ran right into the back of him. Hot, hard and sturdy.

His hand shot out to steady her and excitement flowered inside her as he smiled wolfishly down at her. She wrenched her arm away, glaring at him.

She held her breath.

'Helicopter,' he said simply.

Helicopter? Once they reached the roof Ava was unable to take her eyes off the rotating blades.

She couldn't go up in that.

Moreover, what sort of man had a helipad on the roof of his house?

If you could call this palace a home.

She'd only glimpsed it this morning, in her run for safety, but in the broad light of day, following Gianluca's confident stride up the stairs, along a brightly lit hall, passing an enfilade of windows, she realised it was indeed close to being a palace—in the centre of Rome. No wonder he behaved as if he'd invented the word entitlement.

And here on the roof, with the wind stirring up from the rotorblades roping her hair around her neck, Ava was struck by the view of the city.

Somehow seeing the *palazzo* in broad daylight made it all too real.

But it was the rotating blades that held her in thrall.

'I'm not climbing into *that*!' she shouted as Gianluca gestured for her to follow.

'Too late, *dolcezza*.' His resonant voice was easily heard above the *whup-whup* of the rotors. 'We have an appointment in Ragusa and this is the quickest way to get us there.'

Ragusa. Yes. Of course that was what she wanted too. But he didn't have to make it sound as if he wanted this to be over.

The noise of the rotors put paid to her thoughts as he secured her harness belt. She told herself for the nth time that thousands of people went up in helicopters every year and nobody fell out, and then she had the unexpected thought that he might not be coming with her.

He leaned in. 'Ava, you don't have a problem with heights, do you?'

She shook her head vigorously, finding she didn't have a voice for the words *Don't leave me*, which were sticking in her throat.

'Motion sickness?'

'No,' she choked.

He gave her a long, measured look and then surprisingly lifted one of his hands and stroked her hair.

'Bene.'

She couldn't bear him to be kind to her or she wouldn't be able to do this. Didn't he understand all of this was difficult for her? Being with him after seven years, knowing at the other end of this flight was his family and social scrutiny—something she'd never been able to bear?

Didn't he understand her anger was the only thing holding her together? A welling of hot, harsh fury spouted through her as if in answer to her need, and as he moved to bring the helmet down over her head she thrust her hands up to take it from him.

'I'm not incapable, you know. I *do* ride a bike.'

The pilot beside her let rip a laugh and said something to Gianluca in Italian, too fast and distorted by the noise for her to follow. She imagined it wasn't complimentary.

What she did understand was that he was giving up the controls to Gianluca.

'You're flying this thing?'

'A man should try everything once, *cara*.'

She tried not to enjoy the moment. She really did. But the moment they were in the air her heart almost lifted out of her chest.

Down below lay Rome in all its glory, and beside her, his hands steady on the controls, the scion of one of Rome's most storied families. Beside *her*, ordinary Ava Lord, to whom nothing remarkable ever happened that she hadn't planned, organised and executed herself.

'It's good, yes?'

He was looking at her with those mesmerising eyes, his wide, sensual mouth warm with amusement.

She didn't know what to say without sounding stupid, over-awed, thrilled beyond measure. She felt like a little girl at the top of a rollercoaster.

He gave a husky, appreciative laugh at her baffled expression.

She had to say something. 'When did you learn to fly one of these?'

'In the Marina Militare.'

She hadn't seen that coming. 'You were in the Navy?'

'*Si.*'

'But—' she began, and then stopped. *What? He can't have a life beyond what you allow him, Ava?*

Had she really spent the last seven years with Gianluca Benedetti sitting in a little box marked 'mine'?

'Before or after you were everyone's favourite soccer star?'

'I played football for five minutes professionally, *cara*. It's hardly been my life.'

'I imagined—' She broke off again, because telling him what had been going on in her head for seven years would be far too personal and revealing.

'Ah, *si*, that imagination of yours.'

He reached out unexpectedly and took her hand. His thumb rubbed over her palm, sending sparks shooting up her arm.

'What *have* you been imagining, Ava?'

'Nothing,' she said immediately. *Everything*. All those women! 'I don't have an imagination.' What did he know about her imagination anyway? That had been a long time ago, when she was a little girl who didn't know life was never going to live up to what was in her head.

So she'd faced reality—had to, really—until one day people had begun labelling her as humourless and dull. Always the new girl at school who never got the joke, never made friends, who wore the same unfashionable clothes day after day. It hadn't mattered. She'd been too busy with part-time work, chasing up Josh over his homework and keeping a roof over their heads to worry much about her popularity as a teenager.

She snatched her hand back and he let her go.

'How long were you in the Navy?' she demanded.

'Two years. I flew an Apache on three tours of Afghanistan.'

'You flew in a war zone?'

'*Si*, in a rescue squadron.'

Ava forgot all about her own discomfort. How had she not known this about him?

'Why did you—?'

'Join up? I like to fly,' he said, with a shrug of those wide shoulders. 'I like to challenge myself. The Navy has the best equipment in the world. I wanted to try it out.'

'That's the worst reason I've ever heard for joining the armed forces.'

'There are worse reasons.' He looked grim for a moment. 'Besides, what would I know? I was just a dumb footballer.'

'I doubt you were ever a dumb anything,' she replied acerbically, 'given what you've achieved. And you're not yet thirty-one!'

'I didn't say I wasn't a *lucky* dumb footballer.'

Ava tried not to stare at him. 'So you joined your father's business after all?'

He shot another look at her. 'You do remember a great deal, for a woman who wants to forget, *cara*.'

She could feel herself colouring—and she *never* blushed.

'I didn't join anything,' he continued blandly. 'By the time I got out of the Navy the Benedetti private banking firm was defunct.'

'But you had connections?' she persevered.

He laughed, but it sounded flat, and Ava felt obscurely guilty for bringing up the subject.

'I came out with nothing but a Maserati, which I sold. I invested in a friend's boat-building business…moved on up from there. Venture capital is high-risk, and most people don't have the stomach for it.'

She knew that. She was one of those people.

'I take it you do?' Ava's mouth was dry as paper.

'What do you think?'

Her eyes were glued to his hard-jawed profile. Suddenly so much made sense about him—the big, physically tough body that didn't fit a man who wheeled and dealed on the money markets, the flintiness she sensed at his core.

He had been to war, and it seemed things hadn't quite worked out the way she had imagined. He wasn't just some spoiled boy who had been handed his life on a platter.

Ava didn't quite know what to say. She settled on a very weak, 'You *have* been busy.'

He chuckled.

'What's so funny?'

'Your expression. It's getting hard, isn't it, *cara*?'

'Pardon?'

'Finding reasons to dislike me.'

'I haven't said I dislike you.' It was supposed to come out as a statement, but it sounded far too uncertain for her liking.

'We should look at doing something together.'

Still sorting through her feelings, she found a highly intimate recollection of the things they had done together flash unexpectedly to mind. Ava felt her face heating.

'Do something?' she repeated airlessly.

He gave her a smile, as if he knew where her thoughts had gone.

'*Si.* You're clearly very talented.'

'I am?' *Oh, good grief, he's not talking about sex, Ava!*

'The Lord Trust Company—a full-service brokerage firm, founded four years ago.' He grinned and her stomach flip-flopped. 'You've got some loyal clients.'

Business. He's talking about your business, she reminded herself. She frowned. 'You've researched me?'

'I'm always looking for new companies to add to my portfolio. If you want to expand.'

She had almost forgotten this was a man who prowled the stock markets of the world like a ravening beast.

For the first time in many years she couldn't have given a damn about her business. Her gaze dropped to his hands, so capable on the controls, and she flashed to an image of those hands so dark against her milk-pale flesh. Of herself arching into them, so utterly uninhibited she couldn't quite believe she had ever been that girl.

'Ava?'

She blinked at him, bemused, and his answering slow smile had her heart doing a *pah-pound, pah-pound* rhythm.

'When did you research me?' she uttered, with a suddenly dry mouth.

The slow smile increased. 'This morning over coffee.'

'Funny—I did the same with you.' Her gaze dropped helplessly to his mouth.

'What did you discover?'

'Enough. But somehow not everything…'

His smile faded.

'Benedetti International is a far-flung enterprise, *cara*, even I have trouble keeping track of our interests.'

She highly doubted that—Gianluca Benedetti struck her as a man who knew what he was about at all times and she would be a fool to forget it. But it was a shock to realise she hadn't been thinking about business at all. Her thoughts had been entirely taken up with his private life, which really was none of her affair. She gave him an anxious look, thrown by her own response to him.

The mountainous terrain below was giving way to the coast, and Ava risked craning her neck to see it rather than confront where her thoughts were leading her.

The cliffs were stupendous, falling away into the water. Towns clung to the sides. She had seen picture postcards of the Amalfi Coast, but hadn't quite believed it was this pretty.

'It's beautiful, *si*?' he said softly.

'Yes, beautiful. I wish—' She stopped and his eyes captured hers.

'What do you wish, *cara*?' he asked, like the devil after her soul.

What did she wish? Too many things—and they came over her in a rush.

To be the girl she had been on that long-ago night—softer, willing to share her feelings for the first and only time in her life, instead of being constantly on her guard against being attacked, ridiculed, exposed...let down.

Her early years had taught her too many harsh lessons about showing vulnerability. About people taking advantage, not living up to their promises. She had applied those lessons to business and they had steered her well.

But she had also applied them when she'd climbed out of his bed seven years ago, and right at this minute she wished with all her heart that she had made a different decision that morning—that against all odds something could have come of that night.

Even more fancifully she wished for this to be a romantic trip away together, at the beginning of their relationship, when everything was full of possibility—and for him not to be a playboy, spoilt by too many women, and herself not to be a woman who prided herself on playing it safe.

It was foolish, and her wistful expression was undoubtedly

telling him everything she didn't want him to know, and yet she couldn't stop the feelings from rushing in…

It was a shock when his expression unexpectedly hardened with determination.

With a quiet, 'Hold on,' Gianluca angled the helicopter and without warning they swooped inland.

At first she thought he was giving her a better look at the town clinging to the cliffs, and then she realised they were dropping down just below the mountain peak. Too low. Much, much too low.

Ava's pulse began to surge.

Directly beneath them was a helipad above a grove of pines.

With a sense of inevitability she realised she was going to get her wish. They were going to land.

CHAPTER NINE

THE ENGINE CUT and the rotors slowed and whirred to a gradual halt. Gianluca whipped off his helmet, tackling his harness with the same economy of movement.

'What's going on? What are we doing here?'

'I've got a meeting I should have taken in Rome today,' he responded, as if he were stating the obvious. 'I've decided to take it in Positano.'

Ava's mouth fell open. 'You're *what*?'

But he was already leaping out, leaving her sitting harnessed to her seat. He'd done this on purpose. She felt sure he did *everything* on purpose to undermine and confuse her. Frustrated, Ava began tugging at the belts, getting herself hopelessly tangled up.

She knew she was overreacting, but her own longings suddenly felt entirely too dangerous in this new situation.

'This was *not* what we agreed to,' she erupted as he came alongside her, his capable hands taking hold of the harness.

'Relax, *cara*,' he advised. She wasn't sure if he meant over being kidnapped or to make it easier for him to unhook her.

'The hard part's over.'

A little stunned that he'd recognised her fear of heights when she thought she'd hidden it so well, Ava held still long enough for him to unhook and free her. She wanted to slap away the hand he offered, but falling flat on her face wouldn't be a good look, so she took the assistance he proffered and concentrated on disembarking.

She wasn't sure how it happened, but in stepping down she pitched forward. He caught her, and she was suddenly very conscious of her soft breasts pressed up against his hard chest. A memory of the last time they'd been this close flamed to mind. His hands settled on her hips. Her legs did a little wobble.

'The hotel here is owned by a friend of mine,' he was saying.

She tried to wriggle free, but it only provided friction between them. Friction she didn't need! His mouth felt far too close to her ear.

'We relax, enjoy the amenities, you tell me about yourself and we go from there, *si*?'

Go where? What was he talking about? She trembled as one of his hands drifted to her waist, tightened.

He drew back, his eyes intent on hers.

'Seven years is a long time, Ava. We have a lot of catching up to do.'

Ava's heart stuttered to a halt.

What was he saying? Was he saying what she thought he was saying?

She gave a little gasp. What was he doing with his hand? Somehow her shirt had come a little adrift of her pants and his rough, broad fingers slid underneath. She felt the firm press of his large dry palm shaping the indent of her waist and the flare of her hip under her waistband. Lightly stroking. His long fingers stretched higher over her ribs and Ava caught her breath, her breasts swelling, her nipples tightening with anticipation.

'Stop it!' she hissed. But she wasn't quite sure who she was addressing, and there was a suspicious lack of force behind it.

Two men were coming up the slope to the helipad from the gardens, their voices intruding, and with a powerfully intent look Gianluca released her and turned away to deal with them as if nothing out of the ordinary had happened. When *every-thing* had just happened to her.

She heard him issuing instructions in Italian, something about their luggage, and realised she was still just standing where he'd left her, with her shirt adrift, gazing stupidly after him.

'Oh, good grief,' she muttered, and rapidly began stuffing the hem of her shirt into her waistband, mortified. What was she *doing*, letting him feel her up like a teenage girl? Where was her dignity?

She walked up to him and stopped a good metre away, arms folded. 'What do you think you're playing at, Benedetti?'

He looked her up and down, as if everything about her amused him, but she saw he was noticing where a little of her shirt still hung loose. She tucked it in fast with her free hand, aware she hadn't exactly been fighting him off.

'Glad to see the flight hasn't dented your charm, *cara*,' he observed with a bit of a smile. 'But next time you throw yourself into my arms give me fair warning and I'll try to arrange it so we don't have an audience.'

Ava's gaze shot to the men dealing with their luggage.

'I did not throw myself at you,' she hissed.

But he was already heading down the steps.

'I thought the idea was to get from A to B as efficiently as possible,' she called after him.

'This is most efficient. I conduct a little business; you enjoy a little down time; we keep each other company.'

'Company?'

He shrugged those wide shoulders.

'My brother—' she began, hurrying to keep up with his long strides.

'Twenty-four hours ago you cared so little for your brother you refused to answer his phone calls.'

Ava stared at his back in horror. 'How do you know that?'

'What is more, you never had any intention of seeing him. I cannot help but wonder, *cara*, if this sudden overwhelming need to rush to his side has more to do with spending time with *me*.'

Ava almost choked.

'And, as I have already told you…' He stopped and she almost ran into his back. As he turned around she backed up. 'I am most happy to accommodate you.'

'Accommodate me?'

'My English…' He shrugged, but she caught the amusement lurking in those golden eyes.

His English was bloody perfect, she thought, feeling hot all over.

She followed him out of the hot sun into a southern coastal garden, with a wide, sandy path underfoot, narrowing as it wound down through the trees. But Ava was too focussed on the lean, muscular physique of the man in front of her to pay it much mind.

From his attitude he clearly expected her to fall into line with his wants and needs. *Keep him company!* She eyed his lean, muscular physique resentfully.

He could find all the company he wanted, but it wouldn't be hers.

The minute she was in possession of her belongings again she would make arrangements and be out of here so fast he wouldn't know what had hit his privileged behind.

Unnecessarily her eyes were drawn to that behind… Incredibly taut, it made a masterpiece of those fitted dark jeans.

'I don't know why you ever imagined I would let you get away with this,' she called after him.

He continued walking down the path, moving with that easy, wide-shouldered grace she could only envy. She hobbled behind him.

'Bringing me here like some sort of concubine.'

'You really need to get this imagination of yours under control, *cara*. I have a meeting.'

'And I've already told you I don't have an imagination.

You're unbelievable. *You* have a meeting. What about *my* meetings, my life? That's all on hold!'

'You are on holiday.' He turned around and Ava tried not to be swayed by his warm eyes, his half tilted mouth. He looked completely relaxed, and she felt…she felt…

'Yes, my *holiday*.' She seized on the concept, veering away from those inconvenient longings. 'And you're such a Neanderthal you think you can just hijack it on a whim.'

'That is the second time you have compared me to our early ancestors.' He suddenly looked like a big cat, deciding whether to take a swipe.

Ava felt a little uneasy. She hadn't actually thought he was paying attention to her insults. How worried should she be that he was keeping score?

'I wonder why,' she shot back.

'I have a contemporary outlook,' he said simply.

'Yes, that's apparent,' she snapped.

He raised an enquiring brow.

'You behave like…like a Roman Caesar. You have run roughshod over my wishes from the moment we met. You critique my clothes, as if as a woman I should only be dressing for a man!'

'It is clear you do not,' he responded, resuming his stride.

Ava ignored him. 'You behaved last night as if I'd committed a crime by informing you that we were previously—' she cast about for a suitable neutral description for a night she had never forgotten and came up with '—acquainted.'

'I was naturally cautious.'

She snorted. 'I'm sure you encounter predatory women all the time. How disappointing for you that I'm not one of them!'

'Yes, we would possibly have less trouble now.'

Brought up short, Ava frowned and halted. She wasn't sure if there was an insult in that comment, or a backhanded compliment, but it was clear as day which sort of woman he'd prefer.

'I feel sorry for you,' she slung at his broad back. 'Never knowing if a woman is interested in you or your bank balance.'

He shrugged.

'And you're promiscuous. You lecture me, but *you*, Benedetti, are a playboy of the worst kind. You treat women like playthings. That sort of thinking went out in the Seventies, along with Sean Connery playing James Bond.'

'Connery continued to play Bond into the Eighties,' he inserted dryly as they approached a large gate cut like a keyhole into the stone wall. He gave her a shockingly charismatic smile over his shoulder. 'But do go on. I would like to hear some more of your opinion of me.'

He thought this was funny!

'No, you wouldn't. What you want is to be praised. All men do.'

'*All* men? This would come from your vast experience of my sex, *cara*?'

Ava looked around for a rock. She needed one heavy enough to cause some damage when she threw it at his head.

He turned, folding his arms across his chest. 'Tell me about all these men.'

Ava suddenly wished she'd slept with a hundred men. She wished she had put the last seven years to better use. Right at this very moment it seemed as if bed-hopping would have been a far better utilisation of her time than attaching herself to a dull, self-effacing man and building a business with a national reputation.

She gritted her teeth.

'I don't know how you dare to stand in judgement on my sex life when your own is nothing to brag about.'

He gestured with one hand, as if he didn't have a clue what she was talking about. 'What is this bragging?'

Ava didn't know. She didn't really know anything about him other than how he made her feel. Out of her depth, out of bounds, a little crazy.

Passionate.

Her thoughts came to a juddering halt. *Look at me*, she thought, a little light-headedly. *Burning up like a firework ever since he came strolling back into my life...*

'It's obvious you're proud of your reputation,' she rattled on, desperately holding on to her anger. Because this man might have strolled in, but he would also stroll out. Guys like Benedetti didn't stick.

'You think sleeping with hundreds of women makes you such a man, when really all it makes you is cheap.'

He had been watching her with a slight smile, his big shoulders relaxed, as if she were providing some form of impromptu entertainment, but her last words had hit their mark, because the smile got lost and his jaw hardened.

Right—good. Ava realised she had unconsciously balled up her hands into fists.

'Yes, cheap—to be had by anyone if she hitches up her skirt and bats her eyelashes at you.'

He closed the space between them and Ava had to force herself to hold her ground. The scent of him took up an assault on her hormones, making her a little dizzy.

'As I recall you did both those things last night,' he said in a low voice, his eyes moving over her face, 'and yet still I refused you.'

His words went through her like an Italian stiletto knife, right under the ribs.

'Well, lucky me,' she forced out airlessly. 'What a near miss.'

He bent his head just slightly, because he was already worryingly close, and his breath feathered her ear.

'Nowhere near, *cara*,' he said.

Three little words and everything—her stomach, her anger and her somehow connected fizz of arousal—all dropped away with a clang.

He turned around and unlocked the gate, giving it a good shove. He seemed angry all of a sudden. He had no right to be. *She* was the one being pushed around, insulted.

Yet suddenly all she felt was shut out.

The gate creaked and the door broke open onto a brightly lit road outside. He walked through and waited for her on the other side.

Ava came blinking out into the bright southern light. It was hot, but she felt cold, and her attention wasn't on her surroundings. It was on his words.

Feeling a little lost, she found herself blurting out her uncertainties.

'I did not come on to you. I did not bat my eyes and—and lift up my skirt.'

'As you say.'

'I might have been drunk last night, but I'd remember that.'

'*Si*, you were.'

'Were what?'

'Drunk.'

Ava tried to shake off the feeling that she had lost something she'd almost had her hand on for a moment in that garden.

'Oh, and you were *such* a gentleman!'

'Yes, I was.'

He said it with such lethal quiet that she shivered and really didn't want to hear what came next. She watched him walk ahead of her down the winding road. A vista of pine treetops and a glimpse of blue sea lay before them. It was so incredibly lovely, but all Ava wanted to do was grab him and shake him and…and *prove* to him there was something between them.

The realisation brought her up short.

Was that what this was all about? Was he right? Was she here because she *did* want to spend more time with him?

'I did not take advantage of you,' he repeated, 'and yet you harp on about it as if you are disappointed, *cara*. You can't have it both ways. Either you attempted to avail yourself of this reputation of mine you speak of, or you drank so much alcohol last night you no longer cared. I can't say that either of those scenarios reflect well on you, but go ahead and choose and we will abide by that version.'

Ava gaped at him. The sun suddenly felt harsh and unbearable, beating down on the back of her vulnerable neck.

She began to jog a little to keep up with him.

'It wasn't like that at all. You've just twisted everything!'

He shrugged, boredom implicit in the gesture. 'I am no longer interested in any of this, Ava. If you want to justify your own behaviour go and talk it out with a therapist—isn't that what women like you do?'

'Women like me?' she parroted.

'Highly strung, too much time on your hands, with sexual needs that obviously aren't being met.'

Ava absorbed the impact of his opinion of her. It was wrong. It was *so* wrong. He had it all *wrong*.

But somehow in that moment she thought he might be right.

Playboy. Lothario. User of women. Slave to his libido.

Where did she get this from?

He unlocked the doors and shoved them open, waiting for the dust to settle before he moved inside.

Anyone who hitches up her skirt and bats her eyelashes...

Yet he'd heard those words before, hadn't he? And from thinner, far harsher lips.

His father, yelling so hard his face had turned puce. Spittle hitting the wall. Himself, seven years younger—a lifetime ago, it seemed now, shoving his broad young shoulders back and, for the first time in their disastrous relationship, giving back as good as he got. *Better.* He was signing a second contract with the Italian team, he had no intention of doing military service, and as for his social life if he wanted to screw every last woman in Rome he'd give it his best shot.

Was that when the pains had started? Had his unnatural colour been the first sign? Could he have stepped in even then, put his arm around his father, eased him into a chair, fetched the doctor, an ambulance—assistance?

It was never going to go away—the guilt—and damn Ava Lord for bringing it all up again.

He'd left her on the roadside, not trusting himself with her until his temper cooled off. He'd had to get off the mountain, and the usual scenic way—the steps that plunged down the side of a cliff to the road below—was not available to a woman who turned milk-white a hundred feet in the air.

Maybe that was why he'd landed them both on the coast—the gesture of a man who was used to women falling in with his plans, no questions asked. He'd stumbled badly there. But that glimpse of vulnerability in the air had made him want to look after her.

Throwing her off the cliff in a sack would have been the way one of his ancestors would have dealt with her.

He would have to be more creative.

He pulled the tarpaulin cover off the bike, kicked out the stand and pushed it onto the road.

She wasn't like any woman he'd ever known. Something about fighting with her was turning him on, and he was a man who made it a point of honour not to involve himself in disputes with women. He'd seen too many of them growing up, between his parents. They were inevitably messy and emotional, and a man never won.

No, women didn't fight with him… They pouted and sulked and made silly little threats, but in the end they did exactly what they were supposed to do. Looked good and provided a little light entertainment.

Yet in the last two days he'd been angered, provoked, amazed, and he was in the grip of a powerful combination of feelings—primarily sexual. *Si*, he could vouch for the sexual, and it was definitely starting to become painful.

Dressed as she was, spitting insults at him, the antithesis of everything feminine and polished—he still wanted her with a fierce pull that was beyond his previous experience.

That she seemed utterly ignorant of her power over him was the saving grace.

Although he was beginning to think even that was wilful.

Crazy woman. He started the bike up. It purred like a kitten. A slow smile curved his mouth. She'd love this. She could hardly sulk on the back of the Ducati.

'*Grazie bene. Molto bene.* This has been most kind of you.'

Having exhausted her schoolgirl Italian, Ava waited and waved to the old man as he made his way back down the path towards a stone foundry.

She stood in the dappled sunshine by a water pump, wondering what Gianluca was doing. Probably at the hotel already, kicking back with some sort of exotic drink and a blonde who, in Ava's imagination, resembled to the letter Donatella... He'd probably sent some lackey looking for her when he'd found her gone, so he didn't have to explain to his precious family how he'd lost her.

Screwing up her face, she mimicked the blonde in her mind. *Oh, Gianluca, you're so wonderful, everything you do is wonderful, let me take off more clothing...*

She ground her teeth together.

Far better that she concentrated on what she could improve for herself. It had been a long day, and it wasn't over by a long shot. She should take this time to regroup, not to fixate on Gianluca Benedetti's sex life and her lack of one.

It was private here, cooler too. Paolo had told her she was welcome to stay as long as she wished, but they would be leaving at five, using an old track direct to the village, and she was welcome to go with them. He'd given her a clay jug to fill with water and she concentrated on filling it.

She had no intention of hanging around. She'd essay that track by herself. But first she wanted to freshen up. She felt hot and sweaty in her clothes, but something about concentrating on the water splashing into the jug was bringing her a measure of peace.

After a quick reconnaissance of the area she determined she was alone and removed her shirt. She splashed cold water from the tap all over her arms and back, chest and belly. It trickled into the waistband of her accursed trousers and she was oh so tempted to rip them off too. But that would have to wait until she was behind a closed door. She determined one thing. When she got back to Sydney she was making a bonfire of them—all twelve pairs—and then she was going on a sexual rampage through the adult male population of Sydney. He'd see who was highly strung and sexually frustrated then!

CHAPTER TEN

GIANLUCA COULDN'T BELIEVE what he was seeing.

She was half stripped and pouring water over herself from a jug. Pouring it over bare, gleaming skin. The clear water, shot with gold at this angle, was gushing out of the pump and Ava had bent over to plunge her arms underneath it, splashing water down her back. She stood up and shook herself completely unselfconsciously.

She jiggled. *Everything* jiggled.

He found himself scanning the area for perverts even as he advanced on her, not entirely sure what his purpose was at this point.

He'd come back for her with the bike, only to spend the last half hour tracking her down. Naturally she'd come back into the garden and wound up at the foundry, but instead of finding a contrite woman he discovered a wood nymph.

She must have heard his tread, but she ignored him and ran more water over the back of her neck, then cupped her hands and brought some into her mouth.

It was too much. He reached down and cut off the flow with an aggressive snap.

'Hey!' she coughed.

He shoved her shirt at her. 'Cover yourself up.'

She turned around and his gaze instantly dropped to her breasts, to the gleaming, glistening rivulets of water running down those slopes in a race to see which was going to soak the white cotton bra first.

He recognised that she was saying something but it got lost in the roar of testosterone currently running at full throttle through him—the kind of overload that made a man say, do, be anything required to stay perfectly still, beholding something designed to turn him into a blithering idiot.

His gaze dropped a little further to the revelation of how her ribs narrowed to a beautifully indented waist, and below her hips flared out almost outrageously. The ugly trousers had lost their top button and hung from the widest point of her hips, revealing her navel and a masterpiece of a soft female belly. Like most men, he really wasn't enamoured of a flat female stomach, and his fingers flexed as he resisted the temptation to touch her there, to stroke her, to test the softness, before his hand moved lower…

He distinctly heard her say, 'Get a grip, Benedetti.'

His attention bounced back to her breasts. The bra was definitely opaque now. Strawberry pink nipples were visible.

Astounded by his lack of self-control, he snarled at her, 'Put the shirt on—*Dio*!'

When she just stood there, blinking like a rabbit in a gun's sights, he took hold of one of her hands and began pushing it through an armhole.

She jerked away from him and hurriedly pulled the shirt over her shoulders, turning her back on him.

He took a couple of steps back, struck by the way he was behaving. Like a madman.

So what if she was standing around in her underwear? He'd had girlfriends in the past who didn't seem to possess a bikini top, who paraded around poolside, and frankly he couldn't have cared less.

Why had he complicated something so utterly simple with this farce? He should never have brought her here. He should have withstood his desire to have her to himself and kept to his plan to take her to Ragusa. Instead he now had her halfway up a mountain with very limited options for getting her down. He should be focussing on those logistics, not on this overwhelming need to corral her. He would explain to her about traditional attitudes and the need to respect them. She would keep herself buttoned up. She would behave, in truth, like the twenty-year-old Sicilian virgin his mother would prefer him to marry. Only then could he relax.

He watched Ava fighting her way into her shirt, muttering something about him being a prude, all the while trying to cover herself up. Her head was bent and he could see the soft kiss curls made by her hair at the base of her neck, at odds with her unforgiving clothes.

Tenderness unexpectedly backhanded him.

When Ava had heard him coming her heart leapt because he'd actually come looking for her. But her first instinct—to be modest, to cover herself up—she had thrown aside.

After all, stab-your-heart-out-blondes didn't have a problem with advertising their wares.

Oh, she'd known she was playing with fire, but deep down an entirely feminine part of her psyche had wanted a little payback.

Sexually frustrated, was she? Well, two could play at that game.

But he'd looked at her as if he was made of stone.

She'd thought her breasts looked pretty good in this bra. Not perky—you couldn't be her size and shoot for the moon… although given this man had had close personal contact with some spectacularly beautiful women he was probably used to the stay-up-on-their-own-thanks-to-a-surgeon variety.

Ava shut down on that line of thought. It didn't help.

'The people here are conservative,' he imparted roughly. 'This isn't your Bondi Beach, with its topless women, and nor is it Positano. This is part of a small mountain village. Show some respect.'

Still feeling beleaguered by all those gorgeous women with more noteworthy breasts he had access to—no doubt he didn't yell at *them* and do his best to cover them up—Ava lost her temper.

'Respect?' she muttered, fumbling with the buttons. 'Why don't you start showing *me* some respect? This whole mess is all your fault to begin with. You're the one who wanted to take the scenic tour of Italy…'

She turned around, only to find he was standing right behind her. She looked up and blinked. He had an odd, entirely too satisfied look on his face.

She gave a soft gasp as he picked her up and tossed her potato-sack fashion over his shoulder.

'Put me down!' she shrieked. But apparently one hundred and fifty pounds of wriggling woman didn't deter a man who had been pushed to his limit, and Ava was getting the distinct impression this might be the case.

As he waded through the undergrowth she stopped struggling and sagged a little against him. Gianluca only put her down when they reached the road.

She spotted the red Ducati immediately.

'What's this?'

'Transport down the mountain.'

As he spoke he straddled the bike.

Ava's feet had frozen. She was *not* strapping herself to his back on that thing.

'Sorry, Benedetti. Been there, done that…'

'Get on the bike, Ava.'

Something about the tone of his voice, the fact he was not quite looking at her, and the way she was feeling—tired, confused, and a little overwhelmed at seeing the bike—had her doing as he asked.

He fired up the four-stroke engine. It purred and crackled with energy. She approached and slid carefully onto the seat. There wasn't much room. Her pelvis was smack up against his hard rear, her inner thighs pressing against his lean, muscled hips. She held herself as stiffly as she could, but he was big and warm and solid, and as they took off her hands groped instinctively for his waist. She tightened them over slabs of hard muscle and heat and swore she felt them move.

Her thighs melted as if on cue. This was *not* good.

The bike leapt as they hit the road. He took the corners on the narrow ribbon of mountain road at speed. Without helmets there was some risk involved. But something else was riding him. She could feel the tension in his big body. Which was just fine by her, because none of this was her idea of fun either. Except for the part about her entire body buzzing and tingling like an electrical storm. But she put that down to proximity and friction.

'Next time remind me to take a bus,' she commented as he braked and they pulled over to allow a small car to pass on the single road ribboning down the mountain.

'*Si?* You would last five minutes, *cara*. The minute you opened that fine mouth of yours the driver would dump you on the roadside.'

She relaxed slightly. This was good. This she could do.

'Careful, Benedetti, or I'll jump off—and how are you going to explain *that* to your mother and Alessia?'

'Believe me, *bella*, once they meet you nobody will question me for dumping you.'

He gunned the engine and they took off again.

Ava guessed she deserved that one. If she was going to dish them out, she had to take them. But she knew well enough that neither woman liked her particularly, and the reminder recalled her to the reality of her situation. She'd almost forgotten in the excitement what this was all about, and her heart started to thump to an irregular, painful beat she recognised.

'Hold on,' he instructed, and he angled them off the road where they hit an unsealed track. Within minutes it became increasingly rocky.

Bouncing behind him, she shouted, 'This wasn't your best idea!'

'It's a damn sight safer than the road,' he responded grimly, 'and the benefit is, you get to live.'

'With bruises on my posterior!'

'Keep looking at the upside, *cara*.'

They hit a rut and her bottom came down hard on the seat. She moaned.

'You did that on purpose!'

'Sometimes fate takes a hand.'

This wasn't fun any more. She was tired of all the fighting, mostly engineered by herself, to keep him at arm's length. But he seemed to be taking some enjoyment in shaking her up. She fell quiet, concentrating on not coming down too hard on the seat.

To her surprise he was braking gently, gradually bringing the bike to a halt. His movements were careful, deliberate. The brake, the ignition, the footrest. The dreadful sudden silence.

Ava looked around at the craggy rocks rising up above them and for some reason she panicked.

'What now?' she asked nervously. 'You get off, push the bike into the ravine and I'm never heard of again?'

He shifted around and she jerked back, unable to unhook her legs. She was stuck. On a bike, in the back of beyond, with a man who seemed to be all brawn and muscle. And she'd been poking him with a big sharp stick. All day.

His golden eyes moved over her with unsettling directness, and under his scrutiny she could feel her cheeks starting to burn.

'We need to get this out of our systems,' he asserted roughly.

Ava could have put her hand over her heart in that moment and sworn it was the last thing she'd expected him to say.

'S-sorry?'

'What is the Australian saying? We need to screw like rabbits until the novelty's worn off.'

Ava gaped. 'We *what*?'

'Is the vernacular wrong?'

She was about to tell him exactly how wrong he was, even as her pulse sped up, when she caught the glint in his golden eyes from beneath those sinfully thick black lashes and everything painful and wrong about her life tumbled away.

He wasn't laughing at her, she realised. He was including her in the joke. And with that a very important piece of that long-ago jigsaw moved into place. She remembered—*this was how he'd made her feel.* As if she wasn't on the outside looking in any more. As if it were all about him and her, their own exclusive little club.

'Yes, the vernacular is wrong,' she said a little faintly.

He smiled at her and she felt her heart lift, as if it were attached to strings connected to his wide, sensual mouth.

Her own mouth twitched. She was *not* going to laugh.

'And I can assure you that won't be happening,' she followed up quickly. But as much as she tried to sound prim and decisive it all collapsed as everything tense and painful inside her unravelled.

He reached over and did something so unexpected she stopped breathing. He cradled her cheek with his hand, forcing her to look at him, following the curve of her cheekbone gently with the pad of his thumb.

'So we are agreed?'

She wanted to push his hand away, bristle like a cat under a pail of water, but this sudden gentleness on his part brought her ridiculously ready emotions to the surface. She blinked rapidly.

'You remind me of those little porcupines, rolling into a ball of bristles to protect yourself, but underneath you have this soft, velvety little belly.'

'Porcupines are rodents,' she retorted, wondering if that reference to her belly was because, unlike the women he dated, *she* had one. 'Trust you to compare me to a pest.'

Then she realised she'd just scrambled to protect herself—exactly as he'd said.

'What is it you're running from? What is it that threatens you, Ava?' His voice was quiet and he continued to stroke her.

Her heart was fluttering wildly. She could feel herself wanting to lean against him, of all things wanting to confide in him, tell him how confused she was feeling, being back here in Italy with him, wondering if she had made a terrible mistake seven years ago and not wanting to make a worse one now.

She looked into his eyes and he smiled. 'You find me attractive, *si*? It is nothing to be ashamed of.'

Saved by his ego! She knocked his hand away. Just as all sorts of longings had risen to the surface they were swamped by his incredible arrogance. 'Oh, yes, *all* women must find you utterly irresistible. It just must gall you to know I'm immune.'

'Immune?' His fingers, so gentle on her cheek, drummed lightly on the frame of the bike. 'How much easier this would be if you were. I wouldn't have to put up with your constant attention-seeking.'

'Attention-*what*? I'm doing nothing of the sort.' She looked away, because if she was honest it was a whopper of a lie. She had been enjoying having his whole attention all day. 'It's just your colossal ego,' she muttered.

'I seem to remember you admired my ego seven years ago, *cara*.'

Ava swung around. 'I don't want to talk about that!'

'Yes, you do,' he growled. 'It's all you want to talk about.'

Caught off guard by the truth, she lashed out. 'I was stupid. You took advantage of me!'

'You were the older woman,' he inserted with that incredible cool.

Ava shot him an incredulous look. 'I can't believe you're throwing my age at me!'

He made an impatient gesture of disbelief with one hand and with another movement slid his hand into the backpack strapped behind the bike. He uncapped a bottle and thrust it at her.

'What's that for?'

'To cool you down. I don't have a bucket of water to hand.'

'I'm not the one talking about rabbits,' she grumbled, irritated because she was breathless all of a sudden. Even fighting with him turned her on. This was most unlike her! She took a swallow and handed it back to him.

He didn't wipe the rim, just took a swig. Ava watched the muscles working in his throat and tried not to stare.

It was so unfair. Everything about him made her want to jump him.

She literally *felt* him smile as he recapped the bottle.

'I would never have slept with you if I'd been in the right frame of mind that night,' she muttered, more to herself than to him.

He stilled, and the easy amusement was suddenly long gone. *'Cosa?'*

She hadn't meant it, but she discovered she couldn't back down. If she did he would see too much—her fear of intimacy—and he'd put two and two together. She feared that exposure more than his anger.

'You heard me.' She avoided his eyes. 'I was upset and not thinking straight and you were in like a shot.'

'I think you should get your facts straight, Signorina Lord,' he drawled, those golden eyes watchful, 'before you start making accusations.'

Ava swallowed hard, staring past him, chin up. She *so* didn't want to have this conversation here and now. It was too intimate, there was nowhere to run to, and he was right beside her—seeing too much, holding the power to slice and dice her fragile ego.

'You threw yourself at me,' he observed, as if he were commenting on the weather.

Ava flinched.

'You did it last night, and you did it seven years ago,' he continued remorselessly. 'It seems to be your modus operandi, *tesoro*. I'm guessing I shouldn't feel flattered.'

As she absorbed the impact of his opinion of her the motorbike's engine roared into life again and Ava gripped the hard column of his waist.

He didn't say anything else all the way down the mountain—because, really, what more was there to say?

CHAPTER ELEVEN

THE HOTEL, LIKE EVERYTHING about Gianluca Benedetti, was not what she'd expected. It was subtle and charming and took advantage of the best water views in Positano.

As he crossed the foyer, shirt half unbuttoned, sleeves shoved up to the elbows, hand-tooled shoes dusty and scuffed, Gianluca still managed to look like an advertisement for a high-end men's fragrance—one of those where a guy came out of water or walked down a beach or gazed knowingly over the naked body of a lithe, bronzed woman.

Ava was all too aware she looked like a woman who had been dragged backwards through the underbrush.

A posse of beautiful leggy girls on their way out fluttered and smiled and broke into a flurry of giggles as Gianluca held the door for them.

Completely unnecessary, as far as Ava could see. They had arms and hands, didn't they?

One of the women stopped to speak to him. Did he *have* to linger?

Flirt.

Her heart started to pound, and not in a good way. Well, that was fine. She could look after herself.

She folded her arms and looked around. She spotted the welcome desk and headed over.

She was just handing over her passport when a deep voice intruded, 'She has a room, Pietro.'

Ava ignored him.

'As I was saying, I would like a single.'

But the desk clerk was looking over her shoulder. Frustrated, Ava rounded on Gianluca. 'Could you butt out?'

He merely looked at her, with stone-cold disapproval, and Ava's bravado-meter dipped.

Because she was behaving this way for the most obvious reason. She was jealous.

'Notice me!' was what she wanted to say. But what would he notice? A tired, grubby, irritable woman who had done nothing but snipe at him all day.

'I'm sorry,' she said, sounding stiff and all wrong yet again. 'That was rude of me—'

'It's been a long day already, Ava, and I have business to attend to,' he interrupted. 'I'll have a car made ready for you in the morning to take you on to Rome, or Ragusa. Whichever you prefer.'

What she preferred was to put her head on his shoulder and apologise for every horrible thing she'd said today, to have him cradle her face with his hands again as he had on the bike, and not to look at other women.

That was never going to happen now, and she was feeling too tired and sorry for herself to get mad about it.

In the lift he took out his phone, which was as good a message as any from where she stood. Enclosed in a small space with him, she couldn't help inhaling the scent of him. He smelled so good, even after all the tramping around, the bumping through underbrush on that motorcycle. He smelled of hot male skin and grass and salt and a little bit of petrol fumes from the bike.

It was a heady combination on him, but probably not so entrancing on her, and she held herself even more stiffly, folding her arms, wishing she could just vanish into merciful invisibility.

A furtive glance at their reflection in the mirrored walls only reinforced the contrast, and Ava realised in a rush of self-actualisation that he was right. These clothes did her no favours.

When had she started dressing this way? When had not wanting to draw attention to herself become a kind of self-obliteration? Bernard had said a woman in her position, with her figure, needed to be careful. So she *was* careful. High-necked blouses. No skirts. Nothing that would draw attention to her femininity.

No wonder it was no skin off Gianluca's nose if she was in Ragusa or Rome or wherever.

On their floor, he keyed open a door and stepped back to allow her inside.

She had expected something like the luxury sports car he drove—state-of-the-art, a little bit flashy, lots of grunt. A Gianluca Benedetti signature.

Instead he'd booked her into a boutique hotel which seemed to be something out of a Grimm's fairy tale, with wood inlay on the walls, cool patterned parquet underfoot and a mix of charming antique and quirky contemporary furniture. She took in the arched and vaulted doorways and windows, which would make the occupants feel they were inside something not of this era and quite wonderful. Unexpectedly she felt close to tears.

'This is my room?' she asked in wonder, turning around with an open look on her face. She remembered he had said something about it belonging to a friend. She wondered if she could use it as a conversation-opener, to show him she could be as charming, approachable, *friendly* as those silly girls downstairs.

She cleared her throat and what came out was, 'I really must insist on paying—'

The door shut in her face with a neat click.

For a moment Ava didn't move.

He had never actually been rude to her before, and a part of her brain said it was clearly another message. He had held that door wide for those girls. He had smiled and lingered like

Prince Charming. Then turned around and slammed a door in her face.

Yes, it was difficult to ignore that door now several inches from her face.

She wasn't sure how she got to the bathroom. She wasn't really aware she was taking off her clothes until the buttons felt fiddly under her fingers. When they wouldn't shift fast enough she began ripping her shirt off. It wasn't as if she had to worry about ruining it—she had a thousand more lined up in her closet at home…

She extended her trousers scarcely more care, because really they didn't deserve it.

Standing in her underwear, she gave her reflection in the mirror a good look. Although of simple white cotton, the set cost more than some people made in a week of work.

There was no use denying that after Gianluca had swept in to her hotel room this morning she'd set aside her usual granny undies to shimmy her way into these.

What a fraud she was.

She hit the shower cubicle, snapping on the jets. The water pounded down on her head as she lathered herself up with the luxury vanilla and clove-scented soap—as far from her own scentless plain bar of soap in her toiletries bag as could be. She washed her dust-laden hair with the complementary products and waited for the warm water to work its magic on her tense muscles.

Instead she had to do battle against the memory of hard hips and thighs between her legs, the feel of a long, broad and muscular back, the clench of rock-hard abdominal muscles under her hands.

The ache low in her pelvis taunted her.

What are you going to do about it, Ava? whispered a hateful voice. *He thinks you're uptight and frustrated and in need of a shrink.*

She hung her head and let the water cascade down.

It was no use.

He was a man who dated models and actresses and hosted private parties at ritzy bars where girls wearing almost nothing draped themselves over him... She was a woman who made lists in her head during sex, when she wasn't sucking in her tummy and trying to hide her bottom.

It would never work.

Yet he was also a man who flew helicopters in war zones, and had cared enough to try and calm her fears of the helicopter. She lifted her head. And when it had come to getting her out of a bind today he'd come through.

She tried to imagine Bernard with her on the hillside. She would have been responsible for getting them both down.

Ava snapped off the flow of water and stepped out before she drowned herself. She was feeling truly wretched by the time she'd towel-dried her hair, rubbed lotion into her skin and gone in search of fresh clothes.

She couldn't quite bring herself to pull on another pair of long trousers, and it wasn't as if she was going anywhere, so she stepped into the boy-leg shorts she slept in and a blue stretchy cotton camisole before brushing out her hair.

She'd order room service and phone the office, check in with her assistant, PJ.

Except it was the wee hours of the morning in Australia.

Which meant, robbed of her go-to, she would have to find something else to keep her mind occupied.

The rest of the afternoon stretched out before her...and the rest of her fearful, boxed-up life which she had come to Italy to change.

She plopped down on the bed and looked around unhappily. She'd come to the conclusion she'd stuffed this up. But was she woman enough to fix it?

Gianluca only half listened to the earnest conversation of his lawyer as he sat at a table with his legals and a Russian oligarch.

Most women would be *grateful* to be dropped onto the

Italian Riviera for a couple days of R & R. In point of fact he could think of several just off the cuff who would brawl with one another to have the chance of spending a couple of days in his company in these surroundings… He was known for being generous. He didn't begrudge a woman a little shopping, a little pampering—it always made them far more relaxed and amenable when it came to the point for which they were both here.

Si, there were many women who would appreciate this gesture.

Clearly Ava wasn't one of them.

She had a sharp tongue, that female, and no sense at all of her role as a woman—to smooth the awkward moment, to expect his assistance.

Instead she pushed him to treat her as he would a man—but what she didn't understand was that if a man had behaved as she had today he'd be out cold on that hillside right now, not sitting nice and tight in a luxury hotel.

Basta. He'd spent too much valuable time thinking about this. He'd done his duty by her. He could live with the papers' stories about his supposed latest squeeze—he was used to it, after all. As far as he was concerned there was no need for them to see one another again.

Besides, there was a cure for this. This was Positano. There were beautiful, available women everywhere. Fiery, opinionated Italian women, who knew how to handle a man, knew when to challenge and when to lay down their weapons and offer up some much appreciated docility.

He observed one or two of these paragons as he sipped his vodka.

The Russian, who had flown in for this one-hour face-to-face and would be flying out afterwards to join his mistress on his super-yacht at St Tropez, followed suit.

The lawyers continued to buzz.

When the business of the day was set aside the Russian leaned casually back in his chair and said in his soft, thickly accented Italian, 'Fly out with me this evening, Gianluca. We can look at the plans over dinner.'

The plans. Drinks and dinner. A bevy of the beautiful girls who travelled the world with one of Europe's richest men. The oligarch was infamous for his parties. But Gianluca's thoughts flickered not to tanned skin and lithe, flexible female bodies, but to Australia's answer to Gina Lollobrigida, wagging her finger at him and lecturing him about Seventies-era James Bond. He wondered what kind of response the Russian would get from her.

Which was when he laughed for the first time since she'd accused him of being a playboy. Which was when he knew he wouldn't be going anywhere. What he wanted was right here in Positano.

CHAPTER TWELVE

AVA SAT UP GROGGILY. She was in the middle of the bed and a quilt she couldn't remember drawing over herself was crumpled under her hand.

She hadn't meant to fall asleep. She remembered lying down and feeling so lousy it had almost hurt to take her next breath. She rubbed her eyes listlessly. Clearly she'd underestimated the toll the day had taken on her.

The quality of light drifting through the windows was different—softer. Some time must have passed. Ava froze. There was a sports coat draped over one of the high-backed chairs, and keys and a phone on the table. Even as she kicked her legs free of the quilt she listened. Running water. It was the shower.

Ava propelled herself off the bed, her hands going to her hair, madly smoothing it down.

He was in her shower—*their* shower. Were they sharing a room? He hadn't said anything about sharing a room. Typical! It was a huge presumption on his behalf. Especially when he knew her feelings on the subject…

Ava caught herself mid-tirade.

Her feelings had changed.

Somehow, at some point coming down that mountain, her feelings had changed.

And she was doing it again. Working herself up to avoid facing her fears.

She subsided back onto the bed.

He'd come back to her.

She bit her lip and smiled the smallest smile.

*Think, Ava, think. Remember what he said about you being
sexually frustrated and highly strung? You could show him.
You could make him eat those words.*

There was only one teeny, tiny problem—and, given he
was a sex god, he might not even notice.

She wasn't very good at it.

Sex.

But maybe there was an opportunity here for her...

He had all the skill.

She could take advantage of that.

She was here in this beautiful spot, with one of the sexiest
men in the world. She remembered *very* successful sex the
last time. Was there ever going to be a more perfect opportunity than this?

Gianluca Benedetti wasn't a man who did deep and meaningful. Knowing that going in, she wouldn't attach herself. It
would be sex. If she could just relax and follow the dictates
of her body, not her conscience...nor her heart...she would
be fine.

Just fine.

She eyed the bathroom door. Perhaps if she just *checked*.

Swallowing hard, she approached the door, carefully laid
her ear against the woodwork and listened. Definitely water...
and another sound—was he singing?

Somehow the idea that he was singing lifted her spirits.
He couldn't be very angry with her if he could hold a tune.
Maybe she could just duck her head in and say— What, Ava?
*I'm sorry for being defensive. I just hadn't worked out what
I wanted, and now I have. I want you. I want you so much I
think I might die of it.*

The worst he could do was say no.

He would probably say no.

Would he say no?

The shower partition would be fogged. She wouldn't even

look. And if, say, she glimpsed the shadow of his body behind the opaque glass she'd hardly be breaking any great taboos. Everyone knew men were a lot less modest about these things than women.

Any further reasoning dissolved as she was hit by steam, a partition that wasn't opaque at all, and six feet six inches of naked male, with spread shoulders, a long, broad back and taut, streamlined buttocks above long, powerful legs.

Gianluca stood with his face in the water stream, drenching his hair to black, and he *was* singing. His voice was a deep, rich baritone, and of course the Italian made everything so much more resonant.

He was just about the sexiest thing Ava had ever seen.

If she backed out now he'd never know she'd been there, but she simply couldn't take her eyes off him.

She told herself she was thirty-one years old. She'd seen plenty of men naked in showers… All right, *two*. Two perfectly nice, athletic, healthy men of around six feet—average men.

He turned around, eyes closed, throwing back his head under the spray, drawing one arm up to soap the back of his neck. The breath stuck in Ava's throat as her eyes dropped to the prize.

Gianluca Benedetti wasn't average.

He opened his eyes and hot molten gold stared back at her through black lashes stuck together with droplets of water. His gaze dropped to her unfettered breasts and Ava just knew her nipples were doing all sorts of interesting things as her body went into meltdown.

She drank in his olive skin, the dark shadow of chest hair arrowing down to the hard, compact ridges of his abdomen, and his beautiful penis, swelling, darkening with arousal before her eyes.

How can he find me attractive in my boy-leg shorts when I don't have stick-thin legs?

It was one of those puzzles, like the mystery of the *Mary Celeste*, destined to go unsolved. But there was no doubt he was looking her over with an expression that would have put any woman's body issues to rest.

He said something basic in Italian and Ava gave a little gasp as naked, dripping, pumping testosterone, he picked her up as if she was a featherweight and dragged her into the shower, making a cushion of his arm for her as he flattened her against the tiles and kissed her. Just like that. His tongue was in her mouth, his stubble was rubbing against her skin, and her lips felt caressed and devoured all at the same time. She hadn't known kissing could be like this.

He dwarfed her with the size of his shoulders. They were a wall she couldn't climb. But she wound her arms up around his neck anyway.

Up, up, up... He was the only man she'd ever kissed she'd had to reach up to. It was a completely different experience.

Yes, that was it—his height, and his build...the big, hard, masculine body she was sliding against which made him impossible for her to resist. It was the water that made everything far too slippery. She couldn't help the circular motion of her hips against him, wordlessly encouraging the pulsing industrial-strength push of his erection against her rounded belly.

His hands were around her waist, under her sopping camisole, peeling it up. *'Il seno bello,'* he growled, and Ava was suddenly hyper-aware of the heaviness of her breasts as her erogenous zones leapt into action.

One big hand cupped the underside of her left breast as he bent and sucked her nipple into his mouth through the wet cotton, rubbing it with his teeth until she was positively shaking. He did the same with the other, his hands pushing down her shorts, finding the bare curve of her behind and squeezing with a gratified groan of appreciation.

The water felt warm as it sprayed over her, his mouth was hot and slick wherever it strayed, and all she could do was hang on to him, stroking the hard, hot expanse of his shoulders and back, his chest, wishing she was better at this. It was as if she'd played all her life at local level and had then been recruited into the big league. She wove her fingers through his hair and brought his head up to hers again, kissed him as passionately and wantonly as she felt.

'Are you protected?' he asked her in Italian, his voice almost guttural.

Ava nodded vigorously, even as she kept kissing him.

'Preservativo,' he told her, his mouth moving away from hers, hot against her throat. 'I've got condoms. I'll use one if you'd prefer.'

She almost told him no, and then with a sort of terrible clarity she remembered. He was playboy of the western world. God knew how many other women he'd slept with just this month, let alone this year. It had been seven years since she'd last been in his arms. She'd been with Patrick very briefly—and he had always used condoms—and then Bernard, her plodding, safe relationship. Gianluca had probably worked his way through the adult female population of Italy...

Something pinched inside her chest and Ava felt her pulse begin to speed up—and not in a good way.

Don't think about all that, the new, reckless Ava urged. *Just go for it. Have your little frolic in the shower, enjoy what he has to offer, and move on with your life. Isn't that what this is all about? Putting the past behind you, making things over in a better way...?*

She pushed her hands against his chest. 'I want you to wear a condom,' she told him, making a space between them.

'Si,' he assured her, and then his tongue was in her mouth again.

She shoved at him. 'No—go and do it now.'

He didn't answer. He merely shut off the water flow, picked her up and carried her wet and dripping out into the bedroom.

He dumped her on the bed and dived for his toiletries bag. Ava sat up, pulling down her camisole. Her stomach only began to plummet when he tipped the bag onto the floor.

'You don't have condoms?'

Gianluca hissed out a breath between his teeth and met her

accusatory gaze. He was so beautiful, aroused and predatory—everything she had fantasised about for so long…

It made her furious!

'I cannot *believe* you of all people don't have condoms!'

He was looking at her strangely. 'Calm down, *cara*. I will make a phone call.'

Ava's jaw dropped slightly. 'Room service provides prophylactics?'

'Why not?'

Aching in places she hadn't ached for a very long time, Ava found herself scrambling to her knees.

'Maybe this isn't a good idea.'

Gianluca stilled. 'What has changed?'

Ava crossed her arms over her breasts. She might as well be topless in the wet fabric, and suddenly everything didn't seem so spur-of-the-moment any more. She felt exposed and wanted to hide away.

He looked incredible. He made her knees wobble, her heart shake, rattle and roll in her chest. She shook her head, knowing she had to be strong and resist.

She felt like bursting into tears.

What was *wrong* with her?

Without a word Gianluca strode to the wardrobe, yanked out a pair of jeans and shoved his legs into them, easing them over what ailed him. Then he grabbed a shirt, punching his arms through the sleeves.

'Wh-what are you doing?'

'Wait there.'

Ava scrambled off the bed, but in a single step, with an outstretched arm, he had her up against him—masculine, potent, dangerous. She trembled, but didn't resist as he clasped her chin and planted a fierce kiss on her amazed mouth.

'Wait,' he said.

'I'm not—' she began, but he was gone.

She heard the main door slam.

She slumped on the bed for a full minute, just thinking

about consequences, and what might happen tomorrow, and how if she didn't have him inside her a part of her might shrivel up and die. But if she did she would have to give something else up. The memory of that shining night when she'd shared her soul with him. And that had meant something.

Because she was going to stuff this up.

Sex wasn't something she was any good at. Patrick and Bernard had found her disappointing; it could only be catastrophic with a sex god like Gianluca. All her earlier feelings of being sexy and wanting something more had shrivelled down to a pile of self-doubt.

She briefly considered making a run for it, packing up her things and vanishing before he returned. But she'd been a coward once before, and how was she going to face him in Ragusa on Sunday if she ran now? No, she had started this, and she always saw things through. When he realised she was no good all this would just *stop*.

Wiping at her damp eyes, she stripped off her wet things and wrapped herself in her big white robe. She had barely covered up when the door banged open. Gianluca was framed in it, looking like every fantasy any red-blooded woman could have, and all the arguments she had assembled collapsed as he threw several boxes onto the bed.

'Where did you get those from?' Her tongue suddenly felt too big for her mouth.

'Farmacia,' he said.

'You went into a chemist's?'

'Si.' A slight smile edged his mouth. 'Why aren't you naked?'

She ignored that, even though her knees felt wobbly. 'Are you planning on sleeping with a lot of women while you're here?'

'I think my time will be taken up with you, *bella,*' he said, advancing on her.

'But four boxes?' She backed up and her bottom hit the wall. How had she ended up all the way over here?

'I was in a hurry,' he said, shrugging it off.

Ava's fears, arguments and nonsensical reasoning dried up.

He hadn't planned this. He hadn't planned any of it! Wouldn't a man with seduction on his mind have armed himself with the necessaries? Didn't a guy like him come with a kit they handed out at Playboys Incorporated? All of her preconceptions were breaking down because this didn't feel standard or routine. He wasn't acting as if this meant nothing.

He'd gone out and found a chemist—*like an ordinary person.*

Ava saw the fierce urgency in his expression, the way he was watching her—like a lion eying a gazelle he was preparing to take down. It reminded her there was nothing ordinary about Gianluca Benedetti, and although they had been together before he was older now, a great deal had changed, and she had spent the last seven years learning how disappointing she was in bed.

Yet he'd brought back condoms. She felt as if he'd gone out and slain dragons for her.

'What about your meetings?' she asked on a deep swallow.

'What meetings?'

He leaned over her, one arm caging her in as he pressed his hand to the wall above her shoulder, the other deftly dealing with the knotted belt around her waist.

His fingers brushed against her bare belly as the robe fell open, circling her navel. Every sensible thought in her head flew out, probably never to be heard from again.

He drew his fingertips up through the valley between her breasts all the way to brush over her clavicle, then he gently nudged the robe over the curve of her shoulder until it fell a little way down her back, revealing her shoulder and most of one breast.

His eyes grew intent under that heavy fringe of lashes as he traced the edge of the robe on its descent to the outer rim of her nipple.

'Are you sensitive here?'

Ava trembled as he rubbed softly over the puffy pink of her areola. 'Y-yes.'

Why was he asking these questions? Why didn't he just get on with it?

She watched him deftly nudge the cloth west and circle her nipple with his thumb. She gave a little start. She wanted him to use his teeth, like he had in the shower, suck on them hard, make the muscles of her inner thighs clench. She needed him to overwhelm her before she lost her nerve.

She didn't have his confidence. She wasn't very good in bed.

Yet his gentleness was what she wanted too. She hadn't expected it, and she found she wanted it like her next breath.

God help her, it didn't feel like seduction.

He pushed the robe off her other shoulder and it fell heavily to the floor. Ava hoped the dusky light would be kind to her. She was aware of him lightly fondling her breasts as he simply looked at her, as if memorising the fullness of their shape above the narrow span of her waist, the gentle curve of her belly below and the more dramatic rounding of her hips, the tiny dark brown curls guarding her secrets between the solidity of her thighs. Ava knew all of these things about herself. She also knew it was hard for her to be naked with someone and arousal was not an easy thing for her. Yet here she was, humming all over, with energy moving through her body like light, warming her, setting her aglow.

She forced herself to meet his gaze head-on and…

'You are *perfetto*.' His hands smoothed over her breasts, glided down her ribs to spread over the flare of her hips, and he brought her in so close she could feel the tremble in his body.

Okay. This was nice. He was looking at her as if she was a goddess and that just made her feel…

Good. It made her feel good. Strong. Female.

Except shouldn't she be touching him too? She didn't want to be accused of being cold.

Bernard had always complained about her lack of participation, but she would always get lost in her head, start making lists for the next day, and really it had begun and finished too fast for her to warm up.

She wouldn't mind going a little faster right now, because she was feeling extremely warm at this point, no lists in her head. She rested her palms on his chest, her fingers tackling the few buttons he'd managed to do up, touching his chest lightly at first and then with more confidence. He felt so hard—springy flesh over steely muscle. She wasn't used to muscle. She wasn't used to feeling smaller, daintier, *feminine*.

He laid her down on the bed and, holding her hands on the mattress, began to kiss her. Long, slow, mind-blowing kisses, seducing her beyond reason with only his mouth, for the moment denying her his body.

She was aware of him pulling off the shirt, could feel his chest hair abrading her breasts, and she gave an involuntary gasp as his thumb ran over the seam of her sex, parting the folds, dipping inside. She stopped thinking.

Oh, God, everything about her was conspiring to make this easy for him. She gripped him around the neck. She didn't want it to be easy. He didn't deserve easy—not after what he'd done to her.

She felt him kiss the curve of her neck, murmur endearments in Italian, felt his big hands splay over her breasts, tugging at her nipples as he lifted his head to kiss her. The feel of his mouth was so compelling on hers—the slide of his tongue, hers joining his, in an echo of the feel of his fingers against her intimate flesh. He made a low, thrilling growl when she found the bare skin of his chest and tangled her fingers in his hair, dragged circles around his flat male nipples, pressed her mouth there and licked him.

He tasted like salt and male skin and Gianluca. The reason she knew the taste of him flew out of her head, but she did, and it made her crazy with want for him. She slid her hand down to unzip him, but he was doing it himself, shucking his jeans and moving over her with all the predatory grace of a man who knew what he wanted and how to get it.

Ava flexed her hand over the rigid length of him and watched as his beautiful features grew taut and pronounced. She circled the head with her thumb, wondering if she should be worried or happy about his size.

She needed to tell him she wasn't always able to let go, that she might disappoint him. Tears built up in the back of her eyes and she blinked rapidly to stop them from falling. She didn't want this to be a failure. She didn't want to wreck it like she wrecked everything else.

Even as her anxieties drove through her thoughts like an express train her thighs fell open naturally to cradle him. But he wasn't in a hurry. He smoothed her hair off her shoulder, fingered it as if the silky texture fascinated him, and then laid the gentlest kiss on the top of one breast, moving agonisingly slowly to her nipple, to the curve of her hip, her belly…

'If you could just—' she began.

He lifted his mouth momentarily. 'If I could what, *dolcezza*?' he asked, and rimmed her belly button with his tongue.

Ava's stomach convulsed and she gripped the sheets. 'It takes me a while,' she asserted breathlessly, even as it occurred to her that it wasn't taking her very long at all. She was throbbing like a heartbeat between her thighs. 'There are certain things you need to do—ways I need to be touched—*oh*.'

He slid a finger inside her, and then another, and she closed her eyes, lost for a moment in the sensations.

He was speaking to her in Italian again as she shuddered under him.

'Is that good?'

She recognised that bit of English amidst the Italian. 'Good—yes. Oh, yes,' Ava whimpered, and bit her lip as she tried not to cry out. More sensation streaked through her. But his other hand was stroking her face. He was dragging his thumb over her mouth until she was sucking on it, biting down on him as her lower body arched off the mattress.

'*Mia ragazza bella,*' he told her in a hushed rough voice. '*Lasciarsi andare.*'

'Luca,' she sobbed, and the moment before she cascaded into a million pieces of pleasure she had the satisfaction of seeing his watchful expression turn wild.

He was still watching her with fierce, glittering eyes as he positioned himself, powerfully male above her, and Ava could see the telltale tension in his body as he held himself back. She lifted her body in response, reaching up to push her fingers through his hair.

As he filled her his careful restraint was almost as erotic as the sensation of her tender tissues expanding to encompass him. He watched her the whole time.

'Luca…' she breathed as he sank deep.

'Good, my sweet Ava?'

Her emotions did a figure-eight in her chest, tying her up in knots.

He pushed and their hips locked.

He said something in Italian, in such a way that she knew this was as good for him as it was for her. Perhaps better. His body tremored with the strain of holding back and she smoothed her palms over his hair-roughened chest, wanting the intimacy of this to be preserved in her memory.

For a moment everything seemed to slow down. *It's not your first time.* A faint voice rippled through her senses. *Your body remembers him. You remember him…*

'Now,' she breathed. 'Oh, Luca, now.'

Her hips lifted of their own accord as he began to move deeper. His eyes didn't leave hers and he wasn't asking her if it was good this time. He was driving her to where they both wanted to be and she found she didn't have to think about his rhythm. Her body took it up like a drumbeat.

Oh, God. I feel like I was born to do this with this man.

Having him inside her, she could feel herself building towards the impossible, rarely ever more than a faint echo for her before, but becoming stronger and stronger, pulsing through her nerve endings as he bore down upon her. God, this *never* happened to her. But it was happening. She dug her nails into his back as if she'd never let go, as sensation exploded in long, pulsating ribbons of intense pleasure that went on and on. He thrust again, once more, and gave up his release with a deep groan of satisfaction before slowly, heavily, he came down on top of her.

Ava could feel his heartbeat pounding against hers. He rolled onto his side, taking her with him, smoothing his hand along her thigh, stroking her as they both still trembled with the force of what had happened in this bed. Ava was all too aware that he was still pulsing inside her, and she was experiencing sweet aftershocks.

She buried her face in his shoulder, feeling hot and sweaty and shuddery, definitely *not* in control.

'*Mia bella*, Ava,' he said hoarsely.

His beautiful Ava.

And she was.

CHAPTER THIRTEEN

Now what?

The questions started the minute he left the bed.

Ava's eyes went a little round and glassy as she watched him move from the bed to the bathroom, his easy steps sending the musculature of his body into a stretching, look-at-me-and-learn rhythm of bunching and contraction. His naked body was truly a masterpiece of the male form.

The empty expanse of mattress stretched out around her. Instinctively she pulled the rumpled quilt over her naked body, wondering how to dial down this overwhelming need for him to hold her.

In his arms she stopped thinking, she just *felt*—and God knew she hadn't felt this good in years.

He'd given her the holy grail of sexual joy—an orgasm during sex.

Not one, Ava, but two—maybe it was three.

Was that it? Was that why she was feeling so…emotional? Because that was how she was feeling—soft and clingy and a little bit weepy.

Clearly she was a lunatic!

The bed dipped as he slid in beside her, as at ease with his nakedness as she was not.

Don't panic, her good sense told her. It was what she told her junior associates. *You have the tools to get out of this. You just need time to process what's happened and a solution will come to you...*

Oh.

Ava's eyes went wide as he encircled her with his arms and splayed his hand in her hair, stroking her, looking at her as if she belonged to him. He began to croon things to her in Italian. Sweet things. She knew they were sweet because of his tone, because of the way his hand smoothed the back of her neck, his lips brushed against her temples. His voice was so deep, yet he spoke so softly, and he touched her as if she were something infinitely precious.

The saliva built up in the back of her throat and Ava swallowed painfully hard.

No one had ever treated her like this. She didn't know what to do. She couldn't let this go on. It wasn't right. It wasn't *her*.

'Gianluca?' Her voice was all scratchy, she didn't even sound like herself.

'Luca—I want you to call me Luca, *innamorata*.' He touched her ear with his lips and an involuntary little whimpering sound escaped her. She felt him smile.

'Is that the drill?' she forced out, her heart just about hammering out of her chest. 'Once you get a woman into bed she gets access to the secret name?'

If she'd thought she could cloak her anxieties in a joke it had backfired.

It came out too snarky, too aggressive. But how could it emerge as anything else when all she was feeling was exposed and, under that, soft and fuzzy...and terribly, terribly vulnerable? If this man dropped her she could break into oh so many pieces.

He said something under his breath in Italian. She knew it was a curse because she could feel the freeze shoot through his bigger body before so warm and enveloping against her own. He eased himself up abruptly onto his elbow and she was instantly thrown into the even more vulnerable position of having to gaze up at him and having nowhere to go.

'Why are you doing this?'

His tone brooked no argument, and the man who had whispered sweet nothings to her was suddenly the man she had insulted.

Like a flash of light in a dark room she understood her caustic comments had hurt his pride. His very old-world Latin machismo, which made him seem impenetrable, was also what made him vulnerable to her attacks. She didn't mean to attack him. She only wanted to protect herself...

'I'm not doing anything,' she said in a small voice.

'You speak of other people while you are in my bed. You speak of me as if I am some sort of predator.'

His features were pulled taut and Ava could see she had drawn blood.

'I don't think that. I—I just wanted us to be...honest with each other. You're acting as if—'

'As if what, Ava?'

'As if I mean something to you—and how can I when we've only known one another a few days?' She brought out the big guns. 'What about Donatella?'

It took Gianluca a moment to work out who the hell Donatella was, and when he did it made even less sense. Apparently it made sense to Ava. She was glaring at him. He made a manful effort not to laugh.

'Ava, I have never been intimate with Donatella. She was a—how you say?—a prop.'

'Prop?'

'Some women—they go out, they take a man with them to hold their handbag, *si*?'

Ava looked at him suspiciously. 'I don't know any women like that.'

'Donatella carried my drink,' he supplied dryly.

'You made a woman follow you round a nightclub carrying your drink?'

'It's a euphemism, Ava. I did not want to be hassled by anyone, so I chose the lesser of the evils—Donatella.'

Ava was clearly considering this. Gianluca watched several emotions cross her face. Felt himself relax as she sank back onto the pillow.

At last. Progress.

'You must think I'm a complete idiot!'

She shot up out of the bed, dragging the sheet with her, but he wasn't having that. He grabbed it with one hand and she was left naked beside the bed. She did what he thought of as the classic pose—one arm strapped across her breasts, the other across the sweet little mop of curls at the juncture of her thighs—and backed away from the bed.

'Cara…' he said, making a placatory gesture.

'Don't you darling me, you liar!'

He stiffened and toyed with the idea of just picking her up and rolling her back into bed. But he told himself she was overwrought, and that if he wasn't careful she might hurt herself. Or him. He tried not to smile as he bounded out of bed.

She had backed herself into the wall, but not before spotting her robe. She had it on in a trice.

'How stupid do you think I am?' she snapped, securing the belt with a violent yank. 'She was beautiful. She was wearing nothing.' Her voice trembled. 'She wasn't a handbag!'

'Prop,' Gianluca amended under his breath, advancing cautiously on her.

'She wasn't that either. Is that how you're going to describe me to the next fool woman you kidnap and hold hostage? A prop?'

Ava was holding herself so rigidly it was a shock to her system when he threw back his head and laughed. The rich, raw, *edgy* sound of it hemmed her in. They stood much as they had when they begun this dance earlier.

'Why are you laughing?'

'Ava, if I don't laugh I'll throttle you.'

'I don't understand,' she said, more to herself than to him.

'I know, *cara*.' He rested one hand on the wall beside her head. Big, naked, magnificent, he made her feel entirely too girly for her own comfort. He was looking at her as if she were something he was making alterations to, and perhaps he was—cutting her right out of the picture.

Ava braced herself. This was the fall-out of giving in to the fantasy, of letting one's emotions rule. It always brought about bad things. This was what she had lectured Josh about—leading with his head, not his heart, taking only considered risks, not coming to Italy and marrying an Italian girl from an old family and *ruining his life*.

But who had ruined her life?

She was a woman who had thrown it all away seven years ago with this man, and up until a blissful five minutes ago she had been lying in his arms—only to find herself once more in the process of dismantling the tiny scrap of wonderful she'd scraped back.

'I'm sorry,' she said awkwardly. 'I shouldn't have lashed out at you.'

Gianluca wasn't really listening. He was distracted. No man would blame him. He could feel her warmth, smell the vanilla scent on her skin. He knew intimately now the softness of that skin. All women had soft skin—it was what made them wonderfully different—but with Ava it felt...*she* felt... softer...more pliant.

She just felt *better*.

He was so hard it was a special kind of torture.

He'd come back to the room and his idea had been to pull on soft old jeans and a T-shirt and do some work while he waited for Ava to wake up. He'd planned to order food. They'd eat, talk. He'd apologise for bringing her here without consulting her, she'd apologise for being a shrew and foolishly reckless, and perhaps something could be salvaged from the wreckage that was today. Perhaps he had been marginally high-handed with her, but he wasn't accustomed to women who made his life difficult.

Finding her curled up, looking so sexy-sweet in her skimpy shorts, he'd lost interest in talking. A hitherto unknown part of him had wanted to wake her up and shake her, tell her she had all the sense of a deer in headlights when it came to looking after herself with men.

She shouldn't have been curled up in some baby-doll outfit like Dorothy in a sea of poppies. She should have insisted on separate rooms. She should have shifted to another hotel. She should be halfway back to Rome! She sure as hell shouldn't trust him! If she were one of his sisters…

Which was when he'd shrugged off his sports coat, removed his watch and phone, drawn over her the quilt folded at the end of the bed to keep her warm.

He'd stood there, looking down at his handiwork, and then asked himself what the hell he thought he was doing.

When no answer had been forthcoming he'd hit the shower.

Right now he felt the same way he had when she'd uttered those immortal words, 'Maybe this isn't a good idea.' Had he *really* sprinted from the hotel, across the road, and grabbed enough protection to keep the birth rate down on a small island?

All he'd known was that he needed a chemist, needed condoms—needed to make this right for her.

It had only been when he saw her, wrapped up in that robe, looking fearful, that he'd recognised he needed to slow this down, coax her back out into the open. It had almost killed him, but taking the time to dismantle Ava's protective mechanism had possibly been one of the most erotic encounters of his life.

He wasn't going to make any sudden moves now.

'Will you answer a question?' He made sure he held her eyes seriously, hard as it was not to let his gaze drift down.

She was looking up at him, all her anxiety stamped on her expression.

'I guess I don't have a choice,' she said begrudgingly.

He almost smiled. 'Ava, you've always had a choice. You continually exercise it. You exercised it right into our bed, and now you want to pretend I have once more taken advantage of you when we both know this was what you wanted from the moment I offered you my services.'

'Services?'

She gave a start as he leaned down and brushed his mouth against her ear, 'Gigolo, escort, servicer of women.'

He drew back a little, enough to see that her lashes had drifted down, her lush mouth was quivering. She looked softened, delicious.

'Is that the fantasy you want?' he murmured over those full lips. 'Do you want me to be those things for you? Because I will do it, Ava. I'll be whatever you want me to be in this bed. But don't ask me not to be tender with you—don't ask me not to be passionate, to pretend this isn't important to you.'

'How do you know it's important to me?' Her voice was husky, her eyes downcast.

'Because…' he bent a finger around the edge of the robe '…my little porcupine…' he nudged it down until the shadowy cleft between her breasts came into view '…otherwise you wouldn't be curled up so tight right now all I can see is bristles. Ah, look—there it is.' He dragged the robe open and spread his hand over her stomach. 'Your velvety little belly,' he said, and felt the muscles in her stomach contract beneath his hand.

Ava felt the muscles in her pelvis do a similar dance, but if her insides hadn't been trembling from his declaration of intent—*to be tender, to be passionate*—she would never have nestled a little closer. Any awkwardness she felt was far outweighed by unhappiness with her own behaviour and trying to make sense of his. This man had not been careless with her feelings, she marvelled. He had, in fact, been careful and incredibly tender.

'I told you—a porcupine is a rodent,' she mumbled, moaning as he pressed his mouth softly, coaxingly to hers.

'You haven't answered my question.' He nibbled on her bottom lip.

Ava suspected she might pass out from anticipation.

'Ask me, then.' Her voice was full of longing.

'Why did you come to Rico's the other night?'

'I wanted to see if you'd changed.' She hesitated before throwing herself over the cliff. 'I wanted to spend time with you.'

He didn't seem surprised. He pressed a kiss to the corner of her mouth.

'*Si*, and why do you think I brought you here, hmm?'

Could it be that simple with a man as complicated as this?

Once again Gianluca Benedetti had taken her assumptions and sent them scattering like marbles.

She didn't have the energy to go chasing after them.

Instead she put her hands on his shoulders as he kissed the soft seam of her mouth, parted her lips. He stroked his tongue along the inner curve of her bottom lip. He *seduced* her mouth. He was the most *beautiful* kisser and when he was inside her he made her see stars.

Ava gave a little sigh and heard the rumble of a chuckle in his chest.

Yes, she was a pushover—and he knew he had her in the palm of his hand.

They emerged into the sunny street in front of the hotel around noon the next day.

Gianluca, showered and shaved and completely energised, looked incredible in a simple pair of dark trousers and one of those shirts he wore that seemed to be tailored to his powerful body.

He held her hand and walked right past the posse of pretty girls who yesterday had taken up so much of his time. Ava glanced at them and hoped her little smile wasn't too smug.

As he moved ahead of her to open the car door she caught her reflection in the mirrored surface of the window and knew beyond doubt that she had to purchase some new clothes.

Gianluca had said nothing about her trousers this morning, and she'd picked her girliest top—a short-sleeved cotton blouse with a scooped neckline. But if clothes maketh the woman they didn't reflect at all how she was feeling.

The shiny black Italian sports car shot out into the traffic, with Gianluca driving with the insouciance for which the Italians were famous—one hand on the wheel, the other playing with her hair, as if he couldn't stop touching her.

Ava's heart was pounding like a bird gone crazy in its cage.

She wanted to tell him how different this was for her—the Amalfi coast, driving in a sports car with her lover...*her lover*... Nobody back home would believe it.

A flutter of nerves swept through her. There were so many things that could go wrong.

Heck, she didn't believe this—not after the long hours she'd worked back in Sydney, the routine that had become her safety zone in an unsafe world. How had she managed to break out of that?

But she didn't feel unsafe with Gianluca. As they drove in this mad way past scooters and pedestrians and other gazillion-dollar sports cars her sense of unreality was Technicolor, but the command of the man beside her, not only over the car but his environment, was reassuring.

Gianluca Benedetti...maybe not so much playboy of the western world...maybe not at all... She looked at him with soft eyes. Maybe the man to get a crazy lady out of a fix.

'If you keep looking at me like that, *tesoro*,' he growled, 'we won't be getting where we're going.'

'And where *are* we going?'

'I thought a little touristing around the coast. There are some pretty sights I'd like to show you.'

'I'd like that too, but—'

How did she broach this? *I need to stop at some boutiques because all the clothes in my suitcase look like I've just stepped out of a business-is-us catalogue!*

'But...*tesoro*?'

'Can I have an hour? To myself?'

He gave her a curious look. 'You will not run off?' he asked, quite seriously.

'No!' Ava shot back just as seriously. 'Why would you think that?'

He grinned. 'Just checking.'

She relaxed and felt foolish. She wasn't used to this kind of banter, although she could quickly grow used to it. Her heart felt light and fluttery in her chest, as if she'd run a race and stopped and her heart didn't know it yet.

'Where should I drop you? When should I pick you up?'

Ava bit her lip. She wanted clothes—except she didn't know where to begin looking.

'Ava?'

She scanned the road, spotted some well-dressed women coming out of a shop with bags. *Bingo!*

'Anywhere here,' she instructed nonchalantly.

He grinned at her, as if she hadn't fooled him in the least, and double-parked.

'Are you sure I'm not wanted?'

He was, but she needed to do this herself. How embarrassing to ask a man to shop for her because she didn't have the first clue about what really suited her.

She had no doubt Gianluca was an expert, but the thought of him with a bevy of other far more fashion-conscious women before her wasn't something she wanted to dwell on.

'Come back in an hour.' That should give her enough time. She hoped.

As the sports car shot off once more into the traffic she felt a pang of regret, but she needed to do this for herself.

The stores seemed uniformly ordinary—and then she entered a boutique where instantly she saw what she was looking for. A long pale blue silk dress with an overlay of gossamer material embroidered with tiny blue forget-me-nots. As a little girl she had missed out on having a mother who liked to dress her up. She'd grown up in jeans and T-shirts, a real tomboy, not through preference but necessity.

This was the sort of dress she'd always thought was too girly for her even as she'd admired the look on other women.

Ignoring the price tags, Ava finally walked out with three bags, laden with her purchases. She was feeling better about her body and it gave her more confidence, trying on clothes that suited her. She made a few more purchases down the road, ditching her trousers for good and feeling much freer in a pair of white capris.

She spotted the sports car in the traffic and waved a bag at him.

Even an hour away from him and she felt her heart expand when she dived into the car. He was looking at her as if checking she was in one piece.

'Shopping? I should have guessed.'

'What do you mean?' she asked uneasily as she strapped herself in.

'Women and shopping.'

She relaxed. 'Oh, yes. That old chestnut. You know, studies have shown—'

He leaned over and kissed her.

'Oh.' She gazed back at him. 'That was nice.'

'You look beautiful,' he said, and he wasn't looking at her new capris.

'I just picked up a few things more suited to the coast,' she wittered.

He was looking at her and she couldn't take her eyes off him. A horn blasted at them from the road but Gianluca continued to stare.

'What?' she asked self-consciously.

'I was thinking,' he said slowly, 'I was in a hurry the other day. I almost didn't stop in at Nero's.'

'Nero's?'

'The coffee bar in Rome. I would have missed you—*this*.' He reached out and stroked the line of her cheek, down around the curve of her jaw.

Unaccountably Ava's eyes filled with tears. 'But you didn't miss me,' she said huskily.

'Then why are you crying, *tesoro*?'

Ava gave a self-conscious little laugh. 'I don't know.'

But she did. Her heart felt full to overflowing. He wasn't anything like the way she'd made him in her head—the self-defensive picture she'd created of a spoiled, privileged aristocrat who didn't care about the women he slept with, only the conquests he made. He wasn't arrogant either. He just possessed confidence in who he was, what he could do. Travelling with him, she felt incredibly safe and also relaxed.

All of her life *she* had been the one to take charge.

It was nice knowing she didn't have to.

He would take care of it.

The fact he expected to take care of it should have lifted her hackles, but it was difficult to begrudge him a role he assumed so naturally.

'Where will we go now?' she asked.

He gave her a supremely masculine smile. 'My turn to surprise you.'

CHAPTER FOURTEEN

'No, I couldn't—I can't. It's too much, Gianluca.'

'On the contrary. It's perfect.' He held the necklace, with its tiny tourmalines, green beryls, amethysts, pink sapphires and diamonds delicately wrought through a white gold chain, against her throat.

The jeweller in the exclusive little shop hovered discreetly in the background.

Ava was all too conscious of their audience—until Gianluca's shoulders blocked them out and he bent his head close to hers.

'Let me spoil you, *tesoro*,' he said, his eyes intent on hers.

'But I don't need you to buy things for me,' she answered. 'I have my own money.'

His mouth twitched. 'It is not the cost, Ava, it is the sentiment.'

She looked anxiously at the divine glittering string he hung before her and the thought flittered through her mind that it was a very expensive piece of rope she might easily hang herself on.

'Then it is a no?' he said, with that infinitesimal Latin shrug.

She wanted it so badly. Not because it was beautiful—although it was—but because he wanted her to have it. And he was being so sweet in letting her have her way although it disappointed him. He wasn't pushing it on her, and he could have no idea how good that made her feel.

Gianluca always gave her a choice, and after a lifetime of struggling and fighting to make her own choices, to have her voice heard, it was a true gift well beyond the glitter of an obscenely priced piece of jewellery.

'No.' She laid her hand on his arm. When he gave her a quizzical look she smiled and blurted out. 'I mean, yes. Yes, I want you to spoil me. If you want to.'

She'd officially handed in her Miss Independent, Miss Stand Alone card in at that moment, but Gianluca didn't seem to see the significance. He merely placed the necklace back in its box and with a barely discernible nod of his head had the jeweller and three members of his staff transferring the tiny purchase to an exquisite box.

As they emerged into the bright day after the hushed, strategically lit environs of the jeweller's Ava said, a little haplessly, 'But we left it behind.'

'No, *cara*, it will be delivered to the hotel. I didn't think you would want to carry it around all day in your handbag. Am I right?'

'No, of course not,' she muttered, feeling a little foolish. Why didn't she know these things? And now Gianluca knew she didn't have a clue.

He was the first man who had ever bought her jewellery. Not unexpectedly her mind shot to the little engagement ring she had secreted away in her suitcase. She had bought it in preparation for Bernard's proposal from an estate jewellers near her office, on her own.

She'd forgotten it in all the excitement.

Unease formed a stagnant pool in her stomach. She didn't want to think about the woman who had made that purchase, the woman who had seen nothing wrong in shelling out for their holiday *and* the ring, as if by paying for everything she could control what happened. ·

'You are really very sweet,' he said, putting his arm around her.

Ava disliked public displays of affection. She disliked anything that drew attention to her, so someone could say, *Look at her—what's wrong with her?* but her judgement seemed out of place at this moment, with this man…and Italy seemed to be full of canoodling couples. In fact love seemed to be a part of the public display along with dressing up and that charming custom *passeggiata*—walking every evening through the town simply to be seen.

'So are you,' she said, resting her head against his shoulder.

'I am sweet, *tesoro*?' He sounded amused.

'Yes, you always have been. I remember—' She broke off, aware she had broken her own rule not to speak about seven years ago.

But it was too late. He bent his head close to hers. 'You remember…?'

'When you were twenty-three. When we first met.' She touched his chest with her hand. 'You were so gentle, kind and sensitive, and yet strong. I felt safe with you.'

'Tesoro,' he said, capturing her hand in his and bringing it to his lips, 'you must never tell an Italian man he is *sensitive*. It just won't do.'

'I think you were—are.' She could feel that heavy weight of seven years lifting off her chest.

'If it pleases you to think so, then I'm glad,' he said neutrally.

But she sensed his resistance. He was more than simply uncomfortable with the description.

Cautiously Ava reached up and touched his jaw, running her fingertips lightly over the incipient stubble.

'It is a nuisance,' he said in a low voice, capturing her hand. 'I need to shave twice a day. Even then I will probably mark your soft skin.'

'No,' Ava said with feeling. 'I like it. I—' She broke off.

A wave of embarrassment swept through her and she didn't know what to say. She was standing in the middle of a busy street, on the other side of the world from where she had always lived, in the arms of this amazing man, saying out loud all sorts of things she would usually only whisper to her pillow, and he was listening to her and looking at her with those eyes as if…as if…

'What else do you like?' he prompted.

'I like *you*,' she said, wondering what on earth had got into her.

'*Si*, this did occur to me,' he said as he angled her towards the car, 'but I didn't like to push my luck.'

They drove the winding coastal road out of Positano. They drank limoncello and ate clams for lunch on a terraced restaurant looking out over the bay at Amalfi. They walked through the town and in the early evening strolled with half the inhabitants along the waterfront.

Gianluca had found he wanted to know everything about her.

Where she'd gone to school. Too many to count.

What was her first job? Sweeping up hair clippings in a hair salon.

Her favourite colour? Blue. Her favourite song? Anything with Billie Holliday singing it.

She'd laughed then and asked some questions of her own.

Where had he gone to school? A military academy, aged eight.

Maybe the Twenty Questions wasn't such a hot idea, he realised now, as the smile was wiped off Ava's face.

'Eight?' she repeated.

'It is how it is done in my family, *cara*. All Benedetti males have attended the same military academy for five generations.'

'Is *done*?'

'*Was* done. As I don't intend to have children the question for me is moot. But my sisters have not followed the custom with their male children.'

'No?' Her voice sounded a little hollow.

Gianluca recognised stony ground when he stood on it. Was she referring to his sisters or his comment about himself?

'You have sisters?'

Si, definitely about him.

'Two—four nephews, two nieces.' He tried not to look uncomfortable by tugging on the neck of his shirt.

'You don't like children?'

'Sure. I love kids.'

Ava regarded him with those sea-green eyes and he braced himself for the feeling of annoyance and sheer frustration a woman badgering him on this topic always aroused.

'Hmm,' she said.

It was all she said. Swishing her hair over her shoulder, she turned to look out over the water.

Just *hmm*?

Inferno, what was that supposed to mean? He didn't have to explain himself. It was a long, boring story—*Dio*, he'd told it to himself so many times even *he* was bored with it! But perhaps Ava should hear it so that she understood, so that she didn't make any plans involving him…

'This is magical. I can see why people turn out in the evening to promenade,' she said unexpectedly, turning up eyes made soft by the light. 'We should go out on the water tomorrow.'

Tomorrow he had planned on meeting with some investors.

'Unless you've planned something else?'

Could a woman look more guileless? All her anticipation and uncertainty flickered in those few words.

What could he say?

'Anything you desire, Ava *mio*.'

The next day he took her out in a motorboat along the coast, around the Galli Islands. The day after they drove into the Lattari Mountains cradling the Amalfi Coast.

A light rain began to fall and, hand in hand, they ran to shelter in a local church. In the dim incense-scented light he couldn't take his eyes off her. He didn't know what it was—perhaps it was the coastal light—but she seemed to shimmer in the gloom. Her dark shoulder-length cloak of hair, her pearly skin, the deep pink of her mouth—all hot colours on a rainy day. She rested against him, looking out at the rain, with his hands hooked around her waist, his head resting against hers.

The weight of her was perfect.

She smelled like vanilla and cloves.

She smelled like Ava.

'Do you see that hill?' She pointed dead ahead. 'It looks like a rabbit's head.'

He couldn't see the rabbit.

'Si, *innamorata*. A fluffy little bunny.'

She eyed him wryly.

'And over there—the forest. That's a boot.'

'*Si*, a boot.'

'I made that one up to see if you were humouring me! And it's not a forest—it's a wood.'

She shoved her shoulder into his chest playfully and then gave a little cry of delight.

'Oh, look—is that a fox?'

The whisk of red across the pasture was indeed a fox.

He felt her thrill and realised that although he knew this area like the back of his hand, from boyhood summers with his maternal grandparents, looking at it through her eyes made him feel as if he was seeing this place for the first time.

He didn't have the heart to tell her that the fox was probably on its way to gobble up any real rabbits foolish enough to be darting around in the rain. She was a true city girl. She was...

Making him crazy. *Pazzo.* Why was he discussing furry animals, in a church in a little village no one had ever heard of, when he had a hotel suite waiting for them? He wasn't a tour guide, and he sure as hell didn't think foxes were something to be delighted over rather than thought of as the vermin they were.

He'd tell her that in a minute. He'd drag her out of here and they'd make a run for the car, rain or no rain, and drive all the way back to Positano at speed. And when they got to the hotel he'd strip her clothes off her and do what a *sensible* man would be doing with a beautiful woman—not hunkering down in churches on a day custom-made for more adult indoor activity.

Then he'd get around to organising their transport south, because tomorrow was D-Day and all he'd been doing was dragging his feet round these tourist traps for days.

She turned in his arms and looked up, her eyes shining. 'I've never seen a fox before—at least not so close.'

'*Si*, they're shy little animals,' he found himself saying. 'You have to play your hand carefully around them…no sudden moves.'

Which was when, instead of whisking her off for some debauchery, as he had done a hundred times before with other women, he bent his head and kissed her soft, delicious mouth. He forgot about D-Day and tourist traps and the idiocy of delighting in foxes and accepted he was possibly the luckiest *bastardo* in the world.

In town, he let her out to run another one of her mysterious errands, idling the car above the waterfront. He caught sight of her coming across the grass, the sun as bright here as it had been banished by cloud cover in the hills, shining on her chocolate hair.

She looked *Italian*—there was no other word for it—in her simple button-front sundress. She even wore it sliding slightly over one shoulder, with the top two buttons undone over her cleavage and the bottom three buttons undone to reveal a portion of her long thighs with each step as the skirt opened over her knees. She looked happy and earthy and incredibly sexy, and Gianluca became aware his wasn't the only pair of eyes on her.

As he got out of the car a piercing wolf whistle had her looking around, and him looking too, to hunt the perpetrator down.

He knew he hadn't stopped thinking about her since she'd walked back into his life. He knew he would never forget her as she had been last night, wearing the string of pretty stones—wearing *only* the pretty stones—in his bed.

Even before she'd accepted them, as he'd held them up against her pale throat in the jeweller's, watched her breasts below her clavicles rise and fall, he'd seen them draped on her naked.

He'd also seen the tremble in her hand as she took the string from him, and the vexation that had sent her dark brows together as she wrestled with her conscience.

There could be a hundred and one reasons why a woman would not accept a gift from a man. Ava's reason had been as transparent as those green eyes of hers. The gift meant something to her.

As you wanted it to, idiota.

He shifted uneasily on his feet. It wasn't a pledge…it wasn't a *ring*. It was just a token—no, more than that. It was a gesture—a sign of his esteem…his affection.

And why shouldn't he feel affectionate towards her? It was easy to stumble into putting labels on things, on feelings—and, yes, he *did* have feelings for her. Fairly strong feelings.

Perhaps he always had.

It didn't mean this was anything beyond his experience… although it was.

She was.

He watched Ava bending down to pet a small dog. She was speaking to the owner, her face turned up like a sunflower.

What would she think about his plan?

If she said no, if she insisted on continuing with this ridiculous excursion to Ragusa…

She stood up and turned her head.

Her smile made his heart turn over in his chest.

It crashed through him as he stood on a pavement in Positano, amidst scooters and tourists eating gelato and a hundred other peripherals that had never touched his everyday life—until this woman stepped into it and brought it into his world.

The simple happiness of being with this woman.

The way she made him feel.

'Ava.'

She turned to him, oblivious to what had just occurred in his world, and said, 'Luca, this gentleman breeds Lhasa Apsos—'

He framed her face with his big hands.

'Come back to Rome with me.'

Her mouth opened. No sound. But her eyes went soft and round and a little soulful.

'No family. No Ragusa. No pretence, Ava. Just you and me. Say yes, *innamorata*.'

She didn't hesitate.

'Yes,' she said.

He flew them back to Rome.

A small jet from Naples, in deference to Ava's needs.

They shot down the highway in his beloved Lamborghini Aventador roadster at dusk. He dropped the speed as they hit the drowsy late afternoon streets of the city he loved and everything became larger than life—the crumbling façades of old buildings, the ruins among the new that was Rome.

It was the old that hung like a millstone around his neck.

But *this* was new. This surging feeling—this certainty of purpose about a woman.

He didn't want to share her with his family. He didn't want her to have to deal with her brother.

To this end he'd arranged for two hundred red roses to land on his mother's lap tomorrow morning by way of apology, and Ava had phoned her brother.

'He asked me to put in a good word with you,' she'd said in a bemused fashion when she had emerged from the bedroom with her phone.

'You told him we were together?'

Even now he couldn't believe he'd been tactless enough to say it.

Ava's expression had neutralised in an instant. 'I didn't know it was a secret.'

No, not a secret—but how to explain that in the past the women in his fishbowl world had appreciated his discretion?

This wasn't like that. It wasn't a liaison. It wasn't anything either of them should be ashamed of.

He didn't intend to hide her away in the *palazzo*. He hadn't exactly formulated a plan, but he wanted to show her Rome, and naturally that would include meeting people—people who mattered to him—introducing her as…as…

He looked over at her now. She was scrolling through her phone, checking the e-mails from her business.

He cleared his throat. 'Ava—'

Ava said a rude word.

'*Cara…?*'

'Stop the car.'

When he continued to drive she wailed, '*Please*, Benedetti!'

It was the please that worked. Braking and pulling over, he barely had the car to a standstill before she sprang out.

Swearing fairly colourfully himself Gianluca leapt out after her, stalking around to where she stood with one hand on her hip, the other waving her phone at him.

'Guess who spotted us on a celebrity gossip site on the internet? *Guess?*'

He hadn't seen this side of Ava since—well, since she'd been in his bed. All her fire had been directed one way, and now it was going another. He couldn't say his life had been dull since her advent into it.

'The Pope?'

'My personal assistant! Do you know what this means? Everyone in the bloody office is talking about me and "the Italian Prince"—like I'm Mary Donaldson or something.'

'*Cosa?*'

She waved the phone again. 'Mary Donaldson from Tasmania—married the Crown Prince of Denmark. Big wedding. He cried. Australia finally got itself a royal!' Ava shook her head. 'You really need to pay attention to the news.'

Gianluca considered telling her he'd been at the wedding, but there were more important things under consideration.

'You are unhappy because your employees know you have a personal life?'

'This is hardly a personal life. Seedy is how it looks!'

Gianluca stilled and looked at her. She stood with one hand on her hip. The white capri pants showed off her long legs. The pale blue T-shirt moulded to her like a second skin.

It was impossible to imagine her in those ugly black trousers, that mumsy silk blouse, with her mouth drawn into a tight, suspicious line. *Go away. I don't want you.*

She might be steaming at him, but she seemed to be having a good time and she was undeniably sexy doing it.

This thing between them had softened her, tempered her, and it had touched him too…

He was happy, and he had no idea how it had happened.

'You'll have to fix this,' she said imperiously.

'Fix it?'

'Yes—issue some sort of statement, make up a story like you said you would about us being related and it being some sort of trick of the photo…'

Gianluca believed this was called being hoist with his own petard.

He strode back to the car.

'What are you doing?' she called after him.

He gunned the engine and Ava moved *rapidamente*, sliding in beside him. She barely had her seatbelt on when he took off, damn sure of one thing—this needed sorting out once and for all.

'What are we doing here?'

Ava was aware her voice was a little shrill but she'd had a fright. The e-mail from PJ had shaken her. The knowledge that people were talking about her, that those photographs were floating around in the ether, had thrown her. She didn't know why it bothered her so much, but suddenly what had seemed romantic felt entirely out of her control.

She'd never had romance in her life, never allowed herself to be vulnerable enough to a man to let her guard down. Now she had and look what had happened—people were talking about her.

She could guess what they were saying...that she was just the latest in a long line...

It made her feel unimportant to him, and this less than what she'd thought it was.

And, really, what was she doing with this man? Where did she think this was going?

Ava, you need to be sensible.

This last was the voice of her past. The little girl who'd had the responsibility for both her mother and her baby brother on her shoulders from far too young an age.

Gianluca had her door open and he took her hand, none too gently.

'Benedetti, I will not go any further until—'

He almost yanked her off her feet and she had to struggle to keep up with him.

The café he took her into was crowded. It was also terrifyingly elegant, and Ava felt under-dressed—especially as heads turned.

'Gianluca, *darling*!'

This seemed to come from a variety of women. Her already shaky confidence did a nosedive.

'Where have you been, my friend?'

A man rose from his table but Gianluca didn't stop, didn't deviate from his course.

Ava tried to loosen his grip, but now he had a hand around her waist, was propelling her in front of him as they were shown by the busboy to a prominent table.

He pulled out her chair.

'Sit down, Ava.'

She sat, too astonished to do anything else. She looked

around and wished she hadn't. People were staring at them. 'How can you just walk in and get a table? Why are we here?' she hissed, all the while trying to keep a social, nothing-to-see-here-people expression on her face.

She tried not to react as she recognised a film director. Undeniably this was a glamorous crowd, out to be seen.

Gianluca leaned across the table and took her hands.

There was a sudden lull in conversation at the tables around them.

'What are you doing?'

He gave her a warm smile. 'If I kiss you now, Ava, it will mean we are an item. Everyone will be talking about us—all of Roman society. You will be the girl who has taken Prince Benedetti's heart. So think carefully before you answer me. We can have a drink together, some food, and nothing needs to change. Do you understand?'

She found herself nodding, then shaking her head. *What was he saying?*

'But I would like to kiss you, Ava *mio*, if you would let me.'

She understood that bit.

And, gazing into his eyes, she began to understand the rest.

Almost as if in a dream she moistened her lips, dropped her lashes, softened her mouth in readiness.

She felt his smile as one hand curled around the back of her head and his mouth met hers in a kiss so tender, so sincere, she could only read it as a pledge.

A light smattering of applause broke out at the tables around them.

'Now you are mine,' he said, with his smile against her lips.

He showed her Rome.

He introduced her to his home, his friends, his life.

He took her to restaurants, to theatres, to parties.

They ate together, slept together, and made love as if they'd just discovered the newness of the world and wanted to celebrate creation.

What did it mean?

Ava didn't know and it was killing her—the sense that around the corner waited something large and ferocious, something she couldn't define or defeat.

She stood now in the studio of one of Rome's leading couturiers, being fitted into a strapless midnight blue gown of such sumptuous scale Ava couldn't imagine an event grand enough as its backdrop. But she had trusted Gianluca when he'd explained the Black & White Ball, this year in aid of a breast cancer charity, was one of the highlights of the social calendar. It was an international affair and ballgowns were a requirement.

This dress was certainly going to make a statement. She only hoped the right kind.

She nervously voiced her fears to the three women circling her.

The seamstress at her feet looked up through the folds of satin and said, 'This is a fantasy dress, *signorina*. All you need is the confidence to carry it off.'

'You have the height,' said one of the others.

Ava translated the fulsome gesture from the third towards her breasts with her schoolgirl Italian. 'And the necessary *vavoom.*'

As she stepped out into the street in her civvies she wanted to pinch herself. These had been the most magical, wonderful, inspiring four weeks of her life. If nothing ever happened to her again half as good she would treasure this time, keep it locked up in her heart always against the hard winter when she didn't have love in her life.

Because she suspected it *was* love. As she slid into the plush confines of the limo Gianluca had put at her disposal she acknowledged the truth. She might not have had much of it in her life, but she knew what it looked like when it arrived.

CHAPTER FIFTEEN

ACROSS TOWN, GIANLUCA was in the elegantly appointed offices of Benedetti International from where he ran the world, as Ava put it.

He only half listened to his lawyer on the other end of the line as he stood at the window, looking down on the busy square below.

Everywhere he looked there were couples, old and young. Even the pigeons roosting outside the window came in a pair.

Two generations ago his family's marriages were still being arranged. It was different now. His father had chosen his mother of his own free will—the beautiful Sicilian model Maria Trigoni, who at that time had had her own small moment of fame in a Fellini film. Fidelity had not been high on either of his parents' minds when they made that merger. Prince Ludovico had wanted a beautiful woman on his arm and Maria had liked the title.

At thirty, Gianluca was very accustomed to women who liked the title. They liked the idea of having *Principessa* dangling in front of their name. They saw the *palazzo* in the middle of Rome, the house in Regent's Park, London, the Manhattan apartment, and started ordering monogrammed napkins for the wedding.

All his life he had imagined that when he came to choose a wife his choices would be constrained by the world in which he moved. Watching his parents tear each other apart had not encouraged him to look beyond the highly stratified and stage-managed relationships he'd engaged in all of his life.

Until now.

In Positano they had discussed their work lives—his offices in Rome, New York and London. The deals that put him over the edge, the rush of trade that she so well understood. Ava had spoken about her difficulties with clients—a mining magnate who'd insisted on meeting with her when he came to Sydney at his gym, so she ended up on a stationary cycle talking about his hedge fund. Worse, he was competitive and had insisted she match his rpm.

'Do I *look* like a cyclist?' she'd asked.

'You, *cara*, you look like a goddess.'

But now they were in Rome, spending all their time together, and the conversations were deepening. Last night in bed he'd told her about his childhood fascination with flight, his godfather's encouragement, his father's impatience. Deeply private things.

'He didn't want you to fly?'

Ava had been propped up in his arms, her head beside his. She'd been wearing that little ice-blue lace thing he'd bought her.

'My father wanted me to come into the family business—the banking group. It was all he wanted for me. He saw the planes as a hobby, at worst, a distraction.'

'But it was your passion.'

'It meant nothing,' he said bluntly. 'My entire upbringing was based on discipline—being tough, being a man. What I wanted didn't much come into it.'

'Yet you pushed for it? For what you wanted?'

'*Si.*' He had noticed how fierce Ava looked in that moment. 'You had to fight for something too, Ava *mio*?'

'Working class girl, left school at fifteen,' she'd said, lifting that stubborn chin of hers. 'Damn right I did.'

He'd kissed her then, and made love to her until the memory of how hard he'd had to push for what he wanted and the consequences of that had been wiped out by a deep sense of having something special at last within his grasp. Something far more important than his passion for flight, his ability with the stock market, all the decisions right or wrong that he'd taken in life. Something that had nothing to do with duty or the family name.

Lying in his arms afterwards, she'd told him more about her business back home—a firm that turned over multi-million-dollar accounts—and how she'd drudged full-time to put herself through university in a variety of jobs, the three years she'd worked for other companies as a broker, setting up her connections as ruthlessly as a Roman emperor assembling legions, until at the incredibly tender age of twenty-eight she'd taken the plunge and set up her own firm.

He had told her in turn one of his other secrets—the breaks he took in Anguilla in the Caribbean, at the place he owned down there, the hideaway nobody knew about. And once he'd told her he'd found himself wanting to show it to her. When he'd asked her if she had somewhere she went to drop out of sight for a time she'd admitted it had been a while since she'd been on a holiday.

'Define "a while"?' he'd teased, kissing her neck.

'Never.'

'You've *never* been on a holiday?'

'I'm here now, and I came here for Josh's wedding. I've travelled for business, but just for me, getting away from it all—no.'

She'd looked embarrassed, but also defiant, as if daring him to pass comment.

A knot had formed at the base of his throat.

That knot was still there now.

His lawyer said intrusively, 'If we move now we'll have them over a barrel.'

He flicked his thoughts back to the present. 'Then we move. Let me know when it's done.'

He turned away from the window and the display of happy couples everywhere.

Thinking about Ava, he focussed not on the future but on the now, where he was most comfortable—on the rather narrow, unrelieved tedium she'd described—and it galvanised him.

Certamente he'd take her to Anguilla. He'd take her around the world if her heart desired it. But right now he wanted to play hooky with her. Take the day off. Stand on top of the world.

But first he had an important errand to run. He got his assistant on the line and asked her to notify the bank that he'd be paying a visit to the vault in around half an hour.

He picked her up in the Aventador and headed for Palatine Hill.

They took a picnic with them and in the late afternoon climbed through the ruins of the imperial palace complex, looking down over the Circus Maximus.

Ava had fallen quiet when they'd first arrived. It wasn't the spot they'd come to seven years ago, but there was the same view of the city, the long grass, the pencil pines. Not that he was in a hurry to rake over *those* coals. Whenever he remembered waking that morning to reach for her, only to grasp emptiness, anger rolled through him—and he didn't want to be angry with her.

Not today.

'When my grandparents were courting they came up here,' he said. 'My grandmother was an archaeologist and very much obsessed with this place.' He found himself adding, 'It was a love match, not at all arranged.'

'Does that make a difference?' asked Ava, picking her way over the rocky ground.

'If it had been arranged there would have been respectful afternoons at one another's parents' houses, chaperoned trips to the opera and summer on the coast where the two families would discuss terms.'

'All so two strangers could marry?'

'Not strangers, *cara*. All the families knew one another. I should add that my grandmother came from another old family, so it wasn't a difficult concept for the two sets of parents to accept.'

Ava didn't say anything.

He cleared his throat. 'It's somewhat different now.'

'I guess Josh came as a bit of a shock, then,' she said out of the blue.

Josh who? His normally razor-sharp brain took a few seconds to register the name.

'Your brother,' he concluded reluctantly, aware that the afternoon was going places he hadn't intended it to. 'I won't lie and say there was universal joy, but that had less to do with him not being Italian and more to do with his ability to provide for Alessia.'

'*Provide* for her?' Ava gave a nervous laugh. 'Last time I looked this was the twenty-first century, Benedetti, or hadn't you noticed?'

Si, he'd noticed. If it wasn't she'd be over his shoulder and halfway back to the *palazzo*, where she'd stay locked up.

'I forgot...' she glanced back at him over her shoulder '—you live in a cave.'

'A *palazzo*,' he drawled, 'but close.'

She needed to accept he was a man who would look after her, that he was not one of these excuses for men she had been putting up with—this brother of hers, who clearly had so little regard for his sister that this was the first time in seven years she had been mentioned. Her ex-boyfriend, whom Gianluca hoped one day to cross paths with. The man who had left her fearful of intimacy—so fearful, in fact, that she'd fought him like a wildcat all the way down that mountain at Positano.

His woman now. She would never be that woman again.

He followed the sway of her hips as she stepped carefully over the broken ground.

He heard himself say, 'Look around you, Ava. There have

been people living on the Palatino for a thousand years, and I'm sure back then, as now, a man's worth could be judged on his ability to protect his family.'

Ava stopped and drew herself tall, but didn't turn around. 'A woman protects her family too.'

'Naturally.' He stepped up close behind her. 'You protected your brother all his life. But at some point he had to stand on his own two feet, Ava.'

'How do you know I protected him?'

'You told me here, on that night, about your mother's fragile mental health. How you worried for her, how you'd had to puzzle out the best care for her as she lay dying, how guilty you felt, how alone. And I remember wondering why you didn't have any help.'

Ava's turned around, her face pale.

'I had no idea you were the groom's sister. If I'd known I would have sorted him out for you.'

'Sorted him out?'

'Reorganised his priorities. A man should be responsible for his mother and sister.'

Her mouth formed a tight line. 'I don't need anyone to be responsible for me, Benedetti.'

He understood her resistance. She wouldn't be Ava if she didn't struggle against any incursion on her independence. He understood that too.

'I get it. You don't like my brother. You think he's beneath your high-and-mighty family. Well, newsflash—I wasn't happy about the damn wedding either. I did my best to talk him out of it. I told him he was making a big mistake. Alessia was far too young, and so was he, and I knew your family didn't approve. Your mother—' She broke off, pursing her lips.

'My mother was most vocal, I understand. I suspect she was not kind to you.'

She turned away. 'I don't wish to say anything critical about your mother.'

'Then allow me.' He turned her in his arms. 'She's a manipulative woman who likes everything to revolve around her. She is also highly emotional and not above using a little blackmail to get what she wants. My sisters act as her ladies-in-waiting, so I imagine the women of my family made your life miserable.'

'They were not welcoming,' Ava said tightly. 'That's why I elected to move to a hotel.'

He had to ask. 'Where were you staying?'

Ava dropped her gaze to the base of his throat.

'The Excelsior,' she said in a tight voice.

The same hotel he'd picked her up from last month. The same hotel he'd driven past that day on his way to the hospital...

He couldn't believe it—the Excelsior!

'I stayed there all day...' She lifted her eyes to his. 'Hoping you'd call.'

She'd hoped he would call?

'How?' It burst aggressively out of him and he let go of her, because he didn't trust the strength in his hands. 'How was I supposed to call?'

She staggered back as if hit by a blast furnace.

'You didn't leave a number. But you knew who *I* was. There was nothing stopping *you*, Ava.'

She looked stricken. 'I know.'

'Not. Good. Enough.' The words stamped through his brain, made him want to pound something. He held on to the edges of his self-control as a tidal wave of anger swept everything he'd planned for this afternoon out of reach. He hadn't known until this moment how strong his feelings were.

Ava had wrapped her arms around herself. But her chin was up and she looked defiant, not scared.

'I know that too,' she said. 'But, really, what would have happened? Had you fallen head over heels in love with me? Were we going to spend the rest of our lives together? It was just a night, Luca, and I knew you'd had many just like them.

I only had that one. *One.*' Her voice cracked. 'I wanted to take it with me—intact, perfect.'

'Perfect?' He snarled. 'What was perfect about it? Casual sex with a guy you didn't know? Didn't want to know afterwards?'

She flinched, her eyes reproachful.

'Oh, and you have never done that? You have never just had sex with a woman you had no intention of seeing again?'

'Si, I have done that.' He looked into her stormy green eyes, more dark blue than green in this light, in this mood. 'But I had no intention of doing that with you.'

Ava's sharp intake of breath was the only sound, but in his head Gianluca was hearing himself on this subject for the first time.

The excited voices of a group of children coming up from below had Ava reacting first, looking around as if realising where they were. Without even glancing at him she bolted for a gate to the winding walkway that wound down to the base of the incline.

He was breathing hard by the time he reached her at the car, but it had nothing to do with the exercise. She had her arms folded and she looked murderous.

'I can't believe you would lie to me like that,' she flung at him.

Fury pumped through his veins. At himself, at his father, at this woman who demanded too much from him.

'I do not lie, I do not cheat, and *you*—' he stabbed a finger at her '—you do not run from me again!'

'So speaks Prince Benedetti, Prince of—'

'Of all he surveys—*si*, I got it the first time.'

He took hold of her elbow and jerked her around, dragging her up against him. The scent of her—vanilla and female skin—filled his senses. But the warm, fragrant softness of her body didn't remind him of all the times she had cleaved to him naked; it only served to enrage him more.

She *did* this to him. She made him crazy and furious and

then she sucker-punched him with the fact that she was a woman he would do anything for, and that just left him with nowhere to go.

He wanted her in ways that weren't just sexual—ways that would make any single man nervous—and it was beginning to make him *pazzo*...crazy.

Maybe he *was* crazy. Especially now, as he hauled her up and kissed her. He didn't make it tender or easy or any of the things he'd done with her before. He kissed her with all the wildness of his lust for her, and Ava's body sprang up against his as if this was what she had been waiting for.

A lot of things were different in both their lives. It was time to take the gloves off and see what this thing between them was made of.

He had her up against the car, her skirt worked high on her thighs, and his hand found her hot, wet welcome. She jumped and cried out when he touched her, lifting one leg to his hip, dragging him in against her, rubbing her sensitive inner thigh over his jeans, inviting what was inevitable... He knew right there and then that he had a matter of seconds to make up his mind before his body did it for him. He was a heartbeat away from freeing himself from the purgatory of denim and thrusting inside her.

He cursed, reefing away from her. They were in the middle of a car park! No one was around, but that didn't mean they couldn't have company in the next five minutes.

Ava's eyes were unfocussed, dark, and her colour was high. Her chest rose and fell as, visibly shaken, she drew her stretchy cardigan around her shoulders. Some of the buttons were loose at the top of her dress but she didn't seem to notice.

'Come on,' he said, trying to exert some control on the situation, pressing her into the car. 'We need to get out of here.'

But Ava's head was down, she looked fragile, and although he told himself it was her own fault—she'd created all this—it wasn't true.

He was just as responsible as she was for that night, and she hadn't just run from him—he'd lost her.

He'd been so caught up in what his family wanted from him he'd let this—*Ava*—go.

And maybe that was the price his father had finally exacted—not the stint in the military, or the loss of his football career. The true legacy of being a Benedetti was wanting a woman and not being able to hold on to her. Not the way he wanted to.

The small square box lay heavy inside his jacket.

Without speaking another word he put her in the car and took her home.

Ava stripped off her clothes and immersed herself under the water jets in the wet room. She found she couldn't cry, although the feeling was a pressure in her body, one she couldn't relieve. As the warm water ran down her back she didn't make any effort towards washing her hair, which had been her plan, just let the water sluice through it.

She felt fragmented—as if all the pieces of the Ava she had built up so carefully over the years not only to survive but to flourish had broken apart and she now had to work out which parts went where.

I had no intention of doing so with you.

Those words had hurt her. Because they hinted at what she suspected was true—she could have had all this seven years ago and she'd thrown it away because she'd been afraid to reach out for it and have it disappear.

The only delusion, it seemed, had been her own.

'Ava.'

He was stripped, bigger than her, muscular, his broad shoulders, narrowing to his lean hips, those long, powerful legs. His expression was intent on her.

He often shared her shower, but right now she felt too raw, too exposed to be naked in front of him. She turned towards the splashback, feeling trapped.

She wanted to weep when his hands slid over her hips. As if sex would make everything all right—more likely the emotional turmoil of this afternoon hadn't affected his attitude to that part of their relationship at all. He was a man—what did she expect? Sensitivity? Cry on another woman's shoulder for that.

Yet as he smoothed one hand around her inner thigh and the other cupped her breast, and as he played his mouth hot and teasing over the back of her neck, Ava could feel her body delighting in his touch, eager to experience this yet again.

She had never thought herself a sexual creature. She had often wondered late at night when Bernard had gone home—she had never let him stay overnight—if she had enhanced that night with Gianluca in her memory. But now she knew better. Memory couldn't supply the heat of his body, the scent of him on her skin, the hunger of his mouth, the demand, the way he stretched her with his size and his sheer stamina. Nor could it replicate the gentleness with which he held her afterwards and how supremely female she felt—replete, wanted, loved.

All illusory, of course. It was just the way you felt after good sex—*great* sex.

She'd never had great sex before, so she was bound to get confused.

Just as her body was confused now, as he turned her in his arms and heat rushed up from her sex and set her whole body alight.

'Gianluca…' she said on a sigh, her brain trying to assert itself.

They were toe to toe and his erection nudged her belly.

He kissed her, his mouth hot, wet under the spray. He tasted so good. Her fingers tried to get purchase on the hard ridges of his shoulders, slipped to his biceps, silk over steel. His physicality did it for her—the hardness of his honed body, so different from her own. His hair-roughened chest felt so good riding against the sensitive tips of her breasts.

Too easy—too easy to lose herself in this.

'Things have been too intense over the last few weeks,' he explained as his mouth roamed over her neck, her shoulders, found her nipple. His voice was slurred with lust. 'Let's just do this—this works for us, *tesoro.*'

Ava wanted to weep as he sucked her nipple into his mouth. There was so much to say. But this—for now—would do.

He thought this would do.

He picked up a cloth, soaped it up and began to drag it over her until she was wobbly-kneed and leaning back against the tiles. He slid to his knees and found the soft heat between her legs. Ava shoved a fist to her mouth to stifle the scream building inside her, her other hand tangling its fingers in his hair. She pulled hard as she convulsed, and screamed anyway. He picked her up and, dripping water, took her to the bed, rolled her onto her belly and entered her from behind with a swift certainty that had her senses firing again.

He was impossibly deep inside her and she climaxed with a shocking immediacy.

His expression as he turned her over was almost feral in its wildness. There was none of the gentleness he was usually so careful to show to her, handling her as if she were somehow less robust than him, easily bruised, needed special consideration.

Ava was damn well aware she was going to have bruises tomorrow, and she didn't care.

He thrust so deeply inside her that she gasped, and then again and again, until there was no room for thought, no doubt, only the tension coiling once more, coming like an earthquake from a long way away.

Her mind orbited separately from her body as she wrapped her legs around him and clung until she was sobbing out her pleasure. He made a deep, gratified sound and then there was just their bodies joined, her heavy breathing as she lay with her head plastered to his shoulder, his harsh breathing as his chest rose and fell.

Ava slowly became aware that tension still inhabited her

body, despite the most intense orgasm of her life. Feeling unbearably heavy, she lifted herself up and rolled onto her back, gasping for breath as if she'd just run an endurance race.

She flopped her head to one side and his eyes met hers, still glowing with that intense explosion of desire she'd seen in them as he thrust inside her. It was banked down now, but it was there. Feral, hot, intensely male.

This works for us. That was what he had said. No soft words, no promises, no mention that she would be going home soon. Just, *Things have been too intense…this works for us.*

The tension pulled wire-tight and she knew she had two choices. She could kill him…or she could kill him.

'Again,' she said.

Hours later, when it was still and dark and the only sound was the cicadas through the open windows, he said slowly, 'That night we met I had a lot on my mind.'

He felt her shift but she didn't say a word.

'My father and I had had an argument the day before. God knows it didn't seem important at the time.'

'What did you argue about?' Her voice was soft.

'I had responsibilities and I was trying to evade them.'

'What sort of responsibilities?'

'Look around you, Ava. I'm a Benedetti.'

Around them was a vast bedchamber. A great empty marble fireplace, lights in sconces, frescos on the wall, heavy bedhangings. He wondered if she understood the weight of having all this history around your shoulders.

It wasn't exactly subtle.

'I was eighteen when I graduated from the military academy and went away to the States to start an Economics degrees at MIT. My father assumed I would be using that degree to work in the family business and he turned a blind eye to my life in the US. I was almost twenty-one when I graduated and was recruited to the professional football league.'

He scrubbed his jaw where the beard was already growing in.

'Tell me about the soccer. It must have been very glamorous.'

'Sometimes. Mostly it was training and keeping my nose clean.'

'And parties, and girls...' she trailed off.

'It was a wild time,' he admitted, not about to lie to her. 'But for me it was all about the freedom. You can't know what it was like after all the years of toeing the line.'

Ava made a soft snorting sound. 'Oh, I think I can, but go on.'

'We had a confrontation the day before Alessia's wedding. I told him this was my chance and I wasn't giving it up. My father said I should be by his side at the meetings with the Agostini Banking Group. It was time I showed him I was serious. I told him they were nothing better than organised criminals, and he struck me. I said things I could never take back. I told him I hated him, that he was weak. I hated him for what he'd done to my mother and that my whole purpose in life was never to be like him.'

He pulled himself up a little straighter in the bed.

'He told me I was to put on a suit and go to Naples with him for the meeting. I laughed at him and chose instead to go to my cousin's wedding.'

'Our night,' she said softly.

'The night of the reception, the night we were together— yes, our night.'

Now there was only the sound of the cicadas. They both seemed to be holding their breaths.

'Tell me,' she said.

'He had a massive heart attack. He was only fifty-three.'

'I'm sorry.'

'I never got to take any of it back. He was under tremendous strain. He'd dug himself a hole stretching back twenty years, full of debt and corruption. The entire banking group collapsed, two of his business partners were gaoled, and most of the property was sold to meet the debts.'

'And you joined the military after all,' was all she said.

'For the honour of my family, for my father. It was what he wanted,' he said softly. 'I know it's hard to understand, and I don't entirely understand it myself, but ours was once a good name. It represented service to the state, an integrity that could not be compromised, and in two generations that had been destroyed. I wanted to build something from the ashes, and the military seemed as good a place as any to start.'

'That's why I couldn't contact you,' she said slowly. 'I rang all those numbers you gave me and only one of them, the one to your office, was connected. I guess the message was never passed on.'

Gianluca stilled. 'The media went after our family like piranhas. All the numbers were changed. You left a message, *cara*?'

'A number and my name.'

Gianluca was silent.

Ava moistened her lips. 'That's why you never came for me.'

'Came for you?'

'When I left that morning I thought you knew who I was.'

'But how, *cara*? You only gave me your given name, and even that I got wrong.'

She lifted her head, blinked at him. 'Wrong?'

'I thought you said Evie.'

'Excuse me.' She began to roll off the bed.

He caught her hand. 'Where are you going?'

Ava pulled her hand away. She grabbed her silk robe from the chair and pulled it around her nakedness.

'To get a drink.'

Gianluca had a nice range of spirits in his study, but Ava reached straight for the sherry.

He might not have known her name, but she was the one who'd got everything wrong! Making believe that night was special only to her, holding on to it in her hot little hand as if it belonged to her. Cutting him out of the picture completely.

Life had taught her to keep her feelings locked up. Her father leaving. The upheaval her mother's illness had wrought as she and Josh were farmed out to friends and neighbours.

She remembered all too well as a small girl believing her mother's assurance that their father would come back to them. As she'd grown older she had learned to rely only on what she could quantify, and she had worked hard to pull herself up out of the poverty cycle their mother's illness had put them in.

But that need to guard herself and shred reality of all illusion had done her no favours when it came to her personal relationships. Josh had fled the country to get away from her, she'd wasted two years of her life in a relationship with a man she would never love, and as for her one chance at having something truly magical—she'd destroyed it simply through fear.

She'd run when she should have stood her ground.

Cowardly Ava.

She splashed a little sherry on the sideboard.

'Ava.' His deep voice cut through the shadows.

'I'm sorry,' she said, in a voice she barely recognised as her own because it was so deep with the weight of emotions she hadn't allowed herself to feel in so long—perhaps ever. She tried to think of something else to say, but what came out again was, 'I'm sorry.'

She almost dropped the glass as he came up to her.

He took it out of her hand, lifted it to his nose. 'This won't do, Ava. *Sherry?*'

He put the glass on the sideboard and drew her into his arms.

'I'm sorry,' she said yet again.

'For what, *innamorata*?' He seemed bewildered.

'What do you think? Everything—everything you went through.'

'It's life. These things make us stronger, make us appreciate what we have in the now, don't you think?'

He wasn't only talking about his father. He was talking about them.

Not love, sex. Sex was what they had. Love might have had

a chance once—but she had thrown it away without knowing what she'd almost had.

All her life she'd picked her battles and won them. But this battle she hadn't chosen. It had come along and taken her on and she didn't know how to fight it. Then or now. So she'd lost without even knowing she'd once had a chance with her magnificent, proud lion in their own personal Colosseum.

CHAPTER SIXTEEN

THE BALLROOM WAS ALIGHT with thousands of tiny candles and four hundred people who had all paid a premium price to be here.

Ava's heart was like a trapped bird inside her, fluttering desperately to get out. She had needed help tonight to get into the dress. A hairdresser had been flown in from Paris to style her hair, and a make-up artist from Milan. The fragrance mingling with her skin had been mixed for her by a perfumer here in Rome, based on details Gianluca had provided. Nothing about tonight was natural.

'Relax, Ava,' Gianluca said softly, whirling her in his arms. 'You are the most beautiful woman they have ever seen. It is taking people time to become accustomed.'

But there was nothing reassuring in his voice. It was edged with that same tension she was feeling. Had been feeling since that explosion among the ruins and the fallout.

Yet with her hair swept up in an elaborate configuration, drop sapphire earrings hanging low, and a large sapphire framed in tiny white diamonds nestling just above her cleavage, it was true she looked a million dollars.

And no doubt was wearing that sum.

She had felt a little awkward wearing jewellery that had belonged to his grandmother, but Gianluca had assured her the pieces were so rarely worn it was almost a service to give them a showing.

As she spotted Maria Benedetti through the crowd it suddenly felt more like theft.

It was on loan. *Everything* was on loan.

Even her time with this man.

The only thing she could call her own was the dress.

Because, dammit, she had money. She'd earned it by being smart and canny and—yes—ruthless.

Why was it she couldn't be as ruthless about this man as he was clearly being with her?

'You didn't tell me your family were going to be here.'

'I didn't know.'

One glance and Ava could see the muscle ticking in his jaw. She realised Gianluca wasn't any more relaxed about this discovery than she was.

She guessed introducing her to his friends was one thing—to his family was another.

It hadn't occurred to her until she'd looked up into his beautiful face, recognised his set expression, that there had been a method in the madness of their dash from Positano to Naples, their flight from Naples to Rome.

It wasn't romantic. It was pragmatic. It was what a man did when he could feel the walls closing in around him. If the man was Gianluca Benedetti and had a jet and a *palazzo* at his command.

He'd dazzled her, wooed her, done things to her body she couldn't imagine doing with anyone else, and when this was over—whatever *this* was—he would walk away. He wouldn't be so crass as to do it by phone call, but the time would come. It wouldn't be in the near future. His desire for her was too present in their lives at this point.

This was where it was at for him. *This* was what worked for them, apparently. *This* being sex. Long-distance wasn't really going to work, then, was it?

Oh, she suspected once she was back in Sydney they would drift on a little longer together—he would fly in, she would fly out—but other women would cross his path and, really, without anything stronger to bind them how long would he lie in sheets grown cool? One day it just wouldn't work any more.

She'd accepted all this last night—told herself to toughen up, to take it like a man. Men didn't confuse the issue. There was sex, and there was emotional attachment, and apparently they could exist separately. He might have given her the whole package once, but those waters had flowed by.

But it was hard to be a tough operator in a glamorous ball-gown that made her feel so intensely feminine it was all she could do not to spin around like a little girl and send her skirts flying just for the joy of it.

It was hard not to yearn when you found yourself swaying to the romantic strains of Strauss as interpreted by a symphony orchestra, dancing in the arms of the man you had longed for all your life.

It was hard not to cry when the man you loved had had no intention of introducing you to a single member of his family until tonight, when he was being forced into it. He had gone out of his way four weeks ago to make sure that couldn't possibly happen.

Oh, yes, now she knew why she'd always been so wary of dresses. They had a way of transforming you into someone you didn't recognise.

'My mother always gets an invitation,' Gianluca informed her tightly, 'but this is the first time she's come.'

With the air of a man condemned Gianluca steered her across the room. Ava became aware they were the sinecure of every eye.

And with that the last of her confidence fell away.

She felt like a circus freak in her glamorous gown. Every inappropriate outfit her mother had paraded in down their suburban street, every time some teenager had hung out of a bus or car window and shouted, 'Freak!,' at her mother—everything bad about being Tiffany Lord's daughter came rushing back.

Knowing she had to keep it together, Ava stopped listening to Gianluca's quiet instructions. As if he thought she needed guidance on how to be with his mother. She wasn't an idiot. She knew how to behave.

Maria Benedetti looked faintly surprised as Gianluca leaned down and kissed his mother's hand. Ava noticed there was an odd stiffness between mother and son, but then the Principessa was regarding her curiously.

Gianluca introduced them and Ava heard herself offering a polite, 'How do you do?'

'Ava, how much like your brother you look. So, *you* are the young lady who has bedazzled my son?'

It wasn't what she had expected the Principessa to say and Ava immediately floundered.

'Are those the Principessa Alessandra sapphires, Gianluca?'

'Ava carries them off well,' he said tightly.

The older woman gave a insouciant shrug, eerily reminiscent of her son. 'It's nice to see them out of the vault.'

Some other conversation was going on, and Ava didn't even try to follow it. The smile pasted to her face felt paper-thin.

'You look as if you're having a wonderful time, Ava.'

'I am,' Ava lied.

'We will have lunch tomorrow, yes? I would like to know how you are enjoying Rome.'

She looked properly at Maria Benedetti and realised the woman who had so disapproved of Josh was offering her an olive branch.

'Yes, I would like that,' she fumbled, thinking of Friday. Thinking of her ticket. Thinking of the man beside her who still hadn't asked her to stay. She knew now that he wouldn't.

But she had relaxed, and she realised it probably had less to do with the Principessa and more to do with the chip on her shoulder which had been whittled down in the weeks she'd spent with Gianluca.

She wasn't standing out in this crowd. She belonged here every bit as much as Maria Benedetti.

And it wasn't just the dress. Although it helped.

Smiling a little for the first time all evening, she looked around the room, taking in the crowd—and then she saw him.

'Ava?' He lifted his hand in a half wave.

Josh appeared like a mirage in front of her, tall and thin in his tux, tugging on his bow tie.

'I can never manage these things. Alessia fiddled with it in the car and now look at it.' He wasn't quite meeting her eyes and she could see the nerves in him.

Her first instinct was to straighten it for him, but then she remembered he wasn't her little brother any more. He was a grown man. She should treat him that way.

Not even questioning why, she threw her arms around him.

He hugged her back awkwardly.

'It's okay, sis,' he muttered in her ear. 'I'll get you out of this.'

She looked at him in surprise, about to tell him there was nothing to get her out of, but instead she hugged him again. It was so good to see him. It was so good to have the courage to show him that.

The curse had been broken, she thought a little fancifully. She hadn't realised until this moment how she had carried his sentiments around with her for seven years. *Rich, disappointed and alone. I'm not going to spend my life alone and unloved*, she thought, *because no matter where life takes me my brother will always love me.*

She had a big smile on her face when a small hand touched her elbow and she recognised Alessia, five feet of crackling energy. She had hardly changed.

'Your gown is so beautiful. You look like a princess. Gianluca, she looks like a princess! Why have you been keeping her locked up? I thought we'd have to come up to Rome and break you out, Ava.'

'Gianluca has been very kind,' Ava heard herself say sincerely, and caught the look of surprise on his face.

'He *stole* you,' Alessia accused.

Well, what did she say to that?

Gianluca put a glass of champagne into her hand.

Other people joined them. Gianluca's cousin Marco and his wife, Valentina—the couple she had already met. She liked Tina. There was something down-to-earth about her that made her wish all of this were real. She would have made a good friend.

A very pregnant good friend.

'I miss champagne,' she said, indicating Ava's glass.

'It's not very good,' Ava lied.

Tina smiled and, nudging her elbow, steered her away from the group.

'I saw you being introduced to Aunt Dragon. How did it go?'

'The Principessa was most kind.'

'Really? How odd. She's usually brutal to other women. I guess it's come as a shock to her to be introduced to one of Gianluca's girlfriends.'

Ava was about to blurt out, *I'm not his girlfriend*, when Tina said cheerfully, 'In fact you're the first. You're not Sicilian, are you?'

Baffled, Ava shook her head.

Tina moved a little closer. 'A virgin?'

'Pardon?'

'No, you've got that look. That well-loved look.' The other woman gave her a little smile. 'Don't turn around, Ava, but Gianluca hasn't taken his eyes off you. I think he's worried about what I'm telling you. So I'll make it quick. He's a nightmare for women. Looks gorgeous, and he's got the title, all that money. Willing women for Gianluca are like—I don't know… ice in Siberia. Too much of a good thing, yes?'

Yes, she knew. But she felt it like another punch to her chest wall.

'I've never seen him so happy.'

'Happy?'

Gianluca stepped up to her and for a moment Ava wondered if he'd heard. He took her hand and wordlessly drew her away from the group.

'You need air,' he said, almost offhand.

Ava gave Tina a little shrug, but the other woman gave her a wink.

On the terrace he removed his jacket to cloak her shoulders. Ava shook her head, backing up.

'We need to talk.'

She was incredibly beautiful tonight.

But it wasn't like the beauty he had seen in her unguarded moments—waking up first thing in the morning, her eyes sleepy-soft, murmuring silly things to him that made him want to move mountains for her…or just kiss her.

Tonight it was a beauty that came at a cost—the kind he had grown up around. He wanted to mess up her hair, smudge her lipstick, take those heavy jewels and throw them into the Tiber.

He didn't want the Benedettis taking her over. He didn't want her to become one of those weights he carried around his neck.

'We need to talk,' she said softly.

He cleared his throat. '*Si*, this is why I have brought you out here.'

'I want to tell you something first.'

She clasped her hands together as if going to her execution.

For some reason it irritated him. But he'd been frustrated all night. He didn't want to be in a crowd with Ava. He wanted to be somewhere they could be alone, just the two of them, and then perhaps this twisting in his gut would stop.

'Have you ever seen *Three Coins in a Fountain*?' she asked unexpectedly.

He shrugged. 'Maybe. Maybe not. I know the song.'

She gave him a tentative little smile. 'I used to watch that film as a girl and I wanted that life. Some other life, so different from my own it was unrecognisable.'

With a sigh she walked away to the stone railing. Somewhere down there in the darkness the Tiber lurked.

Gianluca found himself thinking about all the carved-up

bodies of the people who had got in his ancestors' way, floating up on its banks. Where Ava saw romance he saw reality.

'You've given me that fantasy, but I think it's time to go,' she said.

Go? She couldn't go.

'Before the spell wears off. Before you wake up one morning and I'm just Ava again.'

What in the hell…? She *was* Ava. Ava who had made him laugh, had made him furious, had made him…*love her.*

He shoved that brutally aside. Loving her wasn't going to work. Benedetti men didn't love their women. They bred from them and then walked away—or as in the case of his father, were driven away.

He'd long ago decided not to continue that nasty little tradition, but if he was going to make the mistake of his life he might as well make it with Ava.

If she thought she was going to walk out on him he'd like to see her try with a ring on her finger, with those heavy jewels around her neck. He'd weigh her down with so much of his history she wouldn't be able to move.

'This life you speak of.' His voice was deep, rough-cut, fraught with a freight load of emotion that seemed to be coming at him too fast. 'Why can't you have it?'

She looked over her shoulder at him carefully, anxiety written in every line of her features.

As well it might be.

The ring was weighting his jacket pocket and right now it felt like a dagger. He reached in and closed his hand over it, made a fist of it.

'Have it, then,' he said, almost aggressively. 'Have this life.'

He reached for her and jerked her around roughly.

Ava cowered back, trying to retrieve her hand. He wasn't letting go.

'I don't know what you're talking about. You're not making sense. Why are you angry with me?'

He took out the ring, held it up to the light.

'Does *this* make sense to you?'

For a moment she looked utterly confused, and then fell utterly still.

'This is the ring my grandfather gave to my grandmother. She only took it off on the day she died, to pass it to my eldest sister.' He took her hand; it was cold and tense in his. She tried to snatch it back but he was so much stronger. 'She chose not to use it and it's been in a vault with the rest of the family jewellery since then. I would be honoured if you—' he forced the ring over her finger, only to realise his hand was shaking, and not in a good way '—would be my wife.'

'It's too small,' she said, in an even smaller voice.

'It can be altered.' He was furious with her. Why was she cowering like that? Why was she acting as if he'd done something unforgivable when she was the one talking about fantasies and here he was fulfilling them?

She began tugging at it. 'I don't want this. Take it back.'

'Gianluca, what are you doing out here? There are people who've come halfway around the world to see you tonight. We all have to do our bit— Oh, I see I've interrupted something.'

Gianluca turned to snarl at their hostess, only to hear Ava make a choked sound of distress. With a flurry of those extravagant skirts she shoved past him and made her way back into the ballroom.

'I need help,' Ava babbled to Alessia. 'This dress won't fit in the back of a taxi and I can't go back with him. I need somewhere to stay…'

'Calm down.' Alessia stroked her arm. 'You'll come and stay with us, of course. We're in a hotel only two blocks away.'

Ava wondered why she didn't feel any better.

'What's going on, Av?' Josh was looking at her with something approaching concern.

In the past she had always fobbed him off. *She* was the protector, the one who kept the wolf from his door, but right now all she could think about was how isolated she was. She'd landed right back where she'd begun—alone in the world.

'You were right, Joshy,' she said, using her old name for him. 'I am destined to be alone.'

She couldn't stay there a moment longer. Picking up her skirts, she made her way to a set of doors. As she ran down the steps outside the *palazzo* it did cross her distressed mind that all she needed at this moment was to lose a shoe, but her Jimmy Choos were holding on as she skirted past security guards who watched as a woman in a fairy-tale dress ran out of the bright lights and into the shadowy road beyond.

Two blocks, Alessia had said.

She could run that far.

Gianluca couldn't find her.

He had made mistakes in his life. This wasn't one of them.

This was a catastrophe.

Had he really pushed a ring onto her finger?

Bullied her like that?

Whatever her reasons for being here with him, it didn't change the single, life-changing fact that he was in love with her, and he'd allowed his anger and resentment with his past to interfere in the way he had treated her.

The one person who made him want a future.

But why the hell had she said she wanted to end it?

Where the hell was she?

'Benedetti?'

Right accent. Wrong Lord sibling.

'Have you seen Ava?' he demanded.

Josh reached back and made a right-hand swing that Gianluca instinctively blocked. He shoved the younger man away.

'*Dio*, what's your problem, Lord?'

'*You're* my problem, Benedetti. You and the way you've treated my sister.'

Gianluca tensed.

'Yeah, that's right. I'm calling you on it. Some loser dumps her and you move right in. She might be smart as a whip, but she's like a deer in headlights when it comes to men.'

'*Si*, we are agreed on that.'

The younger man frowned.

'I want to marry your sister,' Gianluca said impatiently, aware that he was only wasting time. 'I'm in love with her. Does that clear things up?'

There was a sharp female intake of breath. Both Valentina and Alessia were standing behind them.

'Where is she?' asked Valentina.

'That's what I've come to tell you,' announced Alessia, clearly enjoying the drama. 'She ran out of here in a state. Possibly to our hotel.'

Gianluca was already pushing his way across the reception area, his head roaring with blood.

He was going to kill her—but only after he made sure she was all right first.

'Benedetti!' Josh Lord was breathing hard as he reached him on the steps. 'You need to hear this, man. She came to Rome expecting a proposal.'

'*Si*, she's told me,' he growled impatiently.

'No, you don't understand. She paid for the tickets, she booked the hotel, she arranged some damn fool tour of Tuscany—and she bought the ring.'

Gianluca stared at the other man as if he were speaking some language hitherto unknown.

And then he knew what he'd done.

I used to watch that film as a girl and I wanted that life. Some other life, so different from my own it was unrecognisable...

And he'd given her a shoddy proposal at a charity ball. He'd forced a ring onto her finger. He'd made a mockery of her romantic dreams after she'd confessed them to him.

If he didn't find her in the next five minutes he was going to go tear this city apart.

'She won't be at our hotel,' said Josh in a low voice. 'Not if she's hurting. When we were small, and Mum was off her meds and at her worst, Ava would take me for a walk. We'd walk to the end of the road and then she'd say, "We'll just go to the end of the next road, and the next…" as if she were looking for something. She did the same thing the night of my wedding. According to one of Alessia's friends, she didn't come back till the crack of dawn.'

With those words everything fell into place.

'*Grazie.* I know where to find her.'

I stayed there all day, hoping you'd call.

He started to run. She was on foot. He was foot. But one of them was running for his life.

The bar of The Excelsior was dark, lit here and there by lamps, but he saw her the moment he stepped inside.

Gianluca was supremely fit, so he couldn't blame the run for the heaving of his chest as his heart hammered home just how important this moment was.

The heavens had opened on the last block and his hair was plastered to his head, the shirt of his tux was damp, his jacket lost along the route. It had taken longer than it should have, for he'd had an unexpected stop, thumping on the door of Luigi Favonne. Everyone in this section of Rome knew Luigi. He could turn a diamond into living fire and for Principo Benedetti he had found, in his bed robe and bath slippers, a green emerald so true its heat licked his fingers as he held it tight in his hand.

She was sitting at the bar, her ballgown surging around her, her bare arms and shoulders above the midnight blue satin alabaster in the soft white light of the neon-lit room. The bartender was watching her as he polished glasses, and people were giving her curious looks, but no one had approached her.

She seemed to be in a world of her own.

He was within a metre of her when he said, 'Ava *mio*.'

Her head turned slowly. Her face was pale and ravaged with tears.

'I am not your Ava,' she said in a low, terrible voice. 'And I never was.'

She threw something at him. It hit him in the chest and he caught it.

The ring. The heavy, ugly, baroque ring. With all the history attached to it.

He strode up to her and stood there, resolute but unsure where to begin.

She looked up at him, her eyes furious. 'Go away. I don't want you.'

'Then why are you here, my love?'

Her chin came out. Her entire face quivered. 'I'm waiting for someone. If he's the man he should be he'll come, and if he doesn't I'm better off without him.'

He knew then how it had been for her. That long day when he'd been at the hospital with his mother and sisters, with the lawyers at the *palazzo* and with the authorities answering questions, she had been here, waiting for him to show.

Frustration shot through him. They had both made mistakes. There was nothing he could do about the past. Nothing. But he wasn't going to let it rule their lives.

In the end it came down to three words. 'I'm here now.'

She looked at him uneasily.

'I want you to forgive me, Ava. I should have moved heaven and earth to find you.'

He braced himself for whatever would come, and then, like a miracle, her chin quivered, her mouth softened and she said, 'I shouldn't have run.' Her hands spread lightly over her lap. 'You found me tonight.'

Relief shuddered through him.

She loves me, he thought. *I know she loves me.*

'And it was only one night,' she added in a low voice.

'It was our night,' he asserted. 'Our amazing perfect night.'

She looked up, something soft entering her eyes. 'It *was* perfect.'

He pocketed the old ring and extended his hand to her.

'Come with me.'

Slowly, swishing her skirts as she slid off the stool, Ava took his hand. Her soft fingers felt incredibly delicate to him and he couldn't believe he'd shoved that ring onto her finger so crudely.

He never did anything crudely. He'd been raised better. He treated women properly, with kindness and consideration. But Ava had brought other emotions to the surface—strange, rough, wild, authentic feelings. She had seen him at his worst.

She had never shied away from that.

If she would have him he would be the most fortunate man in Rome.

The Excelsior possessed a tower, built in the sixteenth century, its winding stairs well-worn from the many thousands of tourists who had climbed it since it had been restored seventy years ago.

It was roped off at this hour, but a heavy bribe enabled him access and Gianluca whisked her up the steps.

'This is crazy,' she said amidst the rustle of her gown, the heavy tread of his shoes, the click of her heels.

The view was breathtaking.

Even on this overcast night.

'Ava *mio*.' He drew her close. 'To the east of here is the Benedetti summer residence. It's old, and the drains aren't good, but every summer I would be dragged there. I hated it. I hated what it represented—hundreds of years of oppression. I vowed when I was young that I wouldn't marry, I wouldn't have children, I wouldn't continue the legacy.'

He stroked her cheek.

'Then I met you.'

Ava's black lashes were stuck starfish-fashion to her skin as she gazed up at him.

'Do you see that hill to the west? The first tribes ever to inhabit Rome lived there. I want to build a home for us there. Something that belongs only to us and our children.'

'But you don't want children.'

'I want them with you.'

Ava made a little sound.

He fell to his knees before her.

'My love, will you spend the rest of your life with me?'

She swayed slightly and before he could leap up to catch her dropped to her knees in front of him. She clutched at his shoulders. 'Oh, yes.'

He framed her precious face, kissed her temples, her eyelids, her sweet nose, her magnificent cheekbones, the full lush contours of her lips. The face he so loved.

'I love you,' he whispered. 'I loved you from the moment I first saw you in the cathedral, wearing that blue dress with the flowers in your hair. And when I saw you in the old ballroom of the *palazzo*, watching me, I thought, *It's her.*'

'Did you?' Her mouth was smiling, her lashes low.

'So I followed you.'

She shook her head. 'You made me dance with you and I couldn't dance.'

'I don't remember that. I remember I kept pulling you close and you kept trying to put space between us.'

'I didn't know you.'

'You knew enough.'

He chuckled and kissed her—really kissed her—deep and slow.

'I knew it was you that day in the street,' he muttered against her soft mouth. 'I just didn't know I knew.'

'I came to Rome to find you,' she confessed. 'Although I didn't know it at the time.'

It was some minutes before he remembered what was burning a hole in his shirt pocket.

He reached in and extracted the stone, gently laid it in her palm.

Green fire.

'I will have this made into a ring for you, Ava *mio*. It will be yours. *Ours.*'

She looked into his eyes, her heart shining in them.

When they emerged into the street below the rain had stopped, but the roads were wet and there was a pungent smell in the air. He didn't have a jacket to give her, and it wasn't warm, but he was taking her somewhere that didn't matter.

'Where are we going, Benedetti?'

'I thought we'd walk for a while, Ava *mio*, find a little church and get married.'

'Can we do that?' Her voice floated up among the pigeons roosting in the window grooves above them.

'Well, there are banns to be read, and the matter of your citizenship, and I suspect the priest will be in his bed at this hour...' Gianluca drew her in close against him. 'Then again, *innamorata*, this is Rome.'

'Yes,' sighed Ava, resting her head over his heart. 'Anything's possible.'

* * * * *

ROCCANTI'S
MARRIAGE REVENGE

LYNNE GRAHAM

CHAPTER ONE

VITALE ROCCANTI was a banker descended from a very old and aristocratic European family. Opening the private investigator's file on his desk, he studied the photograph of four people seated at a dining table. The Greek billionaire, Sergios Demonides, was entertaining Monty Blake, the British owner of the Royale hotel chain, his highly ornamental wife, Ingrid and their daughter, Zara.

Zara, nicknamed Tinkerbelle by the media for her celebrity status, her silver-gilt-coloured hair and fairy-like proportions, wore what appeared to be an engagement ring. Evidently the rumours of a buyout anchored by a family alliance were true. Most probably Demonides' loathing for publicity lay behind the lack of an official announcement but it certainly did look as though a marriage was on the cards.

Vitale, renowned for his shrewd brain and ruthless pursuit of profit, frowned. His lean, darkly handsome face hardened, his firm mouth compressing. His dark gaze flared gold with angry bitterness because it could only sicken him to see Monty Blake still smiling and at the top of his game. For a fleeting instant he allowed himself to recall the loving sister who had drowned when he was thirteen years old and his stomach clenched at the recollection of the savage loss that had left him alone in an inhospitable world. His sister had been the only person who had ever truly loved him. And the moment that he had worked towards for the better part of twenty years had finally arrived, for Blake looked to be on the brink of his greatest ever triumph. If Vitale waited any longer his prey might well become untouchable as the father-in-law of so powerful a man as Sergios Demonides. Yet how had Blake contrived to catch a fish as big as Demonides in his net? Apart from the little known fact that the Royale hotel chain had once belonged to Demonides' grandfather, what was the connection?

Were the oft-publicised charms of Tinkerbelle, whose brain was said to be as lightweight as her body, the only source of Blake's unexpected good fortune? Was she truly the sole attraction? Vitale had never let a woman come between him and his wits and would have assumed that Demonides had equal common sense. His mouth curled with derision. If he ensured that the engagement was broken the business deal might well go belly up as well and he would bring down Monty Blake, who desperately needed a buyer.

Vitale had never dreamt that he would have to get personal or indeed so unpleasantly close to his quarry to gain the revenge that his very soul craved for closure, but he remained convinced that Monty Blake's cruelty demanded an equal response. Should not the punishment be made to fit the crime? This was not the time to be fastidious, he reflected harshly. He could not afford to respect such boundaries. No, he only had one option: he would have to play dirty to punish the man who had abandoned his sister and her unborn child to their wretched fate.

A man who had always enjoyed enormous success with women, Vitale studied his prey, Tinkerbelle. His shapely mouth quirked. In his opinion she fell easily into the acceptable damage category. And wasn't suffering supposed to form character? Huge blue eyes wide in her heart shaped face, Blake's daughter was undeniably beautiful, but she also looked as shallow as a puddle and was anything but a blushing virgin with tender feelings. Undoubtedly she would regret the loss of so wealthy a catch as Demonides but Vitale imagined that, like her glossy mother, she had the hide of a rhinoceros and the heart of a stone and would bounce back very quickly from the disappointment. And if he left her a little wiser, that would surely only be to her advantage...

'I can't believe you've agreed to marry Sergios Demonides,' Bee confessed, her green eyes bright with concern as she studied the younger woman.

Although Bee was only marginally taller than her diminutive half sibling, and the two women had the same father, Bee was built on very different lines. Zara looked delicate enough to blow away in a strong breeze but Bee had inherited her Spanish mother's heavy fall of dark brown hair and olive-tinted skin and she had substantial curves. Bee was the child of Monty Blake's first marriage, which had ended in divorce, but she and Zara were close. Monty had a third daughter called Tawny, the result of an extra-marital affair. Neither girl knew their youngest sister very well because Tawny's mother was very bitter about the way their father had treated her.

'Why wouldn't I have?' Zara shrugged a narrow shoulder, striving for a show of composure. She was very fond of Bee and she didn't want the other woman worrying about her, so she opted for a deliberately careless response. 'I'm tired of being single and I like kids—'

'How can you be tired of being single? You're only twenty-two and it's not as if you're in love with Demonides!' Bee protested, scanning her sibling's flawless face in disbelief.

'Well…er—'

'You can't love him—you hardly *know* him, for goodness' sake!' Bee exclaimed, quick to take advantage of Zara's hesitation. Although she had met Sergios Demonides only once, her shrewd powers of observation, followed up by some careful Internet research on the Greek tycoon, had warned her that he was altogether too tough a proposition for her tender-hearted sister. Demonides had a very bad reputation with women and he was equally renowned for his cold and calculating nature.

Zara lifted her chin. 'It depends what you want out of marriage and all Sergios wants is someone to raise the children that have been left to his care—'

Bee frowned at that explanation. 'His cousin's three kids?'

Zara nodded. Several months earlier Sergios' cousin and his wife had been killed in a car crash and Sergios had become their children's legal guardian. Her future husband was a forceful, sardonic and distinctly intimidating shipping magnate, who travelled a great deal and worked very long hours. If she was honest, and there were very few people in Zara's life whom she dared to be honest with, she had been considerably less intimidated by Sergios once he had confessed that the only reason he wanted a wife was to acquire a mother for the three orphans in his home. That was a role that Zara felt she could comfortably cope with.

The children, ranging in age from a six-month-old baby to a three-year-old, were currently being raised almost entirely by his staff. Apparently the children had not settled well in his household. Sergios might be a very rich and powerful man but his concern for the children had impressed her. The product of a dysfunctional background himself, Sergios wanted to do what was best for those children but he just didn't know how and he was convinced that a woman would succeed where he had failed.

For her own part, Zara was desperately keen to do something that would finally make her parents proud of her. Her twin Tom's tragic death at the tender age of twenty had ripped a huge hole in her family. Zara had adored her brother. She had never resented the fact that Tom was their parents' favourite, indeed had often been grateful that Tom's academic successes had taken parental attention away from her wounding failures. Zara had left school halfway through her A-levels because she was struggling to cope, while Tom had been studying for a business degree at university and planning to join their father in the family hotel business when he crashed his sports car, dying instantly.

Sadly for all of them, her charismatic and successful brother had been everything her parents had ever wanted and needed in a child, and since his death grief had made her father's dangerous temper rage out of control more often. If in some way Zara was able to compensate her parents for Tom's loss and her survival she was eager to do it. After all she had spent her life striving for parental approval without ever winning it. When Tom had died she had wondered why fate chose him rather than her as a sacrifice. Tom had often urged her to make more of her life, insisting that she shouldn't allow their father's low opinion of her abilities to influence her so much. On the day of Tom's funeral she had promised herself that in honour of her brother's memory she would in the future make the most of every opportunity and work towards making her parents happy again. And it was a sad fact that Zara's entire education had been geared towards being the perfect wife for a wealthy man and that the only way she would ever really please her parents would be by marrying a rich high-achiever.

The children in Sergios' London home had touched her heart. Once she had been an unhappy child so she knew something of how they felt. Looking into those sad little faces, she had felt that finally she could make a big difference in someone else's life. Sergios might not personally need her, but those children genuinely *did* and she was convinced that she could make a success of her role as a mother. That was something she could do, something she could shine at and that meant a lot to Zara.

What was more, when she had agreed to marry Sergios, her father had looked at her with pride for the first time in her life. She would never forget that moment or the glow of warmth, acceptance and happiness she had felt. Her father had smiled at her and patted her shoulder in an unprecedented gesture of affection. 'Well done,' he had said, and she would not have exchanged that precious moment of praise for a million pounds. Zara was also convinced that marriage to Sergios would give her freedom, which she had never known. Freedom primarily from her father, whose temper she had learned to fear, but also freedom from the oppressive expectations of her perfectly groomed, socially ambitious mother, freedom from the boring repetition of days spent shopping and socialising with the right people in the right places, freedom from the egotistical men relentlessly targeting her as the next notch on their bed post...freedom—she hoped—that would ultimately allow her to be herself for the first time ever.

'And what happens when you *do* meet someone you can love?' Bee enquired ruefully in the lingering silence.

'That's not going to happen,' Zara declared with confidence. She had had her heart broken when she was eighteen, and, having experienced that disillusionment, had never warmed the slightest bit to any man since then.

Bee groaned out loud. 'You've got to be over that lowlife Julian Hurst by now.'

'Maybe I've just seen too many men behaving badly to believe in love and fidelity,' Zara fielded with a cynical gleam in her big blue eyes. 'If they're not after my father's money, they're after a one night stand.'

'Well, you've never been that,' Bee remarked wryly, well aware that, regardless of the media reports that constantly implied that Zara had enjoyed a wide range of lovers, her sibling appeared to be sublimely indifferent to most of the men that she met.

'But who would ever believe it? Sergios doesn't care either way. He doesn't need me in that department—' Zara would not have dreamt of sharing how welcome that lack of interest was to her. Her reluctance to trust a man enough to engage in sexual intimacy was too private a fact to share, even with the sister that she loved.

Bee froze, an expression of even greater dismay settling on her expressive face. 'My goodness, are you telling me that you've actually agreed to have one of those *open* marriages with him?'

'Bee, I couldn't care less what Sergios does as long as he's discreet and that's exactly what he wants—a wife who won't interfere with his life. He likes it as it is.'

Her sister looked more disapproving than ever. 'It won't work. You're far too emotional to get into a relationship like that at such a young age.'

Zara lifted her chin. 'We made a bargain, Bee. He's

agreed that the kids and I can live in London and that as long as I don't work full-time I can continue to run Edith's business.'

Taken aback by that information, Bee shook her head and looked even more critical. Zara's parents had simply laughed when Zara's aunt, Edith, died and left her niece her small but successful garden design business, Blooming Perfect. The Blakes had sneered at the idea of their severely dyslexic daughter running any kind of a business, not to mention one in a field that required specialist knowledge. Their father had stubbornly ignored the fact that in recent years Zara, who had long shared her aunt's love of well-groomed outdoor spaces, had successfully taken several courses in garden design. Huge arguments had broken out in the Blake household when Zara stood up to her controlling snobbish parents and not only refused to sell her inheritance but also insisted on taking a close interest in the day to day running of the business.

'I want…I *need* to lead my own life,' Zara confided with more than a hint of desperation.

'Of course, you do.' Full of sympathy when she recognised the tears glistening in Zara's eyes, Bee gripped the younger woman's hands in hers. 'But I don't think marrying Sergios is the way to go about that. You're only going to exchange one prison for another. He will have just as much of an agenda as your parents. Please think again about what you're doing,' Bee urged worriedly. 'I didn't like the man when I met him and I certainly wouldn't trust him.'

Driving away from the specially adapted house that

Bee shared with her disabled mother, Zara had a lot on her mind. Zara knew that it didn't make much sense to marry in the hope of getting a new life but she was convinced that, as a renowned entrepreneur in his own right, Sergios would be much more tolerant and understanding of her desire to run her own business than her parents could ever be. He would be even happier to have a wife with her own interests, who had no need to look to him for attention, and her parents would at last be proud of her, proud and pleased that their daughter was the wife of such an important man. Why couldn't Bee understand that the marriage was a win-win situation for all of them? In any case, Zara could no more imagine falling in love again than she could imagine walking down the street stark naked. A marriage of convenience was much more her style because love made fools of people, she thought painfully.

Her mother, for a start, was wed to a man who regularly played away with other women. Ingrid, a former Swedish model from an impoverished background, idolised her husband and the luxury lifestyle and social status he had given her by marrying her. No matter what Monty Blake did or how often he lost his violent temper, Ingrid forgave him or blamed herself for his shortcomings. And behind closed doors, her father's flaws were a good deal more frightening than anyone would ever have guessed, Zara thought, suppressing a shiver of recoil.

A moment later, Zara parked outside Blooming Perfect's small nursery. Rob, the manager her father had hired, was in the cluttered little office and he got up with a grin when she came in. 'I was just about to call you—we have a possible commission from abroad.'

'From where?' Zara questioned in surprise.

'Italy. The client has seen one of the gardens your aunt designed in Tuscany and apparently he was very impressed.'

Zara frowned. They had had several potential clients who backed off again the minute they realised that her aunt was no longer alive. 'What did he say when you told him she passed away?'

'I told him you do designs very much in the spirit of Edith's work, although with a more contemporary approach,' Rob explained. 'He was still keen enough to invite you out there on an all-expenses-paid trip to draw up a design. I gather he's a developer and he's renovated this house and now he wants the garden to match. By the sounds of it, it's a big bucks project and the chance you've been waiting for.'

Rob passed her the notebook on his desk to let her see the details he had taken. Zara hesitated before extending a reluctant hand to accept the notebook. For the sake of appearances she glanced down at the handwriting but she was quite unable to read it. As a dyslexic, reading was always a challenge for her but she had always found that actual handwriting as opposed to type was even harder for her to interpret. 'My goodness, what an opportunity,' she remarked dutifully.

'Sorry, I forgot,' Rob groaned, belatedly registering what was amiss, for she had had to tell him about her dyslexia to work with him. He dealt with what she could not. Retrieving the notebook, he gave her the details verbally instead.

While he spoke Zara remained stiff with discomfiture because she cringed from the mortifying moments when she could not hide her handicap and colleagues were forced to make allowances for her. It took her right back to the awful days when her father had repeatedly hammered her with the word 'stupid' as he raged about her poor school reports. In her mind normal people could read, write and spell without difficulty and she hated that she was different and hated even more having to admit the problem to others.

But Zara's embarrassment faded as enthusiasm at the prospect of a genuine creative challenge took its place. Apart from the designs she had worked on with Edith, her experience to date encompassed only small city gardens created on a restricted budget. A larger scheme was exactly what her portfolio lacked and, handled well, would give Blooming Perfect the gravitas it needed to forge a fresh path without relying so heavily on her late aunt's reputation. In addition if she made such a trip now it would ensure that Sergios and her family appreciated how seriously she took her new career. Perhaps then her family would stop referring to the design firm as her hobby.

'Phone him back and make the arrangements,' she instructed Rob. 'I'll fly out asap.'

Leaving Rob, Zara drove off to check the progress of the two current jobs on their books and found one in order and the other at a standstill because a nest of piping that nobody had warned them about had turned up in an inconvenient spot. Soothing the customer and organising a contractor to take care of the problem took time and it was after six before Zara got back to her self-contained flat in her parents' house. She would have preferred greater independence but she was reluctant to leave her mother alone with her father and very much aware that Monty Blake made more effort to control his temper while his daughter was within hearing.

Her indoor pet rabbit, Fluffy, gambolled round her feet in the hall, welcoming her home. Zara fed the little animal and stroked her soft furry head. Within ten minutes of her return, Ingrid Blake, a beautiful rake thin woman who looked a good deal younger than her forty-three years, joined her daughter in her apartment.

'Where the heck have you been all afternoon?' her mother demanded impatiently and at the sound of that shrill tone Fluffy bolted back into her hutch.

'I was at the nursery and I had some jobs to check—'

'The nursery? *Jobs?*' Ingrid grimaced as if Zara had said a rude word. 'When is this nonsense going to stop, Zara? The nursery can only ever be an interest. The real business of your life is the wedding you have to arrange—there's dress fittings, caterers and florists to see and that's only the beginning—'

'I thought we had a wedding organiser to take care of most of that for us,' Zara responded evenly. 'I've made myself available for every appointment—'

'Zara,' Ingrid began in a tone of exasperation, 'don't be more stupid than you can help. A bride should take a more active role in her own wedding.'

'Don't be more stupid than you can help' was a comment that could still cut deep, like a knife slicing through tender flesh, for Zara still looked back on her school years as a nightmare. Her lack of achievement during that period was, even now, a deep source of shame to her.

'This *is* more your wedding than mine,' Zara finally felt pushed into pointing out, for she couldn't have cared less about all the bridal fuss and frills.

Ingrid clamped a thin hand to a bony hip and swivelled to study her daughter with angry eyes. 'What's that supposed to mean?'

'Only that you care about that sort of thing and I don't. I'm not being rude but I've got more on my mind than whether I should have pearls or crystals on my veil and Sergios won't care either. Don't forget that this is his second marriage,' Zara reminded her mother gently, seeking a soothing note rather than piling logs on the fire of her mother's dissatisfaction.

In the midst of the dispute, Rob phoned Zara to ask how soon she could fly to Italy and he kept her on the line while he reserved her a flight in only two days' time. Too impatient to wait for Zara to give her her full attention again, Ingrid stalked out of the apartment in exasperation.

Left alone again, Zara heaved a sigh of relief. At least in Italy she would have a break from the wedding hysteria. Nothing mattered more to her mother than the appearance of things. Zara's failure to hog the gossip columns with a string of upper class boyfriends had offended Ingrid's pride for years and her mother had revelled in Tom's escapades in nightclubs with his posh pals. Ingrid, however, was determined that her daughter's wedding would be the biggest, splashiest and most talked about event of the season.

Sometimes Zara marvelled that she could have so little in common with her parents. Yet Zara and her father's sixty-year-old unmarried sister had got on like a house on fire. Edith and Zara had shared the same joy in the tranquil beauty of a lovely garden and the same unadorned and practical outlook on the rest of life. Her aunt's death, which had occurred within months of her brother's car crash, had devastated Zara. Edith had always seemed so fit that her sudden death from a heart attack had come as a terrible shock.

Zara dressed with care for her flight to Italy, teaming a khaki cotton skirt and jacket with a caramel coloured tee and low-heeled shoes. She anchored her mass of pale hair on top of her head with a judicious clip and used the minimum of make-up, apprehensive that her youth and looks would work against her with the client. After all, nobody knew better than a girl christened a dumb blonde at fourteen that first impressions could count for a lot. But, at the same time, as she stepped off her flight to Pisa she knew that her brother, Tom, would have been proud of her for sticking to her guns when it came to Blooming Perfect and making it clear how close the business was to her heart.

A driver met her at the airport and she was whisked off in the air-conditioned comfort of a glossy black four-wheel drive. The stupendous rural scenery of misty

wooded hillsides and ancient medieval towns soothed
nerves left ragged by a last-minute difference of opinion with her mother, who had objected bitterly once
she realised that Zara was flying off to Italy for a long
weekend.

'And how is your fiancé going to feel about that?'
Ingrid had fired at her daughter.

'I have no idea. I haven't heard from him in a couple
of weeks but I left a message on his phone to let him
know that I would be away,' Zara had countered gently,
for Sergios was not in the habit of maintaining regular
contact with her and she perfectly understood that he
saw their marriage to be staged three months hence as
being more of a practical than personal connection.

'He's a very busy man,' Ingrid had instantly argued
on her future son-in-law's behalf.

'Yes and he doesn't feel the need to keep constant
tabs on me,' Zara pointed out quietly. 'And neither
should you. I haven't been a teenager for a long time.'

Ingrid had pursed her lips. 'It's not like you're the
brightest spark on the block and you know how dangerously impulsive you can be—'

Recalling that dig as she was driven through the
Tuscan hills, Zara felt bitter. Only once in her life had
she been dangerously impulsive and had paid in spades
for that miscalculation. Even four years on, Zara still
burned and felt sick at the memory of the humiliation
that Julian Hurst had inflicted on her. She had grown
up very fast after that betrayal, but even though she
had never been so foolish again her parents continued
to regularly remind her of her lowest moment.

The car turned off the road and her thoughts promptly turned to where she was headed, she sat up straighter to peer out of the windows. The lane became steep. If the house stood on a hill, as seemed likely, the garden would have wonderful views. Her first glimpse of the old stone building basking in the late afternoon sunshine made her eyes widen with pleasure. A traditional set of box-edged beds adorned the front of the villa, which was much bigger and more imposing than she had expected. Designing anything for an individual who owned such a beautiful property would be a major creative challenge and she was thrilled at the prospect.

As the driver lifted out her weekend bag the front door opened and a dark-haired woman in her thirties, elegantly dressed in a business suit, greeted her. 'Signorina Blake? Welcome to the Villa di Sole. I'm Catarina—I work for Signore Roccanti. He will be here shortly. How was your flight?'

Ushered into an airy hall floored in pale limestone, Zara smiled and set down her bag. It was obvious that the newly renovated house was empty and she began to wonder where she would be staying the night. The chatty woman showed her round the property. Well over a hundred and fifty years old, the villa had undergone elegant modernisation. In every way it was a stunning conversion. Rooms had been opened up and extended, opulent bathrooms added and smooth expanses of natural stone flooring, concealed storage and high-tech heating, lighting and sound systems added to achieve a level of luxury that impressed even Zara.

Catarina was a blank wall as far as questions concerning the extensive grounds were concerned. She had no idea what her employer might want done with the garden or what the budget might be.

'Signore Roccanti has discriminating taste,' she remarked as Zara admired the fabulous view of hills covered with vineyards and olive groves.

Fine taste and plenty of cash with which to indulge it, Zara was reflecting when she heard the dulled roar of a powerful car engine at the front of the property. Catarina hurried off with a muttered apology and moments later Zara heard heavy footsteps ringing across the tiled entrance hall.

She glanced up just as a man appeared in the doorway and her breath tripped in her throat. Sunshine flooded through the windows, gleaming over his black hair and dark curling lashes while highlighting the stunning lines of his classic bone structure and beautifully modelled mouth. He was smoking hot and that acknowledgement startled her—it was rare for Zara to have such a strong, immediate response to a man.

'A business appointment overran. I'm sorry I kept you waiting, *signorina*,' he murmured smoothly, his dark reflective gaze resting on her.

'Call me Zara, and you are…?' Zara was trying not to stare. She picked up the edge of strain in her voice and hoped it wasn't equally audible to him. She extended her hand.

'Vitale Roccanti. So, you are Edith's niece,' he remarked, studying her from below those outrageously long lashes, which would have looked girlie on any less masculine face, as he shook her hand and released it again, the light brush of those long brown fingers sending tingles of awareness quivering all over her body. 'Forgive me if I comment that you don't look much like her. As I recall she was rather a tall woman—'

Zara stilled in surprise. 'You actually met Edith?'

'I was living at the Palazzo Barigo with my uncle's family when your aunt was designing the garden,' Vitale explained, his gaze momentarily resting on her slender hand and noting the absence of an engagement ring. Had she taken it off?

As he made that connection with the woman who had taught her almost everything she knew Zara relaxed and a smile stole the tension from her delicate features. 'It is the most wonderful garden and in all the professional design books…'

When she smiled, Vitale conceded, she shot up the scale from exceptionally pretty to exquisitely beautiful. The photos hadn't lied but they hadn't told the whole truth either. In the light her pale hair glittered like highly polished silver, her velvety skin was flawless and those eyes, lavender blue below arched brows, were as unusual as they were gorgeous. He reminded himself that he liked his women tall, dark and curvaceous. She was tiny and slender as a ribbon, her delicate curves barely shaping her T-shirt and skirt, but she was also, from her dainty ankles to her impossibly small waist, an incredibly feminine woman. As for that mouth, unexpectedly full and rosy and ripe, any man would fantasise about a mouth that alluring. Vitale breathed in slow and deep, willing back the libidinous surge at his groin. He had not expected her to have quite so much appeal in the flesh.

'Have you been outside yet?' Vitale enquired.

'No, Catarina was showing me the house when you arrived—it's most impressive,' Zara remarked, her gaze following him as he pressed a switch and the wall of glass doors began to slide quietly back to allow access onto the terrace. He moved with the silent grace of a panther on the prowl, broad shoulders, narrow hips and long elegant legs defined by his beautifully tailored grey designer suit. She found it difficult to remove her attention from him. He was one of those men who had only to enter a room to command it. Even in a crowd he would have stood out a mile with his exceptional height, assurance and innate sophistication.

'The garden should complement the house with plenty of outside space for entertaining,' he told her.

'I see there's a pool,' she remarked, glancing at the feature that was at least fifty years old and marooned like an ugly centrepiece in the lank, overgrown grass.

'Site a replacement somewhere where it will not be the main attraction.'

Zara tried not to pull a face at the news that that landscaper's bête noire, the swimming pool, was to feature in the design. After all, every job had its pitfalls and there was plenty of space in which to provide a well-screened pool area. 'I have to ask you—is this going to be your home? Will a family be living here?'

'Aim at giving the garden universal appeal,' he advised, his face uninformative.

Zara felt slightly foolish. Of course if the villa was to

be sold which was the most likely objective for a property developer, he would have no idea who the eventual owner would be. As she began to walk down the worn steps her heel skittered off the edge of one and his hands cupped her elbow to steady her. The faint scent of a citrus-based cologne flared her nostrils in the hot still air. When she reached level ground again he removed his hand without fanfare but she remained extraordinarily aware of his proximity, the height and strength of his long, lean frame, not to mention the unmistakeable aura of raw masculinity.

She needed measurements for the garden, all sorts of details, but Vitale Roccanti did not look like the patient type, happy to stand around and wait while she took notes. She would have to contain her eagerness to start work until her next visit. The garden ran right up to the edges of woodland and merged with the dark shade cast by the trees. But the open view to the south was nothing short of breathtaking.

Vitale watched her face light up as she caught the view of the hills with the sun starting to go down, bathing the trees in a golden russet light. Her habitually wary expression was transformed into one of open enjoyment. She was not at all what he had expected, being neither flirtatious nor giggly nor even high maintenance if that plain outfit was the norm for her. No make-up that he could see either, which was an even more unusual sight for a man accustomed to decorative women, who preferred to present a highly polished image for his benefit.

As Zara turned back to him her unusual lavender

eyes were shining at the prospect of the challenge before her. In such beautiful surroundings this was truly her dream job. 'How much land does this place have?'

The purity of her heart-shaped face, lit up with the unhidden enthusiasm of a child's, made the man watching her stare. *Per amor di Dio,* Vitale reflected involuntarily, what a piece of perfection she was! The unfamiliar thought jolted him and his hard bone structure tautened and shadowed.

'The land as far as you can see belongs to the house. It was once a substantial agricultural estate,' he explained. 'You'll be able to come back here to explore tomorrow. A vehicle will be placed at your disposal.'

Zara encountered stunning dark golden eyes with the shrewd watchful penetration of gold-tipped arrows. Dark-hued, deep-set, very sexy eyes surrounded by inky black lashes and blessed with extraordinary impact. Goose bumps erupted on Zara's arms. Her mouth ran dry, her tummy executing a sudden somersault that made her tense and dizzy. 'Thanks, that will be very helpful,' she responded, striving to overcome the way she was feeling by making herself remember Julian and the pain and humiliation that he had inflicted on her.

'Prego!' Vitale answered lightly, showing her back indoors and escorting her back through the silent house.

In the hall she bent down to lift her weekend bag.

'I have it,' Vitale said, reaching the bag a split second in advance of her.

She followed him outside and hovered while he paused to lock up. He opened the door of the black

Lamborghini outside, stowed her bag and stepped back for her to get in.

'Where will I be staying?' she asked as she climbed into the passenger seat, nervous fingers smoothing down her skirt as it rose a little too high above her knees.

'With me. I have a farmhouse just down the hill. It will be a convenient base for you.' His attention inescapably on those dainty knees and pale slim thighs, Vitale was thinking solely of parting them and he caught himself on that X-rated image with a frown.

What the hell was the matter with him? Anyone could have been forgiven for thinking that he was sex-starved, which couldn't be further from the truth. Vitale scheduled sex into his itinerary as efficiently as business appointments. He had lovers in more than one European city, discreet, sophisticated women who knew better than to expect a lasting commitment from him. There were no emotional scenes or misunderstandings in Vitale's well-ordered life and that was how he liked it. He had not rebuilt his life from the ground up by allowing weakness to exist in his character. He had no expectations of people and he certainly didn't trust them. If there were no expectations there was less chance of disappointment. He had learned not to care about women, especially not to love them. Life had taught him that those you cared about moved on, died or betrayed you. In the aftermath of such experiences being alone hurt even more but it was safer not to feel anything for anyone. That credo had served him well, taking him from extreme poverty and deprivation to the comfortable cultured life of a multimillionaire, who seemed to make more money with every passing year.

CHAPTER TWO

THE farmhouse sat a good distance from the mountain road, accessed by a track that stretched almost a kilometre into dense woods. Built of soft ochre-coloured stone and roofed in terracotta, the property was surrounded by a grove of olive trees with silvery foliage that seemed to shimmer in the fading light.

'Very picturesque,' Zara pronounced breathlessly, belatedly registering that she had allowed herself to be brought to an isolated place in the countryside by a man whom she knew almost nothing about! She mentally chastised herself for her lack of caution.

As her lips parted to suggest that she would prefer a hotel—at her own expense—a plump little woman in an apron appeared at the front door and smiled widely.

'My housekeeper, Guiseppina, has come out to welcome you. Be warned, she will try to fatten you up,' Vitale remarked teasingly as he swung out of the car.

The appearance of another woman relieved much of Zara's concern, although a stubborn thought at the back of her mind was already leafing through various murders in which the killers had enjoyed female companionship and support in which to commit their crimes. Her colourful imagination had often been considered one of her biggest flaws by her teachers. 'I think I would prefer to be in a hotel—I'll settle my own bills,' she muttered tautly.

In considerable surprise, for he was accustomed to women seizing on every opportunity to enjoy his full attention, Vitale recognised her apprehension and murmured, 'If you would be more comfortable staying in this house alone I will use my city apartment while you are here. It is not a problem.'

Flushing in embarrassment, afraid that she might have sounded a little hysterical while also being soothed by his offer, Zara hastened to recant. 'No, that's really not necessary. I think it's the fact I know virtually nothing about you except that you're a property developer—'

'But I'm not…a property developer,' Vitale confided in a ludicrous tone of apology.

Zara studied his lean bronzed features with a bemused frown. 'You're…*not*?' A helpless laugh bubbled out of her throat because there was something very amusing about the way in which he had broken that news.

'I'm a banker,' Vitale admitted.

'Oh…' Zara exclaimed, nonplussed by that level admission, there being nothing flashy, threatening or indeed exciting about bankers in her past experience.

'The property developing is only a pastime.' Her patent lack of interest in his admission set his teeth on edge a little. Had he been spoilt by all the women who hung on his every word and eagerly tried to find out everything about him?

Bubbling Italian like a fountain, Giuseppina was a bustling whirlwind of a woman and she instantly took centre stage. Although Zara didn't understand much of what she was saying, it didn't inhibit Giuseppina's chatter. She drew Zara eagerly into the house and straight up the creaking oak staircase to a charming bedroom with painted furniture and crisp white bed linen. Zara glanced with satisfaction at the en suite bathroom. The walls might be rustic brick and the furniture quirky and antique but, like the Villa di Sole, every contemporary comfort had been incorporated.

A light knock sounded on the ajar door. Vitale set her bag down on the wide-planked floor. 'Dinner will be served in an hour and a half. I hope you're hungry. I bring guests here so rarely that Giuseppina seems determined to treat us to a banquet.'

Zara glanced at him and for an instant, as she collided with dark eyes that glowed like the warmest, deepest amber in the fading light, it was as though her every defence fell down and she stood naked and vulnerable. For a terrifying energising moment she was electrified by the breathtaking symmetry and beauty of his face regardless of the five o'clock shadow of stubble steadily darkening his jaw line. She wondered what it would feel like to kiss him and the passage of blood through her veins seemed to slow and thicken while her heart banged behind her ribs and her breath dragged through her tight throat.

As Giuseppina took her leave, her sturdy shoes ringing out her descent of the stairs, Vitale held Zara's gaze, his eyes scorching gold, lashes dipping low as though to conceal them. 'I'll see you at dinner,' he told her huskily, backing away.

As the door shut on his departure Zara was trembling. She felt too warm. Unfreezing, she darted into the bathroom to splash her face with cold water. Her hands shook as she snatched up the towel to dry herself again. Never before had she felt so aware of a man. The feelings that had drawn her to Julian as a teenager paled utterly in comparison. She stripped where she stood to go for a shower. What was happening to her? She had decided a long time ago that she just wasn't that sexual a being. Only once had a man made Zara want to surrender her virginity and that man had been Julian, but if she was truthful she had only been willing to sleep with him because she had assumed that it was expected. When in fact Julian had put greed ahead of lust in his priorities, Zara had been left a virgin and a very much sadder and wiser one. So what was different about Vitale Roccanti?

After all, in August she was supposed to be marrying Sergios Demonides and, having thoroughly weighed up the pros and cons, she had reached that decision on her own. All right, she didn't love the man she had promised to marry and he didn't love her, but she did respect the commitment she had made to him. Loyalty and respect *mattered* to her. Was it stress that was making her feel edgy and out of sync? Or was Bee's warning that she might fall for another man after she married working on some level of her brain to make her more than usually aware of an attractive man? Vitale *was* an extraordinarily handsome man and very charismatic. That was fact. Possibly she was more nervous about getting married than she had been prepared to admit even to herself. And for all she knew Vitale Roccanti was a married man. Yanking a towel off the rail as she stepped out of the shower, she grimaced at that suspicion. At the very least he might be involved in a steady relationship. And why on earth should that matter to her? Not only did it not matter to her whether he was involved or otherwise with a woman, it was none of her business, she told herself staunchly. In the same way it was none of Vitale's business that she was committed to Sergios. She thought it was unfortunate, though, that Sergios had chosen not to give her an engagement ring. But there was still no good reason why she should bother telling Vitale that she was getting married in three months' time. Why was she getting so worked up?

Releasing her hair from the clip, she let the silvery strands fall loose round her shoulders and she put on the print tea dress she had packed for more formal wear. Dinner was served on the terrace at the rear of the property. A candle flickered on the beautifully set table in the shade of a venerable oak tree. Her slim shoulders unusually tense, Zara left the shelter of the house.

A glass of wine in one hand, Vitale was talking on a cell phone in a liquid stream of Italian. He was casually seated on the edge of a low retaining wall, a pair of chinos and an open shirt having replaced the suit he had worn earlier. Black hair still spiky from a shower, he had shaved, baring the sleek planes of his features and throwing into prominence his beautifully shaped mouth. Her heart seemed to take a flying leap inside her body, making it incredibly difficult to catch her breath.

'Zara,' he murmured softly in greeting, switching off the phone and tossing it aside.

'I used to hate my name but suppose everyone does at some stage when they're growing up,' Zara confided, aware that she was chattering too much in an effort to hide her self-consciousness but quite unable to silence herself.

'It's a pretty name.'

Madly aware of his intense scrutiny, Zara felt her cheeks warm. For goodness' sake, relax, she urged herself, exasperated by her oversensitive reaction to him. He sprang fluidly upright, his every physical move laced with easy strength and grace, and asked her if she would like some wine. He returned from the house bearing a glass.

It was a warm evening. She settled into the seat he pulled out from the table for her and Giuseppina appeared with the first course, a mouth-watering selection of *antipasti*. Her bright dark eyes danced between them with unconcealed curiosity and romantic hopes.

'I'm twenty-nine. She thinks I ought to be married by now with a family and she keeps on warning me that all the best girls have already been snapped up,' Vitale told her in an undertone, his eyes alive with vibrant amusement.

Surprised by his candour, Zara laughed. 'Have they
been?'

'I don't know. The women with wedding rings in
their eyes are the ones I've always avoided,' Vitale volunteered.

Zara reckoned that if she was truly the honest person she had always believed she was she would be telling him that she was within a few months of getting
married herself. Yet while the admission was on her
tongue she could not quite bring herself to speak up. At
the same time she could not help wondering if Vitale
could actually be warning her off. Was it possible that
he was letting her know that he had only ever been in
the market for a casual affair?

Whatever, there was no future or sense in succumb-
ing to any kind of entanglement with him and she was
far too sensible to make such a mistake. In honour of
that conviction and impervious to his polite look of
surprise, Zara dug her notebook out of her bag and
began to quiz him about his garden preferences and
his budget. The main course of steak was so tender it
melted on her tongue and it was served with a tomato
salad and potato and cheese croquettes. She ate with
unbridled pleasure for it was, without a doubt, an exceptional meal, and when she could bring herself to set
down her knife and fork she took notes.

'This is not quite how I envisaged dining with you,'
Vitale remarked wryly. It hadn't escaped his notice that
she ignored any hint of flirtation, preferring to maintain
a professional barrier he had not expected. Of course
she was clever enough to know that lack of interest only

made the average man keener, he decided, unwilling to concede the possibility that she might be genuinely indifferent to him.

Although he was taken aback by her eagerness to work he was pleasantly surprised by her healthy appetite and the way in which she savoured Giuseppina's renowned cuisine, for he was accustomed to women who agonised over eating anything more calorific than a lettuce leaf. 'You should be relaxing. You can work tomorrow.'

'But I'm only here for a couple of days. I need to make the most of my time,' Zara told him lightly as Guiseppina set a lemon tart on the table and proceeded to cut slices. 'And if I do find myself with a spare couple of hours I'm hoping to try and visit the garden my aunt Edith made at the Palazzo Barigo.'

'Have you not already seen it?'

'I've never been to this area before. My parents don't do rural holidays.' Her sultry mouth quirked at the mere idea of her decorative mother in a countryside setting. 'I did ask my aunt once if she would like to come back and see the garden and she said no, that gardens change with the passage of time and that she preferred to remember it as it was when it was new.'

'If I can arrange it before you leave I will take you to the Palazzo Barigo for a tour,' Vitale drawled softly, lifting the bottle to top up her wine glass.

'No more for me, thanks,' Zara told him hurriedly. 'I get giggly too easily, so I never drink much.'

Vitale was sardonically amused by that little speech. She was putting up barriers as prickly as cactus leaves and visibly on her guard. But he was too experienced not to have noticed her lingering appraisals and he was convinced that she wanted him even though she was trying to hide the fact. Erotic promise thrummed through his body, setting up a level of anticipation beyond anything he had ever experienced.

Vitale was as well travelled as Zara and they shared amusing anecdotes about trips abroad, discovering that their sense of humour was amazingly similar. He moved his hands expressively while he talked and slowly but surely she found herself watching him like a hawk. When all of a sudden she collided with his scorching golden eyes, she couldn't even manage to swallow. The truth that she couldn't stifle her physical response to him alarmed her. She was not in full control of her response to Vitale Roccanti and disturbingly that took her back to her ordeal with Julian. She breathed in slow and deep and steady, mentally fighting to step back from her reactions. Vitale was gorgeous but not for her. She didn't want to dip a toe in the water, she didn't want to get her fingers burnt either. Even if it killed her she was determined to retain her self-respect.

'I hope you won't think I'm being rude but I've had a lot of late nights this week and I would like to turn in now so that I can make an early start in the morning,' Zara proffered with a bright smile of apology.

Vitale accepted her decision with good grace, rising immediately to his feet. Her cheeks warmed at the sudden suspicion that he might only have been entertaining her out of courtesy. Not every guy wanted to jump her bones, she reminded herself irritably.

At the foot of the stairs, she hovered, disconcertingly reluctant to leave him even though she had carefully engineered her own exit. 'Will I see you in the morning?' she asked breathlessly.

'I doubt it. I'll be leaving soon after six,' Vitale imparted, watching her slim figure shift restively. His level of awareness was at such a pitch it was not only his muscles that ached.

Still unable to tear herself away, Zara looked up at him, focusing on the irresistible dark glitter of his stunning eyes and his perfect lips. He was downright drenched in sex appeal and she wanted to touch him so badly her fingertips tingled. The hunger he was suddenly making no attempt to hide made her feel all hot and shivery deep down inside.

'But before we part, *cara mia...*' Vitale purred, purebred predator on the hunt as he closed long, deft fingers round her arm to ease her closer.

He took Zara by surprise and she froze in dismay, nostrils flaring on the scent of his cologne. 'No,' she said abruptly, planting both her palms firmly to his broad chest to literally push him back from her. 'I don't know what you think I'm doing here but I'm certainly not here for this.'

Ditching the smile ready to play about his beautifully sculpted mouth, Vitale lifted a sardonic brow. 'No?'

'You have a hell of an opinion of yourself, don't you?' The tart rejoinder just leapt off Zara's tongue, fierce annoyance rattling through her at his arrogant attitude. Evidently he had expected her to succumb rather than shoot him down and the knowledge infuriated her, for she had met too many men who expected her to be a pushover.

His dark, heavily lashed eyes flashed with anger and then screened. 'Perhaps I misread the situation—'

'Yes, you definitely did,' Zara retorted defensively. 'I'm grateful for your hospitality and I've enjoyed your company but that's as far as it goes! Goodnight, Vitale.'

But as she hastened up the stairs and hurriedly shut her bedroom door she felt like a total fraud. Exit shocked virginal heroine stage left, she mocked inwardly, her face burning. He had not misread the situation as much as she would have liked to believe. She *did* find him incredibly attractive and clearly he had recognised the fact and tried to act on it. She was not the undersexed woman she had come to believe she was. But what a time to make such a discovery about herself! Why now? Why now when she was committed to marrying another man? Even though her bridegroom had no desire to share a bed with her, her susceptibility to Vitale Roccanti's lethal dark charisma made her feel guilty and disloyal.

She lay in bed studying the crescent of the moon gleaming through the curtains. Vitale was simply a temptation she had to withstand and maybe it was good that she should be reminded now that being a married woman would demand circumspection from her. In the future she would be more on her guard. But she could not forget that even in a temper she had still not told him that she was getting married that summer.

CHAPTER THREE

At war with herself, Zara tossed and turned for a good part of the night, wakening to a warm room bathed in the bright light filtering through the thin curtains. Seating her on the terrace, Giuseppina brought her a breakfast of fresh peaches, milky coffee and bread still warm from the oven served with honey. Birds were singing in the trees, bees buzzing and golden sunshine drenched the country valley below the house. It was a morning to be glad to be alive, not to brood on what could not be helped. So, a handsome Italian had made a mild pass at her, why was she agonising over the fact? The attraction had been mutual? So, she was human, fallible.

Giuseppina brought her keys to the car and the villa and Zara left the house to climb into the sturdy pickup truck parked outside. In the early morning quiet the garden of the villa was a wonderful haven of peace. Grateful that it was still relatively cool, Zara took measurements and sat down on a wrought iron chair in the shade of the house to do some preliminary sketches. She chose the most suitable site for the pool first and, that achieved, her ideas were free to flow thick and fast. For the front of the house she wanted a much more simple and soft approach than the current formal geometry of the box-edged beds. So engrossed was she that she didn't hear the car pulling up at the front and she glanced up in surprise when she heard a door slam inside the house.

Vitale strolled outside, a vision of sleek dark masculinity sheathed in summer casuals, a sweater knotted round his shoulders with unmistakeable Italian style. She scrambled up, her heart going bang-bang-bang inside her chest and her mouth dry as a bone.

'Time for lunch,' he told her lazily.

Zara glanced at her watch for the first time since she had arrived and was startled to find that the afternoon was already well advanced. It had taken his reminder for her to notice that her tummy was hollow with hunger. 'I lost track of time...'

Vitale moved closer to glance curiously at the sheaf of sketches she was gathering up. 'Anything for me to see yet?'

'I prefer to submit a design only when I'm finished,' she told him evenly, accustomed to dealing with impatient clients. 'I've been working on some options for the hard landscaping first.'

He studied her from beneath the dark lush screen of his lashes. Even without a speck of make-up and clad in sexless shorts and a loose shirt, she was a true beauty. Tendrils of wavy silvery hair had worked loose from the clasp she wore to cluster round her damp temples and fall against her cheekbones. Her lavender eyes were wide above heat-flushed cheeks, her temptress mouth lush and natural pink. The tightening heaviness at his groin made his teeth clench. She looked very young, very fresh and impossibly sexy. He remembered the rumour that Monty Blake had paid a fortune to suppress pornographic pictures taken by some boyfriend of hers when she was only a teenager and he reminded himself that it was quite some time since Zara Blake was in a position to claim that level of innocence.

Disturbingly conscious of his measuring appraisal, Zara packed away her sketch pad and pencils. The coarse cotton of her shirt was rubbing against her swelling nipples. As was often her way in a hot climate she had not worn a bra and in his presence her body was determined to misbehave and she was insanely aware of those tormented tips.

'I'm taking you to the Palazzo Barigo,' Vitale volunteered, walking her back through the house and out to the Lamborghini.

Edith's garden, he was taking her to see Edith's garden! Zara almost whooped with delight and a huge grin curved her soft lips; she turned shining eyes on him. 'That's wonderful—is it open to the public, then?'

'Not as a rule.'

'Of course, you said it belonged to your uncle,' she recalled, reckoning that, had she been on her own, she might not have been granted access. 'Thank you so much for making this possible. I really appreciate it. Should I get changed or will I do as I am? I haven't got many clothes with me. I like to travel light.'

'There is only staff at the palazzo at present. You can be as casual as you like,' Vitale responded lightly.

'What will we do about the car I drove here?' she asked belatedly.

'It will be picked up later.'

The Palazzo Barigo lay over an hour's drive away. Zara used a good part of the journey to sound him out on different kinds of stone and then she discussed the need for a lighting consultant. She found him more silent and less approachable than he had seemed the night before. Had her rejection caused offence? It was probably her imagination, she thought ruefully, but once or twice she thought he seemed distinctly tense. His lean, hard-boned face was taut in profile, his handsome mouth compressed.

'How did you spend your morning?' she enquired when she had failed to draw him out on other topics.

'At the office.'

'Do you often work at weekends?'

'I was in New York last week. Work piled up while I was away.' His fingers flexed and tightened again round the leather steering wheel.

'This landscape is beautiful. No wonder Edith felt inspired working here.'

'You talk a lot, don't you?' Vitale sighed. The views she was admiring were painfully familiar to his grim gaze. He felt as though his world were turning full circle, bringing him back to the place where the events that had indelibly changed his life had begun. Yet conversely he was conscious that only two years earlier he had taken a step that ensured he could never hope to escape that past.

Zara could feel her face reddening. She did talk quite a bit and it wasn't exactly intellectual stuff. Perhaps he found her boring. Annoyance leapt through her as she fiercely suppressed a sense of hurt. He wasn't her boyfriend, he wasn't her lover, he wasn't anything to her and his opinion should not matter to her in the slightest.

'I'm sorry, that was rude,' Vitale drawled softly, shooting the powerful car off the road and below a worn stone archway ornamented with a centrally placed Grecian urn. 'I'm afraid I've had a rough morning but that is not an excuse for ill humour. I find spending time with you very relaxing.'

Zara wasn't quite convinced by that turnaround and when he parked she got out and said stiffly, 'You know, if there's only staff here, you could leave me to explore on my own for an hour. You don't need to stay—'

'I want to be with you, *angelina mia*,' Vitale intoned across the bonnet, whipping off his sunglasses to view her with level dark golden eyes. 'Why do you think I arranged this outing? Only to please you.'

As Zara could think of no good reason why he should have bothered otherwise, the anxious tension fell from her heart-shaped face. 'I'm no good with moody guys,' she confided with a wry look. 'They make me uncomfortable.'

'I'm not moody.'

Aware of the powerful personality that drove him, Zara didn't quite believe him on that score. He might not be subject to moods as a rule but he was definitely a very driven and strong individual. She was convinced that he could be stubborn and tough and a bit of a maverick but she had no idea how she could be so sure of those traits when she had only met him the day before. And yet she *was* sure. In much the same way she read the strain in his dark golden gaze and realised for the first time that he wasn't just flirting with her, he wasn't just playing a sexual game like so many of the men she had met. Vitale Roccanti was keen to soothe the feelings he had hurt. He sincerely cared about her opinion. Heartened by that conviction, she tried not to smile.

Vitale lifted out the picnic basket Giuseppina had made up and tossed Zara a cotton rug to carry and extended his free hand to her. 'Let's find somewhere to eat…'

'The orchard,' she suggested dreamily, already mentally visualising the garden design she had often studied.

In the heat of the afternoon they strolled along gravelled paths. The clarity of her aunt's talent as a designer was still as clear as it must have been forty years earlier when it was first created. 'The garden's been replanted,' Zara registered in surprise and pleasure, for she had expected to see overgrown shrubs and trees, the once noticeable lines of her aunt's vision blurred by many years of growth.

'Eighteen months ago.' Vitale's explanation was crisp, a little distracted. As she stood there against the backdrop of a great yew tree he was remembering his sister dancing along the same path in a scarlet silk gown for a fashion photographer's benefit, her lovely face stamped with the detached hauteur of a model, only the sparkle of her eyes revealing her true joyous mood. 'For a while the house and garden were open as a tourist attraction.'

'But not now,' Zara gathered.

'The owner cherishes his privacy.'

'It's almost selfish to own something this beautiful and refuse to share it with other people,' Zara contended in a tone of censure, lavender eyes darting in every direction because there was so much for her to take in.

His handsome mouth quirked as he watched her clamber unselfconsciously onto a stone bench in an effort to gain a better overall view above the tall evergreen hedges. 'The temple on the hill above the lake offers the best prospect.'

Zara's fine brows connected in a sudden frown. 'There was no temple in the original scheme.'

'Perhaps the owner felt he could add a little something without destroying the symmetry of the whole,' Vitale murmured a tinge drily.

Zara went pink. 'Of course. I think it's wonderful that he thought enough of the garden to maintain it and secure its future for another generation.'

Vitale shot her a searching glance, much amused against his will by her quick recovery. She was a lousy liar, having something of a child's artlessness in the way that she spoke and acted without forethought. She had no patience either. He watched her hurry ahead of him with quick light steps, a tiny trim figure with silvery pale hair catching and holding the sunlight. When he had seen the photos of her he had assumed the hair was dyed but it looked strikingly natural, perfectly attuned to her pale Nordic skin and unusual eyes. He would have to get her clothes off to explore the question further and that was a prospect that Vitale was startled to discover that he could hardly wait to bring about.

Monty Blake's daughter had an unanticipated charm all of her own. Even in the casual clothes her quintessential femininity, dainty curves and deeply disconcerting air of spontaneity turned him on hard and fast. It was years since any woman had had that effect on him and he didn't like it at all. Vitale much preferred a predictable low level and controllable response to a woman. He did not like surprises.

Beyond an avenue of cypresses and the vista of a picturesque town clinging to the upper slopes of a distant hill, the garden became less formal and a charming winding path led them to the cherry orchard. Wild flowers laced the lush grass and Zara hovered rather than spread the rug because it seemed almost a desecration to flatten those blooms. Vitale had no such inhibitions, however and he took the rug from her and cast it down. He was wondering if she could possibly have chosen the private location in expectation and encouragement of a bout of alfresco sex. No way, absolutely no way, Vitale decided grittily, was he sinking his famously cool reputation to fool about in long grass like a testosterone-driven teenager.

Seated unceremoniously on her knees and looking not remotely seductive, however, Zara was already digging through the basket and producing all sorts of goodies. 'I'm really hungry,' she admitted.

Vitale studied her and decided that he was becoming too set in his ways. Maybe he could bite the bullet if the only option was making out in the grass. He poured chilled white wine while she set out plates and extracted thin slices of prosciutto ham, wedges of onion and spinach frittata, a mozzarella and tomato salad and a bowl of pasta sprinkled with zucchini blossoms. It was a colourful and enticing spread.

'Giuseppina is a treasure,' Zara commented, digging in without further ado to a wedge of frittata washed down with wine from a moisture-beaded glass.

'I'm an excellent cook,' Vitale volunteered unexpectedly. 'Giuseppina is a recent addition to my household.'

'I can just about make toast,' Zara told him cheerfully. 'My older sister, Bee, is always offering to teach me to cook but I'm more into the garden than the kitchen.'

'I didn't know you had a sister.'

Zara kicked off her shoes and lounged back on one elbow to munch through ham and a generous spoonful of the juicy tomato salad with unconcealed enjoyment. 'Dad has three daughters from two marriages and one affair. He's a bit of a womaniser,' she muttered, downplaying the truth to an acceptable level.

'Is he still married to your mother?'

Worrying at her full lower lip, Zara compressed her sultry mouth. 'Yes, but he's had other interests along the way—she turns a blind eye. Gosh, I don't know why I'm telling you that. It's private.'

'Obviously it bothers you,' Vitale remarked perceptively.

It had always bothered Zara. Several years earlier, Edith had gently warned her niece to mind her own business when it came to her parents' marriage, pointing out that some adults accepted certain compromises in their efforts to maintain a stable relationship. 'I think fidelity is very important...'

Thinking of the wedding plans that he already knew were afoot in London on her behalf, Vitale almost laughed out loud in derision at that seemingly naïve declaration. He supposed it sounded good and that many men, burned by female betrayal, would be impressed by such a statement. More cynical and never ever trusting when it came to her sex, Vitale veiled his hard dark eyes lest he betray his scorn.

Zara could feel hot colour creeping across her face. She believed fidelity was important yet she had agreed to marry a man who had no intention of being faithful to her. Suddenly and for the first time she wondered if Bee had been right and if she could be making the biggest mistake of her life. But then, she reminded herself quickly, she would not be entering a real marriage with Sergios. In a perfect world and when people loved each other fidelity was important, she rephrased for her own benefit. Feeling panicky and torn in opposing directions by the commitment she had so recently entered, Zara drained her wine glass and let Vitale top it up.

'How do you feel about it?' Zara pressed her silent companion nonetheless because she really wanted to know his answer.

'As though we've strayed into a dialogue that is far too serious for such a beautiful day.'

Was that an evasion? Vitale was very adroit with words and Zara, who more often than not said the wrong thing to the wrong person at the wrong time, was reluctantly impressed by his sidestepping of what could be a controversial subject. More than anything else, though, she respected honesty, but she knew that some regarded her love of candour as a sign of immaturity and social awkwardness.

'I could never, ever forgive lies or infidelity,' Zara told him.

Watching sunshine make her hair flare like highly polished silver, her eyes mysterious lavender pools above her pink pouting mouth as she sipped her wine, Vitale reflected that had he been the susceptible type he might have been in danger around Zara Blake. After all she was a beauty, surprisingly individual and very appealing in all sorts of unexpected ways. That radiant smile, for instance, offered a rare amount of joie de vivre. But most fortunately for him, Vitale reminded himself with satisfaction, he was cooler than ice in the emotion department and all too aware of whose blood ran in her veins.

Barely a minute later and without even thinking about what he was going to do, Vitale leant down and pressed his sensual mouth to Zara's. He tasted headily of wine. His lips were warm and hard and the clean male scent of him unbelievably enticing. Zara stretched closer, increasing the pressure of his mouth on hers with a needy little sound breaking low in her throat.

Her hands curved to his strong, muscular shoulders and, as though she had given him a green light to accelerate the pace, the kiss took off like a rocket. His hot tongue pierced between her lips and she shivered violently, erotic signals racing through her slight length. A flood of heat travelled from the pinched taut tips of her breasts to the liquid tension pooling at the heart of her. Her heart thumping out a tempestuous beat, she dug her fingers into his silky black hair and kissed him back with a hunger she couldn't repress.

Within seconds she was on her back, Vitale lying half over her with one lean thigh settling between hers. On one level she tensed, ready to object the way she usually would have done if a man got too close, but on another unfamiliar level his weight, proximity and the fiery hunger of his kiss somehow combined in a soaring crescendo of sensuality to unleash a powerful craving she had never felt before.

'You taste so good,' Vitale growled huskily, '*so* unbelievably good, *angelina mia*.'

He was talking too much and she didn't want him talking, she wanted him kissing, and she pulled him back down to her with impatient hands. He reacted to that shameless invitation with a driving passion that thrilled her. His mouth ravished hers, his tongue darting and sliding in the tender interior and the thunderous wave of desire screaming through her was almost unbearable. Long fingers slid below her top, travelling over her narrow ribcage to close round a small rounded breast. He found the beaded tip, squeezed it and she arched off the ground, shattered by the arrow of hot liquid need shooting down into her pelvis. And that jolt of soul stealing desire was sufficient to spring her out of the sensual spell he had cast.

Eyes bright with dismay, Zara had only a split second to focus over his shoulder on the trees around her and recall where she was and what she was doing. Shot back to awareness with a vengeance, she gasped, 'No!' as she pushed at his shoulders and rolled away from him the instant he drew back.

Still on another plane, Vitale blinked, dazed at what had just happened. *Almost* happened, he corrected mentally. *Dio mio,* they were lying in an orchard and there wasn't even the remotest chance that he would have let matters proceed any further. She was like a stick of dynamite, he thought next, dark colour scoring his high cheekbones as he struggled to catch his breath and withstand the literal pain of his fully aroused body. A woman capable of making him behave like that in a public place ought to carry a government health warning. Overconfident, he had underestimated the extent of her pulling power, a mistake he would not repeat, he swore vehemently.

'I'm sorry…' Zara's teeth almost chattered in the aftershock of having called a crushing halt to that runaway passion. 'But someone might have come along,' she completed lamely, wondering if she seemed dreadfully old-fashioned and a bit hysterical to a guy of his experience. After all he had only kissed her and touched her breast and she had thrown him off as if he had assaulted her.

'No, I'm sorry,' Vitale fielded, reaching for her hand,

the nails of which were digging into the surface of the rug in a revealing show of discomfiture, and straightening her fingers in a calming gesture. 'I didn't think.'

It was an admission that very nearly choked Vitale Roccanti, who, with the patience and power of a Machiavelli, had planned and plotted his every move from the age of thirteen and never once failed to deliver on any count. Zara, however, was soothed by his apology and his grip on her hand. In her experience not all men were so generous in the aftermath of thwarted desire.

In seemingly silent mutual agreement they put away the picnic and folded the rug to start back to the car. She had barely seen the garden but it no longer had the power to dominate her thoughts. Her entire focus was now centred on Vitale. Was this what an infatuation felt like? Or was it something more? Was he a man she could fall in love with? How did she know? Was she crazy to wonder such a thing? Julian had been her first love but he had never had the power to make her feel the way Vitale did. Sadly she had been too young at eighteen to understand that there should be more said and more felt in a relationship with a future.

Just before she climbed back into the car, a gardener working at a border across the front lawn raised a hand to acknowledge Vitale. Of course, his uncle's employees would know him. She watched him incline his head in acknowledgement. Her fingers had messed up his black hair and as he turned his handsome dark head, stunning golden eyes locking to her as if there were no other person in the world, she felt a fierce pride in his acknowledgement and refused to think beyond that.

As he drove her back to his house she was in a pensive mood and slightly dreamy from the heat, the wine and the passion.

'You're very quiet,' he murmured.

'I thought you would like that.'

In a graceful gesture he linked his fingers briefly with hers. 'No. I miss the chatter, *angelina mia*.'

Zara thought crazily then that engagements could be broken and weddings could be cancelled. That possibility momentarily put paid to the guilt and assuaged her conscience. It had never been her intention to deceive either man but now it was too late to tell Vitale the truth, that she was supposed to be getting married. She shifted uncomfortably at the knowledge that an honest and decent woman would have spoken up much sooner and certainly before the first kiss. Now she could not bear the idea that Vitale might think badly of her and she hugged her secret to herself in silence.

Not surprisingly, with her unusually optimistic mood interspersed by anxious spasms of fear about the future controlling her, the journey back to the farmhouse seemed very short because she was so lost in her thoughts.

She wandered into the sunny hallway. 'I didn't even explore Edith's garden properly,' she remarked with regret.

'Someday I'll take you back to see it,' Vitale promised and then he frowned.

'I'm leaving in the morning,' she reminded him helplessly.

His beautiful dark deep-set eyes lingered on her anxious face and he lifted a hand, brushing her delicate jawbone with his knuckle in an unexpected caress. 'Let your hair down,' he whispered.

The look of anticipation gleaming in his eyes made her heart race and the blood surge hotly through her body. 'Why?' she asked baldly.

'I love your hair...the colour of it, the feel of it,' he confessed huskily.

And like a woman in a dream, Zara lifted her hand and undid the clip. Vitale need no further invitation, angling his proud dark head down as he studied her and used his hands to deftly fluff her rumpled hair round her shoulders. 'I even like the smell of it,' he admitted, a bemused frown tugging at his ebony brows even as his nostrils flared in recognition at the vanilla scent of her.

He was gorgeous, Zara thought dizzily, the most gorgeous guy she had ever met and he seemed equally drawn to her. It was a heady thought, and not her style, but she was basking in the hot golden glow of his appreciative appraisal. It was the work of a moment to mentally douse the sparks of caution at the back of her mind and instead stretch up on tiptoe as if she were free as a bird to do whatever she liked and taste that remarkably beautiful mouth of his again. He lifted her up in his arms and began to carry her upstairs.

CHAPTER FOUR

ZARA surfaced from that kiss to discover that she was on a bed in an unfamiliar room.

It was a larger, more masculine version of her room with bedding the colour of parchment. Unfortunately the last time that Zara had been alone in a bedroom with a man she had been handcuffed half naked to a metal headboard and it was thanks to that terrifying experience that she remained a virgin at the age of twenty-two. Momentarily transfixed by that chilling recollection she turned pale as milk and studied Vitale, reminding herself that she had kissed him, and encouraged him entirely of her own free will. She was not under the influence of alcohol this time around either.

'What's wrong?' His shirt already half unbuttoned to display a dark, hair-roughened wedge of muscular torso, Vitale regarded her with observant eyes, reading her tension and her pallor and wondering at her mood.

He was too clever by half to miss her nervous tension, Zara registered in dismay. A blush of discomfiture warmed her face as she struggled to suppress the apprehension that was a direct result of the betrayal she had suffered. Vitale wasn't a blackmailer, she told herself urgently. He wasn't going to whip out a camera either…at least she hoped not. He was a wealthy successful man in his own right with no need to target her as a potential source of profit.

'It's all right…it's not you,' she told him awkwardly. 'I had a bad experience once…'

Vitale spread his hands in a fluid soothing movement. 'If you want to change your mind I'll understand.'

Her wide eyes prickled with tears at that considerate offer because she knew it could not have been easy for him to make. He was not selfishly putting his own needs first, he *cared* how she felt and that meant a great deal to Zara. After all, in spite of all his protestations Julian had never cared about her, he had only seen her as a means to an end, a convenient conduit to her father's bank account. Her chin came up and she kicked off her shoes in a statement of intent. It was time she shook off the shadows cast over her life by Julian Hurst; it was time that she accepted that not every man was a user or an abuser.

'I'm staying,' Zara informed him unevenly, fighting her nerves with all her might. Twenty-two and a virgin—no, she absolutely was not going to share that embarrassing truth with him. She had read somewhere that men couldn't tell the difference so he would never guess the level of her inexperience unless she made it obvious by parading her insecurity.

Vitale wanted to tell her that she wouldn't regret sharing his bed but he was no hypocrite and he knew that she would. But what was another one-night stand to a woman with her level of experience? Unhappily for him, however, nothing seemed as cut and dried as it had before and he was suffering stabs of indecision directly in conflict with his usual rock-solid assurance and resolute focus. When and how had the business of avenging his sister contrived to become a guilty pleasure?

How could a little pixie-like blonde threaten to come between him and his wits? Vitale always knew what he was doing and controlled his own fate every step of the way. Time after time in his life he had made tough choices and he had never flinched from them. He might loathe the fact but he wanted Monty Blake's daughter much more than he had ever dreamt possible. Even knowing that she was engaged to another man and a heartless little cheat didn't kill his desire for her. Did it matter how he felt though? Surely all that mattered was that he took revenge for his sister's pitiful death at the hands of a filthy coward? And the woman on his bed was the magic key to that much desired objective.

'Take the shorts off,' he urged huskily.

Tensing, Zara was very still for a moment before she scrambled off the bed. It was a modest request, she told herself. He hadn't asked her to take off everything. But she was all fingers and thumbs as she undid the button at the waistband of her shorts and shook her slim hips clear of the garment, finally stepping out of them to reveal a pair of high cut blue satin knickers.

There was something wrong. What, Vitale didn't know, but his instincts were good and he sensed it. Her face was pink, her eyes evasive below concealing lashes and her movements curiously stiff. This was not a woman confident in the bedroom and the suspicion sparked a sense of unease in him for once again she was defying the picture he had of her. Her lavender eyes met his with an unmistakeably anxious glint and her arms were crossed defensively. He recalled that bad experience she had mentioned and wondered just how bad it had been to leave a beautiful young woman so unsure of herself. Disconcerted by the train of his thoughts, Vitale reminded himself that he only wanted to spend the night with her, not step into her mind and psychoanalyse her. He never went deep in relationships, never got involved. He liked his affairs light and easy, with sex the main event and no bitter aftertaste. What was it about her that continually off-balanced him?

Zara had always worried about displaying her body to a man. Unforgettably Julian had laughed at her very slight curves, remarking that she might as well have been a boy as she would never make a centrefold. She had once considered getting a breast enlargement but had feared that with so slim a body she might end up looking top heavy and unnatural. Now all of a sudden she wanted to be perfect—she wanted to be perfect purely for Vitale.

'What *is* it?' he prompted, crossing the floor to grip her taut shoulders.

'I'm feeling horribly shy,' she told him in a rush.

He lifted her off her feet and set her on the side of the bed and then he kissed her, knotting one hand into the soft silky fall of her hair to hold her steady. It was a hungry, demanding kiss, his tongue flicking against the sensitive roof of her mouth to fire a response that raced through her like an explosive depth charge. She forgot who she was, she forgot who he was, she even contrived to forget that she was a virgin. Her palms skated up over the hard muscular wall of his powerful chest and with a groan deep in his throat he caught her hand and, in a stark expression of need, brought it down to the thrust of his erection beneath his trousers.

Pleased to recognise that he wanted her that much, Zara stroked him and struggled to run down his zip. Her slim fingers skimmed beneath the fabric to find the long, thick evidence of his arousal. He pushed against her hand, hard, eager, and hungry for her touch and it fired her up, finally convincing her that in spite of her inexperience she was sexy enough to turn him on hard.

Vitale yanked off her T-shirt with impatient hands and kissed her again while pushing her back across the bed. His urgency, as he dispensed with his trousers while exchanging hard, driving kisses that stoked her hunger higher and higher, was undeniable. He couldn't get enough of her, couldn't get close enough. Zara knew exactly what she wanted for all her lack of experience. She wanted him on top of her, she craved his weight, but instead he found the petal-soft pink tips of her small breasts and used his mouth on those delectable buds with a skill that wrung a gasp from her parted lips.

'You're very sensitive there, *gioia mia*,' Vitale breathed thickly, raking her dainty breasts with eager, admiring eyes.

No longer concerned about the size of her attributes, Zara trembled, insanely conscious of the wet heat building at the heart of her, but for an instant, when he skimmed off his boxers and she saw the powerful upstanding proof of his excitement, her nerves almost betrayed her. Her body craved him but she was afraid it might hurt. Irritated with herself, she suppressed that fear and then all such thoughts fled her mind as he explored her most private place that she was tempted to hide from him. But the desire was too strong, the sensation he gave her too intense to be denied by modesty.

He lay on the bed teasing at her lower lip with tiny little bites that only inflamed her more while he touched her most tender flesh with a skill that made her back arch and her hips lift off the mattress. He eased a finger inside her and groaned against her swollen mouth. 'You're so tight, so wet…'

Her face burned and an ache bloomed between her thighs, an unbearable yearning for much more. With his thumb he found her clitoris and all thought and awareness fell away, reducing her to a much more elemental level. She pushed up to him and kissed him wildly for herself, shivering when the straining buds of her nipples grazed his warm hard chest.

All masculine dominance, Vitale leant over her, dark golden eyes ablaze with desire as he kissed her long and hard. 'I want you so much I'm burning…'

'So what are you waiting for?' Zara urged breathlessly, because he had brought her to an edge of anticipation that was intolerable and without her volition her hips were shifting up to him in tiny needy movements.

He tore the foil off a condom and eased it on while she watched, madly curious about what she had never known but rather apprehensive as well, although she was striving to suppress that feeling. He would fit, of course he would. Nature had designed men and women to fit. He leant over her, strong and sure, and she felt the head of him against her slick, damp entrance. Her body trembled with expectation when he plunged into her.

It hurt and a moan of protest escaped Zara. When he froze, staring down at her, his eyes full of enquiry and confusion, she was mortified.

'Zara?' he began, 'I hurt you. I'm sorry—'

'I don't want to discuss it,' Zara told him hurriedly. She could feel the tension draining away, the pain already receding, and suspected she had made a lot of noise about nothing. 'You can continue…'

It was that prim little command now, in the most inappropriate of circumstances, that nearly sent Vitale into a fit of laughter. With difficulty he restrained his amusement, for her lovely face was a picture of disquiet and embarrassment. 'But I hurt you—'

'Some things are just too private to talk about,' Zara assured him.

'You really want me to continue?' Vitale queried in a strained undertone, wondering why no other woman had ever made him want to laugh as she did.

'You might as well now,' Zara pointed out prosaically, abandoning all hope of receiving much enjoyment from the act now.

Just as she thought that, Vitale sank into her up to the hilt and an erotic thrill sizzled through her like the touch of a firebrand on naked skin. As he began to move she struggled to swallow back a gasp of surprise. She felt truly extraordinary, as if her body were directly attuned to his. A sweet torment of pleasure built as he withdrew and then thrust deep again, jolting a low cry from her. She no longer had the ability to rein back her response. Intense, all-consuming pleasure gripped her and she panted for breath, her urgency rising in exact proportion to her need. Her excitement climbed higher and higher, spiralling through her like a bright light fighting to escape. Then, just when she thought she couldn't bear it any more, she reached a peak and fell apart in an exquisite agony of sensation, eyes opening, lips parting in wonderment as he shuddered over her in the throes of his own climax.

Eyes brilliant with gratification, Vitale claimed her mouth one more time. '*Ebbene*…now then, you amazing woman,' he growled hoarsely. 'That was a worthy continuance.'

Feeling wonderfully at peace, Zara pressed her lips gently against his satin-smooth shoulder. He lifted her wrist and let his tongue glide along the pulse there, making her quiver helplessly. She glanced up at him from below her lashes, recognising that this was a guy who knew every button to push. He kicked back the sheet and got up to stride into the bathroom, and she turned over onto her side, still stunned by the power of what she had experienced in his arms.

The aftermath of that wondrous pleasure was still engulfing her. Great sex, she labelled dizzily, but she wanted more and was already wondering if Vitale planned to continue what they had begun. Or was she

just a little weekend distraction? That humiliating possibility had to be considered. After all, theirs had been a
chance attraction, rather than a more conventional one.
Ironically she had sacrificed so much more to be with
him, she recognised ruefully. There was no question of
her marrying Sergios Demonides now. Furthermore she
could barely believe that she had been so blind to the
risk of temptation when she agreed to marry a man she
neither loved nor cared for simply to please her parents.
How immature and foolish was that? Oh, how much
easier life would have been now had she paid more heed
to Bee's warnings and told Sergios that she was very
sorry but she had changed her mind!

Well, she supposed wryly, a change of heart weeks
before the wedding invitations even went out was better
than a marriage that failed. No doubt Sergios would be
annoyed with her for wasting his time. She had wasted
everyone's time and no doubt the cancellation of all the
wedding arrangements would cost her parents a great
deal of money. She had been very foolish and short-
sighted about her own needs. But what was done was
done and now everything had changed. There was no
going back to the mindset she had cherished before she
came to Italy and met Vitale Roccanti. He had blown
everything she thought she knew about herself to smith-
ereens. She wanted more from a marriage than Sergios
could ever have given her.

'Join me in the shower,' Vitale husked from the doorway.

She slid out of the bed as though he had pulled an
invisible piece of elastic that had her attached to one

end. Being naked without even the coverage of a sheet or his body was a challenge for her, but already the demeaning memories of what Julian had done to her were being replaced by more positive ones. What went without saying was that she wanted to be with Vitale and felt as though she had waited all her life to feel as strongly about a man as she felt about him. Moreover she was overpoweringly conscious that she was flying back to London in the morning and that then the ball would be in his court as to what—if anything—happened next. There was no way she would chase after him—she had way too much pride for that.

Having finally shed his shirt, Vitale caught her up in the doorway and lifted her high against his lean bronzed body. 'I could easily become accustomed to a woman your size, *gioia mia*. You're so easy to move around!'

A smile as bright as a solar flare lit across her face and all thoughts of the future fled to the back of her mind. Right now she would live for the moment. Why not? She was young, she was, if not technically free, morally free in her own mind to enjoy herself. The only cloud on the horizon was the fact she dared not be honest with Vitale for fear of how her explanation about Sergios might alter and indeed destroy his good impression of her.

The shower was already running and Zara gasped as the cascade of water hit her, then Vitale kissed her and nothing else mattered but the need to get as close to him as possible. He sank his hands below her bottom and hoisted her high so that she could wrap her arms round his neck and kiss him back with passionate fervour. As her fingers moved across his strong back she felt the surprising roughness of his skin there and wondered if he had been in an accident, for she was sure what she was feeling was some sort of scarring. But her curiosity was soon overwhelmed by the heat of his mouth on hers. Just as quickly she discovered that she wanted him again for her nipples instantly pinched into prominent aching beads and the slick heat pooled between her legs again.

'You are so hot you burn me,' Vitale rasped, lowering her back onto the tiles again, his strong erection brushing her stomach.

Shower gel foamed between his hands and he transferred it to her sensitised skin. His expert fingers glided over the pouting mounds of her breasts, lingered over her straining nipples, toying with them before slowly delving lower to graze the most tender bud of all in the most indescribably arousing way. Trembling, she leant against him for support, making no attempt to pretend that she was still in control, surrendering entirely to the tingling, taunting need pulsing through her. With a hungry groan, Vitale hoisted her up against him again and swung round to brace her spine against the tiled wall.

'I can't wait,' he breathed, spreading her thighs and bringing her down on him so that her lush opening sheathed his shaft in a single stunning move.

Hands anchored to her hips, he drove deeper into her and then lifted her to withdraw again before thrusting back into her quivering body again. It was incredibly exciting. She couldn't think, couldn't speak, she just hung onto his broad shoulders for what felt like a wildly exciting roller-coaster ride. At some stage he lifted her out of the shower and laid her down on the floor so that he could continue to pleasure her there with tireless vigour. She writhed in a frenzy of abandon and hit another breathtaking climax that sent her spinning off into the stars.

'Wow…' she whispered weakly in the aftermath, belatedly aware of how hard the floor was below her and how heavy he was.

'That wasn't very well planned,' Vitale breathed abruptly, freeing her from his weight and pulling her up with him.

'Planned?' In a sensual daze, Zara blinked and reached for one of the towels on the rail. 'How… *planned*?'

'I forgot to use a condom. Do you take contraceptive pills?'

Zara froze and looked up at him. His devastatingly handsome face was suddenly very serious. 'No,' she said, the size of the risk they'd just taken slowly dawning on her. 'And I'm about halfway through my cycle.'

'I'll be more careful from now on…I promise,' Vitale asserted, running a fingertip caressingly below her sultry lower lip, swollen from his kisses. 'But I do find you incredibly tempting. You make me dangerously impulsive.'

Meeting the urgent appeal in those stunning golden eyes, Zara could barely put one foot in front of another, never mind think logical thoughts. 'I'm sure I'll be fine,' she muttered, suppressing her concern that she might fall pregnant and thinking that if she took after her mother, who, in spite of her longing for more children, had only ever conceived once in her entire life, she probably had nothing to worry about.

As he turned away to reach for a towel she saw his back and her shocked breath caught in her throat. Line after line of raised scars like welts criss-crossed his long, muscular back and there were little round darker marks as well across his shoulders and spine. 'What on earth happened to your back?' she asked abruptly.

Momentarily, Vitale froze in the act of towelling himself dry and shot her a glance over one broad shoulder. 'Ancient history,' he said dismissively.

And he did not offer to share it.

He pulled on boxers and a shirt to go downstairs with her to raid the fridge. It was Giuseppina's day off but she had left the cabinet packed with goodies. They were both very hungry. He lit a candle on the terrace and they sat eating cold spicy chicken and salad washed down with wine and lively conversation. She wanted to ask him about his back again but was reluctant to snoop. Somehow he manoeuvred her back onto his lap and his hands travelled below her tee to cup her breasts. She stretched back against him, helpless in the grip of her instantaneous hunger and they went back to bed where he made love to her twice more. Afterwards, she lay spent on the bed watching Vitale sleep and feeling ridiculously happy.

Even in the moonlight he had the most amazing bone structure, from his high cheekbones to classic nose and his hard, angular jaw line. She wanted to touch him, trace the winged ebony brows, the sensual firmness of his mouth, but she curled her hands into fists of restraint instead. She was thinking and acting like a teenager, a lovesick teenager, she scolded herself impatiently, deliberately turning away from him and lying back again. Somehow she had never got to play it cool with Vitale the way she usually did with men and that made her feel very insecure. They had bypassed the calm getting-to-know-you phase and plunged straight into meaningful looks and passion. He was as attracted to her as she was to him, she reflected wryly, so at least the spell she was under was a mutual one...

Vitale couldn't sleep. When he woke it was still dark and he reckoned that it was the awareness that he had company that had made him feel uneasy. After all, he always slept alone. He never stayed the night with anyone. He didn't like that kind of closeness. By nature he was a loner and after the childhood he had endured he thought it was hardly surprising that he should be uncomfortable with any form of physical intimacy that went beyond sex. But she was very affectionate, hugging and kissing and snuggling into his lean hard frame. His eyes bleak, he eased away from her, resisting that togetherness. It would soon be over. He couldn't work out why he didn't feel happier about that. But then he had never been given to introspection.

'You should have woken me up sooner!' Zara complained several hours later as she struggled to close the zip on her case.

While Vitale had risen early, he had let her sleep in

and it had been a rush to get dressed and packed ready
for the time he had said they had to leave. At first it had
pleased her that he was making the effort to personally
drive her to the airport, but even the most insensitive
woman could not have missed out on noticing how polite and almost distant Vitale seemed to be acting all of
a sudden. Zara had never had a one-night stand but it
struck her that her vision of how a morning after such
a night would feel best described Vitale's behaviour.
The awkwardness in the atmosphere was not solely
her fault. And maybe she *had* just enjoyed a one night
stand, she reasoned painfully, maybe this was it for her
and Vitale Roccanti.

What were the chances of him trying to conduct a
long-distance relationship with her? Did he even visit
London in the course of his work? For the very first
time she acknowledged that the odds were that she
might never see Vitale again.

Her potential client had become a lover and that
could well have destroyed any chance of him seriously
considering her for the job.

'Do you still want to see a set of plans for the villa?'
she enquired stiffly.

'*Sì*, of course,' Vitale confirmed, shooting her a
muted glance, his tension palpable as he swept up her
case in a strong hand and carried it downstairs for her.

All Zara's suspicious antennae were on alert. Had
Vitale already toyed with the idea of telling her not to
bother with the plans? Wouldn't that provide a neat
end to a potentially embarrassing situation? *I'm never
going to see him again. I'm never ever going to see him*

again. The conviction cast a pall over Zara's spirits. She told herself she didn't care, that it didn't matter to her, that a few days ago she had never even heard his name before. And while those thoughts whirled round and round in her mind, pride forced her head higher. With brittle efficiency she discussed arrangements for submitting plans for his inspection while ascertaining the exact level of detail he required. As he seemed to have little to say on that score she was convinced that he would reject the plan, but as Blooming Perfect always charged for putting in a basic design her time would not have been entirely wasted.

His lean, strong face set in forbidding lines, Vitale opened the front door and took her small case out to his car. Standing in the porch, she donned her jacket, her delicate features blank as she fought for composure and blamed herself bitterly for having abandoned her professionalism in the first place. This sense of discomfiture, this sharp sense of loss were the payback for her reckless behaviour.

'Zara…' And as she looked up she was taken aback when Vitale closed his arms round her and bent his head to kiss her, because the way he had been behaving actual physical contact had to have been about the last thing she expected from him.

But in the emotional mood Zara was in, his carnal mouth had only to touch hers for her hands to delve possessively back into his black hair. In fact she held him to her for a split second before she yanked her arms away again and angled her head back, having finally recognised in some disconcertion that he had offered her more of a peck than a passionate embrace.

But even as she released him it seemed all hell broke loose. She stared in shock and flinched at the sight of two men wielding cameras only yards away from them. The men leapt up from crouching positions, clearly having taken photos of Vitale and Zara in each other's arms, and tore off into the trees surrounding the property to speedily disappear from sight.

'Where on earth did they come from? Who are they, for goodness' sake?' Zara demanded angrily. 'Why the heck were they taking pictures of us?'

CHAPTER FIVE

'PAPARAZZI. They must've staked out the house to await their chance.' It was the incredible calm with which Vitale made that explanation that first alerted Zara to the idea that something was badly wrong. He didn't seem surprised by the invasion of their privacy or even particularly bothered by it, which shook her.

'But what on earth for?' Zara queried, marvelling at his seemingly laid-back attitude when everybody she knew in the public eye hated the intrusion of muck-raking journalists into their private lives.

'Obviously you know *why* the paps would find photographing you with another man worth their while,' Vitale countered with a harsh edge to his dark deep drawl, his intonation cold enough to make him sound momentarily like a stranger.

Taken aback by that tone, Zara frowned up at him. 'If they were paps, how would they know I was here with you? *Another* man? What are you saying?'

Vitale quirked a derisive brow, stunning eyes dark as pitch and harder than she had ever seen them. 'Have you forgotten your Greek fiancé? The fact that you're marrying Sergios Demonides this summer? In the light of that, proof of your obvious intimacy with me is more than sufficient to sell a grubby tabloid story for a profit.'

Air rasped in Zara's throat and the muscles there tightened, making it hard for her to catch her breath. She was deeply shaken by the level of his information. 'You *know* about Sergios?'

'Obviously,' Vitale admitted drily.

'We're not engaged,' she said limply, not really even knowing why she was troubling to make that distinction since it was painfully obvious that Vitale Roccanti had already judged her badly for her silence on the score of her marital commitment. 'There was no ring, no engagement…it's not like Sergios and I are in love with each other or anything like that—'

Vitale shifted a silencing hand, his lack of interest patent and like another slap in the face. 'Whatever—'

'No.' Zara refused to be silenced, determined to defend her behaviour as best she could. 'As soon as I got back to London I was planning to tell Sergios that I couldn't go ahead and marry him. I wasn't fooling around behind his back. I'm not like that. I had already decided that I couldn't go ahead and marry him after meeting you—'

'It's immaterial to me—'

'You knew about Sergios and yet you said nothing?' Zara pressed, struggling to understand and not linger on that last lethal statement, for nothing positive could be gained from the words, 'It's immaterial to me.' He didn't care that she was supposedly marrying another man? Didn't care in the slightest? That was a declaration of towering lack of interest that cut her to the quick.

'If you're to make your flight, we have to leave now.' Vitale delivered the reminder without any emotion at all.

'I'll catch a later flight at my own expense,' Zara fielded with a slight shake in her voice. 'I'm more interested right now in finding out what's going on here. I went to bed last night with one guy and this morning it's like I've woken up with his nasty identical twin. If you knew about Sergios why didn't you mention it?'

Vitale resisted a strong urge to ask her why she hadn't mentioned it. Why should he care? She was faithless, pleasure-loving. She meant nothing to him, less than nothing. He breathed in deep and slow, suppressing any hint of an emotional reaction. He was keen to be done with the dialogue and it struck him that honesty was probably the best policy in the circumstances. It would draw an efficient line under their entanglement as nothing else could do. 'I was willing to do whatever I could to ensure that your marriage plans fell through as I believe it will have a detrimental effect on your father's hopes of selling the family hotel group to Demonides.'

Zara was so startled by that explanation that her legs wobbled beneath her and she sank down heavily on the low wall surrounding the shrubbery beside the porch. Her lavender eyes narrowed in bemused concentration when she stared up at him. 'What on earth are you talking about?'

'I set you up,' Vitale volunteered grimly, spelling

out the facts without hesitation. 'From start to finish. Contacting your design firm, bringing you out here—'

In receipt of that admission, Zara had slowly turned white as snow. 'Sleeping with me?' she interrupted jerkily, distaste scissoring through her like a blade. 'Was that part of the set-up? If you wanted Sergios to dump me, ensuring embarrassing pictures of his future bride misbehaving appear in some tabloid rag would be a good start.'

'I thought so too but, believe it or not,' Vitale imparted grittily, 'I had no wish to hurt you personally. Your father has always been my target—'

'My father?' Zara could feel her muscles stiffen in shock as she sat there, spine rigid, feet set as neatly together as a small child told to sit still at church, her hands so tightly clasped together in an effort at self-control that her fingers ached. 'Why would my father have been your target?'

A bleak expression entered his eloquent gaze. 'Sixteen years ago, your father took my sister, Loredana, out on a sailing weekend and when the yacht got into trouble he saved his own skin and left her to drown. She was twenty years old and pregnant with his child.'

In shock at that horrible story, Zara slowly shook her head as though to clear it. Sixteen years ago her father had been divorced from Bee's mother but still a single man. Zara had been born quite a few years before her parents actually wed, but then a wedding ring or indeed a child had never kept the older man faithful. She did actually remember something happening, some kind of an upheaval, which had resulted in rows between her parents... What was it? What had happened? Her smooth brow furrowed. But no, her memory seemed to have packed up and gone home. Sixteen years ago, after all, Zara had only been a child of six. Yet Vitale had still targeted her for something he believed Monty Blake had done to his sister?

'So now you know the truth.'

Her teeth set together so hard that her jaw thrummed in punishment but she did not want to break into impulsive speech. Yes, now she knew that once again a man had made a colossal fool of her. Maybe all the people, including her parents, who had called her dumb were right—she had not had the slightest suspicion of Vitale while he had been executing his charm offensive.

Not until this very morning, at the last possible moment, had she recognised his change of mood and attitude. So what did that say about her? That when it came to men she was criminally stupid and blind and ought not to be let out on her own, she thought painfully. To follow a Julian Hurst with a Vitale Roccanti suggested seriously bad judgement. Twice she had fallen headlong for the flattering approaches of men programmed to hurt and use her for their own purposes. And now she felt as if the bottom had fallen out of her world, as if she had been deserted and left utterly lost in alien territory. This guy, who had shamelessly used and abused her, was the guy she had actually believed she might be falling in love with? That was the lowest blow of all and it decimated her pride.

'Call me a taxi to get me to the airport,' Zara told him curtly.

'There is no need for that.' Vitale flung wide the passenger door as if he expected that she would still scramble into the car like an obedient dog.

The delicate bones of her face prominent below her fine skin, Zara fixed scornful lavender eyes on him and ignored the invitation. 'So you slept with me to try and wreck my Dad's big business deal with Sergios. At least I know what a four letter word of a man you are now,' she breathed. 'You used my business to lure me into a trap, deliberately deceived me, took inexcusable advantage of my trust and stole my virginity—'

'Your *virginity*?' Vitale stressed with incredulous bite. 'You couldn't have been a—'

'I *was*. You were my first lover. I don't sleep around. Were you foolish enough to believe all the rubbish printed about me in newspapers?' Zara demanded fierily, standing up now, narrow shoulders thrown back as she voiced her feelings without embarrassment. 'Of course now I wish I hadn't slept with you but I'm even more relieved to find out firsthand what an unscrupulous bastard you are, so that I can ensure that I have nothing more to do with you—'

'Zara—'

'No, you listen to me for a change!' Zara told him, interrupting with raw driving determination. 'I didn't do anything to harm you or your sister. I didn't even know you existed until I met you. If you had a problem with my father you should have had the courage and decency to talk to him about it and left me out of it. You had no excuse whatsoever for dragging me into your vengeful attack on him.'

Vitale withstood that verbal onslaught in brooding silence. Perhaps, she thought wildly, he realised that she was entitled to her say.

'Are you getting into the car?' he enquired flatly.

'No, call me a taxi. I wouldn't take a lift off you if I was dying!' Zara flung back at him, stepping forward to reach into the car and yank out her case again with a strength born of pure anger.

Vitale made use of his cell phone. 'The taxi will be here in ten.' He lowered the phone again and studied her. 'Was I truly your first lover?'

Zara used two very rude words to tell him where to go and she shocked him with that succinct retort almost as much as she shocked herself, for she was not in the habit of using that kind of language. At the same time, though, she was not prepared to stand there exchanging further conversation with a man who had deliberately set out to ensnare and hurt her.

'You might as well sit down indoors to wait,' Vitale advised curtly.

Zara shot him a look of loathing and remained where she was. 'You ensured that the paps saw me here with you—that's why you kissed me!' she suddenly realized. Her eyes were full of bitter condemnation and contempt but she was ashamed as well because even though Sergios would not be marrying her now he would surely be embarrassed by that sort of publicity and he had done nothing to deserve that from her.

The truth, Vitale had pronounced, when he told her the story about his sister—was that what it was? She knew there could be many shades of the truth and she doubted his version. Had Monty Blake honestly stood by and let some young pregnant girl drown? It would surprise her if it was true. She didn't like her father and feared him when he was in a temper. He had adored her brother, Tom, the clever son he had longed to see follow in his narcissistic footsteps, but Zara had only ever been a disappointment to him. Her father was obsessed with money and social status. He had a mean amoral streak, a violent temper and a tendency to lash out physically, but he had never done anything, to her knowledge, that suggested he might be downright evil.

It dawned on her then that her father would kill her for getting involved with another man and offending Sergios. Even in the sunshine, a chill of genuine apprehension ran down Zara's taut spine and turned her skin clammy and cold. Only the brave crossed Monty Blake. Her mother would be outraged as well. And Zara would have to avoid Bee to ensure that her half-sister did not get involved in her troubles because her father would go spare if Bee supported her. In fact, Zara recognised painfully, she wasn't going to be anybody's flavour of the month after that photo of her kissing Vitale appeared in print. She might not have been engaged to Sergios, but even without an official announcement lots of people had guessed that a wedding was in the offing.

Vitale watched the taxi disappear down the wooded lane. It was over and, honour satisfied, he could return to his smooth, civilised existence, organising multimillion-euro deals and travelling between the apartments he owned round the world. He had done what he set out to do, smoothly and effectively. He should be pleased that after so many years the only kind of justice that a man of Monty Blake's greed would understand was finally about to be served to him. But impending victory had a strangely hollow and unsatisfying feel.

In his mind's eye the banker renowned for his cold calculation and emotional detachment could still see Zara Blake's pale heart-shaped face and the incredulity etched in her eyes. In a sudden movement he punched the wall with a clenched fist. It was a crazy thing to do and he was not a man who did crazy things and it hurt like the very devil. Blood from his bruised and scraped knuckles dripped on the tiled floor but that aberrant surge of violence did serve to vent a little of the raging sense of frustration Vitale was struggling to suppress. He had no idea why he felt this way.

Had Zara been a virgin? He saw no reason for her to lie on that score and he had only dismissed the suspicion because it had seemed so unlikely that a rich and beautiful party girl could still be that innocent at her age. He recalled her lack of assurance in the bedroom and his wide, shapely mouth twisted as he acknowledged that he *had* been guilty of believing what he had read in the media about her. Few party girls were virgins, but she had been and he had ignored his suspicion precisely because it had suited him to do so. Had he known the truth about Monty Blake's daughter would he still have used her as a weapon to strike at her father? He could not answer that question. He still wondered why there had been no man before him and then he shook his head, killing the thought as well as that dangerous seed of burning curiosity. It was done and there was no going back. Now he only had to wait for Demonides to ditch the buyout of the Royale hotel group at an inflated price and he would have achieved his final goal.

Even so, for the very first time Vitale was tentatively questioning the desire for revenge that had driven him since the age of thirteen. It was like probing a ragingly sensitive tooth. As a boy he had known it would be a foolish waste of time to stage a personal confrontation with his sister's former lover. Monty Blake would simply lie to him as he had lied at the inquest. He was a vain and devious man, not to be trusted with women. Vitale shut out the reflection that the end might not always justify the means. He had done what had needed to be done. The scornful condemnation in those amazing lavender eyes could not destroy the painful memories of his innocent and trusting sister or his powerful need to hit back on her behalf. Loredana hadn't been a 'someone'. She had had no powerful connections—at least, Vitale adjusted grimly, none who *cared* enough to question the judgement of accidental death made at that inquest.

In comparison, Zara Blake meant nothing to him, less than nothing, he affirmed with vigour. He was not an emotional man. In all likelihood he would never see her again. Unless she proved to be pregnant, he thought abruptly, and, after what he had done, wouldn't that be a disaster to end all disasters? He still could not credit that he could have taken that risk with her. Since when had sex been so overwhelming an event? He had always been proud of his self-control, not a trait that came naturally to those of his bloodline, he conceded grimly. So, how could passion have betrayed him to that extent? In truth it had been an extraordinary weekend—Zara had defied his expectations at every turn and precious little had gone according to plan.

But why was he questioning his behaviour? Why the hell had he smashed his fist into a wall? He was a goal-orientated man and, having achieved his objective, he ought to be celebrating. After all, Demonides was never going to go ahead and marry Zara Blake once he saw that photo of her in another man's arms in the newspapers. Vitale decided that the problem was that he had got too close to his quarry. He had found her intensely desirable and quite impossible to resist, and all that was wrong was that the shock of that was still ricocheting through a man who rated his strength of mind and self-discipline as exceptional.

'Ignore them, darling,' Jono advised Zara in a tone of crisp dismissal as he helped her stack another box in the van he had borrowed to help her move into her new home. Fluffy was peering out of her carrier, little round eyes full of anxiety. The rabbit hated change and travel of any kind.

A pair of enormous sunglasses anchored on her nose, Zara endeavoured to look indifferent to the pair of reporters shouting rude questions while taking photos to record her departure from her parents' elegant town house. If only she had moved out and embraced independence long ago, she reflected ruefully, she wouldn't be feeling quite so lost. On the other hand, every cloud had a silver lining. This was the first day of her new life, she reminded herself bracingly. Her parents might have thrown their troublesome daughter out and washed their hands of her, but at least she was now free to do as she liked and concentrate on Blooming Perfect.

Jono glanced at Zara's tense profile before he drove off and squeezed her hand in a comforting gesture. 'Things will get better once you can settle into your new flat.'

'They could hardly get worse.' Blond and blue-eyed, Jono, a successful PR consultant, was one of the few friends who had stuck by Zara when the proverbial had hit the fan ten days earlier.

As a well-known socialite and the rumoured future bride of one of the world's wealthiest men, Zara had been extremely popular. Stripped of her father's money and the luxury lifestyle that had accompanied it, she had learned that she was more of an acquired taste in the friendship stakes. She would no longer be able to afford the shopping expeditions, the trips abroad or the expensive pastimes that she had once taken for granted. Of course, given the chance Bee would have stood by her side, but Zara had been determined not to enrage her father even more by encouraging her half-sister to get involved in her problems.

After all, Zara accepted that she had made some very bad decisions and it was the way of the world that she should have to pay the price for her mistakes. That photo of her with Vitale after spending the weekend with him in what had been gruesomely described as a 'love nest in the Tuscan hills' had appeared in one of the murkier tabloids. Sergios had wasted little time in cutting her loose. Her former bridegroom's phone call, Zara recalled with a cringing sense of mortification, had been a masterpiece of icy restraint. Sergios had not reproached or condemned her, he had merely pointed out that it was obvious that they would not suit and that had been that. He had rung off while she was still stuck like a record in a groove trying to apologise for the sort of scandal and behaviour that no woman could adequately apologise for.

In comparison to Sergios' moderation, her parents' fury had known no bounds. Things had been hurled in vicious verbal onslaughts that had almost inevitably led to Monty Blake's raging demand that his daughter move out from below his roof. But, she acknowledged ruefully, at least her enraged father had confined himself to vocal abuse and retained some shred of control over his temper. Sadly that was not always the case.

She had done a search on the Net in an effort to dig up the story of her father and the yacht episode. The sparse facts available had left her none the wiser when it came to apportioning blame. An Asian earthquake and the resulting waves had caused the hired yacht to sink in the middle of the night. Apparently it had happened very quickly. One member of the crew and a passenger called Loredana, described as an Italian fashion model, had been listed missing, presumed drowned. When her father was already furious she had seen little point in mentioning an incident that would only madden him even more. Furthermore, if even an inquest had failed to extract any damaging admission of culpability from the older man she had little faith in the likelihood of her own persuasive powers doing a better job. And why wasn't she being more honest with herself? She had not brought up that business with the yacht because she was frightened of pushing her father's temper over the edge. No, she had been too much of a coward.

The studio apartment she had rented was a masterpiece of clever design in which the minimum possible space was stretched to cover the essentials but it covered nothing well, Zara conceded ruefully as she unpacked, aghast at the lack of storage space. If there was little room for the requirements of ordinary life, there was even less for Fluffy. A neighbour had already informed Zara that no pets were allowed in the building and had threatened to report her to the landlord. Just then that seemed to be the least of Zara's worries, though. By the time she had finished shopping for bed linen, food and kitchen necessities, the balance in her bank account had shrunk alarmingly. Bearing in mind that she had only the small salary she could draw from her late aunt's business, she would have to learn to do without things if she didn't want to run into debt. Now that she was in a position to work full-time it would have suited her to dispense with Rob's services as manager, but, owing to Zara's dyslexia and the restrictions it imposed, Rob had become an essential component in the successful running of the business.

She went to bed early on her first night in the apartment. The instant she closed her eyes in a silence disturbed only by the sounds of traffic the anguish she had fought off to the best of her ability all day flooded back: the intense sense of loss and betrayal, the conviction that she had to be the most stupid woman ever born, the swelling, wounding ache of deep hurt. And she walled up that giant mess of turmoil and self-loathing, shut it out and reminded herself that tomorrow was another day.

That same week in his Florence head office, Vitale's oft-admired powers of concentration let him down repeatedly in meetings when his mind would drift and his shrewd dark eyes would steadily lose their usual needle-sharp focus. The teasing image of a tiny blonde haunted his sleep and shadowed his working hours with unfamiliar introspection. By night he dreamt of Zara Blake in all sorts of erotic scenarios doing all sorts of highly arousing things to his insatiable body. Evidently with her in a starring role his imagination took flight.

Even a resolute procession of cold showers failed to chase the pain of his constant lingering arousal and, being innately practical, he immediately sought a more effective solution to his overactive libido. Since Zara had returned to the UK he had dined out with two different women, taken another to the opera and accompanied a fourth to a charity event. All were extremely attractive and entertaining. Any one of them would have slept with him without attaching strings to the occasion, but not one of those women had tempted him and for the first time he had found himself actively avoiding intimate situations. He had also discovered flaws in all four women and now asked himself when he had become so very hard to please. But while he loathed constant female chatter one of the women had proved too quiet, another had had a very irritating laugh, the third had talked incessantly about shopping and the fourth had constantly searched out her own reflection in mirrors.

Every day Vitale had all the key English newspapers delivered to his office and he skimmed through them mid-morning over his coffee without once admitting to himself what he was actually on the lookout for. Yet every day he contrived to take his coffee break just a little earlier. During the second week, however, he finally hit the jackpot when he saw the photo of Zara with another man. He frowned, at first wondering who the good-looking blond male by her side was. She looked tinier than ever pictured with a suitcase almost as big as she was. He read between the lines of the gossip column below. Her family was angry enough with her to throw her out of their home? What else was he supposed to think?

Vitale was very much shocked, mentally picturing a puppy being dumped at the side of a busy motorway, a puppy with no notion of how to avoid the car wheels racing past. Monty Blake's daughter, surely spoiled and indulged all her life to date, could have few survival skills to fall back on. Honed to a cutting edge by a very much tougher background and much more humble beginnings, Vitale was appalled on her behalf. He had not foreseen such a far-reaching consequence but he felt that he should have done. After all, the loss of Sergios Demonides as a son-in-law would have been a major disappointment and Monty Blake was not the type of man to deal gracefully with such a setback. Evidently he had taken his ire out on his only child.

Feeling disturbingly responsible for that development, Vitale lifted the phone and organised a flight to London in his private jet that evening. He only wanted to check that she was all right, that was all, nothing more complex, certainly nothing personal, although if she turned out to have conceived, he conceded broodingly, matters would swiftly become a great deal more personal. Vitale, after all, knew that he would be the last man alive to take a casual approach to an unplanned pregnancy. He knew too well the potential drawbacks of such a route. It took another couple of phone calls to establish where Zara was staying and the unwelcome gossip he received along with that information persuaded him that Monty Blake's daughter must be having a pretty tough time.

But why should that matter to him? Vitale frowned heavily, deeply ill-at-ease with his reactions. Why did he feel so accountable for what might happen to her? While Vitale was, at least, a free agent Zara had chosen to betray the trust of the man she had promised to marry. She was a faithless liar without a conscience, the spoilt daughter of a man he loathed. But he still could not shake the recollection that he had been Zara's one and only lover. The reflection that he had been wrong about her on that score made him wonder whether there could be other things he might have been wrong about as well. And for a man as self-assured as he was that was a ground-breaking shift in outlook.

The next day, Vitale called at Zara's apartment at

nine in the morning. Even before he entered the building he was asking himself why the hell he was making a social call on the daughter of his enemy. He might have got her pregnant, he reminded himself with fierce reluctance, his handsome mouth down curving. If there was a child he had a duty of care towards her and until he knew one way or the other he could not turn his back on her and ignore her predicament. Born into a comfortable background, she had enjoyed a sheltered upbringing, so how was she coping without that safety net?

Vitale stepped out of the lift on Zara's floor and right into a heated dispute. A burly older man was standing at Zara's front door saying aggressively, 'This isn't open to negotiation—either the rabbit goes or you move out!'

Zara gave him a stricken look. 'But that's—'

'No pets of any kind. You signed the rent agreement and you're in breach of the conditions,' he pronounced loudly. 'I want that animal out of here today or I'm giving you notice to quit.'

'I don't have anywhere else to take her,' Zara was arguing heatedly.

'Not my problem,' the landlord told her, swinging on his heel and striding into the lift that Vitale had only just vacated.

Only as Vitale moved forward did Zara register his presence and her eyes flew wide, her lips parting in furious surprise and dismay. 'What the hell are you doing here?'

CHAPTER SIX

At first glimpse of Vitale, shock shrouded Zara like a cocoon, so that external sounds seemed to come from a very long way away. The traffic noise, the doors opening and closing in the busy life of the building faded fast into the background. As her landlord stomped angrily away, offended by her combative stance, Vitale took his place. Even at a glance, Vitale looked fabulously, irretrievably Italian in a faultlessly cut grey business suit that had that unmistakeable edge of designer style. From his cropped black hair and staggeringly good bone structure to his tall, well-built body, he was a breathtakingly handsome man.

But it hurt to look at him, and as Zara felt the pain of his deception afresh her anger ignited like a roaring flame. Her eyes cloaked, hiding her vulnerability. He hadn't cared about her, hadn't even really wanted her for herself. He had simply used her as a weapon to strike at her father. 'What do you want?' she asked, her intonation sharp with anger. 'And how did you find out where I was living?'

'I have my sources,' Vitale fielded, his stunning dark deep-set eyes trained on her to track any changes.

Casually clad in cropped trousers and flip-flops, she seemed smaller and younger than he had recalled but, if anything, even more beautiful. Her creamy natural skin was flawless. The wealth of silvery waves falling round her narrow shoulders was bright as a beacon, providing the perfect frame for delicate features dominated by wide lavender eyes and an impossibly full and tempting pink mouth. And that fast Vitale wanted her again. The tightening heaviness at his groin was a response that unnerved him more than a little. He operated very much on cold, clever logic—he had no time and even less understanding of anything uncontrolled or foolish. He could not compute the sheer irrational absurdity of such an attraction when he had remained indifferent to so many more suitable women. In self-defence, he immediately sought out her flaws. She was *too* small, her hair was *too* bright, she talked like an express train rarely pausing for breath and much of it was totally superfluous stuff. But in defiance of popular report, he recalled abstractedly, she was anything but stupid. She had a quirky sense of humour and very quick wits.

While Vitale looked her up and down as though he had every right to do so, his face sardonic and uninformative, Zara's resentment merely took on a sharper edge. 'You still haven't told me what you're doing here.' Her heart-shaped face had tightened, irate colour stealing into her cheeks as she belatedly grasped the most likely reason for his reappearance, and she winced in discomfiture. 'Oh, of course, you want to know *if*—'

'May I come in?' Vitale incised, not being a fan of holding intimate conversations in public places.

'I don't want to let you in but I suppose I don't have much choice,' Zara countered ungraciously, reflecting that far from worrying about the possibility of an accidental pregnancy she had shelved the concern in Italy and had refused to think about it again when it seemed that she had so many more pressing things to worry about.

A thumping noise broke the tense silence. At Vitale's entrance, Fluffy thumped the floor with her hind feet in protest and let out a squeal of fright before hotfooting it for her hutch.

Vitale was even more taken aback by the display. 'You keep a…rabbit indoors?' he queried, his only prior experience of rabbits being the belief that people either shot them or ate them and sometimes both.

'Yes, Fluffy's my pet. She's nervous of men,' Zara remarked, wishing she had been as sensibly wary as Fluffy when she had first met him, for it might have protected her from harm.

Indeed in a rage of antipathy, she was looking fixedly at Vitale. Somehow she couldn't stop looking and all of a sudden and without the smallest warning she was recalling much more of that night in the love nest in the Tuscan hills than was necessary or decent. She remembered the early morning light gleaming over the black density of his tousled hair. She had run her fingers through that hair before she ran them over the corrugated flatness of his incredibly muscular torso and traced the silken length of his shaft, exploring him in a way she had never wanted or needed to explore any other man. Her heart was beating so fast in remembrance of those intimacies that she wanted to press a hand against it to slow it down before it banged so hard it burst loose from her chest.

'I don't know if I'm pregnant or not yet,' she admitted frankly, descending straight to the prosaic in the hope of bringing herself back down to planet earth again, safe from such dangerous mental wanderings. He might be gorgeous but he was her enemy and a callous con artist and she hated him for what he had done to her.

Still disconcerted by the presence of a bunny rabbit whose quivering nose was poking out of the elaborate hutch, Vitale frowned, uneasy with a situation he had never been in before. The sort of lovers he usually had took precautions and accidents didn't happen, or at least if they did they were kept quiet, he acknowledged cynically. 'I believe there are tests you can do.'

'I'll buy one and let you know the result when I've done it,' she muttered carelessly. 'But right now I've got more important things to worry about—'

Vitale raised a brow. 'Such as…what exactly?'

'Fluffy, my pet rabbit—what am I going to do with her? My neighbour has already lodged a complaint and you heard the landlord! He wouldn't budge an inch. He's going to chuck me out of here if I don't rehome Fluffy!' she exclaimed.

'Rules are rules,' Vitale pronounced, a little out of

his depth when it came to keeping pets because he had never had one of any kind. It was a challenge for him to understand the depth of her attachment to the animal, but her distraught expression did get the message across. Growing exasperation gripped him. 'Perhaps you could give the rabbit away.'

Zara dealt him a furious look of condemnation. 'I couldn't give Fluffy away!' she gasped. 'She's been with me since my sixteenth birthday and I love her. Thanks to you I've been put through an awful lot of grief over the last couple of weeks but I can cope with it because I'm strong.'

Vitale was still very much focused on what was most important to him and detached from the rabbit scenario. 'I'll buy you a pregnancy test and bring it back here—'

'Don't put yourself out!' Zara slung him a seething look of hatred that startled him, for he had not appreciated that those lavender eyes could telegraph that amount of aversion.

Vitale compressed his sensual mouth and heaved a sigh. 'I must. I'm equally involved in this situation and I can't relax until we have found out where we stand.'

'Well, if wondering about where you stand is all you're worrying about I can help you right now!' Zara fired back at him. 'I hate you. If I find out I'm pregnant, I'll hate you even more. What will I do? I'll trail you through every court in the land for financial support and I'll hope it embarrasses the hell out of you!'

Vitale dealt her a seething look of impatience. 'If you are pregnant you won't have to trail me through a court for financial support. I would pick up the bills without argument.'

Unimpressed by that declaration and cringing at the unhappy thought of being beholden to him, Zara stood so straight her spine ached and her eyes glowed like embers in a banked down fire. 'Then I'll fight *not* to accept your financial support!' she slung back.

Vitale was not slow on the uptake and he got the message that whatever it took she was currently out for his blood. As there was nothing that whet his appetite more than a challenge, a sardonic smile slashed his wonderfully well-shaped mouth. She didn't know who she was dealing with. 'I'll be back soon,' he warned her before he turned on his heel.

'You're not the Terminator,' she told his back acidly before the lift doors closed on him.

Vitale, her sleek sophisticated banker, had gone to buy her a pregnancy test, surely a humble task beneath his high-powered notice? He was not hers, she scolded herself angrily, marvelling that such a designation had even occurred to her. Why was she even speaking to him? Her period was already four days late, a fact she had kept pushed to the back of her mind because she already had more than she could handle on her plate. Usually, however, she was as regular as clockwork in that department, so her disrupted cycle was a source of concern. She stroked Fluffy, inwardly admitting that she really didn't want to do a test yet because she much preferred to keep her spirits up by concentrating on sunnier prospects. My goodness, she reflected with a creeping feeling of apprehension, becoming a single parent in her current circumstances would be a nightmare.

Within the hour, Vitale returned and handed her a carrier bag. Zara extracted, not one, but four different boxes containing pregnancy-testing kits.

'I had no idea which you would prefer,' Vitale declared without a shade of discomfiture. Zara dug into the biggest box and extracted the instructions. The print was so tiny she couldn't read it and the diagram just blurred. Her hand shook, a sense of intense humiliation threatening to eat her alive and turning her skin clammy with perspiration. 'Go home,' she told him shakily.

'Why? I might as well wait.' Vitale's impatience to know the result was etched on his face and hummed from his taut restive stance. He lifted one of the other boxes. 'Use that one. From what I read on the box I understand it can give an immediate result.'

Grateful for that information, Zara took it and unwrapped it, spreading out the instructions on the table with a careful hand, squinting down at it as calmly as she could in an unsuccessful attempt to focus on the minuscule print. All she could see was a blur of mismatched symbols. She thought it was most probably her mood and the awful awareness that she had an audience that was making her dyslexia even worse than it usually was. She needed to stay calm and focused but just at that instant her self-discipline was absent.

'What's wrong?' Vitale queried rather curtly.

Zara breathed in slow and deep. 'The print is so small I can't read it,' she complained.

Assuming that she had imperfect sight but was not

prepared to own up to the fact or indeed have anything done about it, Vitale suppressed a groan and lifted the sheet to read the relevant sentences. Zara would have much preferred to have read it herself. Her cheeks flared red and hot but, veiling her gaze, she made no comment. As she locked herself into the tiny shower room with the kit she thought that anything was better than him discovering the truth about her affliction.

Only when Zara reached sixth form had a concerned teacher asked her mother to allow an educational psychologist to test her daughter. Identified as severely dyslexic, Zara had finally been offered the assistance that she needed to catch up with her peers. Unfortunately by that stage her self-esteem had sunk to rock-bottom and she had been unable to believe that reasonable exam grades might be within her reach. Her father, after all, had immediately dismissed her dyslexia as a 'poor excuse for stupidity' and had refused to credit the existence of such a condition.

Although a speech-language therapist had been recommended to teach Zara how to handle the problem, her father had refused to consider that option, saying it would be a waste of time and money. Unsurprisingly Zara had never recovered from her father's shame and disgust at the news that his daughter suffered from something labelled 'a learning disability'. It was a subject never ever mentioned in her home but she often suspected it was the main reason why her parents continued to look on her as some sort of perpetual child, rather than the adult that she was.

Zara stood in the shower room with her attention on

the novelty wall clock left behind by a previous tenant, refusing to allow herself to simply stare at the test to see if it had changed colour. The waiting time up, she straightened her shoulders and finally directed her gaze to the tiny viewing window on the test wand and there was the line of confirmation that she had most feared to see. Her legs almost buckled beneath her and she broke out in a cold sweat of horror.

Wrenching open the door, Zara reeled out. 'It's bad news, I'm afraid,' she proclaimed jaggedly.

'Let me see.' Accustomed to trusting in only his own powers of observation, Vitale insisted on checking the test. He might have paled had his attention not been on Zara, who was displaying more than enough shock and consternation for both of them.

'You can leave now,' she told him woodenly.

But Vitale stayed where he was, his attention involuntarily fixing to her flat stomach. A baby, she was going to have *his* baby. He was going to have a child with Monty Blake's daughter. He was utterly appalled at the news. A selfish moment of inattention in the heat of passion was all it had taken to permanently change both their lives. Yet he more than anyone had known the potential cost of such negligence and had the least excuse for the oversight, he conceded with stormy self-loathing.

'I can't simply leave you like this,' Vitale declared with a harsh edge to his deep drawl.

'Why not?' Zara gave him a deadened look, still too traumatised to think beyond what she had just learned about her own body. 'Don't you think you've already done enough?'

In the face of that unnecessary reminder, Vitale stood his ground. It was a bad moment but in almost thirty years he had lived through an awful lot of bad moments and he would not allow himself to flinch from anything unpleasant. But for him the worst aspect was that this was an event outside his control and he liked that reality least of all. 'I'd like to deal with this before I leave.'

Zara folded her arms and lifted her chin, suspicious of that particular choice of wording. '*Deal* with it?' she questioned, astonished by the current of protectiveness towards her unborn child that sprang into being inside her and stiffened every defensive muscle. 'I should tell you now—I'm not prepared to have a termination—'

'I'm not asking you to consider that option,' Vitale countered, exasperated by her drama, craving a sensible solution even though he already knew there probably wasn't one. 'You don't trust me but I assure you that I will only act in my child's best interests.'

Zara was unimpressed. How could she trust anything he said? How did she know that getting her pregnant hadn't been part of his revenge? Hadn't he accused her father of getting his sister pregnant? How much faith could she put in Vitale's promises now?

'That's quite a sudden change of attitude you've had,' she remarked in a brittle voice.

His lips set in a firm line, his eyes flaring bright and forceful before he cloaked them. Even though she tried not to, she found herself staring because, regardless of her hatred and distrust, nothing could alter the reality that he was sleek and dark and beautiful as sin.

'Whether I like it or not the fact that you're going to have my child does change everything between us,' he responded darkly.

Zara released a tart laugh of disagreement. 'Even though you believe that my father is the equivalent of a murderer and hate me for being his daughter?'

Anger lent a feverish hint of colour to his exotic high cheekbones and gave Vitale's appearance such striking strength and magnetism. 'I do *not* hate you.'

Scorn crossed Zara's heart-shaped face. 'You're not being honest with yourself. You hate me for the blood that runs in my veins. How else could you think it was acceptable to treat me so badly?'

Vitale did not think in the emotive terms that came so naturally to her. He was in a stormy mood, naturally resentful of the predicament they were in, but still logical enough to accept that anger would do nothing to solve the problems they faced. He saw even less sense in harking back to the past. 'The day we learn that you are carrying my baby is not the time to discuss such issues,' he told flatly. 'We have more important matters to consider—'

'The fact that I hate and distrust you tends to overpower every other impression,' Zara shot back at him, furious at being targeted by that superior little speech and wishing that she knew exactly what he was thinking. Unfortunately that lean darkly handsome face was uniquely uninformative.

'At the very least I would ask you to see a doctor for a check-up as soon as possible,' Vitale advised.

'When I can find the time.' Zara glanced at her watch. 'You really do have to leave. I have an appointment with a client in an hour and I'm not even dressed yet! Oh, my goodness, I forgot, what am I going to do about Fluffy?'

Vitale's sculpted lips parted. 'I'll take her,' he said, startling himself with that announcement almost as much as he startled his companion.

'Are you serious?' Zara stared back at him in stunned disbelief.

'Why not?' Having made the offer, Vitale refused to back down from the challenge. She had quite sufficient thoughts to occupy her without stressing about her pet's impending homelessness. She needed peace of mind to concentrate on her own condition and if removing the wretched rabbit could deliver that he was willing to take care of the problem for her.

'You can't give her away to someone, you know,' she warned him doubtfully. 'Or have her put down or anything like that.'

Vitale dealt her a grimly comprehensive scrutiny, now fully acquainted with how low she feared he might sink even when it came to a dumb animal. 'In this instance you can be confident that your pet will enjoy the best of care.'

Zara frowned, glancing worriedly at the little animal. 'You're not planning to just dump her in a pet-care place, are you? They're always full of dogs and she's terrified of dogs.'

As that was exactly what Vitale had planned to do with Fluffy, it was a tribute to his ability to think fast that he didn't betray a shred of discomfiture. 'Of course not,' he insisted as though such a thought had not even occurred to him.

Vitale then learned a great deal more than he ever cared to know about bunny rabbits. Fluffy did not travel light either. Even with Zara helping it took two trips down to his car to transport all Fluffy's possessions.

'I'll look after her,' he asserted, challenged to retain his patience.

'I'll need your phone number,' Zara told him. 'I'll ring you later to see how you're getting on.'

If ever there was a moment when an unprecedented attack of benevolence on his part had paid off this was it, Vitale recognised with fearless self-honesty. Ironically the mother of his unborn child was more concerned about her pet than about herself, but an avenue of communication had at least opened again. He was going to be a father. The shock of that thought suddenly engulfed Vitale like an avalanche. A baby, he was thinking in a daze of lingering horror as he installed Fluffy in her three deck condo in the corner of his open plan lounge. The brightly coloured plastic rabbit version of a palace with all mod cons looked incongruous against his elegant décor.

On learning that the rabbit was there to stay for the foreseeable future, Vitale's part-time housekeeper told him thinly that she was allergic to animal fur, and when he failed to offer an immediate solution she handed in her notice on the spot. Zara phoned briefly just to tell

Vitale that Fluffy liked MTV for company, apparently being a bunny with a musical bent.

'Tough luck, Fluff,' Vitale breathed, switching on the business channel to catch the most recent stock figures. 'The guy with the remote calls all the shots.'

Fluffy sidled into view like a bunny with a very good idea of how welcome a house guest she was. She slunk along the skirting and then settled down happily to munch at the corner of a very expensive rug. As Vitale rose to intervene and Fluffy took fright at the movement and fled back to her condo it occurred to him that a young child would, at times, be equally trying to his reserves of patience.

That was, if Zara Blake *allowed* him anywhere near their child. His blood ran cold with apprehension as he pictured that possible scenario of parental powerlessness. He cursed the situation he was in. He had several good friends supporting children they rarely, if ever, saw. He knew that a child's mother generally controlled how much access a father might receive and he was well aware that some mothers preferred not to share. As an unmarried father he would have virtually no rights at all over his own flesh and blood. Vitale had been the son of an unstable mother and the defenceless victim of an abusive stepfather. That he might have little say in his own child's upbringing was a prospect that Vitale could not bear to contemplate. How would he ever be able to protect his child from the risk of abuse? His appetite for work suddenly abating, Vitale shut down his laptop. He fed Fluffy, who had the fine taste of a gourmand, and then he paced the floor to consider his options with a new driving urgency.

In the meantime, Zara was having a very busy day. She spent an hour chatting to a potential client before checking out the current job that Blooming Perfect was engaged in and finally returning to the firm's office to finish a plan.

'It really is quite something,' Rob remarked when he saw the plan she had completed for the villa in Italy.

Zara smiled as she rolled it up and slotted it into a protective cardboard tube. 'Well, we'll see.'

'When will the client get it?'

'This week. He's staying in London.'

'Convenient,' Rob commented, already engaged in closing up for the night.

Only as she drove back to her new apartment and struggled to find a parking spot was Zara at long last free to think of the tiny seed of life growing inside her. A baby, *her* baby. She could still hardly believe it was true and could not suppress a sense of wonderment over the conception that embarrassed her. After all, she could hardly celebrate falling pregnant by a man with whom she no longer had a relationship. That was very bad news for her child. Or was it? Thinking about her own father, Zara was not sure that she had ever enjoyed a single advantage from his presence in her life and he was a fearsome man in a temper. On the other hand she had friends who adored their fathers and found them very supportive and good at giving advice, she conceded fairly.

Her unplanned pregnancy would also give her parents yet another reason to criticise her, although they would have fewer grounds than most to complain, because Zara and her brother had been eight years old before their parents even moved in together. Certainly her father had been in no hurry to commit to the mother of his twins. Indeed even at that point Monty Blake must already have been involved with her sister Tawny's mother.

But Zara was not like either of her parents and she told herself that there was no reason why she shouldn't make a good single mother. As she had no trust fund to fall back on she was lucky to have Edith's business to help her survive on the financial front. She was strong and sensible. In a crisis she would bend, not break, and she was willing to make the best of things. So, she had been more than a little foolish over Vitale? She just had to learn to live with that as he was no doubt learning to live with Fluffy. The serious expression on Zara's face slid away and she almost smiled at that incongruous image. Now that offer of his to look after her pet had come as an enormous surprise. But then Vitale was deep, so deep and complex that she couldn't fathom him and she quite understood how she had been taken in by him. Vitale did not wear his true and tricky nature on the surface.

As she was wondering what to make for her evening meal her cell phone beeped with a text.

Join me for dinner? I'll cook. V

No, absolutely not, Zara thought in dismay and annoyance. What was he playing at? And then a more responsible inner voice reminded her that she was set to have a relationship with Vitale through her child that would stretch quite a few years into her future. Ignoring him, refusing to see him or speak to him might be tempting, but it would not be the sensible path to follow. Sadly, on one issue Vitale was correct. Her pregnancy did mean that everything had changed, although her feelings towards him hadn't changed in the slightest: she still hated him like poison. Bolstered by that conviction, Zara texted back her agreement. After all, meeting up with Vitale would also provide her with an easy way of delivering the plan for the grounds of the Italian villa.

CHAPTER SEVEN

FLUFFY was watching television on the leather sofa when Vitale returned to his apartment that evening. He wouldn't have believed it if he hadn't seen it with his own eyes: the wretched bunny was watching music videos while basking in the comfort of a well-upholstered seat! But no sooner did Zara's pet hear the noise of the front door closing than it raced like a furry streak for the safety of its home in the corner. And there, in spite of the food Vitale brought it, the rabbit stayed firmly out of sight.

But Fluffy had not spent an entirely lazy day, Vitale noted grimly, because the rug had been chewed and the wooden foot of a coffee table had been gnawed. It was a destructive bunny rabbit, utterly unsuited to civilised life in a luxury apartment. On the other hand, Zara had agreed to come to dinner, most probably because she wanted to see how her pet was doing.

The plan for the villa tucked below one arm, Zara arrived sporting an ice-blue dress teamed with incredibly high heels. The pale shade accentuated her eyes and her hair shimmered round her shoulders. For the first time

ever Vitale admired a woman's legs and then, quite un-
nervingly for him, thought of her safety instead. What
if she stumbled and fell and got hurt?

'Those shoes are like stilts,' he remarked before he
could think better of the comment, only to watch in
amazement as Fluffy bounded out into the hall to greet
her mistress and gambol round her feet in a welcoming
display.

Zara petted Fluffy and talked to her. Anything was
better than focusing on Vitale, breathtakingly handsome even casually clad in jeans and an open-necked
black shirt. She decided that she was horrendously overdressed and felt as though she had lost face in some secret contest of who could act the most laid-back. Her
·heart was doing that bang-bang-bang thing again but
that was just the natural effect of Vitale's manifold at-
tractions hitting her defences with all the subtlety of a
ten-ton truck.

He served the meal immediately in the spacious dining annexe off the lounge. He had made steak and salad,
nothing fancy, but she was impressed all the same, her
one and only attempt to cook steak having resulted in a
lump of tough and rubbery meat that nobody could eat.
The silence stretching between them seemed to shout
in her ears, reminding her with a painful pang of regret how easily they had once talked in Italy. That, of
course, she recalled, had only been part and parcel of
his deception.

'How do you feel?' Vitale asked her levelly.

'Like I'm stuck inside a soap bubble. The baby

doesn't really feel real yet, probably because it's such an unexpected development,' she admitted.

'I intend to give you all the support that I can.'

At that austere unemotional promise, a tight little smile formed on Zara's lips. 'Then give me space.'

Space was the very last thing Vitale could imagine offering her at that moment. In one of those infuriating shifts of awareness that infiltrated his formidable calm a surge of heat consumed him as he focused on her luscious mouth and recalled what she could do with it. Subjected to an instant erection, Vitale breathed in deep and slow, furiously willing his undisciplined body back under control and deeply resentful of the effect she could have on him. 'I don't think I can do that. I feel responsible for you now.'

Her eyes were cool and flat as glass. 'But that's not how I feel and not what I want.'

'Don't make our child pay the price for what I did in Italy,' he urged her forcefully, already concerned about a future in which he might not be in a position to ensure that his child received the very best of care.

'Maybe I'm thinking that after what you did to me you might be a bad influence to have in a child's life,' Zara told him honestly.

In receipt of that admission, his strong bone structure showed prominently below his bronzed skin and his jaw line clenched hard. In one sense he was outraged that Monty Blake's daughter could question his integrity when her father had none whatsoever. But he could hardly expect her to appreciate that when he had deceived her in Tuscany. He should be grateful, however, that she refused to see him as her only support in a hostile world just because she had fallen pregnant by him. After all, just how much was he prepared to sacrifice to ensure his child's welfare?

'I'm trying to forge a new and different relationship with you,' he delivered tautly.

She gazed into his stunning dark eyes and it was as if a thousand butterflies fluttered free in the pit of her stomach. Instantly she closed him out again, refusing to be entrapped by his raw physical appeal. 'I can't give you a fresh start with me. I don't forgive men who try to use me.'

His brows drew together as he picked up on the pained note she could not suppress. 'There was someone else? Who? What did he do?'

Zara dealt him a bleak look and then wondered what she had to hide. Maybe if she explained he'd understand that there was no way back into her good graces. 'I met Julian when I was eighteen. He was twenty five and he told me he loved me. After he had asked me to marry him he took me away for a weekend. The first night he got me drunk in our hotel room…' Her strained voice ran out of steam and power, her heart-shaped face drawn, her eyes haunted by unpleasant memories. 'I must've passed out. When I came round he had me handcuffed half naked to the headboard of the bed—'

'He had you…*what*?' Vitale repeated in thunderous disbelief.

'When I opened my eyes he had a camera trained on me. All he wanted was sleazy photos of me undressed, so that he could blackmail my father with them. He took my clothes off while I was unconscious. He hadn't even bothered to wait until after he had slept with me—but then he wasn't that interested.' A laugh that had a wounded edge fell from her lips. 'In fact he said I wasn't really his type, he preferred curvy brunettes—'

'Per amor di Dio!' Vitale had a disturbing image of her naked and bewildered, innocent and frightened. The newly protective instincts he had formed since he learnt of her pregnancy were inflamed by the idea of her being stripped of her dignity and at the mercy of a man who only saw her as a source of profit. Julian had badly betrayed her trust when she was still very young and naïve. Vitale refused to think about the damage he might have done pursuing revenge on his sister's account. Regretting the past was always, in his opinion, a waste of time.

'My father may be a womaniser but he's a complete dinosaur when it comes to the behaviour of the women in his family and very conscious of his public image. He paid up and the photos were destroyed although I still haven't heard the last of that disaster even now,' Zara confided painfully. 'I got Julian thrown in my face again last week and the week before. I was young and stupid and too easily impressed, but that's twice I've seriously embarrassed my family now.'

'But what Julian did was criminal. He assaulted you. You father should've reported him to the police.'

'Dad didn't want to risk the newspapers getting hold of the story. It's ancient history now.' Zara's tone was dismissive and she lifted her chin. 'And I thought I had learned my lesson with Julian, but then I met you.'

'What happened between us in Italy is over and done with—'

'Is it? It may be over but it's not forgotten,' Zara pointed out, her quiet voice harshening with the antipathy she was struggling to restrain. 'And I'm not going to give you the chance to cause me any more grief.'

Vitale realised that in the light she saw him now, only the ultimate sacrifice was likely to convince her of the strength of his intentions. With every fibre of his being he baulked at that option, for marriage was a hell of a price to pay for a contraceptive oversight. Yet how else could he make sure that he had a permanent place in his future child's life? How else could he acquire the legal rights with which he could always protect his child from any threat? And how could she possibly cope well as a single parent without adequate family support? Yet if he married her, he would lose the freedom he valued, the choices he luxuriated in and the privacy he had always cherished. Suppressing his reluctance and his resentment, Vitale recalled his own wretched childhood and accepted that no price was too high if it protected his unborn son or daughter from the risk of growing up in a similar hell.

Vitale studied Zara carefully. 'Will that answer still hold good even if I ask you to marry me?'

Zara jerked in astonishment, her brow furrowing, her eyes wide as she decided that that must be his idea of a joke after what she had told him about Julian using a marriage proposal to gain her trust. 'You can't be serious.'

'I am perfectly serious—I'm asking you to be my

wife,' Vitale countered with cool assurance. 'In the hope that we can raise our child together.'

'Not so long ago you told me that you avoided women with wedding rings in their eyes and that that's why you're still single,' she reminded him ruefully.

'But then you fell pregnant with my child and naturally my priorities altered,' Vitale pointed out drily. 'We can't turn the clock back. We have to look to the future.'

Her appetite having disappeared in tune with the tension rising in the atmosphere, Zara pushed aside the dessert and stood up, her eyes dark with strain. If an offer of marriage was his attempt at restitution he could forget it—she was not about to be taken in again. 'No, absolutely not. You don't need to worry. The baby and I will be fine on our own. Thankfully I'm not a helpless teenage girl with no idea how to manage—'

Vitale was not convinced by that argument. He sprang up to his full commanding height, the vital force and energy of his gaze welded to her. 'We have to talk this out. Don't leave.'

Zara veiled her eyes and fought to recapture the composure he had cracked with his astonishing proposal. 'I wasn't leaving yet. I've brought the villa plan with me. If you've finished eating we can look at it now.'

Desperate for a distraction, Zara removed the plan from the tube and spread it on the unused portion of the polished table. She explained the meaning of various symbols she had used and discussed possibilities. Vitale was impressed by the intricate detail of the design, not having appreciated that she would actually be drawing the plans with her own fair hand.

'Those borders—could some of them be left empty?'

Her brow furrowed. 'Yes, of course, but—'

'The lady whom I hope will be living there,' Vitale began with uncharacteristic hesitancy lacing his dark deep voice, 'may have an interest in the garden and if the planting is not quite complete that may encourage her to get more involved.'

'That's a good idea,' Zara remarked, insanely curious about the identity of the individual, for he had been careful to keep that information confidential when they had been together in Italy. His innate reserve would always seek to impose distance between them, she registered. He was not a man given to casual confidences and he kept his own counsel. Working out what made him tick would always be a challenge for her.

Zara laughed when Fluffy nudged her ankle with one of her toys and Vitale watched in surprise as Zara threw it and the rabbit played fetch. 'She loves games,' she told him, a natural smile chasing the tension from her lush mouth.

Vitale watched her stroke the rabbit's head with delicate fingers. She was so gentle with the little animal and it clearly adored her. 'I was serious about the proposal,' he asserted, exasperated that she could think otherwise.

'Being pregnant isn't a good enough reason to get married,' Zara replied doggedly, her senses awakened by the faint aromatic hint of his cologne assailing her nostrils because he was standing close to her. Even the scent of him was awesomely familiar. Her spine stiffened as tingling warmth pooled at the heart of her, her body instantly reacting to the proximity of his. He was pure temptation but she was too much on her guard to betray the weakness he could evoke.

His frustration increasing, Vitale stared down at her with brooding dark eyes. 'It is very important to me that I should be in a position to play a proper part in my child's life—'

'You don't have to marry me to play that part—'

Thinking of his destroyed childhood with his cruel stepfather, Vitale barely repressed a shudder of disagreement. 'If we're not married, if we stay separate, we will both end up with other partners and it will be much more difficult—'

'But other people manage it,' Zara sliced in flatly even as her heart clenched at the very thought of him with another woman.

It was going to happen, possibly had even happened already, she scolded herself angrily. Vitale was going to be with other women and she had to adapt to that idea. That the idea bothered her was just some weird jealous and possessive prompting, most probably because he had become her first lover. On the other hand, a scheming little voice murmured somewhere in the depths of her brain, if *you* married him, nobody else could have him. She stifled that inner voice, embarrassed by its foolishness.

The following morning Zara attended an appointment with her GP. He confirmed the test results and sent her off to see the practice nurse, who gave her a bunch of leaflets packed with pregnancy advice. They were still clutched in her hand when a man walking past her in the street knocked her shoulder, loosening her grip so that the sheets spun across the pavement in an arc. As the man sped on without noticing Zara stooped to pick up the leaflets.

'*Zara?*' a familiar voice queried and Zara straightened, recognising the elegant brunette. 'I wasn't expecting to see you round this neighbourhood. Didn't I hear that you'd moved to another part of town?'

Meeting Ella's big blue curious eyes, Zara reddened. 'Yes, I have—'

'Oh, my goodness, are those for you?' Ella exclaimed, flicking one of the leaflets, which clearly showed a pregnant woman, with a manicured fingernail and accompanying the question with a delighted squeal. 'Are you pregnant?'

'I'm meeting someone in ten minutes. Lovely seeing you again, Ella,' Zara fielded with a bright smile, stuffing the informative leaflets into her bag and walking on without further comment. Her cheeks were hot as she queried her bad luck at running into one of the biggest gossips she knew at the wrong moment.

Vitale was not having a good day either. He had offered to fall on his sword like a proper little soldier when he had asked her to marry him. The sacrifice had been necessary: she was carrying his baby and he had a deep need to be a genuine part of his child's life. But it would also entail sharing his life. When had he ever dreamt of sharing his life with another person?

When had he ever longed for a child of his own? He had never wanted those things and his entire life had been devoted to achieving emotional self-sufficiency. He told himself that he should be grateful that she had turned him down. He should walk away while he could, avoid getting personally involved. He should be content to ensure that his only responsibility towards her and the child was financial. Why could he not settle for that eminently practical option? Realistically what were the chances that Zara would some day bring a man into her life as brutal as Vitale's late stepfather?

Zara was at Blooming Perfect going through the accounts with Rob when Jono phoned her and drew her attention to a paragraph in a gossip column. Although she was grateful for the warning her heart sank and she went out to buy the paper and there it was, clearly the result of a tip-off from Ella or one of her pals, the loaded suggestion that party girl and socialite Zara Blake might be expecting a baby. Her phone rang again: it was mother asking her to come home for a chat.

Zara knew what she was going to be asked and she definitely didn't want to go and face the music. Unfortunately being adult and independent demanded that she not avoid the inevitable, no matter how unpleasant it might prove to be. Monty and Ingrid Blake were going to be even more disappointed in her than they already were. An unmarried pregnant daughter was no consolation for one who mere weeks ago had been set to marry a Greek billionaire in the society wedding of the year.

'Is it true?' Ingrid Blake demanded the instant her daughter entered the sparsely furnished drawing room where elegance counted for more than comfort.

Her heart beating very fast, Zara glanced nervously at her father standing by the fireplace, his still-handsome face set hard as granite. 'Yes, I'm pregnant.'

'We'll organise a termination for you straight away,' her mother said without an ounce of hesitation.

Zara straightened her slight shoulders and eased them back. 'No. I want to have my baby.'

'Who's the father?' Monty Blake growled.

'I'm sorry but I don't want to discuss that.'

'I bet you don't, you brainless little—' the older man launched furiously at her, a red flush of rage staining his cheeks.

Her tension palpable, Zara's mother rested a soothing hand lightly on her husband's arm. 'Don't let her upset you, darling... She's not worth it—'

'You're telling me, she's not!' Monty Blake seethed, grinding his teeth as he strode forward, his face a mask of fury. 'It's out of the question for you to have this baby.'

Struggling not to back away from her enraged parent as she had so often seen her mother do without any happy result, Zara stood her ground.

'Listen to your father for once, Zara,' Ingrid ordered thinly. 'You simply *can't* have this baby! Be reasonable. Once you have a child in tow, your life will be ruined.'

'Did Tom and I ruin your life?' Zara asked painfully, deeply hurt that her mother could so immediately dismiss the prospect of her first grandchild being born.

'Don't you dare mention your brother's name, you stupid little cow!' Monty Blake spat at her, erupting into a white hot rage at that fatal reference and swinging up his hand to slap her hard across one cheekbone.

Eyes filling with fear and pain, Zara was almost unbalanced by the force of that blow and she had to step back to stay upright. Her hand crept up to press against her hot, stinging cheek. 'Don't you dare hit me,' she told her father angrily. 'I should call the police on you—'

'Don't be silly,' her mother interrupted in alarm at such a threat from her daughter. 'You asked for it.'

'The same way you always did?' Zara prompted shakily before turning scornful eyes on her father. 'I'll never set foot in this house again.'

'We'll live,' her father shot back at her with derision. 'You're no loss!'

Sick with shock in the aftermath of that traumatic confrontation, Zara returned to her apartment. When she climbed out of her car she could feel something trickling down her face and when she dashed it away saw blood on the side of her hand. In her compact mirror she saw the cut on her cheek where the stone in her father's signet ring must have broken the skin. She couldn't still the shaking in her body, but she was asking herself why she was so surprised by what had happened for, although it was the first time that her father had hit her since she had become an adult, it was far from being the first time that he had struck her.

It was a fact of Zara's childhood that Monty Blake had an unmanageable temper and that he lashed out with his fists whenever he lost control. Usually Ingrid had paid the price of her husband's need for violence to satisfy his rage or frustration. In fact as a terrified child of ten years old seeing her mother beaten up Zara had once called the police and the fallout from that unwelcome intervention had taught her an unforgettable lesson. Branded a wicked liar and winning even her twin's censure for 'letting down' the family, she had been sent away to boarding school. That night she had learned that anything that happened behind the doors of the Blakes' smart town house was strictly private and not for sharing, not even with Bee.

'It's between Mum and Dad—it's nothing to do with us. He hardly ever lifts the hand to either of us,' Tom used to point out when they were teenagers. 'It's only the odd slap or punch—I'm sure there's a lot worse goes on in other families.'

But dread of their father's sudden violent outbursts had created a horribly intimidating atmosphere in Zara's home while she was growing up. All of them had worked very hard at trying to please or soothe Monty Blake. Tom, the apple of his father's eye, had always been the most successful. The aggressive attacks on their mother, however, had continued in secret for occasionally Zara had noticed that her mother was moving slowly and stiffly as if she was in pain and had known that her father was usually too careful to plant a fist where a bruise might show.

By the time she reached her apartment stress had given Zara a nasty headache and her face was hurting her like mad. She was on the brink of taking painkillers before she remembered that she was pregnant and realised that without medical advice it would be safer to do without medication. She examined her swollen cheekbone in the mirror. It was hot and red and a livid scratch trailed across her skin while the darkening of her eye socket suggested that a bruise was forming. When the buzzer on her door sounded she snatched up her sunglasses and put them on.

It was Vitale, long and lean in a black business suit and impatiently about to stab on the buzzer a second time when she opened the door. His hand fell back from the wood and he stared down at her.

'Why are you wearing sunglasses indoors?' he questioned, strolling past her although she had not invited him in.

Just as Zara frowned Vitale flipped the specs off her nose and stilled when he saw her battered face. 'What the hell happened to you?' he growled angrily.

'I fell…tripped at the nursery,' she lied.

'Don't lie to me. I can spot a lie at sixty paces,' Vitale warned her, frowning as he traced the swelling with a gentle fingertip. 'This looks more like someone punched you.'

'Don't be ridiculous,' Zara said in a wobbly voice, her eyes welling up with tears. 'Why are you here?'

Vitale tossed down the newspaper he carried in a silent statement. It was the same edition that had implied that she might be pregnant.

'Oh, that…' she muttered abstractedly as he closed the door behind him. Although she had only read that gossip column this morning it already felt as if a hundred years had passed since then.

'I don't believe that you fell. I want to know who did that to your face. Who hit you?' Vitale breathed soft and low, but there was a fire in his penetrating gaze. 'I think you might have a black eye tomorrow.'

Nervousness made it difficult for Zara to swallow and her throat was tight. She was tired and upset and sore. 'It's not important.'

'You've been assaulted. How can that not be important?' Vitale demanded, cutting through her weary voice. 'Who are you trying to protect?'

Zara paled at that accurate stab in the dark, but the habit of secrecy where her family was concerned was too deeply engrained in her to be easily broken. 'I'm not protecting anyone.'

'You're pregnant. What sort of a person attacks a pregnant woman?' he demanded rawly. 'He could have hit your stomach rather than your face, causing you to miscarry—would you still be protecting him then?'

The hunted expression in Zara's strained eyes deepened as she dropped her head to avoid his searing gaze. 'I don't want to talk about this, Vitale.'

He closed a hand round hers and drew her closer. 'I'm not leaving until you tell me. When you were attacked our child was put at risk and I can't walk away from that.'

Reminded of her responsibility towards the baby she carried, Zara was engulfed by a dreadful tide of guilt. Her opposing loyalties made her feel torn in two and suddenly her resistance washed away in the tide of her distress. 'It was my father...okay?' she cried defiantly as she wrenched her hand free of Vitale's hold. 'But he didn't mean anything by it—he just loses his temper and lashes out—'

'Your…*father*?' His eyes flaring like golden fireworks, Vitale's angry voice actually shook, his accent thickening around the syllables as he yanked open the door again.

'Where are you going?' In consternation, Zara followed him and grabbed his arm to force him to stop in his tracks. 'What do you think you're going to do?'

Eyes veiled, Vitale rested his livid gaze on her anxious face. 'I'll make sure that this never happens again.'

'How can you do that? I don't want you fighting with my father… I don't want people to find out about this—it's private!' Zara gasped, clutching at the well-cut jacket of his business suit with frantic hands.

Vitale closed his fingers round her fragile wrists and gently detached her grip. His face was forbidding in its austerity, his eyes hard as iron. 'I'm not about to fight with your father. I am not planning to tell anyone else about this either—that is your choice to make. But I *am* going to make sure that he never ever dares to lay a finger on you again,' he spelt out in a wrathful undertone. 'I'll see you later.'

Left alone, Zara trembled from the force of all the emotions she was fighting to contain. She was shaking with stress. Her father would lose his head again when Vitale approached him and made his accusation. The older man would know that once again his daughter had talked. A headache hammered painfully behind her taut brow and she sank down on the edge of the bed and breathed in slow and deep in an attempt to calm down. She was appalled by Vitale's interference but even more shocked that she had surrendered and told him the truth. For so many years she had kept that family shame a deep, dark secret. Now all hell was about to break loose because she had just given a man who already hated her father another reason to despise and attack him.

For an instant though Zara was mentally swept back to the elegant drawing room where she had been rocked back on her heels by her father's blow. Whether she liked it or not she had to admit that Vitale had made a valid point. Had she fallen she might have injured her baby or even miscarried. There was no excuse for her father's violence; there never had been an excuse for his behaviour. But while she accepted that truth, intellectually dealing with something that had become so much a part of her family life was altogether something else. It had been her mother's refusal to condemn her husband's violence that had set the agenda of acceptance in Zara's home. Although it hurt to admit it, her brother Tom's insistence on ignoring the problem had also given strength to the idea that such violence had to be endured and concealed. Of course, her father had never struck Tom. Monty Blake had always aimed his violence at his womenfolk.

Feeling too sick to eat, Zara lay down on the bed and eventually fell asleep. Vitale's return wakened her and she answered the door barefoot, her hair a tousled silvery cloud round her face as she blinked up at him drowsily. She was startled to see her father standing by

Vitale's side. In the shadow of Vitale's greater height and raw energy, Monty Blake looked pale, wretched and diminished.

'Your father has something he wants to say to you,' Vitale proclaimed harshly.

'I'm sorry I hurt you—it will never happen again,' her father muttered with all the life of a battery-operated robot.

'I'm not having a termination,' she reiterated in a feverish whisper, wanting her father to know that that was not a price she was prepared to pay for family forgiveness.

In response to that revealing statement a murderous light flamed in Vitale's gaze. 'We're getting married as soon as it can be arranged,' he delivered.

Taken aback by the announcement, Zara shot him a confused glance. After all, he was already well aware of her thoughts on that subject. Dark eyes gleaming with purpose, Vitale stared back at her in blatant challenge. She parted her lips to argue and then decided to wait until her father was no longer present. She felt she owed Vitale that much after he had brought her father to her door to apologise to her. For the first time ever a man had tried to protect Zara rather than take advantage of her and she could only be impressed by that reality.

'You must do as you see fit,' Monty Blake responded flatly, turning back to Vitale to add, 'Are you satisfied?'

'For the moment, but watch your step around me and your daughter.'

Zara watched her father hurry back into the lift, keen to make his escape, and she slowly breathed in and out, the worst of her tension evaporating with his departure. 'How on earth did you persuade him to come here?'

'I didn't persuade him, I threatened him,' Vitale admitted without an ounce of regret. 'He's terrified of being forced to face the legal and social consequences of his behaviour. I'm surprised that you've never used that fear against him.'

Zara lowered her lashes, thinking of how she had been branded a troublemaking liar at the age of ten when she had tried to report her father's violence to the authorities. Nobody had backed up her story, not even her mother, and by the end of it all nobody had believed her either.

'He's hit you before, hasn't he?' Vitale prompted darkly.

'This was the first time since I grew up,' Zara admitted grudgingly. 'I don't think he can help himself. I think he needs professional help or anger-management classes but he wouldn't go to anything like that. He won't admit he has a problem.'

'Does he hit your mother?'

Zara glanced at his lean strong face and then looked away from the condemnation etched there to nod jerkily in reluctant confirmation. 'She won't do anything about it, won't even talk about it. I'm glad you didn't hit him though.'

'I would have enjoyed smashing his teeth down his throat,' Vitale admitted with a casual ease that shook her. 'But it wouldn't have helped anyone. Domestic violence is like an addiction for some men, but I believe that in your father's case the threat of public exposure might have forced him to seek treatment.'

'Did you confront him about your sister? About what happened the night that she drowned?' Zara pressed in a strained undertone.

There was a bitter light in his eyes and his sardonic mouth twisted. 'No, it wasn't the right moment for me to demand those answers. I was more concerned about you.'

Vitale swung away, his last words still echoing inside his head; even he questioned his own restraint. How could he have been more concerned about her? Granted she carried his child, but he had spent half a lifetime dreaming of a confrontation with Monty Blake. Only to discover that, in the flesh, Monty Blake was scarcely a challenging target. Loredana's former lover was a weak man, easily cowed by a more forceful personality and the threat of social humiliation.

Zara was frowning as well, marvelling that Vitale had had her father at such a disadvantage and yet had remained silent in spite of his fierce desire for revenge. 'Did he realise who you were? Didn't he recognise your name from your sister's?'

'Loredana and I had different surnames. Her name was Barigo.' His lean strong face had taken on a shuttered aspect that warned her she had touched on a sensitive subject. Vitale, she realised belatedly, had family secrets as well.

'Why on earth did you tell him that we were getting married?'

Vitale threw back his handsome dark head and settled his moody gaze on her. 'I'm convinced that when you consider your options you'll see that you have nothing to lose and everything to gain by becoming my wife—'

'How?' Zara interrupted baldly. 'I've already told you how I feel about you.'

'Take a risk on me.'

Her lips compressed. 'I don't take risks—'

'But I do. That's why I'm the CEO of a major investment bank,' Vitale told her with savage assurance. 'It makes sense for you to give marriage a chance for our child's sake. If it doesn't work out, we can get a divorce. But at least we'll know that we tried.'

Taken aback by his speech, Zara was momentarily silenced. *For our child's sake,* four little words that had immense impact on her impression of Vitale Roccanti, much as his earlier defence of her against her father had had. Slowly but surely Vitale was changing her opinion of him. Her father might not have added anything positive to her life but Vitale, she sensed, would be a far different prospect in the parenting stakes. Vitale was willing to put his money where his mouth was and put their baby's needs to the top of the pile. He was a handsome, wealthy and successful man yet he was still willing to give up his freedom to provide a more stable background for the child he had accidentally fathered. She could only admire him for that and admit that, given the choice, she would much prefer to raise her child with two parents.

'If we get married and it falls apart, it would be very upsetting for everyone concerned.'

'I would find watching you raise my child with another man infinitely *more* upsetting,' Vitale countered with blunt emphasis. 'All I'm asking you to do is give us the opportunity to see if we can make it work.'

'It's not that simple—'

Vitale released his breath in a driven hiss of impatience. 'You're the one making it complicated.'

Zara's tiny frame was rigid. Could she take a risk and give him another chance? But marriage wasn't an experiment. She could not marry him on a casual basis and walk away without concern if it failed. In her experience failure always bit deep and hurt. And just how far could she trust a man she couldn't read with any accuracy? 'I don't know enough about you. I can't forget that you plotted and planned against me.'

'I can put that past behind us if I have to, *angelina mia*. Our child's needs take precedence,' Vitale contended.

The silence buzzed. Her troubled gaze lingering on his wide, sensual mouth, she recalled the taste of him with a hot liquid surge low in her tummy that she struggled to quell. The tender flesh between her thighs dampened and a pink flush of awareness covered her face. Tensing, she looked hurriedly away from him.

'But I will be honest—I also want you,' Vitale conceded in a dark driven undertone, startling her with that additional admission. 'That's not what I chose, not what I foresaw and certainly not what I'm comfortable with. But it *is* how I feel right now. Ever since we were together in Italy I've wanted you back in my bed again.'

Although she flushed, Zara stood a little straighter,

strengthened by that raw-edged confession. It did her good to know that he was not quite as in control as he liked to pretend. Every time she looked at him she had to fight her natural response to his sleek dark magnetism. The idea that he had to fight the same attraction had considerable appeal. He bent his arrogant head, eyes narrowed to track her every change of expression with a lethal sensuality as integral to him as his aggressive take on life.

'All right, I'll give marrying you a trial for three months,' Zara declared, tilting her chin. 'If we can't make it work in that time we have to agree to split up without any recriminations on either side.'

'A sort of "try before you buy" option?' Vitale drawled silkily.

'Why not?' Feeling as though she was somewhat in control of events again, Zara settled her soft full lips into a wary smile. She could handle being attracted to him as long as he was attracted to her. If she kept a sensible grip on her emotions there was no reason why she should get hurt. Furthermore, after what he had done to her she would never make the mistake of viewing him through rose-coloured glasses again.

His hand curving to her narrow shoulder, Vitale lowered his head and claimed her mouth with his. As he pried her lips apart with the tip of his tongue an arrow of sizzling heat slivered through her with such piercing, drugging sweetness that she shivered violently in response. She dug her nails into her palms to stop herself from reaching out to him and she stood there stiff as a board while the greedy warmth and excitement of desire washed through her every skin cell, filling her with restless energy and longing.

He lifted his head again, dark golden eyes blazing with unconcealed hunger. 'I'll *make* it work for us,' he swore.

But the very fact that he acknowledged a need to work at their marriage was, to her way of thinking, the most likely reason why their efforts would fail. Natural inclinations often outgunned the best of good intentions, she reflected worriedly. Only when the going got tough would they discover how deep their commitment to a practical marriage could actually go.

CHAPTER EIGHT

Two weeks before the wedding, Vitale arranged to pick Zara up for lunch. Not having seen him at all in the preceding week owing to his demanding schedule, she was surprised by the invitation.

'I thought you were always too busy during the day for this sort of thing,' Zara reminded him of his own words on the phone several nights earlier as she climbed into his car.

'As a rule I am but this is rather different. We're going to see your father,' Vitale revealed grimly.

Her head swivelled, eyes bright with dismay and curiosity in her disconcerted face. 'Why the hell are we meeting up with Dad?'

'It's time I asked those questions about my sister's death,' Vitale volunteered tight-mouthed, his brooding tension palpable in the taut lines of his face. 'Now that we are getting married those questions have to finally be answered. He's your father. I can't leave you out of this.'

'I'm not sure I want to be there,' she confessed, disturbed by the prospect of being on the sidelines of such a sensitive confrontation. 'Although it hardly matters as relations currently stand between me and my parents, Dad won't forgive me for being present if you're planning to humiliate him.'

'I see no advantage to doing that,' Vitale admitted flatly fingers flexing and tightening round the steering wheel. 'I phoned your father first thing this morning and told him that I was Loredana's brother and that I need him to tell me the truth of what happened the night she drowned. He's had a few hours to think over his options.'

'And you think an upfront approach will work like some kind of magic charm with him?' Zara pressed doubtfully.

'Your father is not a stupid man. What does he have to lose? He knows I probably can't disprove anything he says. There were only two crew members on board that yacht. The stewardess, who was also the cook, died. Rod Baines, the sailor in charge of the boat, suffered head injuries and remembered very little about that night after he had recovered.'

Monty Blake was in his office on the first floor of the elegant flagship hotel of the Royale chain. He was standing by the window when they entered and he swung round, his mouth tightening with annoyance when he saw his daughter. 'Did you know about this connection when you got involved with the man you're planning to marry?' he demanded accusingly.

'That's not relevant. Why don't you just tell Vitale what happened that night?' Zara replied evenly.

'I told the full story at the inquest many years ago—'

'Yes, I believe you magically found yourself in the rescue dinghy and then fell conveniently unconscious while the yacht sank,' Vitale breathed witheringly. 'How long were you a part of my sister's life before that night?'

The older man grimaced. 'I wasn't a part of her life. I hardly knew her—'

'But she was pregnant—'

'Not by me, as I stated at the inquest,' Zara's father insisted quick as a flash. 'I was never intimate with her.'

Vitale frowned. 'Do I look like a fool?'

'I never got the chance. Check out the dates if you don't believe me. I met Loredana at your uncle's country house, dined with her the following week while I was at our hotel in Rome and invited her to go sailing with me at the weekend. She was a very beautiful young woman but it was a casual thing,' he declared, shooting a look of discomfiture at his daughter. 'I had quite enough complications in my life. Your mother and I were hardly speaking to each other at the time.'

Zara stiffened. 'Nothing you tell us will go beyond these walls,' she promised uneasily.

'Loredana was in a very emotional mood when she joined me that weekend,' Monty Blake revealed. 'Over our meal she admitted that she'd had a row with some boyfriend and that she was pregnant. It was hardly what I had signed up for when I invited her onto the yacht for a pleasure trip and we had a difference of opinion when I asked her why she had agreed to join me on board—'

'An argument?' Vitale queried darkly, his suspicions obvious.

'There was no big drama,' the older man replied wearily. 'Apparently Loredana only accepted my invite because she wanted to make her boyfriend jealous. She hoped he would try to stop her seeing me but he didn't and she was upset about that. When she started crying I suggested she retire to her cabin for the night—and I mean no disrespect when I say that I'd had quite enough of her histrionics by then.'

Vitale managed not to flinch but he did remember his sister as being a very emotional and vivid individual, easily roused to laughter, temper or tears. There had been no reference to an argument, no mention of Loredana's supposedly troubled state of mind during the inquest. But for all that there was a convincing ring of authenticity to the older man's story and he could imagine how irritated Monty Blake must have been when he realised why Loredana had accepted his invitation and that his seduction plans were unlikely to come to anything.

'Your sister made me feel like I was too old to be chasing girls her age,' Zara's father claimed with a curled lip. 'She depressed me. I didn't go to bed. I sat up getting very drunk that night and fell asleep in the saloon. Some time during the night, Rod, the chap in charge of the boat, woke me up, said there was a bad storm. He told me to go and fetch your sister and Pam, the stewardess, while he sorted the escape dinghy. He said the two women were together...' Monty shook his greying head heavily. 'I was drunk and the generator failed, so the lights went out…'

'And then what did you do?' Vitale growled.

'Your sister wasn't in her cabin and I didn't know my way round the crew quarters. The yacht was lurching in every direction. I couldn't see where I was going or keep my feet. I started shouting their names. Water was streaming down the gangway. It was terrifying. I fell and hurt myself. I rushed back up on deck to get Rod to help but Rod had been injured and he was bleeding heavily from a head wound.' Something of the desperation Monty Blake had felt that night had leaked into his fracturing voice and stamped his drawn face with the recollection of a nightmare. 'The boat was sinking and I panicked. Is that what you want me to admit?'

'All I want is the truth,' Vitale breathed tightly, almost as strained as Zara's father.

'Well, I'm sorry I wasn't a hero, but with the sea pouring in I was too scared to go below deck alone again,' he gritted in a shamed but also defiant undertone, as if that was a moment and a decision he had weighed many times over the years that had passed since that fateful night. 'I pulled on a life jacket and helped Rod into his, struggled with the dinghy while he tried to tell me what to do. I can't swim, you know…I never learned. The boat was going down, there was no time for a search, no time to do anything else—'

'You hardly knew her,' Vitale remarked with hollow finality. 'You saved yourself. I don't believe it would be fair to judge you for that. '

Zara never did get lunch. They left the hotel in si-

lence. Neither of them had any appetite after that meeting. She knew Vitale's thoughts were still on his dead
sister. She knew the truth had been hard for him to hear.
Loredana had been very young and agreeing to go sailing with a virtual stranger had clearly been an impulsive act. Her father had been drunk and less than brave
in an emergency, but only a special few were willing to
risk their own life for another person's and it wouldn't
be fair to blame him for falling short of a heroic ideal.

'No, there's not even a hint of a little bump!' Bee declared two weeks later on Zara's wedding day, as she
scrutinised her half-sister's stomach from every angle.
Bee reckoned that only a woman who had never had a
weight problem would have fallen pregnant and then
chosen a figure-hugging wedding gown calculated to
reveal the smallest bulge. Luckily for Zara, she had
no surplus flesh to spoil the perfect symmetry of her
flowing lace dress.

Zara studied her reflection, grateful that her pregnancy did not yet show. True, her breasts were a little
fuller, but that was the sole change in her shape that she
had noticed. Her gown was slender and elegant, max-
imising her diminutive height. 'I hope Vitale doesn't
think I'm overdressed.'

'How can you be overdressed at your own wedding?'
Bee demanded.

'When it's a quiet do with only a couple of witnesses
attending,' Zara pointed out, wincing at that reality,

'Does that bother you?' Bee asked worriedly. 'I know

this can't be the sort of wedding you ever expected to have.'

'It's what I want. I was never into all the fuss and frills of the wedding arrangements Mum insisted on when I was supposed to be marrying Sergios,' Zara admitted, a look of discomfiture crossing her delicate features, 'and this wedding is still only a formality—'

'I think it's a little more than a formality when the man you're about to marry is the father of your baby,' Bee cut in with some amusement.

'I'm very grateful that Vitale's willing to share that responsibility.'

Bee pulled an unimpressed face. 'Which is exactly why you picked a gorgeous dress and got all dollied up in your fanciest make-up and shoes for Vitale's benefit?' she teased. '*Please*, do I look that stupid?'

Zara said nothing, for it was true that she had gone to no end of trouble to look her very best for the occasion. She had not required a church full of guests as an excuse to push the glamour boat out. But it had taken an ironic ton of make-up and every scrap of artistry she possessed to achieve the natural effect she had sought. The natural effect she knew he admired. Her shoes, sparkling with diamanté, were the very cute equivalent of Cinderella's slippers. To satisfy the something-old rhyme she had her late brother's school badge tucked into her bra and her thigh sported a blue garter. If the wedding was only a formality why had she bothered with all those trappings?

The circumstances being what they were, she had only invited her half-sisters to share the brief ceremony

with her. Bee was accompanying her to the church and
Tawny had promised to meet them there. Afterwards
she and Vitale were flying straight out to Italy. She had
packed up her apartment, surrendered it and had spent
the previous night with Bee. She was retaining Rob to
manage Blooming Perfect in London. She was hoping
that there would be sufficient demand for her services
in Tuscany for her to open another small branch of the
business. Fluffy had already flown out to her future
new home. Zara, however, was as apprehensive as a
climber hanging onto a frayed rope: she was terrified
that she was doing the wrong thing. In one life there
was only room for so many mistakes and on this occasion she was very conscious that she had a child's welfare to consider.

The car Vitale had sent to collect her drew up outside the church. She got out with Bee's assistance and
her younger sister, Tawny, hurried towards her.

'Zara!' she exclaimed, pushing a long curl of fiery
copper hair out of her eyes. 'You look amazing! Who
is this Italian? And why didn't I get the chance to meet
him before this?'

'I'm pregnant and we're in a hurry,' Zara confided,
watching her sibling's bright blue eyes shoot wide in
surprise and drop almost inevitably to her stomach.

'Oh…' Tawny grimaced. 'And you're marrying him?
I hope you know what you're doing—'

'When does Zara ever know what she's doing?' Bee
chimed in ruefully. 'She never takes the long view.'

'My sisters are supposed to be universally supportive on my wedding day,' Zara cut in with a warning frown. 'Get supporting.'

And nothing more was said. Her siblings escorted her up the church steps and smoothed out the hem of her gown in the porch. The organ began to play and the doors opened for Zara to walk down the aisle. Marriage, she was thinking on the edge of panic, marriage was such a big complex step. Was she even cut out to be a wife? There was so much she didn't know about Vitale, so much they hadn't discussed. He was waiting at the altar, his head held high, and she needn't have worried about being overdressed because he and the man by his side were kitted out in fancy grey morning suits.

At the exact moment that Vitale turned his handsome head to look at her, his gaze every bit as edgy as her own, her apprehension evaporated because he smiled. A wolfish smile that took him from being a very good-looking guy to an absolutely gorgeous one. There was admiration in his gaze and she basked in it.

'*Like* the dress,' he breathed in a discreet aside before the vicar began to speak. 'You look wonderful.'

The last knot of tension in her stomach dissolved into a feeling of warmth and acceptance. The ceremony progressed and her hand stayed steady as he slid a wedding ring on her finger. And then almost dizzyingly fast the service was over, the organ music was swelling and Vitale was escorting her back down the aisle, a light hand resting on hers. In the porch he met her siblings and she learned that his companion was his lawyer and also a friend from his university days.

They drove straight to the airport.

'Did you mind that your parents weren't part of the ceremony?' Vitale asked her as soon as they were alone.

'Not at all. It wouldn't have been fancy enough for my mother and somehow my father would have found a way of ruining the day by calling me stupid.' Her soft mouth compressed and she shrugged a forlorn shoulder, conscious of his bewildered appraisal and saying nothing more.

'Why would he have done that?'

'I should have told you by now—I suffer from dyslexia. *Badly*,' Zara stressed, her hands tightly curled together on her lap because it took courage to confess a weakness that had been regarded with such disgust by her family. 'Regardless of what my father thinks, though, I'm not slow-witted. I have some difficulty reading, writing and spelling but I manage most things fine with the help of a computer.'

Vitale frowned because he was recalling her blank appraisal of the instructions on the pregnancy test and suddenly he was rethinking that scene with a tight feeling inside his chest. The anxiety, the fear of rejection, in her gaze screamed at him. He realised that, regardless of her attempt to refer casually to the condition, what she had just admitted was a very big deal for her. 'I went to school with a couple of dyslexics. I know you're not slow-witted and fortunately dyslexics can get a lot of help these days.'

Zara grimaced. 'My father doesn't believe dyslexia exists. He just thinks I'm stupid and he wouldn't allow me to have speech-language therapy.'

'That's ridiculous. Didn't you get help at school?'

'I was sixteen before I was diagnosed and I left a few months later. Although I dropped out of my A-level studies, I do manage,' she said again, clearly keen to drop the subject.

He remembered how pale and tense she had been while she struggled with those instructions, clearly terrified of him realising that she had a problem, and his rage with Monty Blake roared up through him like volcanic lava. Instead of being taught how to cope with the disorder, she had been taught to be ashamed of it and left to struggle alone. He wondered why that image bothered him, why he should feel so angry on her behalf. When had he ever felt protective about a woman? Only once before and even then his intelligence warning him to keep his distance had warred with more natural instincts.

'It's never too late to learn. Some sessions with a professional would help you handle the condition now,' Vitale remarked evenly. 'And lift your confidence.'

Zara went pink. She bit back the tart comment that she was sure he hadn't expected to take a wife still in need of lessons, because she was well aware that when she put herself down she was revealing low self-esteem. Furthermore she recognised that he had seen shrewdly right to the heart of her problem. Her family's attitude to her dyslexia had imposed secrecy on her and her subsequent fear of exposure had only made the problem worse.

'I thought you'd be embarrassed that I'm a dyslexic.'

'It would take a great deal more to embarrass me, *gioia mia*. Your parents overreacted. Albert Einstein

and some very famous people were also dyslexic,'
Vitale fielded casually.

They boarded a private jet and as Zara settled into a
cream leather seat in the cabin she was thinking once
again about how very little she knew about the man she
had married. 'I had no idea that you owned your own
plane,' she confided.

'I travel a lot. It speeds up my schedule and ensures
that I can move quickly in a crisis—'

'Where are we heading?' she prompted.

'It's a surprise, hopefully one which will please you.'

Lunch was served. After several sleepless nights
spent worrying about the unknowns in her future, Zara
was too exhausted to do more than pick at the food on
her plate. Finally she pushed the plate away and closed
her heavy eyes to rest them. That was the last thing
she registered until the jet landed and Vitale shook her
shoulder to rouse her from a deep sleep.

She was torn between pain and pleasure while he
drove her through the Tuscan hills, for although she
loved the Italian landscape she could not forget how
much he had hurt her on her last visit.

'Isn't this the road we took to the Palazzo Barigo?'
she pressed at one point.

'*Sì.*' His classic profile was taut, his response clipped.

When the car actually turned beneath the arched
entrance to the palazzo, Zara turned with a frown to
exclaim, 'What are we doing here?'

'You'll see.' Vitale parked at the front of the palazzo
and, filled with curiosity, Zara scrambled out. Was he
planning to introduce her to his uncle? Smoothing her

dress down while wishing he had given her some warning of his intentions, she mounted the shallow flight of steps to the front door, which was already opening. She came to a sudden halt when she saw the domestic staff assembled in the marble hall, clearly waiting to greet them.

Joining her, Vitale curved a hand to her elbow and introductions were made. There was no sign of any member of the family and she was confused when a middle-aged manservant called Edmondo showed them into a spacious reception room where once again she expected to meet Vitale's relatives, only nobody awaited them there either.

'What on earth are we doing here?' she demanded of Vitale in a perplexed whisper. 'Is this where we're going to stay?'

'I own the palazzo,' Vitale told her flatly, breaking the news with the minimum possible fanfare.

CHAPTER NINE

VITALE's blunt confession hit Zara like a brick thrown at a glass window, shattering her composure. She recalled the tour of the gardens that he had said he had arranged. She remembered the gardener waving at him .that same day and she turned pale before a flush of mortified pink mantled her cheekbones.

'Oh, my goodness, what an idiot I am!' she gasped, her temper rising hot and fast because she felt exceedingly foolish. 'But you told me this place belonged to your uncle—'

'No, I didn't. I only told you that I was staying here with my uncle and his family when your aunt worked on the garden—'

'Semantics—you *lied*!' Zara shot the furious accusation back at him. 'You're so tricky I'll never be able to trust a word you say!'

Vitale stood very still, reining back the aggression that her condemnation threatened to unleash. 'I bought the palazzo two years ago when my uncle decided to sell up but, while I have instigated repairs and maintained the property, I have not attempted to make personal use of the house until now,' he admitted without any expression at all.

He watched her, the daylight flooding through the tall windows burnishing her eye-catching hair and illuminating the fine lacework on her dress while enhancing the slender, striking elegance of her figure. He wondered when her pregnancy would start showing and experienced a glimmer of excitement at the prospect that shook him. But the awareness that her body would soon swell with visible proof of *his* baby turned him on hard and fast, no matter how fiercely he fought to repress the primitive reaction. Once again in her presence he was at the mercy of feelings and thoughts that were foreign to him and he hated it, craving the cool distance and self-discipline that were more familiar to him.

Zara settled furious lavender eyes on her bridegroom. 'Why not? If you bought the palazzo why haven't you used it?'

'I didn't feel comfortable here. When I was a teenager I stayed in this house during my term breaks and I have no good memories of those visits,' he admitted with a hard twist of his eloquent mouth.

'So what are we doing here?' Zara demanded baldly, still all at sea.

'You love the garden—I assumed that you might also like the house. It is a fine one.'

Zara was more confused than ever. An ancestral home was right off the grid of her scale of experience. To talk of it in terms of liking or disliking seemed positively cheeky. Yes, she had friends who inhabited such properties and she had occasionally stayed in them for the weekend but it had never occurred to her that she might one day actually live in one. 'Why did you buy a place this size if you don't even like it?'

'The palazzo has belonged to the Barigo family for centuries. I felt it was my duty to buy it and conserve it for the next generation.'

'But your name isn't Barigo…' Zara was still hopelessly at a loss.

'I have chosen not to claim the name but I am a Barigo.'

The penny of comprehension dropped noisily in Zara's head and she was embarrassed that it had taken her so long to make that leap in understanding. That was why he and his sister had had different surnames. They must have had different fathers. Evidently he was an illegitimate Barigo, born outside marriage and never properly acknowledged by the rest of the family. Yet he seemed so very much at ease against the grandeur of the great house, she mused. He had the education, the sophistication, the inborn classy assurance to look at home against such a splendid backdrop. He also had a level of worldly success and wealth that the most recent of the palazzo's owners had evidently lacked. Yet in spite of all that, deep down inside himself, Vitale had still not felt good enough to stay in the palazzo he owned and relax there and that disturbing truth twisted inside Zara's heart like a knifepoint turning.

'If you buy a house, you should use it,' Zara told him squarely. 'You seem to have a lot of staff employed here and you maintain it. My aunt used to say that a house that isn't lived in loses its heart.'

'I'm not sure that the Palazzo Barigo ever had a heart,' Vitale contended wryly. 'My sister grew up here. It was different for her. This was her home until her father died and my uncle inherited.'

'Why didn't your sister inherit?'

'The palazzo only goes to the men in the family. Loredana got the money instead,' he explained.

'So, why did you have to buy it to get it?' Zara pressed curiously. 'Because you're illegitimate?'

'I'm *not* illegitimate…it's too complicated to get into now,' Vitale countered with a dismissive shrug of a broad shoulder.

He didn't want to talk about his background and the shutters came back down. He was shutting her out because he didn't want to tell her any more. But these surroundings, his evidently troubled early life and what had happened to him since then were the key to Vitale's complex personality. Just then she recalled the strange scarring on his back and wondered once again what had caused it. At the same time, Zara was mystified by the depth of her longing to understand what drove Vitale Roccanti. Once she had thought he was a cold, callous guy focused purely on revenge, but the tiny seed of life inside her womb had steamrollered over that conviction and triumphed. As had her own personal safety, she conceded, recalling how he had brought her father to her door.

'Let's take a look at the house,' she responded lightly,

eager to distract him from the bad memories that he had mentioned.

'You're hardly dressed for a grand tour—'

'I can change.'

'I was rather looking forward to taking that dress off for you, *cara mia*,' Vitale admitted with a charismatic smile playing attractively at the corners of his beautifully shaped mouth.

'Well, you're going to have to help me get out of it. Getting into it was a two-person job,' Zara confided, thinking of the complex lacing that ran down her spine. 'I would never have managed without Bee's help this morning.'

As they reached the imposing marble staircase Edmondo appeared to show them the way and set off ahead of them at a stately pace that very nearly gave Zara a bout of irreverent giggles. Her dancing eyes meeting Vitale's in shared amusement, she had to swallow hard. The massive bedroom Edmondo displayed for their benefit was full of such extravagantly gilded furniture, embroidered, tasselled and fringed drapes and grandeur that Zara thought it would have been better suited to a reigning monarch. But there was no mistake because their luggage awaited them beside a pair of monumentally vast mirrored wardrobes.

'Wow…' she framed in a fading voice once they were alone again, unable to even imagine sleeping in that huge bed festooned in crimson drapes falling from a giant ceiling-mounted golden crown.

'What do you really think?' Vitale prompted as she bent to open her case and extract a change of clothing.

'It's hideous but I'm sure the antiques are worth a fortune and very historic,' she added in a rush, recognising that she might just have been tactless in the extreme.

'We could put them in storage and refurnish. It's not my style either,' Vitale admitted, stepping behind her to unknot the satin lacing closing the back of her dress. 'But Edmondo is a stickler for tradition and this is where the owner of the palazzo has always slept.'

'My goodness, your predecessors must've enjoyed their pomp and ceremony.' Zara shivered a little as cooler air brushed her bare shoulder blades and the fitted bodice of her gown loosened and fell forward. 'While you're a dab hand at unlacing.'

Vitale bent his head and pressed his lips to the tender side of her throat where a tiny pulse was going crazy. Lingering to enjoy her smooth, delicately perfumed skin, he used his mouth to nuzzle the soft skin there. His attention to that particular spot was unbearably arousing and a helpless gasp was wrenched from her as streamers of fire shot to every erotic zone she possessed. Stretching back against him for support, she caught her reflection in one of the wardrobe mirrors. She looked wanton, possessed, her hair shimmering round her shoulders, her face turned up eagerly to his, her breasts swelling and straining over the slightly too small cups of her lace strapless bra.

'I look like a shameless hussy,' she cried in embarrassment, her hands reaching down to pull up her dress again.

'Shameless works a treat for me, *angelina mia*,'

Vitale told her, his hands releasing her hold from the fabric so that her gown slid off her hips and down to her ankles. He lifted her out of the entangling folds and brought her down on the bed where he studied her scantily clad body with smouldering appreciation. 'You look gorgeous, Signora Roccanti.'

Self-conscious heat seemed to flood Zara from her head to her toes. She felt as though she were burning up inside her skin while her nipples tingled into straining buds and the tender flesh at the heart of her tingled with awareness. Dispensing with his tie, his waistcoat and his jacket and shoes, he lay down beside her, eyes full of anticipation. Zara propped herself up on her elbows, secure in his admiration, satisfied that she was both wanted and desired. He captured her lips with devastatingly erotic urgency so that even before he eased a small breast free of the bra her breath was parting her lips in rapid, uneven gasps. He rubbed the stiff rosy peak between thumb and forefinger and then dropped his mouth there to tease the throbbing tip with his lips and his tongue. As he simultaneously stroked the band of taut silk fabric stretched between her legs and felt the dampness there he groaned out loud. 'I've been fantasising about this moment for weeks,' he confided in a roughened undertone.

Only as he undid her bra to remove it did he spot the small blue badge she had attached to it. 'What's this?' he questioned.

'The something blue from the wedding luck rhyme and to remind me of my brother. He got it at school for playing rugby or something,' she muttered vaguely.

'I didn't even know you had a brother.'

'Tom was my twin. But he died in a car crash two years ago.' Flinching from her poignant recollections, she let her fingers delve into his tousled black hair to draw his mouth back to hers again and when he took her invitation to stop talking and kiss her it was so exhilarating that all sad memories left her head.

Her bra melted away, quickly followed by her panties. Vitale reared back on his knees to shed his remaining garments with a great deal more haste than cool. She revelled in his impatience, his eagerness to make love to her.

'I wanted this to be slow and perfect, unlike the last time,' Vitale admitted in a tone of frustration.

'Human beings don't do perfect,' she quipped, lifting a slender hand to run her fingertips gently down his cheek. 'And I don't expect it.'

'But you should,' Vitale informed her, eyes welded to her like padlocks.

With a gentle laugh of disagreement she arched her back below the hands curving to the pert swell of her sensitised breasts.

'Is it my imagination or is there more of you than there was a few weeks ago?' he teased.

'Falling pregnant does have some advantages,' she told him seductively. 'Alcohol may not be a good idea but I'm getting very bosomy indeed.'

Vitale laughed and kissed her breathless. She quivered as he found her clitoris with the ball of his thumb and pleasured her, gently delving and stroking until she moaned in helpless response to his stimulation. She was twisting and turning, her hips rising long before he rose over her and eased into her honeyed depths in a long deep thrust that sent a wave of excitement currenting through her.

'Don't stop,' she told him at an ecstatic peak of pleasure when it was a challenge to even find her voice.

She couldn't lie still as his fluid movements grew more insistent, more passionate and the intolerable tightness and tension within her gathered with every heartbeat and then exploded into an earthshaking climax. She hit that high with a startled cry of delight that she muffled by burying her mouth in a strong brown shoulder. She was as weak as a kitten once the tingling ripples of rapture had slowly coursed away from her again.

'I don't want to stroke your ego but that…*that* was perfect,' Zara whispered shakily, her hands sliding down from his shoulders to his back and instinctively massaging the roughened skin there with a gentle touch. 'What happened to you?' she asked him abruptly.

His muscles jerked taut below her fingers, and he stared down at her with bleak eyes. 'I was beaten, tortured as a child by my stepfather. He went to prison for it.'

A surge of horror swiftly followed by tears of sympathy flooded Zara's eyes. She lowered her lashes before he could see and when he tried to pull away from her, she held on tight to him. 'I thought I'd bottomed out in the parenting stakes,' she remarked tightly. 'But obviously you did a lot worse.'

Vitale realised that it would be more dignified to

stop fighting the comforting hug being forced on him. There was a ghastly moment when he just didn't know how to respond and he froze in her arms. She was always petting the rabbit, he reminded himself grimly; affectionate gestures were second nature to the woman he had married. He would have to learn how to handle them. He dropped a brief and awkward kiss on her brow, watching in dismay as a single tear inched down her flushed cheek on his behalf. 'We may not have done well in the parent lottery but that won't stop us being amazing parents,' he stated with powerful conviction. 'I'm sure we both know what *not* to do with our child.'

Zara thought of the mess that had been made of his back, the pain he must have endured and the despair he must have felt until he was removed from that cruelly abusive environment and she wanted to weep, but she had to confine herself to a subtle sniff or two and a comparatively modest hug. He saw hope in the future and refused to dwell on past suffering, she recognised with respect. Their marriage truly did have all the potential it needed to survive.

'My mother, Paola, married a wealthy businessman when she was eighteen. His name was Carlo Barigo and he was twenty years older,' Vitale said in a charged undertone, finally caving in and telling Zara the story that she had longed to hear since the day of her arrival as a bride at the palazzo.

Unfortunately prising that tale out of a male as reserved as Vitale was had taken determination and spot-on timing even from a wife of almost eight weeks' standing. At that instant, Vitale was at his most relaxed in a post-sex sprawl in the tangled sheets of their bed and her fingers were gently engaged in smoothing through his black hair.

'Go on,' she encouraged, quick to react to a hint of hesitation.

'Loredana was born within the first year of the marriage and within five years Paola was taking advantage of the fact that her husband was often away on business. She made friends with the wrong people, got into drink and drugs and started an affair. The marriage broke down. Carlo threw her out and her parents turned their back on her. She had never worked in her life and she was pregnant so she moved in with her lover—'

'The guy who beat you?' Zara cut in with a frown.

'*Sì*…he was a drug dealer to the rich. He married her because he assumed the divorce settlement would be huge—it was not. He also assumed that the child she was expecting was his.'

'That was you,' she guessed.

'I was Carlo Barigo's legitimate son but Paola lied and said I wasn't because my father had already deprived her of her daughter and she didn't want to lose me as well,' Vitale explained curtly. 'That was also my stepfather's excuse for beating me—that I wasn't his kid—but the truth was he got off on brutality.'

'Didn't your mother try to stop him?'

'By that stage all she cared about was her next fix.'

'There must have been someone who cared,' Zara said painfully.

'Not until Loredana decided that she wanted to meet

her mother after Carlo Barigo died. But when my sister visited us Paola was out of her head on drugs and Loredana got to know me instead. When she saw my bruises she notified the authorities of her suspicions. I went into the foster system and my stepfather eventually went to prison. I owe my life to Loredana's intervention,' he breathed heavily. 'I was eleven when she became my guardian. I went to boarding school while she worked as a model.'

For the first time she understood the foundation of his deep attachment to his late sister and her memory. Although his mother had failed him Loredana had saved him from a life of abuse.

Zara gazed down at his strong profile, so beautiful, so strong and yet so damaged, she conceded painfully. 'So how did you manage to visit this house as a teenager?'

'Loredana was an heiress, *gioia mia*. My uncle encouraged her to continue treating the palazzo like her home because he hoped that she would marry one of his sons and bring her money back into the family. That's why she was allowed to bring me here. It was that or leave me at school all the year round,' he proffered with a rueful sigh. 'My sister accepted me just as I was and I *was* rough round the edges. It never occurred to her that her snobbish cousins would be outraged to have a drug dealer and a junkie's son forced on them as a guest.'

Her brow furrowed. 'But that's not who you were.'

'It's what they believed. My cousins used to drag me out of bed in the middle of the night and thump and kick me and, thanks to their desire to ensure that I didn't get too big for my boots, I learned that my mother was selling her body to survive.'

Zara was pale. 'I bet you didn't even tell your sister what was happening.'

'Of course I didn't. I idolised her. She thought I was being treated to a slice of the family life she couldn't give me.' His mouth quirked. 'She was very trusting that way, always thought the best of everyone—'

'What age were you when she died?'

'Thirteen.'

'And how did you find out who your father really was?'

Vitale grimaced. 'The DNA testing that had to be done to identify Loredana's body revealed that we were full siblings. I chose to keep that news to myself. She hadn't changed her will to include me but a portion of her estate was set aside by the courts to cover my educational and living costs. My uncle got the rest and, being conscious of what people might think, he insisted that I continue to spend my term breaks at the palazzo.'

'Your sister was part of your life for such a short time.' Zara could only imagine how painful that loss must have been for a boy who had never known love and caring from any other source. It was even sadder that their true relationship had only been discovered after his sister had drowned.

'She first met your father here at the palazzo,' Vitale volunteered abruptly, his tone harsh. 'The grounds were being used for a fashion shoot and your aunt, Edith, was still working on her design. Loredana was modelling and your father flew in to see your aunt and he was invited to stay to dinner.'

'Oh,' Zara pronounced, it being her turn to pull a face, for she did not wish to tackle that controversial issue again at that moment for she was too well aware that, had her father been a braver man, Loredana might have survived the sinking of the yacht. 'Let's not discuss that now. Give me one positive thought about the palazzo, Vitale.'

'That is *so* childish, *cara mia*,' he groaned, looking at her in reproach.

'It's not…you can be very prone to taking a negative stance.'

A rueful smile chased the tension from his well-shaped mouth and he threw his untidy dark head back on the pillow. As dark, bronzed and glossy as a tiger at rest, he looked incredibly handsome. 'I commissioned the temple above the lake as a tribute to Loredana. The top of that hill was her favourite place—'

'That was a cheat thought…a sort of positive and negative together,' Zara censured.

'I won't need to commission anything to remember you,' Vitale teased with sudden amusement. 'Everywhere I look you've made your mark on this household.'

The huge pieces of gilded furniture had already gone into storage in favour of contemporary pieces in oak, which looked surprisingly well against the silk-panelled walls. Welcoming seating had arrived along with cushions, throws, unusual pieces of pottery and flower arrangements to illuminate dark corners and add comfort and character. Edmondo, who thoroughly approved of such nest-building instincts, had cheerfully described the new mistress of the palazzo to her husband as a 'force of nature'.

'You don't need to remember me,' Zara countered. 'I'm not going anywhere.'

His attention suddenly fell on the little jewelled enamel clock by her side of the bed and he stiffened and sat up in an abrupt movement. 'I didn't realise it was almost six!'

Within ten seconds of that exclamation, Vitale had vacated the bed and the shower was running in the adjoining bathroom. Zara lay on in the bed as stiff as a wooden plank while her mind whirled off on a wheel of frantic resentful activity. Sadly, she knew exactly why Vitale was in such a hurry. Well, at least she knew and she didn't know...

Once again, after all, it was a Friday night and every Friday night for the past five weeks Vitale had religiously gone out alone and not returned home until around two in the morning. He would only say that he visited a longstanding female 'friend', who lived near Florence, for dinner and if Zara tried to extract any more details from him he became irritable and broodingly silent. She suspected and had asked if that female friend was living in the villa for which she had done the garden plan but, rather tellingly, he had ignored the question.

'You must learn to trust me. You may be my wife but that doesn't mean I have to tell you *everything*!' he had argued without hesitation the previous week.

But Zara thought marriage should mean exactly that even though she had backed off from the looming threat of a row for the sake of peace. When Vitale returned to the palazzo tomorrow, however, she already knew that he would be grim and distant and that it would probably be at least forty-eight hours before he so much as touched her again. His Friday nights away from her, it seemed, did not put him in a good mood.

Was he spending that time placating another woman who mattered to him? A woman he had reluctantly set aside so that he could marry Zara because she had fallen pregnant? It was Zara's worst fear but what else could explain his tense, troubled attitude in the aftermath of those evenings? Vitale was betraying every sign of a man being torn between opposing loyalties.

It had to be admitted, though, that his mysterious Friday outings were the one and only storm cloud in Zara's blue sky and at first she had not been at all concerned when he left her to her own company one evening during the week. Her concern had grown only in proportion to his reticence. She did not like secrets and did not feel she could sit back and quietly allow him to maintain his secrecy.

Yet at the same time she had lived in Tuscany with Vitale for eight long weeks and had during that period discovered a happiness and a sense of security that was wonderfully new and precious to her. He had devoted the first three weeks of their marriage entirely to her, but after that point had had to return to the bank and his travels abroad. While he was away she had flown back to London on several occasions to catch up with business at Blooming Perfect and see clients.

Round her neck she wore a teardrop diamond pendant on a chain that Vitale hated her to take off. He had said the flash of the diamond in sunlight reminded him of her hair and her luminous smile. He had said loads and loads of romantic flattering stuff like that, words that she cherished, compliments that she took out and analysed whenever she was on her own or worried about the depth of his commitment to her and their marriage. He was very generous, had bought her innumerable gifts, everything from jewellery to flowers and artworks to pieces of furniture he thought she might like. Even more impressive he had also quietly engaged a speech-language specialist to visit weekly and help Zara overcome the problems caused by her dyslexia. She was already able to read more easily. Even Fluffy had benefited from Zara's move to Italy, having acquired more toys than even the most spoilt bunny could play with.

Vitale had become Zara's whole world without her even noticing it until she began to panic on Friday nights, worry about where he was and who he was with, and it made her realise her heart was more vulnerable than she had ever really appreciated. She was hopelessly in love with the guy she had married and to whom she had foolishly suggested a three-month-long trial marriage. Three months? Seriously, what sort of a stupid idea had that been? She already knew that she would not willingly give Vitale up after even a thousand months. What would she say at the end of the trial period if he was the one who turned round and jumped through that escape hatch she had handily provided to ask for *his* freedom back? It was a prospect that made her blood run cold.

She didn't know when she had fallen for Vitale or when she had first overcome that bad beginning when he had set her up for the paparazzi. But she was crazy about him and she really did understand that she had landed herself an extremely passionate, 'all or nothing' guy, who had switched his original allegiance to his sister's memory to their child instead. At heart she really did grasp what motivated Vitale more strongly than any other factor.

And what did inspire him was his movingly strong concept of what a man owed to his family. Her pregnancy had shot her right up the pecking order in his mind and brought her out at the top of the pile. She was carrying his baby, she was his wife and he really did treat her as though she was something incredibly precious. It touched her to the heart that even after the horrific experiences he had endured as a child he could still set such a very high value on the importance of family.

His cell phone rang and he emerged from the bathroom, a towel anchored precariously round his lean hips, to answer it. He frowned, thrust long impatient fingers through his damp black hair, spiking it up, and spoke in fluid Italian for several minutes, clearly issuing instructions. Setting the phone down again, he glanced at her. 'I'm afraid I have to fly to Bahrain this evening to meet a major investor. I won't be home until late tomorrow.'

As he broke the news Zara found herself smiling. If he had to be in Bahrain he couldn't also be dining somewhere near Florence with his unknown female friend. But if he didn't make it there this week he would presumably make it there at a later date. He walked over to the window and made another call, his attractive accented drawl apologetic, gentle in tone. Zara knew in her bones that he was talking to another woman and it wounded her, plunging her straight back into her uneasy thoughts.

Exactly what did Vitale get up to on Friday nights? He was risking their relationship by maintaining such secrecy. Didn't that bother him? Did he think this woman was worth that risk? Was he keeping a mistress in that luxury villa? A mistress he needed more than he needed his pregnant wife? She had to know. Who was he protecting her from? Or was it that he was protecting another woman from her?

Suddenly, Zara was determined to satisfy some of the questions that Vitale had refused to answer. Once he had left for the airport, she would drive over to the villa, make the excuse that she had come to check on the garden and discover who lived there. She had to know, she *needed* to know, and tough if he didn't like it when he found out that she'd gone behind his back to satisfy her curiosity...

CHAPTER TEN

THE local landscaping firm hired by Vitale to bring Zara's plan for the villa grounds to fruition had done an excellent job. A wide terrace girded by graceful trees and elegant shrubs had removed the old-fashioned formal aspect from the original frontage. Her heart beating very fast, Zara parked the car and approached the front door.

Whatever she discovered she would deal with it quietly and calmly, she reminded herself bracingly. She was ready to handle any eventuality. There would be no distasteful scene, no tears, certainly no recriminations. Hadn't she promised Vitale that before she married him? She was engaged in a trial marriage, which either one of them could walk away from without a guilt trip. If he *was* keeping another woman at the villa, if he *was* maintaining an extra-marital relationship, she had to set him free and get on with her life. Those far-reaching reflections were all very well, she reasoned in sudden dismay, as long as she didn't acknowledge that the very thought of having to live without Vitale, or raise her child without him, was terrifying.

It was a shock, therefore, while she hovered apprehensively on the doorstep, when without her even knocking to announce her presence the front door suddenly shot open and framed Giuseppina. Zara frowned when she recognised the housekeeper, who had looked after her and Vitale at the farmhouse where she had stayed several months earlier.

'Buona sera, Signora Roccanti,' Giuseppina greeted her with a welcoming smile and a further flood of Italian, which Zara did not understand.

With a display of enthusiasm that suggested that it was very unlikely that Vitale could be engaged in an improper extra-marital relationship with the villa occupant, Giuseppina ushered Zara into the hall. Quick light steps echoed across a tiled floor somewhere nearby and a woman appeared in the doorway.

She was an older woman, trim and not particularly tall with short silvery grey hair, anxious dark eyes and a heavily lined face. When she saw Zara she came to a sudden halt while Zara continued to stare, ensnared by a fleeting physical resemblance that took her very much by surprise.

'You must be Zara,' the woman breathed in accented English, her discomfiture unhidden. 'Did Vitale tell you about me? I made him promise that he would keep me a secret but I knew it would be difficult for him—'

'He didn't break his promise,' Zara admitted tautly, suddenly wishing she had stayed home, suddenly wishing she did not still suffer from that impulsive streak that invariably got her into trouble. 'I must apologise for dropping in without an invitation. I'm afraid I couldn't rest until I knew who was living here, who Vitale was seeing every Friday night...'

In the face of that explanation, the anxious expression on the other woman's face eased somewhat. '*Naturalmente*...of course. Come in—Giuseppina will make us English tea.' She spoke to the housekeeper in her own language before extending a hesitant hand. 'I am Paola Roccanti.'

'I thought you might be,' Zara almost whispered, shock still winging through her in embarrassing waves as she lightly touched that uncertain hand. 'Vitale has your eyes.'

Smiling as though that comment was a compliment, Paola took her into the lounge, smartly furnished now in contemporary style. 'I should have allowed Vitale to tell you I was here. I can see now that I put him in a difficult position. That was not my intention. I simply didn't want to embarrass you or him. I didn't want you to feel that you had to acknowledge me—'

'How could you embarrass me?' Zara asked in bewilderment. 'Why wouldn't I acknowledge you?'

Paola sighed. 'You're married to my son. You must know how badly I let him down as a child. Many people despise me for the life I have led and I understand how they feel. I've taken drugs, lived on the streets, I've been in prison for stealing to feed my addiction—'

'If Vitale wants to see you that is enough for me,' Zara broke in quietly, feeling that such revelations were none of her business.

'Since I came out of rehabilitation my son and I have been trying to get to know each other. It is not easy for either of us,' his mother confessed with a regret that she couldn't hide. 'It is hard for Vitale not to judge me and sometimes I remember things that make it almost impossible for me to face him.'

'I think it's good that both of you are trying, though,' Zara responded with tact as Giuseppina entered with a tray of tea.

Paola compressed her lips. 'Coming to terms with my past and facing up to the mistakes I made is part of my recovery process. I attend Narcotics Anonymous meetings regularly,' she explained. 'I have a good sponsor and Vitale has been very supportive as well.'

'That's good.' Still feeling awkward, Zara watched her companion pour the tea with a slightly trembling hand, her tension obvious.

'On Fridays we usually go for a meal and we talk, sometimes about difficult things…like my daughter, Loredana,' Paola continued quietly. 'I have no memory of her beyond the age of six or seven when I left my first husband, Carlo. She visited twice when she was grown up but I was in no condition to speak to her and I can't remember her—'

'Vitale told me…'

'You must know some of the bad things at least.' Paola's eyes were moist, her mouth tight with anxiety. 'He could have died when he was a child. I think he often wished he had when he was younger. I deprived him of his true father and his inheritance and yet he puts me in a house like this and takes me out to dine in fancy restaurants as if I was still the respectable young woman who married his father…the woman I was before I became an addict. He says I can be whoever I want to be now.'

'He's right. You can be,' Zara said gently, soothingly. It was impossible not to recognise how fragile Paola was and how weighed down she was with shame for her past mistakes. She found herself praying that the older woman did make it successfully through the recovery process and managed to stay off drugs.

Paola asked her about the garden and then offered to show it to her. Zara began to relax as they discussed the design and Vitale's mother asked for advice on what to plant in the empty borders behind the villa. Paola had already visited a garden centre nearby. Zara was quick to suggest that they should go back there together the following week and she agreed a date and time while hoping that Vitale would approve and not think her guilty of interference.

It was late afternoon the next day before Vitale returned to the palazzo. Dressed in a simple white sundress, Zara was arranging an armful of lavender in a fat crystal vase in the hall. He strode through the door and came to a halt, brilliant dark eyes locking to her tiny figure, picking up straight away on the troubled look she shot at him. Her pregnancy was becoming obvious now, a firm swell that made her dress sit out like a bell above her slender shapely legs.

'You can shout if you want,' Zara told him ruefully.

An ebony brow rose. 'Why would I shout?'

'I went to see your mother. I assumed you'd already know.'

'I did. Paola rang me as soon as you left the villa,'

Vitale confided with a wry smile. 'She likes you very much and thinks I did very well for myself, which I already knew—'

'But I went behind your back quite deliberately,' Zara pointed out guiltily, keen to ensure that he had grasped exactly what she had done. 'I just had to know where you went on Friday nights and who you were spending time with—'

'It was hell not telling you but I didn't want to spook Paola by forcing the issue. It took a lot of persuasion to get her to move into the villa. She's afraid of encroaching on our lives and of embarrassing us—'

'Are we that easily embarrassed?'

'I'm not, if you're not.' His sardonic mouth hardened. 'She lost thirty years of her life to drug abuse and she's made a huge effort to overcome her problems. I think she deserves a fresh start.'

'But you've found seeing her…difficult,' she selected the word uneasily.

'I didn't like the secrecy and it does feel strange being with her. I never knew her when I was a child and from the age of eleven until this year I had no contact with her, nor did I want any. We have a lot of ground to catch up but I've learned stuff from her that I'm grateful to have found out,' he admitted levelly, accompanying her up the marble staircase. 'Do you mind if I go for a shower? I feel like I've been travelling all day.'

'Not at all. What did you learn from Paola?' she probed curiously as he thrust wide the door of their bedroom.

'That my father kept a mistress throughout the whole

of their marriage.' Vitale raised a brow with expressive scorn. 'He only married my mother to have children and he didn't treat her well. It's not surprising that the marriage broke down or that she was suffering from such low self-esteem that she went off the rails.'

'But it was a tragedy for both you and her…and your sister as well,' Zara completed. 'How did your mother come back into your life again?'

'I was first approached on her behalf by a social worker several years ago but at the time I refused to have anything to do with her,' Vitale confided as he shrugged free of his jacket. 'Then I met you and I began to realise that human beings are more complicated than I used to appreciate.'

'What have I got to do with it?' Zara prompted with a frown.

'I used to be very black and white about situations. People, though, are rarely all good or all evil but often a mixture of both and we all make mistakes. After all, I made a big mistake targeting you to get at your father,' Vitale volunteered grimly. 'That was wrong.'

'I never thought I'd hear you admit that.' Zara curled up on the bed and looked at him expectantly. 'When did you reach that conclusion?'

Vitale dealt her a sardonically amused appraisal. 'There were quite a lot of helpful pointers after I met you, *angelina mia*. How about my discovery that you could get under my skin in the space of one weekend when I had already wrecked my chances with you? How about when you learned that you were pregnant and told me at the same time that you hated and distrusted me? Or even how about your need to impose a ridiculous three-month trial on our marriage so that you could get out of the commitment again if you had to? Do you think I'm so slow that I couldn't learn from those experiences?'

'It has never once crossed my mind that you might be slow—'

'But I was when it came to recognising and understanding my emotions,' Vitale interrupted, trailing his tie loose and tossing it aside. 'When I was a kid, it was safer to squash my feelings and get by without them because anything I felt only made me more vulnerable.'

'I can understand that,' Zara conceded, picking up the tie he had dropped on the floor and frowning at him.

'So I'm untidy,' he conceded with a flourish of one dismissive hand, well into his stride now with his explanation. 'As an adult I didn't recognise emotions for what they were, the same way as I didn't recognise what I felt for my mother until it was almost too late for me to get the chance to know her. By the time a priest who worked with Paola in rehab came to see me this year you were in my life and I was more willing to credit that I might not know everything there was to know and to listen to what he had to tell me.'

'I don't get my connection,' she admitted freely, draping the tie over the back of a chair in a manner that she hoped he would learn to copy.

'Well, once I fell in love with you it opened the floodgates to the whole shebang!' he pointed out mockingly. 'I mean, I've even learned to be reasonably fond of Fluffy now. Going from loving you to trying to understand my mother's need to make amends and be forgiven wasn't that difficult...'

Zara blinked and stared at him in disbelief, lavender eyes huge. 'You fell in love with me...*when*?'

A wicked grin flashed across his beautifully shaped mouth as he realised he had taken her by surprise. 'Oh, I think it probably happened that first weekend when I was playing at being the evil seducer and setting you up with the paparazzi. In fact, as I later appreciated, I was setting myself up for a fall. I didn't know I was in love back then, I just felt like you had taken over my brain because I couldn't get you out of my head, nor could I stay away from you.'

'So when did you decide it was love?'

'Slowly, *painfully...*' Vitale stressed ruefully, his face serious. 'When I'm with you I'm happy and secure. When I've been away from you and I'm coming home I'm downright ecstatic. Everything has more meaning when you're with me. Loving you has taught me how to relax, except when I'm worrying about you.'

'What have you got to worry about me for?'

'It's that naturally negative bent my thoughts suffer from,' Vitale confided ruefully, shedding his shirt. 'The more you mean to me, the more scared I am of losing you, and sometimes when I look at you I am terrified of what I feel—like when I came through the front door and saw you standing there with those purple things—'

'The lavender,' she slotted in.

'Whatever, *angelina mia*.' With a fluid shift of one hand he dismissed an irrelevant detail. 'You were standing there looking so beautiful and pleased to see me and yet worried and I had this moment of panic that something had happened, that something was wrong—'

'I was just worried that you would be annoyed at my having gone behind your back to see who was living in the villa.'

'No, I was touched by your compassion. You spent time with Paola. You didn't make her feel bad. You even invited her out—'

'She needs company,' Zara pointed out. 'It's no big deal.'

'It would be a very big deal to some women. There will be gossip, even scandal if Paola becomes a part of our lives. Some people will approve, others will not.'

'That doesn't matter to me. Let's see how things go,' Zara suggested, knowing that the older woman still had a long way to go as part of her recovery process and that the continuing success of her rehabilitation could not be taken for granted.

'She needs us to have faith in her—she's got nobody else.' Naked but for his boxer shorts, Vitale ran a knuckle gently down the side of Zara's face. 'But I've been hell to live with while this was going on, haven't I?'

'You were a little moody after seeing her.'

'And you don't like moody guys,' he reminded her with a grimace. 'It was tough at first. But although seeing Paola roused bad memories it also made me view my past in a more even light.'

'I really like the fact that you're making that effort for your mother,' Zara confided softly, her tender heart touched. 'It would have been easier for you to turn your back on her.'

'I think it's actually harder to hang onto the prejudices, as I did over Loredana.' Vitale compressed his handsome mouth. 'I will never like your father—he is not a pleasant man and he hurt you. But speaking to him about the night my sister drowned did show me that I was still thinking of that incident with the vengeful attitude of a teenager distraught over his sister's death.'

'Yes,' Zara agreed feelingly.

'Someone else isn't always to blame for the bad things that happen,' he acknowledged heavily. 'Although your father, in fact *both* your parents are very much to blame for your unhappy childhood. To have stood by and allowed you to be branded a liar at the age of ten to conceal your father's violence towards your mother and you was unforgivable. That was a huge betrayal of your trust.'

'I got over it.'

'And I don't think I will ever understand why you were still willing to marry Sergios Demonides just to cement a business deal and win your parents' approval.'

'It was very foolish but I had spent so many years craving their approval without ever getting it. I didn't have enough self-respect,' she admitted wryly. 'I had to come to Tuscany to realise that to marry a man I didn't love or care about was a very bad idea.'

'I had an identical moment of truth when I met you. You changed my outlook, *gioia mia*,' Vitale confided in a tone of immense appreciation. 'I didn't like emotions, didn't trust them, preferred not to get involved with anything or anybody that made me feel too much. But you taught me how much of a difference love could make to my life and then you taught me to want your love…'

Heaving a delighted sigh at that assurance, Zara rested a small hand on his shoulder. 'You know that three-month trial marriage I mentioned?'

'Don't I just?'

'I won't keep you in suspense,' Zara told him teasingly. 'I've decided to keep you for the long haul.'

The beginnings of a smile started to tug at the corners of Vitale's mouth. 'Finally she lets me off the hook.'

'I'm not convinced it did you any harm to be on that hook in the first place.' Zara mock-punched his shoulder. 'Sometimes you're far too sure of yourself. But I do love you,' she whispered, suddenly full of heartfelt emotion. 'I love you very much indeed.'

Vitale did not make it into the shower until much later that evening. In fact he didn't even make it out of the bedroom, for Edmondo was instructed to bring dinner to his employers upstairs. Having declared their love and revelled in the wonder of sharing the same feelings and opinions, Vitale and Zara made passionate love. Afterwards they lay on in bed for ages talking about the why and the how and the when of those first seeds of love until even Zara was satisfied that they had talked the topic to death.

It was definitely not hard for her to listen, however, to how enraged Vitale had felt on her behalf when he appreciated how little her parents valued her in comparison to the twin brother whom they assumed would have been perfect had he lived beyond his twentieth year. In turn, Vitale was hugely amused by the news that his kindness to Fluffy had alerted Zara to the idea that he might have a softer centre than his initial behaviour towards her might have suggested.

'So, I'm not on probation any longer,' Vitale commented with a hint of complacency.

'And how do you work that out?' Zara enquired, surveying him questioningly.

'You said you wanted me for the long haul.'

'Depends on your definition of long haul,' she teased.

'For ever and ever just like the fairy tales,' Vitale hastened to declare, spreading a large hand across the swell of her stomach and laughing in satisfaction as he felt the faint kick of the baby she carried. 'You and the baby both, *angelina mia.*'

'That's an ambition I'm happy to encourage,' Zara told him happily.

EPILOGUE

THREE years later, Zara watched her daughter, Donata, play in the bath in their London town house before scooping her out into a fleecy towel and dressing her little squirming body in her pjs. Her dark eyes were so like Vitale's that the little girl was very talented at wheedling things out of her mother.

'Daddy?' Donata demanded, first in Italian and then in English, demonstrating her bilingual language skill with aplomb.

'Later,' Zara promised, tucking the lively toddler into bed and reflecting that it would be the next morning before Donata saw the father she adored.

Vitale had spent the whole week in New York and, although Zara and occasionally their daughter sometimes travelled with him, she had taken advantage of his absence to catch up with plans needed for Blooming Perfect clients in both London and Tuscany. Business was booming in both countries to the extent that Zara had been forced to turn down work. Media interest and an award won for a garden she had designed for the Chelsea Flower Show had given her an even higher profile and resulted in a steady influx of clients. Rob had become a permanent employee and Zara had hired a junior designer to work under her in London.

Vitale's mother, Paola, had made it safely through her rehabilitation and as time went on had gained in confidence. Having undertaken training as a counsellor, Paola had recently found her feet in her new life by volunteering to work with other addicts. Vitale had also agreed to sponsor a charity for former addicts and their families. The older woman was now very much a part of Vitale and Zara's life and was a very fond grandparent—a fact that Zara was grateful for when her own parents had little to do with their lives.

While Vitale had managed to come to terms with his mother's malign influence on his childhood and had since established a more relaxed adult relationship with the older woman, little had occurred to improve Zara's relations with her parents in a similar way. Her father could not accept the fact that Vitale knew about the domestic violence that had cast such a shadow over Zara and her mother's life. In turn, Zara's mother, Ingrid, was too loyal to her husband to challenge his hostile attitude to their daughter and son-in-law.

Although Zara occasionally accompanied Vitale to social events in London that her parents also attended, and the two couples were always careful to speak for the sake of appearances, there was no true relationship beneath the social banter. Sometimes that hurt Zara a great deal more than she was willing to admit to Vitale. At the same time she did have reason to cherish some hope of a future improvement in relations because her mother made a point of phoning and asking her daughter when she would next be in London so that she could see Donata. Ingrid would then visit her daughter's home and play with her grandchild, but it was tacitly understood that those visits took place without Monty Blake's knowledge.

On the other hand Vitale had taught Zara that life by its very nature was imperfect and that nothing was to be gained from fighting the fact. Her sadness over her poor relationship with her parents was more than compensated for by the deep and happy bond of intimacy she had forged with her husband and child. Her confidence in his love made her smile when she wakened and smile again when she often fell asleep in the safe circle of his arms.

Their closeness had grown by leaps and bounds in the wake of Donata's birth. Vitale travelled less so that he could spend more time with his family. He was also very much a hands-on father, who enjoyed playing with his daughter and reading her stories. Zara could see that he was striving to give Donata the safe, loving childhood that fate had denied both of them and it touched her heart. On this particular evening, though, Zara gave her daughter less time to settle into bed than she usually did because it was the couple's third wedding anniversary and she and Vitale were going out to celebrate.

Zara donned an elegant blue designer dress that skimmed her slight curves and made the most of her height. As she did her make-up she was thinking of the announcement she had to make and smiling to herself, thinking of how different it would be this time from the last time when everything relating to her pregnancy had seemed so uncertain and scary.

Vitale strode through the door with all the impatience of a man who was always eager to see his wife after being away from her.

Zara appeared in the bathroom doorway. 'Vitale...' she murmured, skimming over him with helpless admiration, for she still marvelled over the fact that this gorgeous man was her husband and the father of her child.

'You look fantastic,' he breathed, his dark gaze running over the chic dress and lingering on that luminous smile echoed by the superb diamond pendant she always wore. 'Do we really have to go out?'

Her sultry mouth quirked. When Vitale was away from her for any appreciable length of time it took determination to get him out of the bedroom.

'I didn't go to all this trouble dressing up just to stay home—'

Vitale groaned, amusement and frustration etched in his lean dark face. 'I just want to grab you and unwrap you like a gift but I know this is a special occasion.'

'Our third anniversary,' Zara reminded him very seriously.

Her husband dug into his pocket and handed her a little box. 'A small mark of my appreciation and love...'

It was an eternity ring, composed of a hoop of beautiful diamonds that slotted onto her finger next to her wedding ring as though it had been made for that spot, which, as Vitale was very good at detail, it probably had been. 'It's gorgeous,' she carolled, pink with pleasure that he had made the effort to celebrate the occasion with such a present.

'I'm sorry, I'm going to have to wreck your make-up, *angelina mia*. I'm in the control of forces stronger than I am,' Vitale teased, closing his arms round her and claiming a passionate kiss.

And he did a lot more than wreck her make-up, for the passion that never failed them burst into being on contact with a strength that could not be denied and they happily gave way to pleasing each other in the oldest way of all. Afterwards, the dress was a little creased and the dinner reservation had to be moved to a later time.

They ate at their favourite Florentine restaurant by candlelight and somewhere between the first course and the final one Zara made her announcement and Vitale did not dare tell her that because she had refused the wine he had already guessed. Instead he gripped her hand and told her that the news she was carrying their second child was amazing, before adding quite truthfully that their three years together had been the happiest years of his life.

Meeting those dark golden eyes resting on her with adoration, Zara's gaze misted over. 'And mine…I love you so much.'

'And with every year that you are with me, I love you more, *angelina mia*.'

* * * * *

LET'S TALK
Romance

For exclusive extracts, competitions
and special offers, find us online:

f facebook.com/millsandboon

🐦 @MillsandBoon

📷 @MillsandBoonUK

Get in touch on 01413 063232

For all the latest titles coming soon, visit
millsandboon.co.uk/nextmonth

MILLS & BOON

THE HEART OF ROMANCE

A ROMANCE FOR EVERY READER

MODERN

Prepare to be swept off your feet by sophisticated, sexy and seductive heroes, in some of the world's most glamourous and romantic locations, where power and passion collide.

HISTORICAL

Escape with historical heroes from time gone by. Whether your passion is for wicked Regency Rakes, muscled Vikings or rugged Highlanders, awaken the romance of the past.

MEDICAL

Set your pulse racing with dedicated, delectable doctors in the high-pressure world of medicine, where emotions run high and passion, comfort and love are the best medicine.

True Love

Celebrate true love with tender stories of heartfelt romance, from the rush of falling in love to the joy a new baby can bring, and a focus on the emotional heart of a relationship.

Desire

Indulge in secrets and scandal, intense drama and plenty of sizzling hot action with powerful and passionate heroes who have it all: wealth, status, good looks…everything but the right woman.

HEROES

Experience all the excitement of a gripping thriller, with an intense romance at its heart. Resourceful, true-to-life women and strong, fearless men face danger and desire - a killer combination!

To see which titles are coming soon, please visit

millsandboon.co.uk/nextmonth

JOIN US ON SOCIAL MEDIA!

Stay up to date with our latest releases, author news and gossip, special offers and discounts, and all the behind-the-scenes action from Mills & Boon...

 millsandboon

 millsandboonuk

 millsandboon

It might just be true love...